THE
HEARSE
CASE SCENARIO

·

Other Books by Tim Cockey

The Hearse You Came In On
Hearse of a Different Color

THE
HEARSE
CASE SCENARIO

•

TIM COCKEY

To Kathy

Tim Cockey

❦HYPERION

New York

Library of Congress Cataloging-in-Publication Data

Cockey, Tim.
    Hearse case scenario / by Tim Cockey.
        p. cm.
    ISBN 0-7868-6711-6
    1. Sewell, Hitchcock (Fictitious character)—Fiction. 2. Undertakers and undertaking—Fiction. 3. Baltimore (Md.)—Fiction. I. Title.

PS3553.O277 H35 2002
813'.54—dc21

                                                    2001024188

FIRST EDITION

10 9 8 7 6 5 4 3 2 1

For Julia C. Strohm
If I can locate any more love, it's yours

THE
HEARSE
CASE SCENARIO

•

Apparently I was the first person Shrimp Martin called after Lucy Taylor shot him. It was a Saturday afternoon. Early June. The sun was high and I was low. I had a wicked toothache and I had just gotten off the phone with a guy named Roger, who was taking my regular dentist's calls while my regular dentist was away at his vacation house in Jackson Hole, poor guy. Roger sounded gung-ho to see me. He was going to fit me in that afternoon, between a root canal and an extraction. Well, good for Roger. Me, I had no gung-ho at all, just the sore tooth. Just before we hung up, Roger had asked me quite earnestly how my gums were. I didn't know how to answer that question. I was still pondering it when the phone rang.

"Sewell and Sons."

The voice on the other end was raspy and hoarse. Like someone whispering and gargling with glass at the same time. "Who's this?" it rasped.

"Excuse me?"

The voice croaked again. "Who's . . . this?"

"You called me," I pointed out. "Sewell and Sons Family Funeral Home. Now. Your turn."

There was a pause. I leaned back even farther in my chair and recrossed my legs, which were up on my desk. Lately, that's where they had been spending a lot of their time. Up on my desk. Not a lot of people were dying these days. My aunt and I were suffering a beginning-of-summer drought. Currently we had only one customer on ice, down in the basement. Mrs. Rittenhouse, from around the corner. Shakespeare Street. Her next-of-kin was due by any minute to drop off a dress for the viewing. A fact that was about to make this phone call all the more interesting.

A hissing sound was coming over the phone, like air going out of a balloon. I asked again. "Who is this?"

"Sssssssss. . . . Shrimp Martin."

Shrimp Martin. Nightclub owner. Blatant self-promoter. Borderline sleaze. A legend in his own mind.

"Shrimp? This is Hitchcock Sewell. What's up? What's wrong with your voice?"

"Lucy," he croaked.

"Lucy?" My heart iced. Nine out of ten people who call me at work are calling to talk about a corpse.

"Lucy."

"Lucy. I got that part. What about Lucy?"

"She's . . . not . . . here."

I switched ears and glanced out the window. Sam and some kids from the neighborhood were hosing down the hearse. Actually, the kids appeared to be hosing down Sam. Who didn't appear to be minding much. Sam's just a big kid anyway. Two hundred and ninety pounds worth.

"Shrimp, why don't we start this whole conversation over? I'm not looking for Lucy. I didn't call you, okay? You called me. So what's up?"

Shrimp sighed again. He sounded irritated. "Who's this?"

Now *I* was getting irritated. "I told you. It's Hitchcock Sewell, Shrimp. What the hell is going on?"

"Lucy," Shrimp said again. "She's gone. She . . . left me. She—" He interrupted his own sentence with another groan. This one stretched out in sort of a singsong fashion, almost a humming. It sounded as if Shrimp was channeling a tone-deaf drunk. Which was the conclusion I was beginning to reach. Not that Shrimp was channeling, but that he was definitely coming to us from the Land of Liquor.

"What do you mean, she's gone?"

Aunt Billie had just stepped into my office. She was holding a rat by the tail, at arm's length. Presumably dead. If not, then faking it nicely.

"Who's gone?"

I palmed the mouthpiece. "Shrimp Martin says that Lucy Taylor has left him."

Billie sniffed. "Lucy Taylor has a brain." She leaned sideways and dropped the dead rat into my brass spittoon. I don't spit. I use it to keep the door propped open. And, apparently, for storing dead rats.

"Mrs. Rittenhouse is all done," Billie announced. "Pretty as a picture. I'm just waiting on her dress."

At that precise instant, the front door opened. I could see a pair of arms wrapped around a blue chiffon number. Well, I call it chiffon. I don't really know these things. It was blue. I made the "voilà" gesture (one-handed version) and Billie floated out to the lobby to do her thing. Shrimp was still gurgling into the phone.

"I'm sorry, Shrimp. I missed that. What were you saying?"

He sounded strained and defeated. "Lucy," he mumbled again. For a man who was refusing to come to a point, he was driving one home nonetheless.

"Yes. Lucy. You just said that she left you. When, Shrimp? When did Lucy leave you?" I was beginning to overenunciate, the way you do when you're trying to get through to a foreigner. Or a child.

"Half . . . hour."

"A half hour ago? Jesus, Shrimp, come on. A half hour isn't really an awfully long time."

Billie was coming back into the office. She showed the dead woman's next of kin—granddaughter—to the chair in front of my desk. The young woman plopped down into the chair, the blue dress bunched in her arms like a bag of groceries. I held up a hand to indicate that I'd be right with her. Shrimp finally got to his point.

"She shot . . . me."

"She what?" I don't even remember it happening, but my feet were suddenly on the floor and I was standing at my desk. The phone felt tiny in my hand, like it was a child's toy. My sore tooth exploded with pain. "What are you talking about?"

Shrimp wheezed, "Lucy . . ." I sank slowly back to my chair as

Shrimp struggled to locate enough air to conclude his short sentence. ". . . shot me."

"When, Shrimp?" I said, cocking an eyebrow at my guest. I noticed that there was a smudge mark on her cheek, the ripening of a fresh bruise. "When did she shoot you?"

Shrimp's answer was depressingly deadpan. "Right before . . . she left."

There was a pause, then he added, "I think I've lost a lot of blood."

And the line went dead.

Bad sign.

"Shrimp? Shrimp, are you still there?" I did what they do in the movies. Rattled my finger up and down on the little jiggywazzits where you hang up the phone, then I hung up the phone. The young woman in front of me was shifting the dress in her lap. Her hand emerged from underneath it and she set something blue and ugly on my desk.

"How's he doing?" she asked.

I steepled my fingers and lighted my chin on the tippy top. Undertakers have a knack for being able to draw their faces into a blank. That's what I did. Then I reached down with my index finger and swiveled the barrel of the little pistol so that it wasn't aiming directly at me. We're also not idiots. Then I resteepled.

"Well Lucy, I wouldn't say he's sounding terribly chipper. If that's what you're asking."

CHAPTER 2

Lucy Taylor and I go way back. She's an old friend of mine and of my ex-wife, Julia. We were kids together. The three of us grew up within rock-throwing distance of each other down here in the Fell's Point section of Baltimore, which is where all three of us still live. I mean that literally by the way, the rock-throwing distance. When I was twelve and Lucy was nine I beaned her just above the right eye with a rock as she was stepping out the front door of her father's house on Shakespeare Street to take out the trash. I wasn't aiming at her specifically; I was having an especially bad day and was just throwing rocks indiscriminately at the world. Poor Lucy. It is *so* like her to have this sort of thing happen. Crazy girl was just born to fall into puddles. Anyway, when I beaned her she went down like a small sack of potatoes and I got her up the street to Hopkins as fast as I could. The doctors patched her up with a few stitches then gave me a lecture about how I might have blinded my little friend and should be more careful in the future and all the rest of it. Lucy didn't hold it against me. She knew I had been upset that day and she was completely understanding. But still. I felt terrible, of course, and I doted on Lucy for weeks afterward. I took her to the movies, I plied her with banana splits, I sneaked her down to the basement of my aunt and uncle's funeral home and let her see a dead body. (Let it never be said that I can't show a girl a good time.) I even badgered Julia to badger her parents to let me open a tab for Lucy at the Screaming Oyster Saloon; any old time she wanted, Lucy could go into the Oyster, saddle up to the bar and drink Coca-Colas to her little heart's content. Lucy Taylor loved her Coca-Colas, and in practically no time she was making the trip to the S.O.S. three and four times a day, sometimes more. She'd climb up on the barstool and plant her pointy elbows on the bar and pull nonstop on the twisty straw, then sing out for a refill. I didn't really have the cash to pay my tab, nor did I have the heart to suggest to Lucy that she maybe slow down a little. It seemed to make her so happy, knocking back free Cokes at the Oyster. I offered to Sally, Julia's mom, to do some chores around the place if that would help any, and Sally's response was to hang her large head—no doubt to hide the grin—and ask me only that I'd promise to come visit her and Frank and Julia once they got shipped off to the poorhouse.

One other thing. Julia swears to me that Lucy Taylor was always the way she is, which is something of a hard-luck Harriet. She says that Lucy came into this earth with her fall-in-a-puddle karma firmly in place, that it was already evident well before I cracked her in the head with a rock. As proof, Julia recalls Lucy at age seven, daydreaming so hard on Christmas day that she walked right off the end of the pier and into the harbor. Or a year later, when Lucy went chasing after a stray cat and ended up getting stuck in a drainage pipe and had to be set free with a pickax. And it's true, the general take around the neighborhood has always been that Lucy was a sweet and generous girl—indiscriminately kind (which is what leads a person like Lucy to a person like Shrimp Martin)—but that she was simply born with a card or two already plucked from her deck.

I'm a sucker for a gal in a uniform. This one's name tag identified her as Nancy. Nancy smiled as sweetly as an angel as she plunged a needle into my arm.

"It's very good of you to offer a blood donation, Mr. Sewell. We're in one of those low phases. People just aren't donating the way they used to." Nurse Nancy nibbled on her lower lip as she pulled back on the plunger, sucking the life force out of me. "O negative. We can always use O negative around here." She smiled up at me as she flicked free the knot on the elastic around my arm.

"All done. You might feel a little woozy for a while. We recommend that you don't drive until you've rested and had something to eat."

"Perhaps you'd care to join me," I said, rolling the sleeve of my muslin shirt back down over my elbow. "The Hopkins Deli makes these gargantuan sandwiches. Do you get breaks around here?"

She shook her head. "We don't leave the floor." She labeled the vials of my blood and stowed them in a small Styrofoam carrying case.

"I could get a sandwich and bring it back," I said.

"The sandwich you describe sounds too big to carry."

Big grin. "I'm a packhorse. I can manage it."

Small smile. "Thank you. But no thank you." She zinged open the curtain that had secluded us from the rest of the world. There it was, just as we'd left it. Cradling my blood, the nurse stepped away silently on her white rubber shoes.

Shrimp Martin was still in surgery. When I had arrived at the hospital I had been told by one of the EMS workers who brought him in that Shrimp had been found unconscious in his living room, lying on top of the phone. He had lost a lot of blood, as indeed he had hypothesized to me over the phone. I sensed a touch-and-go vibe. I could probably get away here with pretending that it was the news of how much blood Shrimp had lost that prompted me to offer a donation of my own. It wasn't. It was Nurse Nancy. The uniform. Something perversely sexy about all that starched white. She wore a blond bob and a shy smile and had seemed enthusiastic about taking me up on my offer that she go at me with a needle.

Soon after my blood donation, I got a report. Shrimp was stabilized. They were still working on him, but he was going to survive. He had taken a single bullet in his stomach. It apparently ripped sideways, right to left, and meddled with a few important organs before exiting directly through his left kidney. In all senses, the kidney was shot, and so the doctors were removing it. One of the emergency room surgeons had emerged from behind a pair of automatic doors—his green smock smeared with blood, his hands wrapped in prophylactic—to let me know about the kidney.

"We're going to perform an emergency nephrectomy," he said. He seemed to want to know where I stood on nephrectomies. I stood nowhere. "He'll live a normal life," he added. Apparently this guy didn't know Shrimp.

The doctor excused himself and went back into the operating room to nephrect. A uniformed policeman came off the elevator and beelined for the nurse's station. I beelined into the stairwell. I wasn't in the mood for chatting with the police. Not yet anyway. I pictured poor Lucy slumped in the chair in my office and the Papa Bear in me simply came out. I just wasn't ready to turn her over. Besides which, my tooth was pulsing with a disco beat by this time and I was feeling very cranky. Cops don't generally like cranky. So really, I was doing this for him, too. I went round and round and up and up and up, and came out on a quiet floor. I strolled to the end of the corridor and gazed out a window onto a gravel rooftop several stories below. Two guys in green overalls were smearing tar around some sort of vent, a bubble-shaped aluminum thing with fan blades. Two pigeons on a nearby exhaust chimney were watching them. A blimp was floating, off in the distance. Pimlico racetrack. I remembered. The Anniversary Stakes were today. Technically, I should have been finding a TV. I had a hundred bucks in the Screaming Oyster pool. A horse called Tango Wallop. I'm not really a horse guy. It was names from a hat. Simple bar betting. Tango Wallop's odds were middling to crappy, which was probably why I wasn't scaling tall mountains and fording great seas in search of a TV set.

Eventually I found my way back to the emergency room. The uniformed cop had left. Shame. It occurred to me that I should be hitting the phones, but I really wasn't sure whom to call. I knew Shrimp had a sister. I had met her once down at the club. A big soft overweight girl who cornered me for three years one evening and melted both my ears on the subject of tarts and strudels and hot-cross buns. The Martin family, so I learned, has been running the extremely popular Mabel's Bakeries for several generations, ever since Great-granddaddy Martin opened the first shop down on Preston Street a century or so ago. As I recall the tale, Shrimp's refusal to follow in the footsteps of his father and his father's father's father had resulted in the sister now being groomed to take over the bread and pastry dynasty when the time came for Daddy to step down. Apparently there was bad blood between Shrimp and his father as a result of this bucking of tradition. The sister was clearly both fond of her brother and thrilled to be next in line to run the bakery dynasty. Standing there in the hospital I could conjure her face and her soft doughy presence, but I couldn't snag the name.

I found a phone out in the waiting area and called Billie to let her know that Shrimp was pulling through. I asked her if Lucy had shared with her yet her reasons for taking a shot at him.

"I can't get a peep out of her, Hitchcock. She's just sitting over in the corner staring out the window. I gave her some Coca-Cola and we put some ice on that cheek. She's looking like a very sad raccoon."

"Put her on the phone, will you?"

While I waited for Lucy to come on, I snagged a young doctor who was passing by and asked him what he'd recommend for a sore tooth. He recommended Tylenol. Just like they say on TV. Billie came back on the line and told me that Lucy didn't want to talk.

"Did you tell her that Shrimp is going to pull through?"

"Yes."

"What did she say to that?"

"Very little." Billie's voice lowered. "What about the police, Hitchcock? I believe they like to be told about these sorts of things."

"They know," I said. "A cop has already been here."

"What did you tell him?"

"Well . . . I didn't actually speak with him. I want to give Lucy a chance to snap out of it first. This is going to be rough on her. It's the least we can do."

"I suppose we can plead ignorance," Billie mused. "I mean, I *am* so tragically daft, after all."

"Loopy as a loon," I said.

"There you have it."

"As spacey as Sputnik."

"If you will."

"The queen of the senior moment. Voted most likely to—"

"Okay, young man, you've made your point."

We hung up. I called Roger and left a message with his answering service that an emergency had come up and I wouldn't be able to come in this afternoon after all. Shrimp was just then being wheeled out of surgery. The bloodied surgeon gave me the rundown. Shrimp had pulled through. He'd be in the hospital for a few days at the very least. Henceforth, he'd be filtering all of his toxins through his remaining kidney but the doctor assured me that this should pose no real problem. I returned to the waiting area and dropped into one of the molded plastic chairs. And slumped. The damn tooth was pulsing, more like Morse code now. The TV set in the corner by the ceiling was showing a red-haired chef waving her arms through volumes of smoke and crying out "I live to feed!" I was too lazy to go channeling for the Anniversary Stakes. Tango Wallop didn't stand a chance anyway; I could kiss that Franklin bye-bye. I picked up the only magazine on the glass table in front of me, but decided I wasn't really motivated to learn how to put the zing back in my marriage. A hundred and one ways. My marriage with Julia had lasted exactly one year. We had relocated the zing simply by bagging the marriage. I doubted the magazine was going to offer this sort of advice. I settled in and gazed up at the chef. For no reason that I was able to discern, she had donned a red clown's nose and was wielding her spatula like a microphone.

I tuned my thoughts back to Shrimp Martin. Shrimp, Shrimp, Shrimp . . . Hell, I didn't even know the guy's real name. Why in the world he would have called me instead of 911 was something that I had not yet worked out. It wasn't as if old Shrimpster and I were backslapping buddies. I had only met the guy several months previous, the night that Shrimp's and Lucy's orbits had first crossed. Julia and I had taken Lucy over to Shrimp's nightclub as part of Julia's campaign to help poor Lucy bounce back from her latest romantic misstep. A little music-soothes-the-soul therapy. As it happened, the tactic blew up in our faces when the club's torch singer had opened her set with "I'll Be Seeing You" and Lucy beat a tearful retreat to the women's room. "Old familiar place," Julia noted wryly. A few minutes later—still no Lucy—a bucket full of ice and champagne had arrived at our table, followed by an unctuous fellow in a white dinner jacket, bad skin and a fox-in-the-henhouse smile. Shrimp Martin. I recognized him from his numerous suck-up poses with club patrons and local celebrities in the photographs that were tacked up on the walls just inside the club's front door. I had already noticed a chubby guy with a camera prowling about. Clearly, the nightclub owner had Julia Finney in his sights. Aside from being arguably the sexiest woman on the Eastern seaboard, Julia is also a highly successful and celebrated painter. She's been hung all over the world. It was abundantly clear that Shrimp was a major hobnobber. While Shrimp jimmied elaborately with the champagne cork, Julia had preened and cooed and made such big can-you-believe-this-jerk eyes at me that I thought the lovely brown bulbs were going to fall right out of their sockets. Shrimp finally wrestled the cork from the bottle, losing half the bubbly over his wrist. It was just then that Fate had trotted forward, dressed up this time as Lucy Taylor. Eyes red and childlike from her bathroom crying jag, a big gooey smile grew on Lucy's face as she approached the table. "Champagne? Oh, I *love* champagne!" And the smooth operator holding the bottle hadn't missed a beat, grabbing hold of the empty chair and sliding it back from the table. "My compliments," he crooned as he tucked little Lucy into the table. And then he introduced himself. "I'm Shrimp Martin," he said, giving a slight bow. "*Mi casa es su casa.*" Lucy summarily beamed and blushed and handed over her tiny paw to the next mistake in her life. "Lucy Taylor," she chirped. "Nice *casa.*"

"Lean in folks!"

Flash! The chubby photographer captured the moment.

A phone freed up. I dug out another quarter. I had a date that night that I wasn't particularly looking forward to, but the prospect of trading it in for a hospital vigil seemed a worse bet. I really did need to get someone else to come down here and take over the Shrimp vigil. I called Julia's cell phone. I hate cell phones. Julia loves them. You tell me, was that marriage not doomed?

"Where are you?" I asked when Julia answered, which in the era of cell phones is the greeting that has replaced "Hello." Julia, it turned out, was way the hell out in the county. Our connection sounded aquatic.

"I'm at the Manor Tavern," she burbled.

"What are you doing way up there?" I asked.

"Eating ribs."

"Oh? Whose?"

"Ha ha. I needed to get out of the city, Hitch. It's too darned hot."

I scanned for a song lyric quip but found nothing. "How did you get out there, anyway?" Julia doesn't drive. Generally, she takes taxis. Or she is squired.

"His name is Tom," she said.

I nodded sagely. "His name is Tom."

"He is a gentleman and a scholar."

"He's a polite professor?"

"Telephone repairman."

"Oh. You're having problems with your phone?"

She giggled. It sounded more like a gurgle. "Not anymore."

"Jules, this still doesn't explain why you're out in the county."

"I told you, I wanted some fresh air. Tom was fixing my phone. He had his repair truck. He offered to take me for a drive. He's gorgeous, Hitch. Male. Blue jeans. Tool belt."

"Jules, listen. We've got a situation here. I'm at Union Memorial. Shrimp Martin has been shot and—"

"He's been *what*?"

"Shot. You know. Bullet? Entry wound? The—"

"Holy Jesus. How's Lucy? Does she know? Is she there?"

I took a deep breath. "Here's the thing. Lucy is the one who shot him."

I had to pull back from the phone. "*What?* Lucy *shot* him? Jesus Christ, Hitch! Where is she? Is she under arrest? Oh God . . . this is *so* Lucy."

"Slow down. She's with Billie right now," I said. "Everything's fine. We're going to pretend that we were too scattered to think about calling the police right away. Billie's keeping an eye on her. She's pretty much in shock, I think."

"Poor Lucy."

"Shrimp's going to live, by the way. I know that was your next question."

"Oh, Shrimp Martin is an idiot, Hitch. Someone was bound to shoot him sooner or later. So come on, tell me. What happened?"

"I really couldn't get anything out of Lucy. I have to guess it was some kind of accident. Here's the thing. Can you get your stud muffin to run you back into town? I need you to get over to Billie's. I think you're the person she needs to see."

"Of course. I'll come in right away."

"I also need to get someone to baby-sit Shrimp down here. I've got a date in a few hours."

"Date? It wouldn't be with that dancer, would it?"

"It would."

"Your enthusiasm is underwhelming."

I grumbled. "We'll go to a restaurant and she won't eat. We'll go to this big dance performance she has choreographed and I won't get it. Do you hear the theme of 'unfulfilling' running through this?"

"What about afterward? Have you two knocked knees yet?" Julia has been racking up euphemisms for sex for as long as she has been racking up sex itself. Ergo, she's got a ton of them.

I told her that I didn't know if "yet" was the right word. "Dead end" was pretty much written all over this one.

"Hitch, is there really any reason for you to even go on this date? Why don't you call her up and give her the perfectly acceptable excuse that you have been called to the hospital bedside of a friend in need?"

I had an answer to that. "A bad date is still preferable to a night drinking cardboard coffee from a hospital vending machine. And Shrimp Martin hardly qualifies as my friend. So look, do you have any idea how I might be able to get a hold of Shrimp's sister?"

"The chubby girl?"

"Yes."

"God, she is more tedious than death."

"I'm not asking for someone to come entertain him. I just want to get someone over here so that I can leave."

"Mary Ann."

"Mary Ann! That's right. Mary Ann Martin. Perfect. I'll give Mary Ann a call and you get your big beautiful bucket back to town and over to Billie's."

"Charming."

I hung up and dialed Information. With a little cajoling I got the operator to work with me. There were seven "Martin, M"s listed, and I was able to get them all on one request, rather than the usual limit of two. The first four I called were not Shrimp's sister. This was easy to determine. My opener was "Hi, I'm looking for Shrimp's sister." Three of the four simply hung up. The fourth was a man with an Eastern European accent who started griping to me about UFOs and what they were doing to his dog. I struck gold on the fifth call. Nearly gold.

"Hi, I'm looking for Shrimp's sister."

"This is Mary."

"Mary Ann?"

"Mary."

"Mary?"

"I live here, too. I'm Mary Ann's housemate."

"That must get confusing."

"Who is this?"

"This is Hitchcock Sewell," I said. "Is Mary Ann there? I need to speak with her."

"I'm afraid she's not."

"Do you expect her back soon?"

Mary said that she thought that Mary Ann would be back within the hour. "She went to a matinee of *My Fair Lady* at The Mechanic." That brought back memories. The Gypsy Players botched that little gem about four years ago. I was Higgins. My British accent stank. And I sang like a mule. Julia was Eliza. Of course, she was loverly. And an even worse ham than me. *The rine in Spine fools minely oon the pline.*

I told the woman on the phone that Mary Ann's brother was in intensive care at Union Memorial with a gunshot wound to the stomach, that he was going to be all right but that someone needed to get over to the hospital right away. Mary was duly impressed with my message.

"Shrimp's been shot? What happened?"

I lied. "I'm not sure. But I can't really stay here with him much longer. I've got to be somewhere in a few hours."

"Mary Ann has a cell phone. Maybe I should call her."

I pictured Henry Higgins in the middle of his silly "By jove I think she's got it!" number when out there in the dark a damn cell phone begins to chirp. By jove, *get it.*

"I wouldn't do that," I said.

"What about I come over? It's not that far. I'm just over near Lake Montebello. I can leave Mary Ann a message on the kitchen table."

It seemed an unnecessarily generous offer. I took her up on it. I told her where to meet me at the hospital.

"How will I recognize you?" she asked.

"I'm tall," I said. "Dark hair. I've got one of those little Superman curls that sort of falls —"

"Okay."

"How will I recognize you?" I asked.

"I'm short."

"That's it?"

"I'll be there in twenty minutes," she said. "I've just got to throw some clothes on."

Intriguing detail that it was, I let it pass. We hung up. I went back to the molded plastic chair to wait for Mary Ann's short friend Mary. I went ahead and glanced at the article about putting zing back in the marriage. Guess what? They suggest more frequent sex. Along with candles and wine and surprises. Big shock.

"You must be whatshisname."

A woman with a freckled face and short damp blond hair was standing directly in front of me. Her approach had been pure stealth. Slipped in under the cover of my daydreaming. I stood up. Her freckled nose leveled off around the latitude of my elbow. Pale blue eyes looked up at me. Mine are blue, too. Turns out these were the only two things we had in common.

"And you must be Mary." I offered my hand. Hers disappeared into mine. Like a whale swallowing a bonbon. "That was fast," I said. Though I had no real idea how much time had passed.

"Twenty minutes. As promised." She released my hand and ran hers through her damp hair, which was sun-streaked gold and short enough to get away with a finger-brushing. Her face was apple-shaped. If you can picture that in a good way. Farmer's daughter, with an urban edge. "You're lucky," she added. "I was just getting out of the shower when you called."

I wasn't sure why that made me lucky, but I let it pass. I placed Mary in her early twenties, fresh and well-scrubbed. Maybe it was the freckles, along with the pulsing peach tan. The remaining inventory supported this first impression. Simple white V-neck T-shirt, blue jean cutoffs and flip-flops. She was all of five feet tall if she was an inch, toned and glowing, a trim vertical package with well-carved little hips and intriguing breasts. I realize that I'm coming off like an auctioneer, but these are simply the facts. She looked beach-ready and very sure of herself. And as humorless as a stone.

She caught me staring. At least it seemed she did. She crossed her arms over her intriguing breasts and frowned up at me.

"So what happened?"

I told her. "Shrimp Martin called me up a couple of hours ago and said he'd been shot. I called nine-one-one. They got him here, he lost a kidney and a lot of blood, but he's going to live." I left out the detail that it was a friend of mine who shot him. It's always good to hold something back, in case the conversation sags.

The damp head was tilted and she was squinting slightly. The woman seemed to be judging my credibility. "So where are the police?" she asked. Her tone was clearly challenging.

"The police?"

"He was shot. Where are the police?"

"A cop was here earlier," I said. "He left."

My little friend was unimpressed. "So who shot him?"

"Why would I know who shot him?" I said. I sounded defensive. Which I was. I'm usually good with my poker face. But for some reason the frank blue eyes already had me on the ropes. Also, my neck was cricking looking down at her.

She batted her critical blues. "You said Shrimp *called* you. Maybe he *said* something?"

"It was . . . everything's under control," I stammered.

"What's *that* supposed to mean?" She was making no effort now to conceal her disapproval with how things were being handled. Or not being handled.

"It was a domestic shooting," I said lamely.

The woman's eyebrows went up, like a stretching cat. "Uh huh . . ."

"The person who shot Shrimp is with my aunt." I added, "At the funeral home."

"Funeral home?"

"My aunt and I run a funeral home."

She studied my face. About a three-second deconstruction. The term "tough little cookie" was beginning to form in the judgment corner of my brain. Mary said, "Okay, so now what? You're here in case Shrimp dies? That's a little eager, isn't it?"

I took a step backward and kneaded my neck. Mary took it the wrong way. She took a step back as well. "What are you doing now, *measuring* me?"

"No. I just . . . nothing."

Mary shifted her weight over to one hip and tilted her head in the opposite direction. The eyebrows went up again—this time both—and a look of complete mistrust slotted onto her face. Now I know what Goliath must have felt like. This pipsqueak's body language was pebbling me to death before I even had a chance. I was reduced to a single bleat.

"What?"

"Would you mind not looking at me that way?" she said.

"What way?"

She made a huffy sound. "You big guys. You've got such a thing for small women."

"*Excuse me?* Who said I've got a 'thing' for small women?"

She uncurled her arms and raised a hand. "Down here? That was me?"

I pulled up. My lightning-speed calculation concluded that there was nothing to be gained in joining an argument with a total stranger with a height complex. At least not in a hospital waiting room. In a bar, maybe, but not here. She stood there, slingshot-ready.

"I think we're sliding off the track," I said. "Look. Thanks for coming down. Let me give you my card. When Mary Ann gets here, have her call if she wants. I might not be in, but she can talk to my aunt."

I produced a card and held it out. She glanced at it then tucked it into the rear pocket of her cutoffs. Any thicker and the card couldn't have possibly fit. She rubbed her bare arms. I hadn't noticed, but in fact it was pretty cold in there. They had the AC cranked and she was dressed for the sun. She squinted up at me again.

" 'Bye."

Like that, she turned and walked away. *Poof.* I raised my hand for a half-wave but it was to thin air and I let it drop. I did look to see if I could spot my business card. I couldn't, of course. But the effort was pleasing. My guess was that she knew I was looking. Julia tells me that they always know we're looking.

I traveled the length of the corridor and pushed the button for the elevator. As I waited, I glanced back. Mary was seated in one of the plastic chairs, trim tanned legs crossed, leafing through the magazine. She'd be learning those zing tricks for dulled marriages. I willed her to glance up from the magazine, but she didn't. The elevator arrived and I got on, squeezing in between a pair of gurneys carrying two pale vapors in human form. The doors were slow in closing. I faced front and again willed the irritating woman at the end of the hall to look up. She wet her finger and turned a page of her magazine. She didn't look up. Her foot waggled. The elevator doors slid shut.

I was in love.

Not really.

The doe-eyed boy in tights was shooting invisible arrows in all directions from an invisible bow. His victims clutched their hearts, their stomachs, their necks, flinging themselves to the ground and tumbling in somer-saults, three, four, five rotations, then leaping to their feet to live another day. Or at least another several seconds. The doe-eyed boy himself was a show-off, leaping up onto a boulder, twirling his feet in midair, shooting off-balance, even tumbling along sometimes right beside his victims. His stash of invisible arrows was endless. In all, a very sprightly massacre.

"Here she comes."

"She" was a waifish girl done up in the same tights and the same doe-eyed makeup as the homicidal Cupid. She appeared atop the boulder, up on her toes, her pipe-cleaner arms snaking upward. In her hands was cupped a large opalescent disk. The moon. The nifty part was that when the girl came down off the boulder—her steps were like those of someone sticking their toe in the water to see how cold it is—the disk remained suspended in air. I tried, but I couldn't see the wires.

I'll skip the blow-by-blow. Bottom line is that the boy's invisible arrows had no effect on Moon Girl whatsoever. He fired away at an increasingly frantic pace while she pranced around mockingly, making an easy target of herself. Her invulnerability infuriated the boy, then exhausted him, then finally drove him to tears (invisible, like his armaments). Any minute I expected Moon Girl to sit down on the boulder and start doing her nails, ho-hum. In the end—I could have almost predicted this—the boy made a very melodramatic scene of handing over his invisible bow and an invisible arrow to the waif, and then he got up on the boulder and reached up to take hold of the moon, sticking his bony chest out so that the girl couldn't possibly miss the mark. She took aim and shot him. The moon came out of the sky in the boy's hands as he tumbled off the boulder . . . and the stage went black.

There was a finger-food-and-wine reception after the performance. The performers were there, looking like alien beings at a getting-to-know-you conference. My date for the evening—we'll call her Clarissa because that's what everyone calls her (she was christened Debbie)—spent nearly the entire reception with her fingers laced in a ball that she kept pressed tightly against her breast. Clarissa had only warm words for the performers, the most frequent one being "wonderful." Everything was "*Wonderful!*" Clarissa's face is one of the most expressive I have ever seen and she lavished it on the young performers, most of whom blushed and demurred at her fawning. This was what they had worked so hard for over the past several months. Clarissa had opened a dance studio over on Read Street early in the year and was trying to put a company together. Tonight was the premiere of *Dance of the Protégés* and the dancers had been so eager to please. If you could judge from Clarissa's liberal scatterings of *wonderfuls*, they had succeeded.

Clarissa reserved her largest fawning for the two principals, pulling out an entirely fresh set of superlatives for the doe-eyed boy and his twinlike murderess. Clarissa goosed up the boy in particular, who wallowed shamelessly in his teacher's praise. From the young girl, however, I detected a whiff of coldness. Competition, perhaps. The gristle of ego in a slow grind. The young dancer definitely had a bug up her ass about Clarissa. She was as skinny as a toothpick. Her eyes, which were lined like those of an Egyptian princess, were dark and mean. Clarissa smiled her effervescent pearlies right through the young dancer's pointed indifference, then didn't wait until we were out of the girl's earshot before saying to me, "So what did *you* think of the little bitch?"

Ah . . . showbiz.

This whole snap, crackle, pop was taking place in the lobby area outside the auditorium of the High School for the Performing Arts, where Clarissa had arranged to stage her show. Air kisses were flying with the frequency of the evening's invisible arrows. I wasn't having me an especially bang-up time. Could you tell? And it wasn't just the cheap wine. Part of it was my tooth, which had now begun to take on a personality all its own. And not one that I particularly liked. Khrushchev pounding his shoe at the U.N. comes to mind. But another big part of it was Clarissa. This was our third time going out together and the chemistry was still proving as so-so as on the first two shots. Even so, I had the sense that this was the evening where the mad blind plunge into the sack had now risen to the top of the docket. This was a big night for Clarissa, after all. God knows how much she had spent on the dress she was wearing, but elegance and glitter like that doesn't come cheap. For my part, I had come through in my big bad tux and I looked like a goodly portion of a million bucks myself. A couple as sharp-looking as the two of us—on a night of no small importance to one of us—is not a couple who are expected to peak at a Gallo and Gouda gala in a high school lobby. There are rules about these things, and it was only a matter of whether Clarissa or I— more specifically, I—were going to break them or not.

When the time came for the toasts and the little speeches, I took the opportunity to duck outside for some air. It must have been nearing nine-thirty. Venus and her friends were blinking and twinkling brightly in the night's blue veil. There was a pay phone near the corner. I stepped over to it and dug out a quarter. I dialed my number. After my own voice told me that I wasn't in, I cupped my hands to the mouthpiece and yelled, "Alcatraz! Sit!" Without a spy on the premises, I'll never know if my lowly hound dog actually does sit when I do this. I punched in the code to retrieve my messages. There was only one (besides the one I had just left). It was from Billie, telling me to call her. I had planned to do just that. And I did.

"Oh, Hitchcock, there you are. I've been trying to figure out how to find you." Billie sounded agitated. Billie is hardly ever agitated. "That woman you left at the hospital . . ."

"Mary."

"Yes. Mary. That's her. She called here looking for you. It's Shrimp Martin."

"What about him?"

"He's dead."

"He's *what*!" I switched ears. "What do you mean he's dead, Billie? He was fine when I left him. I mean, they told me he was fine. The doctor told me—"

Billie cut me off. "You'd better get down there, Hitchcock. According to— Apparently they had a little problem."

"A little problem? I'll say. The guy's dead, for Christ's sake. They had a *big* problem."

"That's not what I mean. According to this Mary, somebody went into Shrimp Martin's room and killed him."

"Billie, what are you talking about? Right there in the hospital?"

"That's what the girl told me on the phone."

"This is insane. Who the hell . . . Put Lucy on, will you?"

There was a pause.

"Hitchcock, Lucy's not here."

"Where is she? Did she go down to the hospital?"

"I don't know where she is, dear. I was in the kitchen making vichyssoise and she slipped out. I thought she was still sleeping."

I didn't like this. "Billie, did Julia come by?"

"No, dear. I'm afraid I haven't seen her."

Didn't like it at all. "When did Lucy leave?"

"It's close to two hours now," Billie said.

"And when did you say Mary called from the hospital?" I looked up at Venus. They say that the atmosphere on Venus is so thickly packed that light bends in ways we can barely imagine here on Earth. In theory, you can be looking straight ahead and staring at the back of your own head at the same time. That's about what I felt I was doing right then.

Billie answered, "That was about an hour ago."

I was halfway to Union Memorial before it occurred to me that I had forgotten to ask Billie about the gun Lucy had brought over. To see if it was still there on my desk.

I was three quarters of the way there before it hit me that I hadn't even said good-bye to Clarissa.

A hand grabbed hold of my arm the moment I stepped off the elevator.

"You're under arrest."

I plucked the hand from my arm as if it were a dead rat (which reminded me). "What's the charge?"

"Perfect attendance at all my murder scenes." John Kruk gave me the sneer that for him passes for a smile. He might even have chuckled. Kruk gave an up-and-down to my tux.

"I was just out for a jog," I said as I surveyed the scene. The intensive care ward was like a department store on Christmas Eve. People were going in all directions, yelling to be heard above the din, arms waving, urgent gesturing. If there was any order here, I was missing it. Uniformed police were milling about. Notebooks were at the ready. Questions were being asked. Some mild flirting with the nurses was going on.

Kruk rubbed a hand over his thick neck. "Let's hear it, Mr. Sewell. What do you know and when did you know it?"

"I thought those questions were reserved for the president."

John Kruk is largely banter-proof. He shifted on his flat feet and gave me his bored look. "I'm waiting."

"Who told you that I had any involvement in this whatsoever?" I asked. "Can't a man in a tuxedo just show up in a hospital on a Saturday night and not get harassed by the local constabulary?"

"Are you saying you don't have any involvement?"

"I didn't say that. I'm just curious how it is you're not surprised to see me."

Kruk consulted his notebook. "You phoned in the nine-one-one at approximately three o'clock."

"Yes sir, that sounds about right."

"Where were you when you made the call?"

"In my office."

"You didn't call from the victim's house?"

"From Shrimp's?"

"That's right."

"No sir."

"According to EMS personnel, someone was milling around outside the victim's home when they arrived. That's why I ask."

"Wasn't me. I was milling around a funeral home."

Kruk consulted his notebook. "So after arriving at the hospital, you passed the victim off to a Mary Childs late this afternoon."

"Ah, so it was good old Mary who gave me up."

"Miss Childs said that you knew who shot Mr. Martin." He gave me his whammy-eye. He's got a real winner.

"Miss Childs doesn't like me," I said. "We got off on the wrong foot. She'd say anything."

"Are you saying that she lied?"

"Well, no. I'm just saying the girl doesn't like me."

"So you withheld information about a shooting for . . . what do we have, going on ten hours now? Do you mind if I ask where you have been all this time?"

I thought about describing the dance performance to him, but that would have been cruel. And most certainly unusual. "I had a prior engagement." When he frowned at me, I added. "A hot date." Now I was giving false and misleading information. See how slippery the slope can be?

We were blocking the elevators. Sick people were trying to get off and on. A large hulking man was pushing a gurney. He was wearing a paper shower cap on his head. Anywhere but in here the guy would have looked like a wuss. Kruk and I drifted over to the waiting area. A woman and someone I took to be her daughter were huddled together on the plastic chairs. They looked confused and scared. A black kid in massive jeans and a do-rag was sitting across from them, frowning at his fists. He and Kruk shared a little staring contest as we carried past him and over to the window.

"I think he likes you," I said to the detective.

Kruk ignored me. Years of practice. The stocky detective squared off in front of me. "Let's start at the beginning." He pulled out his notebook. "I want a name, Mr. Sewell."

"You don't like Kruk?" Now I was in a staring contest. Which I lost immediately. "Lucy Taylor," I said.

He wrote it down. "Relationship?"

"Old friend."

"Old?"

"As in 'long time.' "

"How old is this Miss Taylor?"

"Around thirty. Thirty-one?"

"And her relationship with the victim?"

"Lady friend." Kruk scribbled something down. I added, "They met in March."

"And how well would you say you know Miss Taylor?"

"Pretty well."

Kruk asked again, "How well do you know Miss Taylor?"

"How do I answer a question like that?"

"You start with the truth and you end with the truth. Very simple."

"I know Lucy pretty well," I said.

He grunted. "Intimately?"

"Nothing like that. We grew up together. Lucy is like a sister to me." Kruk scribbled something in his notebook. I craned my neck to see if he had actually written "like a sister," but I couldn't make sense of his hieroglyphics.

Kruk asked, "Is there any reason why you would hold back from calling the authorities about this other than simple loyalty to an old friend?" He looked up at me. "Don't give me a glib one here."

"Reasons like what?" I said.

"I don't supply answers for people, Mr. Sewell. Do you need to hear the question again?"

"No sir. And the answer is also no, sir. Lucy was scheduled to show up at the funeral home to drop off a dress. Her grandmother died two days ago. We're handling the funeral. Just before she arrived, I got a phone call from Shrimp Martin. Shrimp was rambling. I had no idea why he was calling. In fact, I still don't quite understand it. But anyway, Lucy came in while I was on the phone to Shrimp. Shrimp told me that Lucy had shot him. Then it seems he passed out. Lucy proceeded to put a pistol on my desk and then pretty much went into shock. I didn't call the police because it didn't occur to me to call the police. I'm sorry. I called nine-one-one. I took Lucy up to my aunt's apartment, then I came here. Shrimp was worked on and then stabilized. The crisis was over, I thought. I phoned Shrimp's sister. Her lovely little housemate came here and took over the vigil. I proceeded to my hot date. The end."

"So your whereabouts the past few hours can be verified."

"I was at a dance program, Detective. I've got the scars to prove it."

"Why do you suppose Mr. Martin called you?"

"I told you, I have no idea. We weren't close friends at all."

He tapped his pencil against his notepad. "Here's a thought, if he knew that Miss Taylor was heading over to your place, maybe he was calling you to warn you."

"Warn me of what?"

"That she had a gun."

"So what if she had a gun? Lucy wasn't going to shoot *me*. Lucy likes me. I'm her friend."

"And according to you, this guy was her boyfriend."

"Look, Detective, this is your area of expertise, not mine. But don't girlfriends shoot boyfriends all the time? And vice versa? Isn't that half of what keeps you in business?"

"I'm just trying to look at all the possibilities here," Kruk said.

"Well, I think you can scratch off the one that says Lucy was gunning for me. Lucy would never hurt me. We're friends. I told you, the first thing she did was hand the gun over."

"And where is that gun right now, Mr. Sewell?"

I wasn't proud of my answer. "I don't know. Last I saw, it was on the desk in my office." I figured he would ask me more about the gun, but he didn't.

"Okay. You said that Miss Taylor was due over at your place to drop off a dress. When had that been arranged?"

"Lucy called about an hour before she showed up. Said she was bringing the dress by."

"How did she sound?"

"She sounded fine."

"Fine?"

"Fine. Normal. Regular Lucy. There was nothing in her voice that suggested maybe she'd be plugging Shrimp with a bullet in the very near future."

"Sad. Upset. Angry. Distant. Confused?"

"You want me to pick one?"

"Only if you detected one in your conversation with Miss Taylor."

"Sad."

"Sad."

"Lucy had been close with her grandmother. Losing her was tough."

He was scribbling something down in his notebook when his attention was snagged by one of the uniformed cops who was over by the elevators. He was gesturing to Kruk with a cell phone. "Excuse me." Kruk went over to the cop and took the cell phone from him. I saw Shrimp Martin's sister wading through the crowd. Thankfully, not in my direction. I don't mean to sound crass, but it's my livelihood to deal with the recently bereaved. I really don't mind avoiding it when I'm off the clock. Mary Ann Martin blubbering against my chest simply wasn't my idea of a nice way to cap off the night. I could tell she was a blubberer. It was written all over her.

Kruk handed the phone back to his minion. The EMS worker I had spoken with earlier was being escorted over to Kruk. Kruk signaled me over. When I got to within about five feet of them the detective held out his hand, signaling me to stop. He turned to the EMS worker.

"Have you seen this man before?"

"Yeah. Right after I got here. He was asking me about the guy who was shot."

"Is this the person you told me about who was outside the victim's home? Who was asking questions?"

"Nah, I told you, that guy had one of those flattops."

"You're sure? This man's hair might have just been—"

"Hey," I interrupted. "Leading the witness."

"This isn't a courtroom, Mr. Sewell."

"Doesn't matter. I told you already, I called from my office. I was nowhere near Shrimp's."

Kruk dismissed the EMS worker. "I just took a phone call from one of my men, down at your place, Mr. Sewell. I sent a squad car over there the moment your name cropped up." He snapped his notebook closed. I remembered this now about Kruk. He had all the moves down pat. "You didn't tell me that Lucy Taylor was no longer at your aunt's," he said. He didn't sound happy saying it.

"I was getting to that."

I could see that Kruk didn't care for my answer. "I asked my man to look in your office, to see if the gun was there. It wasn't."

"Somehow that's what I suspected."

"And why is that?"

"I don't know . . ." I let off a large sigh. "I guess I figured Lucy took it with her when she left."

"Do you have any idea where she might have gone, Mr. Sewell?"

"Off the top of my head, no."

"You will supply us with an address, I hope. Where Miss Taylor lives."

I did. Right then and there. Kruk passed it on to one of his men, who trotted off with it.

"I suppose that's all for now, Mr. Sewell. Naturally, if you hear from Miss Taylor again, I expect you to contact us."

"Naturally."

"Immediately. Not ten hours later."

"You think Lucy Taylor killed Shrimp, don't you?"

"We have the victim's own statement to you over the phone that it was Miss Taylor who shot him. We have your statement that Lucy Taylor came into your office, put a gun on your desk and then lapsed into shock. Or what you've surmised is shock."

"I mean tonight. Here. You suspect that she came over here to the hospital and shot him again."

Kruk rubbed his jaw with his stubby fingers. "Mr. Martin was not shot," he said. "Whoever did this used a sharp object. We've got the M.E. going over the victim. He was stabbed directly in the heart. Plus, all of his tubes were pulled out."

"He wasn't shot?"

"Guns make a loud noise, Mr. Sewell. If you were going to kill someone in a hospital, would you use a gun?"

"I guess not. Never really gave it much thought. So he wasn't shot. But you still think Lucy did it, right?"

Kruk tugged on his ear, passed the back of his hand along the tip of his chin, tapped a finger against his jaw. If crime solving ever sours for him, I guess the guy could always ask the Orioles if they need a new third base coach.

"What would you think, Mr. Sewell?"

I took a deep breath. "I'd wait until all the evidence had been collected and all the related parties had been questioned and their stories checked out."

Kruk grunted. "We could certainly use more fair-minded men like you in law enforcement."

"So what's your take on Lucy?" I asked.

"I'm issuing a warrant," the detective said flatly. "I think the lady's a killer."

CHAPTER 3

Life inside my mouth, as I had known it, had ceased to exist. The silent Jackhammers of Hell had secured the area and it was theirs to do with as they pleased. It was Sunday. Not even eager Roger was going to see me on a Sunday. I could either grin and bear it or scowl and bear it. Frankly, neither seemed to make any difference.

My cupboards were bare. My refrigerator was bachelorized. I emptied the lumpy milk down the drain and took Alcatraz out for breakfast. I dressed for the occasion in my Cat's Eye T-shirt and my shorts-of-a-thousand pockets. Sunglasses on a Croakie. Air-conditioned Keds. No socks. Didn't shave. I was the deuce.

We went to Jimmy's, on Broadway. We sat at the window. I had coffee. And French toast. Dog ate pig. With a milk chaser. Our waitress was Edna. Rumor has it that she once slapped George Washington. This would make her well over two hundred years old, so that's patently absurd. I'd believe Abe Lincoln though. In order for my coffee to be hot, I fetched it myself. Same thing for my French toast. In fact, as Edna toddled off after taking my order I called it out over her head to Sid at the grill. Edna served no real function at Jimmy's. But she collected good tips.

Julia had never shown up. She had not called. She had not answered her cell phone the dozen or so times that I had called her. I didn't like this. Julia's a big girl—as the saying goes—and can certainly take care of herself. But the Lucy factor was another matter. Or rather, the Shrimp factor. I didn't know what to make of the events of the day before, but I had to assume that if Julia was in fact now in Lucy's company, she was at the very least within the orbit of whoever it was who killed Shrimp Martin. I suppose some former husbands might take a secret, or not so secret, thrill in such a turn of events. Not this one. This one put thirty-two stab wounds in his French toast as he mulled over what to do. On the sidewalk outside the restaurant window was a Sunpapers box. The headline didn't read JULIA FINNEY MISSING, unless you had my eyes. The headline said something about China. Well, I'm sorry, three hundred million people would just have to wait.

I finished up my breakfast as Edna was shuffling across the floor with my glass of water. She was humming a nonsense tune. I left her tip on the table and paid Sid directly. Edna was setting the water glass down on the table as I left.

A flea market was being set up in the square. Card tables and junk were blooming on the bricks. Alcatraz and I crossed the square to Julia's gallery. Chinese Sue was sitting at the counter, thumbing through a biography of Wernher von Braun. She had not heard a peep from her boss.

"Sold anything lately?" I asked.

She responded, "Lately?" which except for its being two syllables is a pretty typical Chinese Sue response.

There were a few browsers in the gallery, nobody who looked as if they'd be lining my ex-wife's pockets with gold anytime soon. There was a guy who was explaining to his girlfriend the significance of the flaming pumpkin motif that ran through several of the paintings. He was completely off, but I wasn't about to meddle. Two teenage boys were snickering at one of Julia's polka-dotted nudes. A middle-aged couple in matching Bermuda shorts and pink T-shirts ambled about the gallery, hand in hand, looking a little scared. A nun was coming in as I was leaving, followed by a biker. It was like a sociology experiment in there.

The square had filled. The smarter vendors sat in lawn chairs under beach umbrellas. I turned to Alcatraz. "Junk!" I love junk. I spotted a four-paned stained-glass lampshade that I couldn't possibly use and I bought it. Two bucks. I couldn't pass it up. The thing about flea markets is tail-wags-dog. With a useless glass lampshade, I'd now be in the market for a lamp that I hadn't previously needed. The vendor put the shade in a plastic bag for me. Alcatraz took a few moments to consider a three-foot-tall Mr. Peanut, but I didn't sense a full commitment on his part, so we passed it up. I was letting the plastic bag swing as we left the square and it slipped out of my fingers. It sailed against a fire hydrant and my two bucks shattered. We went back and got Mr. Peanut.

The day was already promising to be a scorcher and I already didn't like it. The logo on my T-shirt—a cat in profile, wearing a pirate's bandanna, and cackling a pirate's laugh—was dark with sweat. Not his, mine. Dog and master popped into St. Teresa's. We took a pew in the rear while a hymn was being murmured. I had to leave Mr. Peanut in the aisle. Alcatraz keened lowly but pretty much in pitch. Which was more than could be said for the sparse congregation. St. Teresa's was baking like a brick oven in hell. Heat wiggles were visible just above the parishioners, putting the altar slightly out of focus. I roused myself to drone along with the "Amen," then dropped onto the bench as Father Ted, dressed in his best Johnny Cash black, climbed onto his high horse. Otherwise known as the pulpit.

Father Ted was pissed off today. Which is not exactly a news flash. Father Ted is always pissed off about something. He is Fell's Point's most beloved crab. The Lord Himself could come down for the long awaited revisit, and Father Ted would still have a bitch and moan at the ready. In practically no time, Father Ted was going off like one of those cartoon teapots. As best I could make out, the theme of today's sermon was "You Had Your Damn Chance and by God You Blew It Big Time!" Or thereabouts. Father Ted is High Pessimist. He pounded the pulpit with his fist and hurled about terms like "moral pygmies" and "fools of the highest order" as his congregation sat passively, nodding their heads occasionally and fanning themselves with anything flappy they could get ahold of.

Alcatraz set his head on my feet and sighed. I had the pew to myself and draped my arms across the back of it. I'm not terribly religious in the organized sense. I'm more of a religious improviser. High Ambivalence. Still, I've racked up some good moments in St. Teresa's over the years, and a few minutes in church usually squares my shoulders. But nothing was really kicking for me today. As Father Ted emptied his spleen I sent up a silent request that Julia and Lucy get their asses safely back from wherever they were. Alcatraz and I waited until Father Ted had finished unloading and everyone's heads were bowed in prayer to make our silent exit from the church. I slipped Mr. Peanut under my arm and out we went. At the door, I stuffed some money into the money box.

Aunt Billie was fussing with her flower boxes as I rounded the corner.

"There you are," she called down to me. "I've been trying to get ahold of you." She snipped off a marigold at the throat and it toppled to the sidewalk. I stepped over and picked it up. I held it up to her.

"Murderer."

"Hitchcock, we have to discuss this Mrs. Rittenhouse situation," Billie said. "She's scheduled for burial tomorrow, but I don't feel right having the service without Lucy present."

"That's a problem," I admitted.

"Did you hear from Julia yet?"

I told her I hadn't. Billie put down her shears and wiped the back of her hand across her brow. "Oh dear. That's a problem, too."

"I suspect it's the same problem," I said.

"You think Lucy and Julia are together?"

"Yes ma'am, I do."

"Well where?"

"Billie . . . *that's* the problem. I'm coming up."

Alcatraz led the way. He loves my aunt as much as I do. They speak a secret language, which consists mainly of scrunchy faces and modulated baby talk. Billie met us at the door. She was in a floral print cotton dress, perfect for window-boxing. Billie doesn't believe in air conditioners, but she does believe in fans. A half dozen of them were working away throughout the apartment, gentle whirring crisscrosses of breeze that managed to give the place a semiweightless feel.

"How's my favorite boy?" Billie sang. It was a song for my dog, not for me. While the two rolled around in the mud together I went into the kitchen and copped a cup of tea. Billie keeps a pot brewing day and night. I dropped an ice cube into the cup and took a few After Eight mints from the freezer. What a party.

My aunt and my dog had calmed down by the time I came back out to the front room. Alcatraz was sitting in front of one of the fans like the RCA dog, though the breeze wasn't quite strong enough to lift his ears. Billie was putting a CD on the stereo. Dave Brubeck. Billie met Brubeck once. He let her sit next to him on the bench while he banged out "Take Five." She adores the guy.

I set Mr. Peanut standing under one of the windows.

"Is that for me?" Billie asked.

"Those late, lonely nights when you need someone to talk to."

Billie sniffed. "I'll talk to Mr. Peanut?"

I dropped into Billie's musty armchair as Billie alighted on the edge of her wooden rocker.

"Lucy has screwed up big time," I said.

"Indeed she has."

"Did she say *anything*, Billie? Anything at all about why she shot Shrimp?"

"I'm afraid not. She was terribly upset, as of course you know. But I'm sure she didn't mean to kill anybody."

"Well, that might be. But then you shouldn't go shooting at them."

"He must have provoked her." I said nothing. Billie leaned forward in her chair. "So do the police really think Lucy had something to do with his murder?"

"Oh yes. As far as they're concerned, Lucy is public enemy number one. But I mean, you can't blame them. She shoots Shrimp in the afternoon, slips away from here a few hours later. Next thing you know some-one has stabbed Shrimp Martin to death in the hospital and Lucy has vanished. If I was doing the math on that one, I'd go after her, too."

"But you don't think she did this."

"Billie, you know Lucy. What do you think?"

"Well, I know you're not supposed to blame the victim, but I don't care," Billie said. "You should never have allowed Lucy to get involved with that Shrimp character in the first place."

"What do you mean, I—"

"You know exactly what I mean. Julia treats that girl like she's her little project. So do you."

"I protest."

"Fine. Protest noted. Doesn't alter the fact."

"Billie, Lucy just can't seem to—"

She held up her hands. "I know, I know. We're all very fond of Lucy, and she does seem to stumble into more than her fair share of calamities—"

"So—"

"So nothing. She's a grown woman, Hitchcock. She should be allowed to make her own mistakes. She doesn't need you and Julia making them for her."

"You wound me."

"You'll recover."

"Billie, all we did was take her down to a jazz club."

Billie sniffed. "Shifty. That man is shifty." She corrected herself. "Was shifty. I didn't like him the first time I laid eyes on him. You know that."

I knew that. It had been just a little over a month ago. I had taken Billie to the club on her birthday. I thought she'd like the music. Which she did. Shrimp had sucked up to Billie for all of fifteen seconds (*flash!* we got our picture taken) before running off to make friendly with a bunch of basketball players from the Baltimore Blues who had just dropped in. The city's brand-new basketball team was knocking them dead this year. Shrimp put the ballplayers at a table right up front where they screwed up everyone's sight lines. Not one of those guys was under six-six. Billie had laser-shot Shrimp with her eyes as he gestured spastically at a waitress to hurry over and wait hand and foot on the local pros. But he didn't fall.

Billie beckoned Alcatraz to her side and took his ears for a ride. She cooed a bit, then looked over at me. "Meanwhile, just what are we going to do about Lucy's grandmother? Do we postpone the burial and hope that Lucy pops back up?"

I had already thought about this. "No," I said. "We don't postpone. I don't know what this is all about with Lucy and Shrimp and all the rest of it. But I don't think we should accommodate Lucy's screwing up."

"That sounds a little harsh."

"Well, I'm angry with her. She shot this idiot and then she ran off and got the police all bothered. Now she's got Julia throwing in with her."

"Julia is her friend."

"She is being loyal to a fruitcake."

"Now *that* is harsh, Hitchcock. Lucy Taylor is no more a fruitcake than you or I."

What could I do, I had to raise an eyebrow to that one. But Billie was having none of it.

"I'm overriding you, Hitchcock," she announced. "We are postponing the Rittenhouse funeral until Tuesday. We'll have the wake tomorrow night, Lucy or no Lucy. One extra day won't kill anyone. I would suggest you get out there and see if you can track her down before the police do."

"Can I tell you that I think it's a mistake to postpone the funeral?"

"Noted. Now go. You're wasting time sitting here."

"Bossy old thing, aren't you?"

Billie lifted from her chair and made her way to the window, where she picked up her trowel and banged some dirt loose on her window box. She looked back at me.

"My suggestion, Nephew: As you exit? Don't look up."

Back at the Hitchcock mansion, I played several sets of tennis, got a massage, drove my golf cart through the wine cellars, then fretted over which ascot to put on, the gold, the chartreuse, the olive, the mauve . . .

I popped open a beer and stood at the open refrigerator door, downing half the beer in one mighty chug. Unlike Billie, I do believe in air conditioners. What I don't believe in is replacing them when they've gone slack, which mine had done the previous summer. So I did as my ancestors must have done and fanned myself with the refrigerator door while guzzling a cold one.

I called Clarissa's number. She was in. Damn. I had hoped for her machine. Her end of the conversation was minimal. And a lot colder than my refrigerator. She heard me out, listened to my explanation ("There was this guy, see, and he was shot by a friend of mine, okay, and then later . . .") and then she opened up a big silent space for me to pour in my apologies. I was able to fill maybe half the space and then we fell silent. I looked down at Alcatraz who had been listening to my end of things. He was unmoved. Finally Clarissa spoke. Frost edged each and every word.

"I will give you another chance."

My response was swift and immediate. I cupped the mouthpiece and spat out at my dog, "I don't want another chance," and then said into the phone, "Great! How about Wednesday?"

Clarissa agreed to a rematch. Wednesday was fine with her. The venue was mine to choose this time. I told her I'd be by around seven then I hung up and finished my beer. "Free will is a crock," I told my pooch. He was unimpressed. Judging by the yawn.

The fact is, free will isn't really a crock. I'm just a guy who can't say no.

I decided to set up headquarters at the Oyster for the afternoon. The S.O.S. is cool, dark and timeless, all of which was quite appealing at the moment. Not to mention the ready supply of anesthetics for my renegade molar. My plan so far was to wait for Julia to call me. Big plan. Or maybe she'd call her mother. If she did, I'd know. Sally was behind the bar all afternoon. And she had a nice surprise waiting for me.

"Who wants to be a thousandaire?"

Ten portraits of Benjamin Franklin in green and black were fanned out on the bar.

"Tango Wallop?" I asked in disbelief.

"By a nose hair. The favorite stumbled coming out of the gate."

"I've done that before," I said, gathering up my winnings. I handed one of the bills back to Sally.

"What's that for?"

"Past and future."

Sally set me up then moved on to her other customers. Sunny Sundays are fairly popular days at the Oyster. I counted thirteen elbows on the bar, not counting mine, several dozen at the tables behind me. An Orioles games was on the television. They were playing New York, which was guaranteeing a familiar chorus from the Oyster clientele.

"He's a bum!"

"Whole city's a bum!"

"His mother's a bum!"

"Yankee *assholes*."

"New *Jerk*, New *Jerk*!"

Baltimore. They call it Charm City.

"I'm spying on you," I told Sally after my second whiskey.

"Well, you're doing a real good job of it, Hitchcock."

"I think so."

She checked an empty glass for chips and tossed it in a bucket on the floor. "Is there any particular reason you're spying on me? My days as a threat to national security are all behind me."

"Actually, there is." I briefed Sally on what had taken place the day before. Shrimp. Lucy. Gun. Hospital. Dead. In the interest of full disclosure, I included the part about Tom the telephone repairman. Sally knows her daughter. She didn't blink. In fact, a twinkle twinkled in her eye. "*My* phone could use some fixing," she said. "Lord God, could it use some fixing."

The game went to extra innings. I didn't. I swam back to Billie's through the heat waves. The flea market was concluding; tables being folded up and slid into vans. Somewhere along the way a hamburger appeared in my hand, which was a good thing; I was starving. Billie met me at the front door with some interesting news.

"We've been asked to handle the Martin funeral."

"Shrimp Martin? Is this a joke?"

We went inside. In the entranceway, Billie fished a peppermint from a bowl and tossed it to me.

"No, dear. This is a job. I received a call from Mr. Martin's sister just after you left. Apparently the two of you have met."

"Mary Ann. We met once."

"You must have impressed her, Hitchcock."

"It didn't take much. She spoke, I listened."

"Well, in any case, she remembers you and she phoned to see if we would handle the arrangements for her brother's funeral."

I unwrapped the peppermint and tossed it into my mouth. I was crinkling the wrapper so Billie plucked it from my fingers. "Isn't there some sort of conflict of interest that plays in here?" I asked. "I mean, I'm friends with the person who the police think killed her brother."

"Miss Martin didn't mention anything about that."

"Maybe she doesn't know."

"Maybe she doesn't."

"Maybe she'd feel differently if she did."

"Are you trying to turn away business, Hitchcock?"

I wasn't sure what I was trying to do. Something about this just didn't feel right.

"So what did you say to her?" I asked.

"Well, I told her that of course we would take care of things for her."

"Then it's done."

Billie told me that the medical examiner had released Shrimp's body. She and Sam had gone down already and picked it up. Shrimp was cooling his heels—along with the rest of his body—downstairs in the basement, alongside Mrs. Rittenhouse. Quite a soiree.

"We have a dilemma," Billie said. "Miss Martin wants her brother prepped for viewing. The father wants him cremated."

I took hold of my auntie's hands. "But Billie, what do *you* want? That's what's important."

She shook free. "Don't start, Hitchcock. I'm not in the mood. The man is unbearable. He picked up an extension while I was speaking with his daughter and he lit into her terribly. I'm expecting the two of them any minute now. I'd appreciate your help."

"Of course."

"You'd better change."

"You don't like my T-shirt?"

"It's lovely, dear. And I've never seen so many pockets on one pair of shorts before either."

I chuckled. "Insane, isn't it."

"And possibly inappropriate for dealing with the bereaved?"

"I guess we'll find out," I said, smoothing down my T-shirt and flattening my cowlicks. "They're here."

Billie muttered, "Oh shit," then slapped on her professional face and stepped forward to meet the couple who were coming in the front door.

Mary Ann Martin I knew, of course. The poor girl. Her shoulders were too broad. Her neck was missing. Her hair was uninspired. Her eyes were too small. She had the figure of a small refrigerator box. She looked like one of her family's pastries. And her brother was dead. She was undone. Her eyes were puffy and red from crying and her bland blue dress was dotted with perspiration.

And poor Hitch. Mary Ann stepped right past Billie and put her arms around me — as far as they would go — and bellowed into the snarling cat, "Oh, it's *horrible*. Poor Shrimp. Can you believe it?"

I patted Mary Ann's shoulder several times and then peeled her back from my T-shirt. She extracted surprisingly easily. She was rubber with grief. Her father was working his scowl over me. Whether Papa Martin was more disgusted with my getup or his daughter's blubbery display, I couldn't tell.

"I'm Hitchcock Sewell, Mr. Martin," I said, coming around his daughter to shake the man's hand. "I'm terribly sorry about your son."

Shrimp Martin's father had *pugnacious* written all over him. A big word for a short man. Red-faced, beady-eyed, somewhat snarling mouth. He was short and barrel-chested. A wrestler's physique. I put him on the approach to sixty. You'd figure that the owner of Mabel's Bakeries could afford better than shoe polish to keep his tight curly locks so forcefully black; whatever this guy was using it sure wasn't state-of-the-art. He was wearing a light blue linen suit, red club tie and cream-colored shoes. There was clearly money floating around here; it was simply ill-spent. The grip was firm. The gaze was mistrustful. The curl of his lips begged for a blunt cigar.

"What's your function here, son?"

Mary Ann answered for me. Or tried to. "This is Hitchcock, Father. I told you. A friend of Shrimp's. He—"

"We phoned to say we were coming," the man said pointedly. His little piggy eyes were glaring at the cackling cat on my T-shirt.

"Hitchcock just dropped in on his way back into town," Billie volunteered. She squeezed in between us, like a referee explaining the rules. She offered her hand. "Wilomena Sewell."

The bakery scion grunted. "Sidney Martin."

"I apologize for the casual dress," I said.

Martin demanded, "Where's my son?"

"Shrimp is downstairs."

"Don't call him that. His name is Sidney. And what's he doing down there?" The question was directed at me. Along with the hostility. Maybe it was more than just the stupid T-shirt. Maybe he also didn't like his daughter hugging strange men. Hey, I didn't like it either.

"My aunt and I are waiting for final instructions from the family," I said coolly. "Before we proceed. This is a terribly difficult time, we know. We're here to help you in any way that we—"

"Yeah, yeah, I know all that," Sid Martin said, cutting me off. Mary Ann started to speak but she was silenced with a withering look.

Billie took a stab. "Mr. Martin, why don't we step into the office. We need to discuss some basic details. Perhaps that would be best."

He muttered "Office" and seemed to like the sound of it. Billie steered him in the direction of my office and at the same time steered me in the direction of the front door.

"I'll be right back," I said.

Ten minutes later, I was. Dressed like an undertaker.

"They're gone," Billie said as I came through the door.

"That was quick," I said.

"There is to be a viewing. Mr. Martin is acceding to his daughter's wishes. I think he just wanted to make her feel bad about it."

"So you didn't find him to be a perfectly lovely representative of roughly your generation?"

Billie sniffed. "He was a pill." She laughed. "And look at you. All dressed up and no one to schmooze."

CHAPTER 4

Bright and early the next day I rolled over and went back to sleep.

A few hours later I parked my bottle green Valiant in front of a large yellow clapboard house across from the Pimlico racetrack, sight of Tango Wallop's recent surprise victory. A bald man in a faded salmon-colored sheet was seated on a tire swing in the front yard, ticktocking lazily, the toe of his sandal making Sandskrits in the dirt. A naked baby crawled in the grass nearby. Wind chimes—currently still—lined the front porch. A second bald guy was sitting on the porch steps. He shaded his eyes from the sun as I approached.

"Well . . . if it isn't Mr. Ghoul."

"What's shaking, Dave?" I said, adding, "Clearly not your hair."

Dave ran his hand over his bald head. Memories. Dave used to have the mane of a lion, red and swirling, along with a Fu Manchu mustache. Without the mop, his head looked half its original size.

Dave grinned. "Here. Pull up a porch."

I plopped down next to him. We lapsed into silence and watched the naked baby slowly crossing in front of us on the grass. It moved like a clumsy grasshopper. The baby was bald, too, but of course this was natural.

"Goddamn, it's good to see you, Hitch," Dave said after a bit.

"Likewise." I turned to him. "Hare Krishna."

"Hare Krishna, buddy." He grinned. "Are you hungry?"

"Starving."

Dave slapped me on the back. "Let's see if we can rustle up some grub for you, cowboy." I stood up and followed him into the house. It was cool inside. Dave muttered "Hare Krishna" to a couple of guys who were drifting down the hallway.

"This is just like old times," I said a few minutes later, mopping up some tahini-tinted slop with a powdery bread. "Who would have figured?"

When Dave and I were in high school we had discovered the Krishna house. Every Sunday they threw the place open to anyone who wanted to come by and feast with them. Naturally, you had to put up with the patter; these guys are always trying to recruit. But I never found them terribly pushy. And so long as the free grub kept coming, what the hell? Little had I known at the time that nearly a decade later my crazy red-haired friend would give up his fabled hell-raising and decide to throw in his lot with the Krishnas. A lot of people at the time had said he was nuts. But then, they hadn't been saying such glowing things about him already anyway.

"Happy, Dave?" I asked as he poured me some more army green–colored juice.

"Hitch, I'm in fucking heaven."

And that's good enough for me.

I wasn't here to see Dave. This reunion with a piece of my past was just one of those coincidences that the Fates toss down every so often just to see if you're paying attention. I was here to see Tom the telephone repairman. Tom wasn't a Krishna. He was scheduled to install some extra phone lines here. I had called the phone company first thing in the morning. Well, second thing.

Dave and I shot the shit and ate the tahini for about a half hour waiting for Tom the repairman to show up. Dave introduced me to his girlfriend. She looked like Mary Ann from *Gilligan's Island*. Only less hyper. She smelled like sandalwood. Her name was Heather. She came into the kitchen carrying the naked baby. Turns out it was hers and Dave's.

"It all just unfolds like an onion, doesn't it?" I said.

They called the kid "Squeak." I don't know if that was the real name.

Tom the repairman arrived. He was just as I had imagined. Paul Bunyan with a tool belt. He seemed a little uncomfortable with a house full of

Krishnas. This probably helped our bonding, the two of us being the only ones with hair and not wearing sheets. I didn't tell him that I was Julia's ex-husband. Could undo the bonding. I just told him that I was a friend of Julia's and that it was very important that I get ahold of her. I followed Tom down to the basement, where he pulled up a stool in front of the phone box and began making sense of a spaghetti of colored wires.

"You brought her back from the Manor Tavern on Saturday. Where'd you take her?" I asked.

Tom snipped off a red wire and a yellow wire and joined them up. "Well, I was taking her back to her place. She said a friend of hers was in some sort of trouble."

"So you dropped her off?"

Tom produced a pair of needle-nose pliers from his belt and began twisting more wires together. "No. I mean, we were on the expressway, right around the old London Fog place, and she got a call on her cell phone. When she hung up she told me to take the next exit and drop her off at the museum instead. You know. Over by Hopkins?"

"And that's what you did?"

"Yeah. I dropped her off right there in front. By the lions."

"Did you see who she was meeting?"

"Nope."

"Man? Woman?"

Tom shook his head and clipped the phonelike thing to a breaker in the wall box. He dialed a number, listened, then disconnected the phone. His gaze snagged on the door leading up to the backyard. A pair of Krishnas were playing badminton.

"What's the deal with these people, anyway?" Tom asked.

"I think it's basically peace, love, reincarnation and a little blue guy who makes it all possible."

"I don't get it."

"It's not for everyone," I said.

"I guess not." He dropped the red phone thingy back into his toolbox. "So what's this all about anyway? Is Julia in some kind of trouble or something?"

"She's fine. It's just very important that I get in touch with her."

Tom stuck his needle-nose pliers back into his belt like he was holstering a pistol. He was finished down in the basement. We went back upstairs. A short ugly guy walked by clicking a pair of finger-cymbals. Tom scratched behind his ear. "This place is creepy."

I left Tom to his work and found Dave in a hammock around the side of the house. The baby was with him, asleep in the crook of his arm. Dave was flipping through a *National Geographic*.

"Bitch of a way to spend a Monday," I observed.

Dave looked up from the magazine. "Somebody has to do it. So did you learn anything about Julia?"

"Not really. It looks like she met up with Lucy at the museum, and that's it. Cold trail."

"Bummer." Dave set the *National Geographic* down gently, open, on his child, like a paper tent. "You said this Shrimp guy was taken to Union Memorial, right? That's where he was killed?"

"Right."

"That's not real far from the museum, you know."

"I know."

"Which doesn't look so good for your friend. I mean, that puts her in the proximity of the crime, doesn't it?"

"You're right. It looks terrible."

Dave's head bobbed thoughtfully. "But you're convinced she didn't kill him?"

I shrugged. "I'm acting as her advocate."

Dave chuckled. "God, Hitch, remind me never to have you act as mine. That's a pretty flimsy endorsement." Dave gently rolled his feet to the ground. Squeak didn't squeak. "When you find Julia, say hi for me. I assume she's still a knockout."

"Dave, they come twice weekly to shovel away the broken hearts."

Heather was rounding the corner with a candle and a smile. The baby stirred under the magazine. Dave plucked up the *National Geographic* like a waiter lifting a tray lid. Squeak cooed. I left them. The wind chimes bade me farewell as I headed for my car.

My rescheduled appointment with Roger was at one. As I had sensed over the phone, he was one of those dentists who aims to please. Nice sentiment, I guess, but wholly dishonest. He would be putting me in pain and that's all there was to it. Offering to stick anything from Bach to the Beatles on the sound system was not going to change anything. He was a tall slender fellow, upper forties, with a pleasant face and a forced laugh. His assistant reminded me of Glenn Close in those dog movies. I begged Roger to be generous with the Novocain. "Novocain's for kids," he joshed. I told him I was tall for my age. He shot me up with about half the dosage I would have preferred and then climbed into my mouth with his pliers. Glenn Close stood behind him, directly in my line of sight the entire time, with an expression that dared me to utter even one peep of complaint.

My jaw was still sore that evening at the wake for Lucy's granny. It sort of crimped my professional smile. Naturally, the buzz was all about Lucy. Fugitive from the law and all that. We're a tight community down here and the majority of the mourners had known Lucy for most of her life. No one believed for a minute that Lucy was capable of murder. Even those who had gotten wind of Lucy's apparent shooting of Shrimp Martin several hours before his actual murder dismissed it as an accident. "You know how Lucy is," ran her defense. "The child wouldn't hurt a flea."

"*Couldn't* hurt a flea."

"She probably didn't know the gun was loaded."

"I'll bet it just went off."

"She could have hurt herself."

"Oh, poor Lucy."

The consensus was that this whole thing must just be a big misunderstanding. Not a few of the mourners felt that I knew where Lucy and Julia were hiding out, that I was even in cahoots with them. Dorothy Slinghoff, who owns the clothes boutique and gift shop where Lucy worked, came up to me and demanded that I fetch Lucy back immediately and straighten out this whole mess. "I need her out on the floor, Hitchcock. We've just slashed prices on nearly everything in the store. This is no time for Lucy to be pulling this kind of stunt." Not really knowing what to say, I muttered my promise to do what I could. Dorothy added, "When you talk to her tell her that the blouses she ordered from Rochester came in but that they're hideous. Find out what she was thinking."

"The Rochester blouses are hideous," I repeated. "I can remember that."

Mrs. Rittenhouse looked okay in her blue chiffon dress. Not great. Any one of her guests could have shimmied into the casket and looked just as okay. A gecko managed to find its way onto the inside of the casket's open lid at one point and it posed frozen there on the white velvet. I didn't want to grab at it for fear that it would flee down into the casket with Mrs. Rittenhouse. Only one guest commented. I told her that it was a logo for the casket company. "So lifelike," she said just as Billie happened to be passing within earshot. "Thank you," Billie replied.

The next day we buried Mrs. Rittenhouse, efficiently and perfunctorily. I had expected a police presence, on the off chance that Lucy would make a surprise appearance at her grandmother's funeral. And there was one. An unmarked car parked about a hundred feet away. A plainclothes detective weighing in at a good three hundred pounds was leaning against the passenger side door, arms crossed on his massive belly, holding a pair of binoculars that he didn't even bother to use. I waved. He waved back. His name is Vernon. We'd gone through this routine before.

There was no sign of Lucy.

Until Death takes an honest-to-God holiday, the turnaround time in the funeral business can sometimes be pretty damn swift. Billie and I had Shrimp Martin's wake to handle later that same evening. I got to the funeral home around six. Shrimp was laid out in Parlor One, dressed in his white tux. I told Billie that I thought he looked like a maître d'. Or a caterer.

"It's what his sister wanted."

I reached down and straightened his tie. "Well, it's his funeral." Oh they laughed and laughed . . .

An hour later, Shrimp's father arrived on the arm of a woman who turned out to be his wife. His second wife. Shrimp and Mary Ann's stepmother. Eleanor Martin wasn't quite young enough to qualify as a bona fide trophy wife (I placed her in her late forties), but in poise and congenial prettiness she was still certainly a decent catch for the old sourpuss.

She was a few inches taller than the bakery king, blond and trim, and as demure as her husband was blustery. They made a generally mismatched couple. Mary Ann arrived with them. She positioned herself between her father and her stepmother and greeted the guests with a brave smile and a small mewing sound. Mary Ann didn't fit in either. Central casting was mangling this one. The three of them—Mary Ann, her father and her stepmother—looked excruciatingly uncomfortable together. It was all I could do to keep from stepping over to them and sending each off to different corners of the room.

The guests stopped coming about forty minutes into the wake. Shrimp got a pretty decent turnout. Mary Childs didn't show. It didn't matter to me either way. Honestly. I had wondered if any of the local celebs whose photos enjoyed a special place in the entranceway to Shrimp's club would make an appearance. I expected not. As it happened, we ended up with two. One was a guy even taller than myself by a good three or four inches. Kit Grady. You didn't even have to follow basketball to know the name Kit Grady. The farm kid from Ohio was making all the magazine covers. He had been a phenom at North Carolina until the brand-new Baltimore Blues had managed to lure him away in his junior year with much fanfare and controversy. Against all odds, the Blues had proceeded to follow Grady's supremely gifted bouncing ball all the way to the NBA championship series, currently under way. Apparently, though, the new "Great White Hope," as some of the sportswriters had dubbed him, was also being referred to as the Great White Dope. And the "dope" here wasn't an allusion to the ballplayer's brainpower but to some of his recreational behaviors. Even as Grady's star was being hoisted up into place, serious questions were already being raised about his ability to cope with the limelight and all the wealth and goodies that come along with it. Grady arrived at the wake wearing a blue suit and a somber expression. He didn't much look like he wanted to be here. But then again, who really wants to be at a wake? I watched as one of the guests approached him and rather indiscreetly asked him for his autograph. The Great White Hope politely—but firmly—shook his head no. Grady didn't seem to know anyone in the room, except Shrimp, of course. He didn't stay terribly long. He sought out Mary Ann and Sid Martin and gave them his condolences. Stood around a few minutes looking too tall and uncomfortable. And then left. I didn't speak with him. And he didn't sign the guest book.

The other notable was Solomon Biggs. If there is anyone in Baltimore who could put up a claim of being as renowned for their paint-slapping skills as Julia Finney, it would be Solly Biggs. Though for vastly different reasons. Talent-wise, Julia is convinced that Solly Biggs couldn't draw so much as a Happy Face. Back when he was still painting, Biggs's work was strictly blobby. Colors. Shapes. Smears. Granted, he picked colorful colors, shapely shapes and smeared his smears with deftness, but still, at the end of the day, it's what the viewer brings to it. Biggs's canvases are all huge. You can't even get a Biggs that would fit through a conventionally sized door. Two things in particular distinguished him as a painter, aside from the size of his paintings as well as his refusal (inability?) to depict anything but the most rampant of abstracts. One is that he never used a paintbrush. What he used was his body. It's the most ridiculous thing I've ever heard of, but it served him insanely well. Biggs would dump his paints into large shallow troughs that he had lined up around the edges of the canvas, which he stretched out on the floor of his studio. Then he'd climb in. The "texture" of each of his paintings was determined by the particular clothes Biggs donned before slipping into the troughs. Denims. Corduroys. Silks. And yes, there are a number of Biggs nudes out there. I am happy to report I've never seen one. Solly Biggs captured all of his "creations" on videotape. So when you bought one of these things, you got the tape thrown in for free. I suppose if you begin to get bored with your gigantic canvas, you could always put in the tape and watch this nut ball rolling around on your canvas.

The other thing that set Solly Biggs apart is that he has served time for aggravated assault with a deadly weapon. Wife number three. Big juicy scandal about five years ago. Biggs el-kabonged her with a gallon can of paint one evening after coming home from an opening, dumped her in a trough of lemon yellow and rolled her around in what still stands as his single least abstract work . . . something that almost looks like a daisy. After the trial—once it was released from the evidence inventory—the painting sold at auction for a huge sum, all of which went to cover Biggs's legal expenses. The painting became known as *The Grisly Daisy*, and its buyer, wisely, remained anonymous.

Anyway, Solomon Biggs served ten months of a two-year sentence. This was nearly five years ago. He came out on his fifty-first birthday and hasn't touched a tube of paint since. The market in his huge abstractions dried up after the stink surrounding *The Grisly Daisy*. Even so, the interest in Biggs himself didn't. Solly Biggs remains an object of fascination to many of the citizens of Baltimore. Criminal transgressions and general debauchery, after all, are more often regarded with fascination than scorn when they are performed by members of the artistic brotherhood. Even more so when the transgressor and debaucher fluffs up the myth with the sort of acts of public flamboyance that Solomon Biggs is all too eager to perform. Biggs's social flatulence is legendary. He is British. He's a brawler, an ass-pincher, and a vivacious, table-pounding pontificator. This was one of the reasons, I assumed, that Shrimp Martin had so eagerly cultivated Biggs's presence in his club. According to Julia, Shrimp fancied the "criminal painter" as his very own Dylan Thomas. A splash of color. A celebrity drunk who brought a whiff of scandal and bohemian energy to the club.

All things being equal, Solomon Biggs was fairly well behaved at Shrimp Martin's wake. His rolling gait contained a little more bounce than usual, and his normally rheumy little eyes looked halfway clear as he made his way across the room. He pedaled over to the casket and made some large wheezing noises, then spotted me standing along the back wall and came over to me. An invisible cloud of gin floated between us.

"Sewell."

"Solly."

"Well, you've got yourself a funeral, mate."

"That's how I butter the bread, Solly."

The criminal painter snorted. "Two things my dear piss of a father always told me. Two things you can count on, Solly, he said. People going to wear shoes. People going to die." He patted me on the arm. "Sewell, you got yourself one of the two guaranteed professions. Good bloody show."

I thanked him. His head swiveled. "Where's the piece, mate?"

"The piece?"

"Finney."

"Oh, that piece." I shrugged. "Julia couldn't make it."

Biggs leered up at me. "Woman's a piece."

"So I'm hearing."

"More god damn talent in her fucking elbow than I've got in my ass, too," Biggs declared. He declared it loudly enough to turn several heads. "I'll never understand you letting a piece like that get away." The rumpled painter patted his pockets for a cigarette. I told him he couldn't smoke inside. "I'll just suck it," he said, and popped a yellowish cigarette into his mouth. Or maybe it was just reflecting his teeth. Biggs looked over in the direction of the casket, then brought his beacons back to me. "What do you think, Sewell? They're saying his lady jimmied him."

"I wasn't there," I said.

Biggs poked me in the chest. Hairy finger. Slightly blue. "Good fucking answer."

"It's good of you to come to Shrimp's wake," I remarked.

Solomon Biggs's crow's feet darkened as his eyes narrowed. "What do you mean by that?"

I shrugged. "Just that. I'm sure Shrimp's family appreciates it."

Biggs snorted. "Don't be so touchy-feely, Sewell. The old bastard over there, he'd as soon piss on his own boy's shoe as give him the bloody time of day. God damn bread maker. Never cared a damn about his own flesh and blood son, that one didn't. If that boy was in a gutter . . . the fucking *gutter* . . . you think the old man would pull him out?"

"Let me guess," I said. "Not on your fucking life."

Biggs poked me in the chest again. His voice was getting louder. "God damn right not on your fucking life! You know what they say about the rich. Cheapest bastards on earth." He pointed over at Sid Martin. "There's one. You think he'd help his own bloody son out of a pickle? Hell no. Flesh and blood's supposed to die for their own flesh and blood. Look at him. Does that bastard look dead to you?"

"Completely vertical as far as I can tell."

Biggs growled at that. "Bloody bakery business," he alliterated. He pointed at the supine Shrimp. "Chap with balls there anyway, you know that? Maybe not the brightest bulb on God's earth, but he put in his effort, didn't he? Treated me like a bloody king, I'll tell you that. Did me all right."

Solly Biggs's face had gone red. At first I thought he was simply working up his head of steam. Then I saw that the tides were rising up in his eyes. It happens fast. I'm used to seeing people crying at wakes, of course. Billie and I both, we're outfitted with hankies for just such occasions. Solly's lips began to quiver, which set his unlit cigarette bobbing. He pawed the air in the direction of Shrimp's casket then broke into a large coughing fit. He snatched the cigarette from his mouth and threw it on the floor. I retrieved it, straightened and did what I could to turn back the stares that were coming our way. I leaned over and whispered to Biggs.

"Why don't you go outside and get some air, Solly?"

Biggs got control of his coughing and looked up at me. Plaintive. Embarrassed.

"What's the food situation, mate? Could use a nibble."

"Negative," I said. "I can whip you up something upstairs, if you'd like."

"Well, you're a pisser, aren't you? Christ. Got anything to drink?"

"Solly, it's a wake."

"Some fucking party."

"We do what we can to keep them dull."

Solly took one last look at Shrimp in his coffin. "Stabbed him, right?"

"That's right."

"I've been stabbed. Hurts like hell."

"When were you stabbed, Solly?" I asked. The painter's biography contained endless adornments.

Biggs gestured vaguely. "Wife number two."

"Why did she stab you?"

An impish grin played over his face. "Caught me with number three-to-be. Tried to stab her, too." He nodded sagely. "Very passionate woman."

He headed off. I watched as he made his way through the crowd. Most parted to avoid his seesawing shoulders. Billie was standing in the parlor door, along with Eleanor Martin. Biggs gave Billie a peck on the cheek as he rolled by. Shrimp's stepmother leaned away from him. He took her hand and made a buffoonish bow. Billie kept watch until Biggs had apparently cleared the front door, then she flashed me an all's clear.

Soon after, Mary Ann drifted over to her brother's casket and quivered awhile. Sid Martin was huddling with some of his cronies. He was a hand-expressive talker and somehow I doubted that all that chop-and-wave had anything to do with the late Shrimp. Besides which, there was occasional laughter.

"Looks all torn up," I observed to Billie, who had drifted over to me to chat tactics.

"Some people hide it better than others," she said.

Sid Martin had one hand in his pocket and he was rapping the back of his other hand against the chest of a man in a blue pinstripe suit. I couldn't hear what he was saying to the guy, who didn't look particularly thrilled with having his chest beaten by the dead man's father, but it didn't seem much like "My son is dead, I'm beside myself with grief and shock." I pictured the sweet little granny face they used for the Mabel's Bakeries logo. Plaster the bulldog mug of the company's current CEO up there and the whole enterprise would go stale in an afternoon.

"I'm going to stick with the 'cold, heartless bastard' assessment for now," I said to my aunt. Billie indicated Eleanor Martin, who had not moved from her spot by the door.

"That's not a happy woman," she remarked.

I pointed out the obvious. "This is not a happy occasion."

"It's not that."

"Did she say anything to you?"

Billie sniffed. "I practically had to goose her just to get a hello. There's something else going on. I just can't deduce it."

I looked over at Sid Martin again. "Maybe the woman still can't believe her luck in having found such a dandy of a husband."

Billie gave me *the look*. "Hitchcock, if you can't say something nice about a person . . ."

Naturally, there was considerable buzz about Shrimp's violent death. Word had indeed seeped out that Shrimp's latest girlfriend was suspected of the murder and that she was on the lam. The jury was already in on one Lucy Taylor. I kept my lips buttoned as I overheard various descriptions of Lucy from people who had never even set eyes on her. Cold-blooded. Vicious. Sadistic. I gathered that Lucy had killed Shrimp for his money, over another woman, for the hell of it, as part of a twisted sex act, and, my favorite, because he wouldn't let her sing at his club. This last one came from the club's chanteuse herself, though it turned out she was only joking. The singer made her comment to Billie when the two had ducked outside for a cigarette. I remembered the woman from my several visits to Shrimp's. She looked like Ida Lupino's older sister. Onstage, she played that card pretty blatantly, with the French twists, the deco dresses, high heels, bloodred nail polish. Naturally, she had toned it down for her boss's wake, taken some of the bounce out of her copper hair. Come down off her high heels. Sort of like Ida Lupino if she had volunteered as a nurse to help the war effort. I placed her at somewhere north of forty. Still holding on to her looks. I purposely didn't make an opportunity to speak with her. Our eyes had met just once across a crowded funeral parlor and then looked away.

Mary Ann sniffled awhile longer at her brother's casket until her father stepped over to tell her to "wrap it up." I did observe him pause to look down at his son. I can't call what fell over the man's red face "grief," but it was probably as close as the guy could get. I sensed a whole raft of unfinished business between father and son as Sid Martin glowered down at Shrimp. I recalled Mary Ann telling me how irritated her father was with Shrimp's decision not to carry on in the family trade. The expression on Sid Martin's face as he looked down at his son suggested that he was *still* not inclined to forgive him. Mary Ann wrapped her chubby arms around her father's elbow and leaned into his shoulder. The sourpuss patted his daughter on the head, then reached down and touched Shrimp lightly on his cheek.

"Cold," he announced, then pulled Mary Ann away from the coffin. They went over and joined Eleanor Martin, who hadn't once moved from her position near the door. It was clear to me from the anxious glances she had kept taking out into the lobby even well after the last person had arrived that she had been expecting at least one more guest.

And whoever it was clearly hadn't showed.

CHAPTER 5

It was her son. Arthur Wisner. Shrimp's stepbrother. I found out from Kruk the next morning. Kruk phoned me just as I had gotten out of the shower to see if I had heard from Lucy. Kruk told me that Lucy had been positively identified by two eyewitnesses just outside Union Memorial on Saturday evening.

"She was spotted sometime around seven o'clock," he said.

"I see."

"And you know what occurred at approximately seven o'clock Saturday night, don't you?"

I had stepped over to the sleeping Alcatraz so that I could drip-dry over him. He didn't stir. "A lunar eclipse?"

The seasoned veteran leapfrogged my nonsense.

"I understand you're handling the Martin funeral."

"That we are. We held the wake last night."

"You know the routine by now."

"You'll be sending Vernon to the funeral to gape at the guests."

"That's right."

"Lucy didn't show up for her own grandmother's funeral, Detective. I'd be damned surprised if she dropped in on this one."

That's when Kruk told me about Arthur Wisner.

"Mrs. Martin's son has not been seen since Friday. The day before his stepbrother was killed."

I gave up on trying to annoy my dog and stretched the cord over to the window. Nice sunny day. Yesterday's twin. "I didn't know Shrimp had a stepbrother," I said.

"Well, he did. And he has disappeared."

"And you think there's a connection?"

"I don't think anything. Arthur Wisner helped manage the victim's nightclub. He worked closely with his stepbrother. I would be interested in talking with him."

"Makes sense to me. So you're hoping maybe he'll show up for his stepbrother's funeral?"

"I'm not holding my breath."

A garbage truck had pulled up outside my window. A large scruffy teddy bear was strapped on the grill. The truck's garbage chomper groaned like a dying dinosaur as the trash men tossed in its feed.

"I guess that's an intriguing coincidence to you!" I yelled into the phone.

"Step away from the window, Mr. Sewell," Kruk said flatly.

I did as I was told. "Detective, you are brilliant."

"Now, what was it you said?"

"I said you must be intrigued, this guy's vanishing the day before his stepbrother is killed."

"I have a better one for you, Mr. Sewell," Kruk said. "According to some workers at the club, your friend and Arthur Wisner had gotten pretty close lately."

"My friend Lucy?"

"Your friend Lucy. The victim's friend Lucy. Everybody's friend. And of course she has vanished as well."

"You think that Lucy and this Arthur fellow ran off together?"

"I just told you, Mr. Sewell, I don't think anything. I'm collecting a lot of questions that I would like answered. Locating Lucy Taylor and Arthur Wisner would certainly help in that effort."

"I wish I could help you."

"Let me throw another name at you," Kruk said. "Greg Snyder. Do you know who he is?"

"Greg Snyder. The name sounds familiar."

"He's a television reporter," Kruk said. "Channel Eleven."

"Right. I know who you're talking about. Big deep fake voice."

"You wouldn't happen to know if Miss Taylor is acquainted with him, would you?"

"Have you asked Snyder?"

"I'm asking you, Mr. Sewell."

"Well, I don't know. I don't recall Lucy ever talking about him, but that doesn't necessarily mean anything. Why? Did someone kill him, too? Is Lucy the fall guy of the week?"

"So your answer is no?"

My answer was a lot longer than that, but apparently Kruk was applying his filter.

"You're not going to tell me what's the connection, are you?"

"No, I'm not," he said. Then he went one better. He broke *our* connection. He hung up without so much as a "Have a good funeral." I nudged Alcatraz awake with my foot.

"Guard the castle. I'm going to work."

Alcatraz raised his head. The bonus in owning a hound dog? They're genetically incapable of giving you a mean look.

Death isn't contagious, but sometimes it feels that way. My car had died. Faster than a speeding bullet one day, next day, kaput. My mechanic is out in the county. He tows for free. Alcatraz and I sat on the curb and bade my valiant Valiant farewell as it moved off on its journey.

The Martin family didn't have a minister of their own. In these cases, we provide Father Ted. The short service was textbook. No one had volunteered a eulogy. Father Ted tossed in a few words alluding to the relatively young age of the deceased and to the suddenness of his departure, but he skipped the spiel about God having called his young servant to heaven for a special reason. What reason would He have? It's not as if the Council had decided to open up a nightclub and thought this Shrimp fellow was just the man for the job. Shrimp was shot by his girlfriend and then knifed in a hospital. You want to keep God out of that picture as much as possible. Father Ted read from the text in as pleasant a voice as he could muster, then we loaded Shrimp's casket into the hearse and headed for greener pastures. I sat in the passenger seat next to Sam, who tried to tell me about a movie he had seen the night before, but he kept bubbling into laughter. I guess I had to be there. Mary Ann Martin, her father and her stepmother followed in a Lincoln Town Car. I suspected the "no laughter" rule was in effect. So far there had been no sign of Arthur. Our procession cruised slowly up Broadway, gliding through red lights, headed west and wound its way to Greenmount Cemetery.

It was a beautiful day for kite flying or heading off to the beach or practically any outdoor activity beside burying someone. I recognized most of the folks here from the wake the night before. Solomon Biggs was a no-show. Which was all for the better. The blue pinstriped suit had turned brown, but I still recognized the man within it. He seemed to be keeping his distance from Sid Martin. I guess there's just so much chest slapping a person can take. The Ida Lupino knockoff was there, too. I had her name now. Lee Cromwell. Billie told me. Miss Cromwell had arrived with a short, slender black fellow who was wearing a pair of sunglasses worthy of Jackie O. and a leisure suit worthy of a consignment shop. Somewhere along the line an alligator had rolled over and died so that this cool cat could slip its patterned hide onto his little dogs. Several colored rocks adorned his fingers and the little tuft of hair beneath his lower lip had been dyed a soft orange. His hair was hidden beneath a large floppy fedora. I'm not describing a pimp, by the way. I'm describing a trumpet player. His name was Edgar Jonz. A midcareer Miles wanna-be. He fronted the house band at Shrimp's. "The Edgar Jonz Experience." His act was patently ridiculous, but his horn blowing more than made up for it. The guy was hopelessly talented.

As promised, Vernon was in attendance again, leaning against his car and sucking on a bottle of root beer. Crowd-scanning was about the extent of Vernon's fieldwork these days. His mammoth Hershey's kiss torso begged for a desk. Or rather, a reinforced chair. His blue plain-clothes suit was a camouflage of sweat spots. His bald head was shining like the sun itself. When I waved, he wearily raised his root beer.

Eleanor Martin's son didn't show at the funeral either. The trio of Martins sat in their folding chairs just in front of the casket, each lost in thoughts they apparently had no wish to share with one another. Father Ted read what was written on his cheat sheet, pausing once to sneeze. In all, pretty uneventful.

That is, until Edgar Jonz decided to do his thing.

Father Ted had tossed his dirt crumbs onto Shrimp's coffin and concluded the service, the awkward milling had just commenced when the distinctive notes of taps suddenly cut the air. The crowd turned as one. It was Edgar Jonz. The lithe hipster had slipped away from the graveside and fetched his trumpet, which he had apparently stashed behind a nearby tombstone. We—all of us—stood stock-still as Jonz stood there some ten feet away squeezing out the baleful notes of taps. We offer a bagpiper if people are hankering for graveside tunes, and Jonz hadn't cleared this with Billie or myself. But there it was, and the best thing to do was to just let the guy have his moment. I glanced over at Sid Martin, afraid that he might not be of the same mind. His red face looked even redder. But he was holding his ground. I figured he figured like I figured.

In the immortal words of Mr. Berra, "It ain't over till it's over." Jonz had an extra little surprise in store for us. As he reached what was *supposed* to be the big finale, the extended final note of taps, the horn player's alligator-shod foot began to tap, tap, tap . . . and in a seamless transition that anyone without a totally tin ear would have to admire, the grandstander launched into a mellow bebop version of the old sad tune. His horn flicked up and down, his head began bobbing side to side. It was a blues-taps. The only thing missing was someone at a trap set behind the jazzman, brushing the skins. The cat was cooking.

The assembled guests remained as still as tombstones. Only Lee Cromwell moved, and this was to roll her eyes before lowering her head in apparent dismay. Clearly she hadn't been aware of what Edgar had been planning. I'll give him this much; he was in a groove. The guy could play. And he got away with it for about twenty-some-odd seconds before Sid Martin snapped out of it and barked out, "Stop that, you asshole!" He came forward but Jonz immediately retreated several steps, still continuing his riff. I closed in, too, and I got there first, placing myself between the trumpeter and the irate Martin.

"Stop that!" Martin snarled again. Behind me, Edgar Jonz responded with an uptick of volume and some squeaks and blaps. I wheeled and grabbed for the horn, but the guy danced deftly clear of my grasp. Sid Martin lunged, but he stumbled into me instead of getting his claws on the renegade trumpeter. At this point Jonz had left any semblance of taps behind. He was segueing into a version of "Freddy Freeloader," when Lee

Cromwell stepped over to him and literally smacked the trumpet out of his mouth. It landed soundlessly on the grass. Jonz was stunned. He slowly lowered his great big sunglasses and gave his singer a look of utter mortification.

"Hey baby . . ."

"Don't 'hey baby' me, Edgar!" the chanteuse snapped. "What the hell do you think you're doing!"

His shoulders hunched in a lazy shrug. "Elegy for Shrimp, baby."

Sid Martin was still wanting a piece of the guy but I was blocking him. Eleanor Martin stepped over to us and took hold of her husband's arm. "Asshole," he hissed at the musician, then pulled free of his wife's grip and marched off toward the cars. Jonz fetched his horn from the grass and stroked it like it was a cat.

Father Ted was lighting up a cigar and loosening his collar. He was off duty. I realized that it was now my responsibility to get the service officially wrapped up. I turned and faced the perplexed gathering.

"Show's over, folks," I announced. "Um . . . thank you for coming."

The man in the brown pinstripe suit was clapping his hands slowly in sarcastic applause.

"Thank you for coming?"

We were at a table on a deck overlooking the harbor. A joint around the corner from the Oyster. Lee Cromwell's cigarette was parked next to her ear. Edgar Jonz was parked next to the singer. He was batting at the smoke every few seconds. I was sitting across from the two of them. It was Lee Cromwell who was busting my chops.

"Thank you for coming?"

I shrugged. "Spur of the moment, what can I say?" I leveled a finger at Edgar Jonz. "You, daddy-o, are a real gas."

Jonz chuckled. "I split some shit out in that graveyard, honey, didn't I?"

Lee Cromwell pulled on her cigarette. Jonz fanned spastically at the smoke. "Baby, you're killing me."

Lee brought out a crocodile smile. "Good thing we've got a mortician here."

Our drinks came. The place specializes in tutti-frutti Caribbean rum numbers. Too damn sweet. Too damn fussy. Plus, you could put an eye out with one of those umbrellas. Edgar and I had beer. Lee took a club soda.

Because of my profession I know more about facial makeup than a guy ought to know. Up close and personal, Lee Cromwell's mask proved a trifle cracked. Her lipstick was a little too red, which is to say that her skin was a little too pasty. She was letting foundation do what sun and healthy living weren't getting a chance to do. Still, I've seen thirty-year-olds who look only half as good as Lee Cromwell. And the woman hadn't seen thirty for well over a decade. I liked her.

"So now what's the story," I asked. "Are you two out of work now?"

Jonz answered first. "Shit, man."

"Was that a yes?"

"I'm working it, baby."

I turned to Lee. "Translation?"

"Edgar's lining something up," Lee said. "The club's been closed since Saturday, but Mr. Jonz is on the hustle. Isn't that right, Edgar?"

"I'm doing it."

"So how'd you two hear about Shrimp's murder?" I asked.

Lee answered. "Oh, we got the word about Shrimp right in the middle of our last set. I was singing 'Starlight.' " She took a drag of her cigarette. "I hate that song."

"Yeah man, the word just rolled up onto the stage like. Shrimp's dead, man." Jonz chuckled. "Shrimp's been cooked."

Lee slapped him on the arm. "Don't be a jerk, Edgar."

He snapped back. "Don't be a bitch, bitch."

"Don't be an asshole, asshole."

"Don't be a—"

I interrupted. "Hey. You two can Heckle and Jeckle later. I'd like to get some information here."

Jonz spread his hands. "What you want to know, bro?"

"Bro. Exactly. Shrimp's brother. Or stepbrother. What do you know about Arthur Wisner?"

"I know he's missing," Jonz said. "Chubby little dude was vapors on Friday and Saturday night, man. I had to get my own glass of water."

"I'm guessing the police already asked you about him," I said.

"Oh yeah, man, they ran their number."

"Arthur's a nice boy," Lee said. "Believe me, there's no way in the world he had anything to do with Shrimp's murder."

"Nice guys can still kill people," I said. "Happens all the time."

"Not Arthur. Arthur was devoted to Shrimp. And between you, me and the lamppost, Shrimp didn't deserve it. Arthur's a good kid. Shrimp just used him."

"Kid. How old is he?"

"I don't know." Lee turned to Jonz. "What do you think? Twenty-two? Twenty-three? Not much more than that."

"Boy's a pup," Jonz volunteered, holding up his beer glass and squinting at it. "I'm with Lee. The kid didn't pop his stepbrother. It don't scrabble up."

Actually, it was Lucy who "popped" Shrimp. Someone else had knifed him. I let it slide.

"What does Arthur do at the club?" I asked.

Lee answered. "Arthur has always done anything Shrimp asked him to do. Arthur is sort of the manager, I guess you can say. He'd do everything. He even ran around the place with that camera of his taking photographs of all the customers."

"The club photographer? You mean all those photos when you walk in the door?"

Lee nodded. "That's Arthur. His idea, actually. He thought it would be good for business. You know, people would know their picture's up on the wall, they might feel a little personal about the place. Not such a bad thought, really. And of course, Shrimp always wanted his picture taken with any of the so-called celebs that came in."

"So then Arthur managed the place?"

"Shrimp put him in charge of ordering supplies, liquor, all that, paying the bills, changing the lightbulbs, you name it. Whatever needed doing that Mr. Big Shot didn't feel like doing."

"I get the picture," I said. "Shrimp said jump—"

"And Arthur would be on the ceiling."

"I could see getting sick and tired of that sort of thing," I pointed out. "Though I don't think I'd consider murder one of my likely responses."

"Arthur didn't murder Shrimp," Lee said again. "I told you, he was devoted to him. The way I heard it, Arthur's mom married Shrimp's father when Arthur was about ten or so. His dad had died suddenly. Some sort of accident or something. I guess Shrimp is around ten, twelve years older than Arthur? Arthur really latched on to him. Big brother. Replacement dad. Whatever you want to call it. Shrimp was his hero. Which, when you think of it, is pretty damn sad."

"You didn't care much for Shrimp."

Lee waved her cigarette . . . too close to Edgar's face. "Oh, Shrimp. He was all right in his way. He thought he was big shit but he was little shit. That's my eulogy."

"Ouch, baby," Edgar murmured.

"He asked the question, Edgar."

The trumpet player leaned in toward me. He whispered for all the world to hear. "My man and my lady . . . they had *issues*."

Lee scoffed. "Issues. Shrimp wanted to sleep with me and I kept reminding him that I had some standards. Not much of an issue in my book. Plus I reminded him he had a girlfriend. As if that made much of a difference."

"I take it Shrimp had a roving eye," I said.

Lee's eye roved right into mine. "More than just the eye."

"He was cheating on Lucy?" I guess this didn't really surprise me. It was one of Lucy's special talents, after all, to locate no-good two-timers.

"You know Lucy?" Lee asked.

"She's a friend of mine."

Lee waved her cigarette again. "I don't mean to insult your friend, but if that girl couldn't read Shrimp the moment she met him, she's illiterate. Shrimp Martin was on permanent cruise control. Especially there at the club."

"And Lucy knew this?"

"I can't say. Seems to me she had to know. Shrimp never put a lot of effort into being subtle. Like I said, he knocked at my door more than once. And he wasn't very sly about it. If Lucy Taylor didn't know she was sleeping with a creep, then she was living in a bubble."

I rolled this one around. One thing about Lucy, she was the undisputed queen of Hope Springs Eternal. She has always been extremely trusting. I wondered if it could have been her discovery that Shrimp was running around on her that had prompted her little gunplay on Saturday. Maybe she just snapped.

"Do you know if there was a particular woman that Shrimp was seeing on the side?" I asked.

Lee took the question into a glance with Edgar. The trumpeter's tiny shoulders affected a shrug. "Dude wasn't hittin' 'em with neon lights and all, you know. Man's got to be a little smoother than that. But yeah, I'd say our man was doing his push-ups when the little Lucy wasn't around."

Lee rolled her eyes. "You are ridiculous, Edgar."

"Undertaker asked me a question, sugar. Cut me some slack. Man's got an inquiring mind."

"Can you give me a name, Edgar?" I asked.

Edgar wagged his head. "Got no name to give."

Lee leaned forward on the table and put a hard look on me.

"So what's *your* story? The police are looking into Shrimp's murder. How come you're nosing around?"

"The police think Lucy killed Shrimp and I just don't think she did it," I said. "Lucy's got no one going to bat for her."

Edgar chuckled. "Step up to the plate."

"Do either of you know if Shrimp had any enemies?"

Edgar shrugged. Lee answered. "I don't know about 'enemy,' but Shrimp did get into it with a TV reporter sometime last week. I can't remember exactly. Monday or Tuesday I guess."

"Is this Greg Snyder?" I asked.

"Yes. Him."

"You're the second person today to bring him up. The police were asking me today if Lucy has any connection with this guy. What gives?"

"He and Shrimp got into a fight at the club. I never did hear what it was all about. I just know that Shrimp caught word that Snyder was out back with a cameraman and he tore out after him. He knocked the guy around pretty hard. I mean, very hard. Messed up the boy's pretty face."

"Edgar, have you got any insights you'd like to share?"

The trumpet player raised a finger and bobbed it at me as he spoke. "Hey, I dug the dude. He wants to chase away a nosy reporter, that's his business. That club was the Shrimp's baby. That was his vision, man. Got his jackass old name up there in lights, you hear me? A joint like that is hard to pull off in this town, don't fool yourself. Man was doing some serious juggling trying to keep that place going. Lots of bills. Dude must've had some nightsweats over that place, but listen. He never stiffed the help." Edgar turned to Lee. "Ain't that right, baby? Shrimp always came up with the clams."

Lee scoffed, "You're funny, Edgar."

"I'm serious shit here. That man wasn't becoming no millionaire. He sweated that place. You see him working to pull in those hotshots? The dude got Mr. Cal Ripken hisself coming in one night. Man was working, so don't go slamming on Shrimp now. Had him some real nerve endings."

Lee Cromwell stubbed out her cigarette partway. Jonz finished the job for her. The singer trained her high beams on me as I sipped on my beer.

"You're a good-looking man," she said.

"Thank you." I set the glass down. "You're a good-looking woman."

It was Edgar's turn to roll his eyes. "Aw shit. We playing the Mating Game now?"

"Shut up, Edgar," Lee snapped. She turned back to me. "I don't know Lucy all that well. But I agree with you. She's no cold-blooded killer. But then, I'm not a cold-blooded killer either, and there were times I could have killed Shrimp. He was awfully good at getting women pissed off at him. He had the gift."

"Lucy's not a murderer," I said.

"So then why did she shoot Shrimp?"

"You just said. The guy probably provoked her. Another woman? Who knows? One way or another, he must have pissed her off."

She pulled another cigarette from the pack on the table and picked up her lighter. "Darling, when they piss me off I slap them, I curse at them and I try to embarrass them in public. A girl picks up a gun, she wants to kill. Anyone can do that math."

"Fine. Attempted murder. Crime of passion. But somebody else went to that hospital and killed Shrimp Martin."

"You're a stubborn one, aren't you?"

"Yes ma'am, I am. Lucy needs someone on her side."

Lee looked at me over the flame of her lighter. "Mr. Undertaker, if I ever go and shoot someone, I hope you'll saddle up that white horse on my account."

Jonz groaned. "Baby, you are embarrassing yourself in broad daylight. I might have to go take me a long walk around the block."

"Look, I'm just trying to get some information here," I said. "I'm not trying to convince either of you of Lucy's innocence."

Lee leaned back in her chair and exhaled a blue cloud. "Innocence. Now what fun is that?"

"That's it." Jonz popped to his feet. "I *am* going to take a walk. I need to spend my day watching white folk being cute together like I need another hole in my head. Good meeting you, Mr. Undertaker." He pointed a finger pistol at Lee. "I'll see *you* later." Lee was waving her cigarette at him.

"Yeah, yeah, just go already."

The musician moved off. He moved like Joan Collins in *Dynasty*. Minus the hip action. It's called a slither.

"Funny dude," I said.

Lee lowered her eyes, then looked up at me. "I'm not really flirting with you. I mean, I don't really mean anything by it. It bugs the hell out of Edgar, though. I can't help myself."

"I understand. Flirting without intent."

Lee laughed. "That's a good one. I'll have to remember that." Lee squinted off in the direction of the water. "I didn't want to say anything while Edgar was here."

"About what?"

"You scratch below the surface, at the club I mean, you're going to find some behind-the-scenes action going on."

"Such as?"

"The usual. A little dope running around. And quite a bit of gaming."

"Gaming?"

"Gambling. Betting."

I thought of my Tango Wallop winnings, most of which were still crowded into my pocket. "Betting. That's practically America's favorite pastime," I said.

"Oh, I know it is. Doesn't bother me one way or the other, really. It's just . . . well, there were some people who could get into it pretty heavily at Shrimp's."

"Edgar?"

Lee nodded. "He's mainly a card player. After-hours stuff. That's all pretty innocent fun as far as I'm concerned. Even though the stakes could get kind of high. But there was more going on than just cards. You name it. Horses. Baseball. Basketball. I heard Shrimp say more than once that gamblers are spenders, win or lose. Also, I just think he liked that kind of crowd. Shrimp liked things a little edgy. He wanted the place to be exciting. Not just a fern bar with a band."

"Lee, are you saying Shrimp was a bookie?"

She shook her head. "I suppose you could call him that. I'm just saying that all this lofty talk Edgar just gave you about Shrimp and his working hard to keep the place going, that's fine, but Shrimp wasn't just sitting around squeezing nickels out of the booze markup. Shrimp was a hustler. There's no other way to put it."

"You mentioned dope."

She waved her cigarette in the air. "It's part of the club scene. Has been since I was in diapers. I'm not saying it was huge or anything. But the place was definitely a little oily below the surface. There were some creeps."

"Any in particular that come to mind?"

"There is this one guy who has been coming around the club recently. He'd usually show up right before closing. One of those after-hours guys. All-torso. Weight-lifter punk, you know the type. Very full of himself. About your age, I'd say. Kept his hair a little long and combed back. A real throwback. The gold chains, open collar. And he had huge hands. Real hams."

"And what about him?"

"I was never quite sure, but he seemed to have a tag on Shrimp. He had a throw-his-weight-around attitude. Shrimp never looked real comfortable when this guy showed up. You know when people just put off that vibe? This guy did. I've never liked that in a man."

"You like your men plain and simple?"

"I didn't say that."

"Do we have a name for this lady-killer?"

Lee let out a chuckle. "I called him Toaster Hands."

"Toaster Hands."

"Yes. That's what his hands remind me of. I mean, they're as big as toasters."

"You're a funny lady."

She stubbed out her cigarette. "I'll bet you say that to all the funny ladies."

"Funny thing," I said. "I do."

A noisy group of kids had just taken a nearby table. They were all drinking the fruity drinks and giving inanity a new lease on life. Lee and I watched them for a bit. One of the boys was playing air guitar, another was on the air drums. Their baseball caps were turned backwards. Lee tipped her chin in their direction.

"I've got one of those."

"One of those?"

"A boy. A son. About that age."

"Oh?"

"He lives with his father."

She put that hard look on me again. She said no more on the subject. The waiter came by to see how we were doing. I ordered another beer. Lee just asked for a glass of ice. I asked Lee about Arthur and Lucy.

"I understand they were friendly with each other," I said. "The police are finding their mutual disappearance most interesting."

"If you're asking was there something going on between Arthur and Lucy, the answer is no. For one thing, it's like I told you, Arthur worshiped the ground Shrimp walked on."

"Maybe he worshiped the girl he was sleeping with."

"Oh that could be. I'm not saying he didn't. But 'worship' is as far as it would go. Arthur would never dare make a move on Shrimp's girl. No way in hell."

"How can you be sure? Love's weird."

"True. But I think I'm right. Lucy's a pretty girl. Lot of spunk. If you'll excuse the expression, she's been around the block. Arthur Wisner? Nice guy. But he'll never get cast as Romeo. Too much baby fat if nothing else." Our drinks arrived. Rather, my drink and her ice. Lee fished out a cube and popped it into her mouth.

"I have no idea where Arthur has run off to. It's sure as hell suspicious, there's no way around it. But I can tell you this, if he has run off with Lucy, they're sleeping in separate beds. For that matter, if they are together, my guess is that Arthur is playing the hero. He's trying to protect his stepbrother's girlfriend."

"This is on the theory that Arthur doesn't think Lucy killed Shrimp either."

Lee nodded. "This is the theory."

"You'll have to excuse me. But until I see otherwise, I'm hanging my hat on Arthur Wisner. I can't explain why he'd want to hurt his stepbrother any more than you can. But if he's with Lucy, I'm not real comfortable."

An explosion of laughter came from the table of young 'uns. The air guitarist was on his chair for his big finale, pinwheeling his arm à la Pete Townshend. His drummer was getting downright spastic. Full Moon. Lee pulled another ice cube from her glass. She didn't pop this one into her mouth. She held this one between her thumb and finger and let their heat slowly melt indentations into the ice. She looked up at me.

"Did you and Lucy ever have anything? It's none of my business of course."

"Lucy's not really my type."

"No, I wouldn't think so."

Water from her melting ice cube was running down her wrist. She flicked the ice cube to the ground and patted her wet fingers against her brow. I caught the waiter's attention and signaled for the check.

"Can I give you a ride somewhere?" I asked Lee.

She reached across the table and placed her wet fingers on my wrist.

"No."

My mechanic had called and left a message that my car needed, among other things, a new universal joint. Or rather, an *old* universal joint that worked as good as a new one. They don't make universal joints anymore for 1964 Valiants. Go figure. It was going to take a few days to scrounge one up. I phoned him back and told him to go ahead in that case and give the car a complete physical while he had it in the garage. "Stick her up on the lift and tickle her feet" was what I said, for which I was rewarded with a long telephone silence.

I got out of my funeral clothes, showered, donned a pair of shorts, a pair of sandals, a pair of sunglasses and a shot-to-hell Brooks Brothers shirt and took my dog out into the sun. I knotted a green bandanna around his neck. The girls didn't exactly flock to get his autograph, but he did leave word where he could be found. I stopped in at Jimmy's for a cup of coffee to go, aged well past perfection, and then circled back to the funeral home and fetched the keys to the hearse. From the day I brought him home Alcatraz has refused to hop into the back of the hearse. He'll happily lie down back there once he's in, but he insists on a side entrance, passenger or driver's, doesn't matter. I respect him so immensely for this I can't even say.

Dog and I hopped into the hearse and made our way down Eastern Avenue to Boston Street, then on past the old American Can Company (now a new American place to shop and eat) and pulled into the deserted parking lot about a quarter mile farther on.

Shrimp's. The place was strictly a nighttime operation, so there was nothing portentous about the empty parking lot and the shuttered windows. Nonetheless, knowing what I knew, I can comfortably say that the place looked dead. The neon sign over the front door—"Shrimp's" spelled out in hot red curlicue at night—was anemic in the bright sun. I parked on the harbor side of the building so that people driving by wouldn't see a hearse sitting there. I got out and plopped down on the hood.

From the outside, Shrimp's was no great shakes. A long, wide flat-roofed building, almost like an oversized shanty. Unadorned. Industrial green. But inside, Shrimp's was fashioned loosely after the clubs you see in the old black-and-white movies, something between the cinema version of the Stork Club and Rick's Place. Lots of slowly chopping ceiling fans. Oversized plants. Checkerboard-tiled floor. A fair amount of moola had been dumped into the place, that's for sure. There was perimeter seating partway around the sunken main floor, and then maybe a dozen tables down on the floor, with a semicircular riser for the band and steps leading down onto the floor so that Lee Cromwell could stroll among the guests and do that Ida Lupino chin-chucking move to the nervous male customers. It was, I had to admit, a pretty classy setup. You had to give Shrimp credit.

I got down off the hood and wandered over to the rear of the club. I wasn't precisely sure what I thought I could get out of swinging by the nightclub; maybe I was hoping for a little inspiration by osmosis. If the walls felt like talking, I was open to it. There was a narrow band of windows that ran along the back wall of the club, behind the band's area. Shrimp usually kept these shuttered—he preferred the out-of-place ambience his club could offer—but on occasion he would go ahead and fold them open so that the band could have a harbor light backdrop.

Now, of course, they were shuttered. Even so, I tried to peer inside. It was because I had my hand up shading my eyes that I didn't see anyone approaching. It was because it was such a damned hot day that the pistol barrel felt especially cold against my neck.

"Don't move."

In the movies, a guy with his arm raised to his face might bring it down in a sudden chopping action, surprising the guy with the gun and knocking it out of his hand. The gun of course skitters across the ground out of both people's reach while the *mano a mano* begins in earnest. The options open up after that.

That's the movies.

I didn't budge one iota. I even willed my stray strands of hair to freeze in place.

"Don't move," the guy with the gun said again. Through clenched teeth I indicated my full compliance with his wishes.

"Bring your other arm up. Slowly. Put them both against the wall. And don't turn your head."

I did as I was told. The pistol barrel left my neck and I took in the cheap thrill of a pat-down. What with shorts and sandals, there weren't many places I could be hiding a howitzer. I felt my wallet being lifted from my pants pocket and the thought flashed in my mind, is this a stickup? Am I being mugged? I had the remaining nine hundred dollars from my Tango Wallop long shot in my wallet. Then the guy let out a snort.

"Is that your name?"

I keep a whole pile of retorts handy for that question. Under the circumstances, I settled for the blandest of the bunch.

"Yes."

"What are you doing here? This place is closed."

"I know that," I said.

"Is that your hearse?"

"That's mine."

"What the hell is that all about?"

"I'm an undertaker," I explained. I glanced up to where the wall met the roof. Tucked into the overhang was a small gray hornets' nest. Abandoned, thank God. I took that as a sign. Things could be worse. "Can I put my arms down now?"

"Why?"

"Why? Because this is uncomfortable, that's why. Look, you're the one with the gun. Little old me isn't going to hurt you."

"Little old you stands about six foot four."

I corrected him. "Six-three, actually."

"Okay. You can bring them down." I sensed him backing away. "Slowly," he added.

I lowered my arms. I was now standing with my arms at my sides, nose-to-nose with the back wall. I felt like a dunce. "Can I turn around?"

"Take one step backwards then turn around slowly and lean your shoulders up against the wall there."

What is this, I thought, the hokeypokey? The thought translated into, "What?"

"You know, tilt back. I don't want you jumping at me."

"I won't jump at you."

"Do like I say and you won't."

I took my step back from the wall, then performed the slow-motion pirouette he requested. I tilted back until my shoulders were stopped by the wall. By God, it was a good plan. I was perfectly off-balance. I crossed my arms and looked over at the gunman.

"Happy?"

The fellow standing in front of me—out of arm's reach—was wiping the palm of his right hand against his slacks. The pistol was in his other hand, aimed roughly in the direction of my groin and wavering.

I cried out, "Hey!"

The guy flipped the gun back to his right hand, clearly the dominant one, and trained it steadily at my chest. He was about five-ten, on the stocky side. Judging from the ratio of salt to pepper, I placed him somewhere in his mid- to upper forties. He was wearing an off-hours five o'clock shadow, a brown sports coat, khakis, white shirt and an ugly green tie. If a face can be both gruff and boyish at the same time, this guy was somewhat pulling it off. He was sweating like the wall of a sauna.

He grunted. "Hay is for horses."

Yes, that is what the man said. I deadened my pan as much as humanly possible under the circumstances.

"I'll have to use that one sometime," I said. Possibly not wisely.

The guy took a beat and I braced for the shot. He didn't shoot. The frown lines shifted and in fact he sort of grinned. One of those Harrison Ford grins where one half of the mouth stays put as the other half does all the work. I take grins, even half grins, as a good sign. I relaxed a little. I saw that my wallet was on the ground by his feet. I really wasn't sure if I was being mugged or not. Regardless, with the pistol still aimed at me I wasn't too willing to enter into repartee with this guy. I've seen too many movies where the big wit-festival ends suddenly with a bang. You just don't want to go there. I conceded the next move to him. He took it. He reached down and grabbed my wallet and tossed it to me. I let it hit my crossed arms and drop to the ground.

"Nice catch."

"You didn't give me permission to uncross my arms," I said. "Seriously. You're getting no sudden moves from me as long as that cannon is pointed my way. I'm in complete Simon Says mode." I added, "Mr. Simon."

He used the gun as a pointer. "Pick it up."

I retrieved my wallet. The money still seemed to be in it. I stuck it in my pocket and went ahead and returned to my position of leaning against the wall. At least I was in the shade.

"So you're not mugging me," I said.

"What are you doing here?"

"I'm snooping. You're not mugging me, right?"

"Get off it already."

"Because you can have the money."

"I don't want the money."

The guy was sweating like crazy. He wasn't exactly out of shape, but he looked like one of these people who keeps himself fairly fit for his first four decades or so and then wakes up one morning to discover that despite it all he is going haunchy and paunchy. From his worry lines to his crooked khaki cuffs, the man needed some serious pressing. He also needed to burn that tie.

"Look," I said. "I know I'm trespassing and all that. I'm sorry. Really. I'll just go. Let's just forget this. It's a beautiful day. Why don't we both just go out and enjoy it."

"I want to know what you're doing here. Snooping for what?"

"The guy who owned this place was murdered a few days ago," I said. "I'm just snooping around for the sake of a friend of mine. That's all. Honest."

"This friend of yours. What's his name?"

"Actually, it's a woman." I went ahead and brought out my big cheesy smile.

He didn't return the smile. "Are you willing to die for her?"

An ice knife went immediately to work on my stomach. "God, I hope that's a rhetorical question."

The guy waggled the gun. "You want to be more careful."

"Can I tell you how uncomfortable I am?"

He slipped his gun hand into his jacket and brought it back out empty, holding it up in a "presto" gesture.

"I'm not going to shoot you."

I finally relaxed. "Good. That's great. Really."

"Makes your day?"

"Big time."

"I still want to know what you're doing here," he said. "I mean, specifically."

"No problem. Why don't we go somewhere else," I said. "You're melting."

The man ran his gun-free hand over his drenched face. "Life's a fucking mess," he said.

Which I found apropos of interesting.

His name was Pete. Pete Munger. He was president of Munger and Associates and clearly in no risk of winning any awards for cleverly named companies.

Munger and Associates was a private investigation company. The guy with the bad tie and the gun was a private detective. The real deal. Registered. Bonded. Licensed to carry a loaded magnifying glass. The only detectives I had ever met before were police detectives. Taxpayer paid. I even got involved with one once. Briefly. Somewhat tragically. Not to insult, but she was a lot better-looking than Pete Munger.

Munger told me that he had been asked by Eleanor Martin to locate her son, Arthur. This was Munger and Associates' first day on the job.

"Arthur Wisner has only been missing a few days," I noted. "Isn't it a little early to be going out and hiring private eyes to look for him?"

"Eleanor is an old friend of mine. She's real worried about her son. The police are suspicious about the timing of his disappearance."

"They think he might have had something to do with Shrimp's murder."

"Or just know something. Could be he's gone into hiding for his own protection. I'm not investigating the Martin murder. That's for the police. I'll give them anything I run across, naturally. That's the deal. My job is to determine the whereabouts of Arthur Wisner. End of story." He tipped his square chin at me. "Now you start yours."

We were at a Tex-Mex place, over in the American Can Company complex. The place was chilled like a meat locker. The detective and I were breaking burrito together. Man's best friend was not allowed inside, so I had begged a piece of twine from one of the cooks and loosely attached Alcatraz to the sign out front. His baleful countenance probably cost the place a few potential customers.

I told him my story. I kept it brief. I reached my bottom line in under a minute.

"I'm trying to find Lucy Taylor before the police do."

Munger spoke with his mouth full. "Then we have something in common. We've each got a missing person."

"I guess we do."

"Except, I'm a paid professional." He pointed a finger at me. "You're a well-meaning busybody who could get himself hurt."

I told him I liked the "well-meaning" part. Munger was doinking on the hot sauce like it was water.

"What you're doing is dangerous. That's all I'm saying."

Witness his poking a pistol in my neck not thirty minutes earlier.

"Well, if that's all you're saying, then thank you. I appreciate the warning."

Munger shrugged. He licked his fingers clean of beans. "Whatever. It doesn't matter to me what you do. Unless you get in the way of my work." He picked up a napkin and destroyed it in three seconds flat. "The hot sauce here isn't much, is it. I like something rips your tongue off."

My standard there is slightly less hostile, but I said "Yeah" anyway. "So let me ask you," I said. "Has your snooping gotten you to the rumor that Lucy and Arthur might have had a thing going?"

Munger's burrito stopped in midair. "Tell."

"My money says they didn't. As far as an actual romantic thing. I know Lucy. Her nose for trouble doesn't often sniff out chubby weaklings, which is the picture I'm getting of Arthur Wisner. But apparently they were friends."

"You're ahead of me here."

"I've been in this since Saturday. Besides, I only just picked this stuff up today."

"So we really do have something in common then. If I find my boy I might find your girl."

"And vice versa."

Munger was about to respond, when he suddenly went on alert. His face froze and the burrito dropped from his hand. Oh God, I thought. Heart attack? Stroke? A message coming in from the home planet?

"What?" I said.

A murmur rolled up darkly. "I'll be damned." He skidded his chair back suddenly and strode purposefully over to the jukebox, which was over near the door. A young couple were standing next to it. They had just plunked in some quarters. I had all of three seconds to recognize the beginning of Dusty Springfield's "You Don't Have to Say You Love Me" before the detective reached down behind the jukebox and yanked the plug from the outlet. The music stopped abruptly. Munger dug into his pocket. Oh God, I thought for a flash, he's going to *shoot* them? It's just a song. Munger didn't bring out a gun. He brought out a paw full of bills, which he put on top of the table next to the stunned couple. He winced an apologetic, if not convincing, smile at them then lumbered back to the table and dropped back into his chair. He shot me a menacing look.

"Don't ask."

Glowering, he waved for the check.

CHAPTER
7

Here's how long my date with Clarissa lasted:

I knocked on the door of her Tyson Street town house, she opened the door, took one look at the deep ruby hearse parked along the cobblestones, one look—one withering look—at me and then slammed the door in my face.

The End.

The old hard-to-get routine. Such a tease.

I pulled the hearse around the corner, parked it on Chase and walked the several blocks up to the Belvedere, where I chewed on a few glasses of bourbon and talked sailing for a while with the bartender. I don't sail and apparently he didn't either. But that didn't stop us. We both knew people who sailed and we each borrowed a few of their stories. After a time I realized that I wasn't even talking about sailing with the bartender anymore, but was locked in a debate with an investment whiz kid over the ethics of human genetics research as a stock market investment. He tucked his card into my shirt pocket as I left. "Call me when you're ready," he said. I slipped him one of mine. "Ditto," I said.

Some hours later I found myself at the Club Charles, bookended by a pair of young women with identical black bangs, tank tops and belly rings. Art students. They were sitting on either side of me giggling at a running private joke of some sort or another. Something to do with François Truffaut. If you really want to know they were pretty uninteresting. They asked me if I wanted to go out dancing with them. "You're so cute," said one. "You're so cute," said the other. "You're so cute . . ." I declined. As they left I gave them the investment guy's business card. "Call me sometime. We'll party," I said.

I probably took one more whiskey than I needed. As midnight approached, I found myself staring at my reflection in the mirror behind the bar. I was deep in thought; not sure how long I had been staring. I was recalling what the EMS worker had said down at the hospital, when Kruk had pulled him over to give me a look. Flattop. He said that there had been a man hanging around outside Shrimp's place when the ambulance arrived, a man with a flattop. I tried to imagine what I'd look like with a flattop. It really wasn't me. I'm the wavy, curly type, I don't do flattop well. That guy who used to get right into Gomer Pyle's face and snarl at him . . . *That* guy did flattop well. He might even be the King of Flattop. Sergeant Carter . . . that was what he was called. I picked up my glass and held it just under my chin. I thought about the guy Lee Cromwell had described, the after-hours guy who seemed to, in her words, "have a tag" on Shrimp. Toaster Hands. I wondered if this could have possibly been the same person, but then I recalled that Lee had specifically described the guy as wearing his hair long and combed back. I looked at my hands in the mirror. Not the size of toasters, not by a long shot. More like one of those large pieces of bread, I thought. Sourdough. Or pumpernickel. Rye, perhaps.

I set the glass back down—unfinished—paid up and left. I made my way back down Charles Street and found the hearse where I had left it. I did fifty jumping jacks, followed by a little shadowboxing, before getting into the car and driving home at a crawl.

As I followed Alcatraz into Billie's apartment the next morning, Billie was delighted with the opportunity to cry out "Look what the dog dragged in!" First thing in the morning, Alcatraz had insisted I accompany him on his bladder run. I had neither showered nor shaved nor brought my hair back from its abstract region.

"How was your date?" Billie asked as I headed directly for the kitchen to kick-start some coffee.

"Aborted."

"How was your evening?"

"Asymmetrical."

Billie looked up from her Alcatraz love-fest. "You'll let me know when I should start worrying about you."

"That's the deal."

Billie fetched Alcatraz's brush and gave him a quick grooming, nose to tail. She stepped into the kitchen as I was pulling a mug from the cabinet.

"Hair of the dog," she said.

"Just coffee."

"No. This." She gave me a small handful of fur.

Once the coffee was made and it was launched on its journey to the far corners of my nerve endings, I summarized for Billie the scraps of what I knew concerning Shrimp Martin and the possible factors that might have played a part in his murder. Billie agreed with me that the sudden disappearance of Arthur Wisner was among the more intriguing pieces of information. While we were talking the phone rang and Billie answered it.

"Yes, it's good to hear you, too, dear. Hold on, he's right here."

She held the phone out to me. "It's someone named Julia, I believe she said."

I snatched the phone from her. "Julia! Where the hell are you?"

"Hitchcock, honey, is that you?"

"Come on, Jules, no more games. Lucy's in enough hot water as it is. You guys hiding out from the law is only going to make it worse. And not just for her. You, too."

"You are such a protector. That's sweet."

"Don't 'sweet' me, Julia. Cough up the fur ball."

"And what a sexy talker you are."

"Where are you?"

"Now Hitch. Please remember. I am out of town for a little R and R, and as such . . . sweetie, I am probably in the dark about anything that might have taken place in my absence, n'est-ce pas? If I happen to have a friend here with me who we'll say hasn't spoken a single word about a certain event that may have taken place back in town but that I may not be aware of then I would have no reason to turn such a person over to the police, which of course would otherwise be my legal responsibility. Does that sound sound?"

Her conditionals and run-ons were giving me a headache. "So long as you can say you didn't know shit, then you didn't know shit. I've got that, Julia. Your bounteous ass is covered. Now where are you?"

She wasn't finished yet. "And so long as I failed to let you know who I might have here with me, then you—"

"Julia, you've covered everyone's ass beautifully. You're a pro. Bravo. But I really need to talk to—"

"Uh-uh-uh. Just listen to me, Hitch." She cleared her thought. "I would like to invite you to come and spend a few days with me. Would you care to join me for a mini-vacation, Mr. Sewell?"

For a woman who has never bothered to learn how to operate a motor vehicle, Julia Finney knows how to squiggle into the driver's seat.

"Yes, dear," I said. "Sounds lovely. Could we get a location, please?"

"Do we have a pen and paper?"

"We do."

"Wouldn't you like to guess first?"

"Jules . . ."

The shadow moved slowly along the sunny streets, traveling at the speed of a brisk walk. Children stopped and stared. Teenaged girls hugged themselves. People of all ages crossing the street with aluminum chairs hooked in their elbows froze as the shadow slid slowly past them. Above and just in front of the shadow, a seagull had fallen into place, hovering on white wings above the dark blot as if it were either caught in the shadow's updraft or towing the obsidious thing along on invisible filament. The bird broke free as the road's dead-end curve took the shadow in a graceful U-turn and fed it deftly between two yellow lines, a parking spot in front of a large white building that sold sticky popcorn, cotton candy and world famous saltwater taffy.

If you've never driven a hearse through a beach town at the height of the season, you don't know what you're missing. I was rockin' in Rehoboth.

I went into Dolly's and picked up a box of their saltwater taffy. The kid behind the counter couldn't find enough ways to say "cool" as he looked out the large windows at the hearse parked there in the sun.

"Are you, like, an undertaker or something?"

"Just like," I said.

"*Man*. Cool. Dead bodies and everything?"

"The deader the better."

"All *right*."

Julia met me at the door in a black one-piece swimsuit, a large flowing white shirt, a big straw hat and a frozen margarita. Her face was electric with beauty, as always. Her pulsing sensuality as alive as a thousand jittering fingers. I handed her the box of taffy.

"I bear sticky gifts."

"Hello sweet man. Welcome to the hideaway." She kissed me lightly on the lips and slipped her hat onto my head. "We must get you native as quickly as possible. Come in, Hitch. I need you to cheer me up." She looked past me at the hearse parked out front. "Nice wheels, daddy-o. Man can make an entrance."

She spun on her bare heel and I followed her into the house. Modern place. All beige and light. Gallery kitchen, open counter to the main room. Sliding glass doors leading out to a deck overlooking the beach and the mighty green Atlantic.

"Where'd you dig this place up?" I asked Julia as she poured a drink for me from a sweating silver pitcher.

"Cheers." We tapped glasses and sipped. She came away with a mustache. If Julia could package her lick-off move, she would make bundles.

"This place? Someone I know."

"I'm sorry, honey. Could you be more vague, please?"

"His name is Ken."

"Like the doll."

"Cute."

"Thank you."

"No, I mean Ken. He's very cute. So is his lover."

"Barbie?"

"Todd."

I saluted with my glass. "I'm up to speed."

Julia topped her drink. "Come outside. Lucy has wrapped herself around a funk and she won't let go."

"Gosh," I said. "Is Lucy Taylor here?"

Julia flashed her big brown cows. "I didn't tell you? How forgetful of me."

Lucy was outside on the deck. She was sitting in one of the deck's two butterfly chairs—the yellow one—wrapped in a ball, brooding, sending silent messages across the sea to Germany for all I could tell. She was wearing an oversized tennis shirt. Mandarin. Probably Ken's or Todd's. She had it pulled down over her raised knees, all the way to her feet. The effect was of an oversized three-year-old. Lucy's mousy blond hair was pulled back with one of those fluffy elastics. Blue polka-dot. The empty butterfly chair was red. The scene was Hockneyesque.

"Hello, Lucy," I said, stepping between her and the ocean. The silent messages slammed into my groin. "Come on, Lucy," I coaxed. "Don't be petulant. I've come all this way. I even brought you and Julia some salt-water taffy. It's inside."

"Hello," she murmured.

"I'm up here."

Lucy made an effort of tilting her head to meet my eyes. The bruise on her face was noticeably reduced. It occurred to me that we should have gotten a photograph of her cheek the other night. Well, it was too late for that now.

"Care for a drink?" I asked.

She blinked slowly.

"Margarita? Mint julep? Coca-Cola?"

She blinked slowly.

"Do you want to talk?"

She blinked slowly again. But I had cracked the code.

"I'm guessing you know that you're a real popular girl back in Baltimore these days," I said.

Julia touched me on the elbow. "Hitch, don't badger."

I squatted down so that Lucy and I were eye-level with each other. She refused to look at me. I spoke gently. "Lucy, we need to try to figure out who killed Shrimp, okay? I'm afraid the police aren't knocking themselves out trying to come up with a suspect. They're pretty happy with you right now."

"I didn't kill him," Lucy murmured.

"Of course you didn't. I know that. But if you want to help yourself, you can't just run away like this. It's only going to make it harder."

Lucy ran her fingers through her hair and looked out over the ocean. I had no idea what her wounded eyes were seeing, but I doubted that it was the water. Her concentration was fierce and far away. Julia leaned in and whispered to me, "Let it go for now."

She was right. I rose and clapped my hands together. "Tell you what. I'm going to change into beach stuff and we can go play in the sand."

Julia said, "I'll mix a fresh pitcher."

I turned once more back to Lucy. "Would you care to join us?" She looked up darkly at me but said nothing. "You know we're just going to be talking about you."

She was monumentally unimpressed. I bounced down once more to a crouch and this time forced a little eye contact. There was precious little animation in Lucy's green eyes.

"We're going to straighten this whole thing out, Lucy," I said. "Trust me."

A blink, a swallow, a slight parting of the lips. I had to settle for that.

I changed into my swim trunks and a T-shirt. Julia draped a large beach towel around my neck and held up a bottle of tanning lotion. "Yum." We went down to the beach, dumped our stuff onto the sand and took our margaritas down to the surf. Though Ken's place was well north of Rehoboth's main beaches, there were still plenty of people around. But no loud radios, no lifeguards, no picking one's way through a minefield of beach towels. Even with the slight breeze it was terrifically hot out there under the sun. The drive from Baltimore had taken just under three hours and it was now the thick of the afternoon. I handed Julia my drink and waded out into the surf and dove under the first wave of consequence. I tried out my various strokes—back, side, crawl—like an otter on a rotating spit, then caught a decent wave to ride back to the feet of my sexy exy, who was standing there like some sort of sensual lighthouse.

"I love a man who frolics," she said, handing me back my drink.

"Must wear pants. Must have heartbeat."

She slapped me lightly on the wrist. "Don't start that slut shit with me, Hitchcock. You know that's not true."

We stood a moment looking out at the ocean. A small plane was flying by, dragging behind it a large banner advertising RIBS, BEER AND ROCK & ROLL at a place down in Ocean City.

"Whatever happened to sex and drugs," I wondered aloud. Apparently Julia hadn't wasted her time on the banner. She ignored my comment.

"Lucy can't seem to snap out of it," she said. "We've been here what, four days already? She hasn't once even come down to the beach. Where you just saw her. In that chair? That's headquarters."

"Why did she shoot Shrimp? Has she told you anything about that?"

Julia blithely stared down a muscle man who, had we been on the street, would have been walking into a telephone pole. She searched my face before she answered.

"Lucy has the worst luck choosing men of anyone I have ever met. You and I both know that. Without exception, they end up being bad to her."

"She's sort of like your opposite," I observed. "Every man you ever meet gives you as much of the world as they can possibly manage."

"We're not talking about me, Hitch." She gave a soft smile. "For once. We're talking about Lucy. You know how she is. So damned trusting. Which is fine, except that it always seems to lead her to trouble."

"Bad things happen to good Lucys."

"That's for sure."

"But you know, Jules, you're not really helping Lucy by hiding her out."

Julia sighed. She bent down and picked up one of those gnarled oyster shells and cupped it between her hands. "You're right. Lucy has to face up to this sooner or later."

"Sooner. This little game of gee-officer-I-just-didn't-know . . . that's over."

"I know."

"So what exactly is it that Lucy has to face up to, Jules? I mean, has she explained at all what happened?"

Julia uncupped the oyster shell and chucked it into the surf. She wiped her hands on her thighs. "That day that Lucy shot him, she says he was totally nuts. Apparently Shrimp had been in a weird mood all last week,

Lucy said. She mentioned something about a fight he got in with a TV reporter earlier in the week."

"I've heard about that."

"Well, Lucy says Shrimp was just on edge. She doesn't know what about. Of course her grandmother's dying whatever day that was, Lucy was understandably preoccupied."

"So what happened?"

"She was on her way over to your place to drop off her grandmother's dress. I guess this was Saturday, right? First she stopped in to see Shrimp. She hadn't seen him for a few days. She says the moment she walked in the door he was all over her. He grabbed her and threw her halfway across the room."

"No hello kiss?"

"Grim, no? Lucy says he was ranting and raving about Arthur. When was the last time she had seen him? What had Arthur told her?"

"Told her about what?"

"Well exactly. Lucy had no idea what in the world that nut ball was talking about."

"He's missing, you know. Arthur is."

"I didn't know that."

"So Lucy's had no contact with him since she's been down here?"

"Not that I know."

"Okay, go on."

"Well, Shrimp was raving on about Arthur this and Arthur that and what did Lucy know about him. And she kept trying to tell him that she had no clue. But he wasn't listening. I mean, it's all ridiculous. Shrimp Martin's a jerk."

"Was. R.I.P."

Julia retorted, "R.I.H. is more like it."

"Rot in Hell?"

She placed a finger on the tip of her nose. "I have no time for bad men. I can't cry about Shrimp Martin. I'm sorry."

"So let's stick with Saturday," I said. "Lucy walks into Shrimp's apartment and he throws her halfway across the room. He's going ballistic about Lucy and Arthur. Totally off his nut. Pick it up from there."

"He pulls out a gun."

"So it was Shrimp's gun."

"Well of course it was Shrimp's gun, Hitch. You think Lucy runs around packing heat? Lucy says what happened was that he got her by the hair and he was screaming at her. 'Where's Arthur? Where's Arthur? What's going on?' Like that. And suddenly he has this pistol right in her cheek."

"A real sweetheart."

"Tell me. If it were me of course I would have kicked the lovely man in his little shrimps. But Lucy was too scared to think straight. She says he kept yelling and yelling and then suddenly he hit her. Lucy thinks it might have been with the pistol, but she's not even sure of that. It was so sudden. All she knows is that something hit her just below her eye and she dropped right to the floor. She says she saw black. And then when she focused, there was the gun, right on the floor in front of her."

"Shrimp had dropped it."

"Maybe it just fell out of his hand when he hit her, who knows? Shrimp was standing a couple of feet away. Lucy says that he went for her and she just grabbed up the gun and fired."

"Went for her?"

"Those are her words. You'll have to get it out of Lucy, Hitch. I'm just telling you what she told me. She said it all happened in an instant. He manhandled her, he pulled out a gun, he whacked her in the face, she picked up the gun and she shot him."

I grimaced. "Members of the jury, we have only the testimony of Lucy Taylor . . ." I trailed off. A pair of little kids—they couldn't have been more than six—had scampered down to the surf just a few feet away from where we were standing. A boy and a girl. The little boy was carrying a green plastic bucket in one hand and a yellow plastic shovel in the other. The girl was wearing pink water wings. When the surf hit her toes she shrieked and began flapping her wings. The boy dropped to his tiny knees and began to dig.

Julia and I went back to our towels. I was as pale as a corpse and didn't trust Julia's sunscreen to keep me from pinking up. We worked on our melting margaritas for a few minutes and then gathered up to quit that crazy scene.

"Wait."

I stood holding the towels while Julia bounded like an Appaloosa down the sand and into the ocean. She was back in thirty seconds, sparkling with sea salt, her hair slicked back, her large feet grinding into the sand as she walked. When she ran her thumbs under the legs of her swimsuit you could practically hear the hearts stopping all up and down the beach.

Lucy wasn't sitting in the yellow butterfly chair when we came up onto the deck. Nor the red one. She wasn't inside either.

"Maybe she took a walk along the beach," I said to Julia.

Julia picked up a piece of paper that was sitting on the kitchen counter. "Maybe not." She handed the paper to me.

I don't want you two to get in trouble. This is all my fault. I'm sorry. I'm leaving.

I looked up at Julia, who was hand-combing her tangles. "Leaving? To go where?"

"Who knows? I need thirty seconds in the shower to get this salt off of me and then we'll go find her."

"She already has a head start."

"Thirty seconds."

I grabbed the outdoor shower while Julia took one inside. I was in and out in thirty seconds myself. Julia was standing there in a white tank top, already buttoning up her shorts. Rinsed and changed, we charged forth. All that was missing was the theme music.

"Should we take the hearse or should we walk?"

"Hearse. She's probably walking into town. We'll catch her on the way."

Julia couldn't resist rolling down the window and waving at people who were gaping as we drove by. She went for the ticktock method, the preferred choice of Kings and Queens.

"Are you enjoying yourself?" I asked.

Julia dipped her head toward the sideview mirror. "Pull over. Let me out here."

"Plan?"

"I'm going to run across the street to the drugstore. That's where the buses leave from. If Lucy's really running away, that's going to be her best bet."

"Do you want me to circle?"

"No. If she's not at the drugstore I want to look for her up on the boardwalk. You saw the state she's in. She might just be wandering around. Why don't you find a place to park somewhere away from the strip and meet up with me?"

"Where?"

I had pulled to a stop. Julia shoved the door open. "Meet me at Funland."

"Wouldn't be the first time," I said.

Julia winced a smile at me. She got out of the hearse and strode across the street toward the drugstore. I turned off the main drag and cruised the side streets until I finally found a place large enough for me to pull the hearse to the curb. An elderly couple were sitting in lawn chairs out in the front yard of their little house. They looked up at me as I got out of the hearse. The man called out, "We're not ready yet." His wife smacked him lightly on the arm with her magazine.

When I got to Funland, Julia wasn't there yet. I wandered about the arcade and watched people riding teacups, swinging in cages, sliding around in bumper cars. My father and I rode these very same teacups once. I had insisted on spinning the wheel to maximize the speed of our rotation, and I spent the next hour weaving on the sand like the world's tiniest drunk. My father weaved with me while my mother sat on the boardwalk railing and laughed.

"Fancy meeting you here."

I spun around. A familiar set of blue eyes were gazing up at me from a familiar face. With a familiar smirk. In an unfamiliar context.

"Mary."

Mary Ann Martin's housemate responded, "And you . . . funny name."

"Mikhail Gorbachev," I said.

"Funny."

"See?"

"Come on, what is it?"

"Hitchcock Sewell."

"Right. Hitchcock Sewell. The undertaker."

"So, Mary Childs. Do you always sneak up on people?"

"I didn't sneak up. You were daydreaming. Same as last time."

"Point made."

She shrugged. "So what brings an undertaker to Rehoboth?"

"I'm here with a friend," I said.

She looked to the left and right. "Is he a big bunny?"

"He's a she. She'll be hopping along in a minute or so. And if I may ask, what brings you to these parts?"

"My parents live down here. Retired. I'm just down for a visit."

"Well, small world, isn't it."

She squinted up at me. Not a friendly squint. "Meaning?"

Oh God. I was damned if I was going to let this woman drag me there again. "It's an expression," I said. "I know damn well you've heard it."

"What's eating you?" The fingers had gone into the rear pockets. Same cutoff jeans. Body Language 101 was back in full force.

"Nothing's eating me," I said. "You just . . ." I trailed off.

Her head tilted as if she were looking at a confusing painting. "You don't like me much, do you?" she said.

"I never said that."

"People don't always say it. You don't have to say it."

"Well, I don't get the impression you like me much either," I said.

She pulled a hand free of her pocket and shot me with a finger pistol. " 'Either.' See? So you do don't like me."

While I took a few seconds to shuffle her sentence and make sure I got it she asked, "You wouldn't be following me, would you?"

"Following you?"

"Stalking."

"What?"

"Because I've had a stalker before. It's no fun, let me tell you. I had to get the police in on it."

"I'm not a stalker."

"My father is an ex-cop."

"Mine was a radio and TV personality."

"You think you're being funny?"

"No, Mary, I don't. But I do think you're being paranoid."

"I'm serious. Stalking is no joke."

"I agree with you. And I'm not stalking you. No joke."

"My father shot the guy."

"The stalker?"

"Yes."

"Did he kill him?"

"No. But he sure won't be stalking anybody anymore." She tapped the side of her head. "Docile as a baby."

"I guess that's what daddies are for."

"Are you making fun of my father?"

"The man with the gun? Absolutely not. No. Guaranteed."

Her eyes narrowed. "Good."

One of those Frisbee rings was wobbling through the air just behind Mary Childs. For an instant it looked like a red halo as it approached her. I reached out over her head and caught it just before it hit her.

"Saved your life," I said.

She smirked. "I owe you."

I tossed the Frisbee back to the kid who was running our way. "Okay, Mary," I said. "I think we've established our parameters here. The chemistry is so bad I can smell it. I say tomato, and you say you hate big irritating men, or at least the one who is standing in front of you right now."

" 'Hate' is a pretty extreme word."

I was kind of hoping she'd take issue with "big irritating man."

"The last guy I was seeing was a big irritating man," Mary said. "Bigger than you, in fact. Big ego to go with it."

"I see. So you've branded the whole lot of us."

She shrugged. "It's an attitude thing."

"I'm sorry. Ours or yours?"

"You swear you're not stalking me?"

"I assure you. This is just a coincidence, running into you." I added, "It's God's idea of a practical joke."

She looked as if she half-believed me. Which I had to take as half a victory. Behind her, a group of teenaged girls were screaming and laughing at a strip of photographs that had just popped out from a photo booth machine. Mary glanced over at them, then back at me.

"Good-bye."

She turned abruptly and walked away. I recalled this same move at the hospital. Mary Childs, Queen of the Sudden Sayonara. My spotlight remained trained on her as she moved off, until she was only about the size of a flea and finally took one of the ramps down off the boardwalk. She never looked back. Someone tapped me on the shoulder. I jumped. It was Julia.

"See anything you like?" she asked.

I turned a perplexed expression to her.

"You know," I said. "I'm not sure."

Julia and I rode the ponies. The merry-go-round. The plastic steeds were so small my legs practically wrapped around them. Julia perched high in the saddle. We took a few revolutions then hopped off.

"It's just not the same without the brass ring," Julia moped.

The sun was beginning its drop to the horizon, slipping into a large yellow rip in the clouds off to the west. The boardwalk was already in shade. I bought two slices of Grotto's pizza to fuel our stroll. The usual array of beach humanity was on display, an elderly couple wearing fuzzy red antennae; a boy walking an invisible dog on a stiff leash; an oiled-up muscleman in a teeny tiny bulging Speedo. . . . People go quietly whacko at the beach.

Lucy had taken the bus back to Baltimore. Or at least the bus that stops in Baltimore on its way south. You can buy your ticket on the bus, so the person behind the counter at the drugstore hadn't been able to say precisely if Lucy's destination was Charm City. But Julia had described Lucy to him and he remembered her. Lucy had gotten there just in time to hop onto the bus. We had missed her by about thirty seconds.

"The showers," Julia said gravely.

There was nothing we could do immediately. Our guess was that Lucy was returning to Baltimore without us so that she could surrender herself in a way that wouldn't implicate us.

"Should we go right back or would you like to stay over?" Julia asked as we sat on the bench eating our pizza. A large seagull had joined us. Julia fed him a slice of pepperoni like it was grapes to an emperor. The damn woman can seduce *fowl*.

"I'd think you would want to be there for Lucy," I answered her.

Julia plucked off a second pepperoni. "I do. But I can't hold her hand forever. Lucy didn't kill Shrimp, Hitch. I know that without question. She's going to have to contend with the fact that she shot him, but they're not going to be able to stick her with his murder. That'll sort out."

"You have great faith in the system," I observed.

"Enough, I suppose." The seagull swallowed, then looked longingly into her eyes.

"I don't," I said. "Lucy put a bullet in Shrimp and a few hours later he was stabbed to death. She was seen near the scene. Where do you see the police weighing benefit of doubt on this one? Lucy needs someone out there looking for the real killer."

"And this would be Hitchcock Sewell, Man of Mystery?"

A thought suddenly occurred to me.

"It would be Pete Munger."

"Pete Munger. You're changing your name?"

"No."

"Good. Because if you were, I was going to put in my vote for Alfonse Valentino. Who is Pete Munger?"

I filled her in on my encounter with the private investigator and how Eleanor Martin had hired him to look for her son.

"Maybe I can convince the good Mr. Munger to expand his scope a little and start looking for whoever it was who killed Shrimp."

" 'Convince him.' That, I believe, is called 'hiring him.' Is that what you're thinking?"

"I don't know. I guess so. Maybe. Maybe not."

Julia mused, "Men and their sense of commitment."

"I won some money on a horse. I might as well invest it in something like this."

"As opposed to?"

"I don't know, pissing it away on some dame."

"Oh, Hitch, piss it away on the dame, please. Dames love it when men do that."

"This is what I've read," I said.

"So then you want to get back to Baltimore?"

"I think we should, yes."

"Even though there's a free place to stay here? Right on the beach? Jacuzzi? Cable? Fully stocked bar? World-renowned sex goddess with all-new tan lines she's just dying to show off?"

I blinked slowly. "You got cable?"

A lesser woman would have slapped me for the impertinence. Julia Finney is no lesser woman. She shifted on the bench to face me a little better. Her expression went blank . . . except for the skyrockets tracing across her brown eyes. She closed her lips. And she *emoted*.

"Don't do that," I said.

She snapped it. "Okay. For a friend."

"Thank you."

We headed off for the hearse. We took the wrong street first, then doubled back and found it. Only one of the lawn chairs was now occupied. It was occupied by Mary Childs. Arms crossed. Legs crossed. Foot wagging irritably. Very irritably. And scowling. I walked across the grass and stopped in front of her.

"Haven't we met?"

She was not amused. "I thought you said you weren't following me."

"I'm not."

She uncoiled her thin arms and pointed at the hearse.

"And that is?"

"That's mine."

She let her arm swing over her head in the direction of the small clapboard house behind her. It was dying for a fresh coat of paint. "And that's my parents' house."

"I didn't know that when I parked here. How could I have known that?"

"My father says you spoke to him."

"That was your father? The one who shoots stalkers?"

She sighed and crossed her arms again. She was like a little queen sitting there in her lawn chair. "So this is coincidence? *Another* coincidence? Your hearse parked in front of my parents' house?"

"That's what it is."

Julia had stepped up beside me. "Hitchcock, are you harassing this woman?"

"Jules, not now."

Julia extended her hand. "Hi. I'm Julia Finney."

Mary Childs hesitated, then leaned forward and gave Julia's paw a terse tug.

"Mary Childs."

"Nice to meet you, Mary."

Mary looked from Julia to me and then to Julia again.

"Can I trust this guy?"

Julia took a step away and gave me a slow up and down. Girl was having fun. "You know, I'm not so sure that you can."

I jerked a thumb at my ex-wife. "Let's go." I took a page from Mary Childs's exit strategy book. I didn't even bother with a good-bye. Julia and I stepped over to the hearse. I opened Julia's door for her then went around to the driver's side. I paused, looking across the roof of the hearse. Mary Childs hadn't budged. The foot was wagging a mile a minute. I got into the car. Julia turned from the window as I fumbled to stick in the key.

"Sexy little thing, isn't she?"

CHAPTER 8

I dropped Julia off at a dance joint near Fort McHenry. A private club. She tried to get me to go with her. "You could stand a little shaking out. You're too stiff lately."

"Is that an undertaker joke?"

"Hitch, you bury people for a living and now you're snooping around a murder investigation. The word could get out that you've got a great big morbid streak. The whole death thing could put a cramp in your sex life."

"I don't know. Maybe some girls dig it."

"Is *that* an undertaker joke?"

"Wasn't supposed to be."

She took hold of the door handle. "When was the last time you saw me dance?"

"Can't remember."

"They write books about it," she said.

"I'll check the library."

"One more chance. All work and no play won't get Hitchcock a frisky chickypoo."

"Is that how that saying goes?"

She stuck out her beautiful tongue at me and shoved the door open. A throbbing salsa beat filled the air. Julia chick-a-boomed down the sidewalk as only Julia can. She is a supreme chick-a-boomer. Her night was young. Nearly underaged.

I drove back to Fell's Point and dropped off the hearse. I had left Alcatraz with Billie as I hadn't known how long my visit to Rehoboth was going to be. I decided to let him sleep over and I went home to an empty apartment. I kicked off my shoes and hit the Play button on my phone machine. I realized that I hadn't checked my messages the night before. I had several greetings from Clarissa. Judging by the passion and the invective, it didn't appear that Clarissa and I were doing too well as a fledgling couple. The tone in each of the messages was pretty much identical, though taken as a whole there was a definite buildup to a crescendo. If I didn't know better, I'd say Clarissa didn't like me. In her last message, however, she told me that she was free on Saturday night and that there was a dance program at The Lyric that she wanted to see. Call me a fool, but I felt I owed her.

"This is a repair-date, Hitchcock," her voice crackled over my machine. "Consider yourself lucky." In my book, the woman was sending mixed messages. I scribbled down the information on a piece of junk mail.

I had two other messages. One was from my mechanic. My car was ready. I would have to knock over a small bank in order to pay for the repairs, but what are you going to do. The other message was from Pete Munger. I could barely make out what he was saying. I had to rewind the tape and play the message a second time. From the general muttering, I plucked what seemed to be his thesis. An apology of sorts for his behavior the other day. Whether he meant the gun or the oddity with the Dusty Springfield tune or both I couldn't tell. My trained ear picked up two irrefutable facts. One, he had called from a bar. The background noise was unmistakable. Two, he had been there awhile.

Before I called Munger, I phoned Lucy's number. The phone rang seven or eight times before it picked up. "Lucy?"

There was a long pause. "Hello, Hitch."

"You know, Luce, I was more than ready to give you a ride back to town today. You didn't have to go running off like that." She didn't respond. "Listen, are you okay?"

"I'm . . . yeah, I'm fine. Hitch, I didn't mean to . . . I'm sorry. I guess it was silly. I just don't want to get you and Julia caught up in this anymore. It's my problem—"

I cut her off. "Lucy, this is no time to play the loner. Have you got that? We'll just go through this thing step by step."

"That's what I'm planning to do. I'm calling the police tomorrow."

"You haven't called them yet?"

"I . . . I just want a good night's sleep. If that's possible."

"All right, that's fair. Look, why don't you give Julia a call? You won't catch her in right now, but she always checks her messages. Just let her know that you're safe and what you're planning on doing."

"But—"

"But nothing, Lucy. Now stop it. You're going to be fine."

"I—" She was beginning to choke on her tears.

"Why don't I come over, Lucy. I—"

"No. Please. I appreciate it and everything, but . . . no thank you."

"You're sure?"

"I'm sure. Really." She paused. "Good night, Hitch." She hung up the phone. I began to redial her number, then changed my mind. I was going to trust that she'd do the right thing. I called Information and got a number for Pete Munger and dialed it up. A woman answered. She didn't answer cheerfully.

"Is Pete there?" I asked.

"Who is this?"

I told her my name. It registered absolutely zero on whatever scale she was using. I asked again if Pete was there.

"Is this an emergency?"

"Well . . . no."

"It's almost midnight."

"I'm sorry," I stammered. "I wasn't . . . Did I wake you?"

"Yes, you did."

I apologized again. "Pete left me a message. I was . . . is he there?"

"He's not here," she said. "Why don't you try his beeper?" She gave me the beeper number, along with a sigh of irritation. I scribbled it down. "Whoever you are, Pete should have given you his beeper number in the first place."

"Don't blame him."

"Too late." She hung up.

I phoned the beeper number and left a message. I put a Gilberto Gil

CD on and imagined Julia shaking her lovely booty over by Fort McHenry. Maybe she had been right. Maybe I should have gone with her and moved my feet in random directions for a while. I suddenly remembered the answer to her question, the last time I had been dancing. Clearly I had blocked it from memory. It had been only a week previous. My second date with Clarissa. Big mistake. She was Martha Graham to my Mr. Bojangles and it hadn't been a pretty sight. Clarissa's dancing included a lot of swooning and fake fainting, as well as some intricate labyrinth building right out there on the dance floor. It was primarily a solo act, and when she tried several times to draw me in we meshed like two cats clinging to an electric fence.

The phone rang. I predicted it was Pete Munger and I was one hundred percent correct. Send this boy to Vegas. Munger speaking noticeably softly. This time there was no background sound whatsoever.

"This is Munger," he practically whispered. "What do you want?"

"I'm returning your call," I said. "This is Hitchcock Sewell."

"My . . . ? I didn't call you."

"Last night. You left a message on my machine. Some of it was even in English."

There was a pause. "Oh. Last night. I called you?"

"Yes sir, you did."

"Was I insulting?"

"Didn't seem to be. But the connection wasn't all that good."

"Sorry. Bad night."

I expected him to say more, but he didn't. So I did. "I'm afraid I woke your wife up just now," I said. "I mean, I'm assuming that was your wife. I called your home."

"It was my wife or my daughter. How'd she sound?"

"Royally pissed."

"That would be wife. Susan."

"Apologize for me."

"For the good that will do."

We shared another pause. The detective broke it. "Well, since you've called, I might as well tell you. Arthur Wisner has been located."

"No kidding."

"No kidding. In fact, I just saw him."

"Just now?"

"That's right."

"Did he throw any light on what happened to his stepbrother?"

"No, he did not."

"Well, his mother must be relieved."

The detective's voice went even lower. "I'm looking at her right now. She looks anything but relieved. She's slumped over in a chair in a hallway. She's crying her eyes out."

"Where are you?"

"I'm at the Medical Examiner's office. Eleanor phoned me the moment she got the word to come down here."

"Arthur Wisner is *dead?*"

"His body was found earlier this evening."

I have no idea what it was that Gilberto Gil was singing. But it was nice and peppy. Too peppy. I lowered myself to the couch.

"Was he murdered?"

"Knife," Munger grunted. "Right in the heart."

"Sounds familiar."

"It certainly does." He paused. "So how are you doing in tracking down your friend?"

"That would be Lucy."

"That would be."

"They really want to talk to her now, don't they?"

"They really do."

Gilberto Gil was practically skipping through posies. I hit the remote and silenced him. "Can I meet you somewhere?" I asked.

I could hear Munger sighing on his end of the line. "I can't get out of this place quick enough. Where?"

The old clock on the wall said: GO HOME. And still the band played on. Fiddles, penny whistles, a mandolin. Cat's Eye Pub. The band had been playing "Midnight on the Water" when I got there, well after midnight. Pete Munger arrived during "Marie's Wedding." He wasn't much in the mood for nuptials. He found me at my table at the far end of the bar and dropped into the chair opposite. His glance around the place snagged on the painting behind the bar. It depicted a street scene in Belfast. Rocks and bottles in the air. Smoke on the horizon. All grays and blacks.

"I.R.A.?"

"It's not just an individual retirement account anymore," I quipped.

"For the price of my beer I'm investing in the cause? I think I'll have water."

Which he did. I was working slowly on a Guinness. "You're going to make me feel guilty," I said.

He shrugged. "Maybe you support the cause."

"If I thought about all the places my money was going when I spent it I'd freeze up. The modern world cannot be grasped," I said sagely, and lifted my glass.

"Look, I apologize for whatever message I left last night."

"You already apologized on the phone."

"I'm having a little trouble with my marriage." He started to say something else, then changed his mind. "I kind of have a lot of triggers lately that set me off. That song the other day."

"Dusty Springfield?"

"Her. Yeah. Big trigger."

"Old memories, huh?"

"I don't want to talk about it."

I didn't bother to point out to him who had brought up the topic in the first place. The band had moved into "Black Velvet Band." Pete Munger looked over at them. Pensively, I thought.

"Another bad song?" I asked.

He shook his head. "No. The girl with the fiddle. She looks a little like my daughter, that's all."

"She's pretty," I remarked.

He gave me a frank look. "She's taking her mother's side in all this. No surprise there, I guess. You married?"

"Was."

"Kids?"

"Us? Nah, we were consenting adults."

If he thought that was anywhere near funny, he kept the thought completely buried. His glower asked the question again.

"No," I said. "No kids."

When Munger sighed, his entire body participated. "It's like . . . it's like someone came in one night when I was asleep and ripped out half the pages in my brain. Does that make any sense to you?"

"Truth? No."

"It's hard to . . . oh, forget it," he grumbled.

I leaned forward on the table. "Pete . . . can I call you Pete?"

He picked up his water glass. "Sure. Or Munger. Doesn't matter."

"How about Alfonse Valentino?"

The glass came back down. "Matters."

"Should we talk about murder, Pete? Maybe that'll get your mind off it."

The detective looked for a moment as if he might take a swing at me. Then he relaxed and sat back in his chair. He gave the chipped wood table a little rat-a-tat. "Murder. Perfect. Good idea."

Munger warmed up as he gave me the scoop. Arthur Wisner's body had been discovered earlier in the evening in the woods out by Loch Raven reservoir. Nature had called a jogger who did a little bushwhacking and had run across the dead body. It was curled in a fetal position and partially covered with twigs and branches. According to Munger, it took no great feats of forensic science to determine that Arthur Wisner had been dead for several days at least.

"How nobody who lived anywhere near didn't catch a whiff of this guy is amazing. The boy was definitely ripe."

I thanked him for the extra color.

"One other thing," Munger said. "There was a camera next to the body."

"A camera?"

"Not one of these little things. Kind of hefty. You know what I mean? Like the old-fashioned kind you've got to hold with both hands. With the big flashbulb. Like you see in the old movies, the news photographers."

"Or the people who take photographs of the customers at their tables," I said.

"Sure. One of those. Except it wasn't really vintage. I mean, it wasn't old like that. Just kind of had that look."

"I'll bet you anything that was Arthur's camera," I said. "That was one of the things that Arthur did. He went around to the tables and took customers' pictures. You walk in the front door, the walls there are covered with them. Apparently it was one of Arthur's ideas for getting repeat customers. They'd also get some celebs. Was this thing a Polaroid?"

"Could be. I don't know. It went off to Evidence."

"I wonder why Arthur would've had his camera with him. I guess it would be asking too much to hope he took a picture of the person who killed him."

Munger scoffed. "You mean he takes the picture, the killer doesn't see it, Arthur falls over dead on top of the picture. Cops show. Roll him over and there it is?"

"You sound dubious."

"You sound like a bad movie." Munger raised a hand and called for a beer. "You want another?"

"I'm nursing," I said. "I thought you didn't want to support the cause."

"*My* cause is more important. Let me tell you how much fun it is to watch an old friend of yours identifying the body of her son."

I was still thinking about Arthur's camera. Or what I was assuming was Arthur's camera.

"What if the killer took the picture," I said. "What if he took a picture of Arthur."

Munger's eyebrows went up. "You mean, dead? A sicko?"

"Okay, maybe that," I said. "But I was thinking . . . well, wait, I was going to say ransom. But you need to have your victim still alive for that."

"Yes, you do."

"Well, how about earlier? Maybe the guy did take a picture of Arthur when he was still alive. The Martins didn't receive any sort of ransom note or anything like that this week, did they?"

Munger answered, "They say they didn't."

"You don't sound one hundred percent convinced."

"I guess I am."

"Pete, that's not one hundred percent."

"The thing is, when people get a ransom note it usually warns them not to notify the authorities. The whole deal is supposed to go down privately and quietly."

"So then you're saying that it's at least possible that someone did nab Arthur and try to shake down the Martins. I mean, it's conceivable."

Munger's beer arrived. He made me wait while he took a hungry sip. He seemed to enjoy it. He set the mug down lightly. "Okay, it's conceivable. But based on nothing more than a camera lying near a dead body? Doesn't really take me there."

"I guess it doesn't add up," I admitted. "I mean, you've got Shrimp being killed right there in a damn hospital. No way there was any thought of ransom involved in that one."

"That's assuming that the two killings are related."

"Well, I'm the amateur here, but that's how I do the math."

"Okay then. So let's stretch it for a minute," Pete said, shifting in his chair. "We've got Arthur as a possible ransom. Maybe a ransom gone wrong. You're right, the camera is an intriguing factor. And we've got Shrimp. No clue there yet, but ransom seems very unlikely. So that could leave the daughter as the next target."

"Mary Ann? What do you think, a full-scale assault on the Martin family? Someone is that determined to shake down the bakery king?"

Munger shrugged. "I'm just speculating." He took his speculation into a long pull on his beer. I happen to be a person who enjoys speculating myself. I was speculating that Pete Munger's satisfaction with his beer carried a little history with it. Just something in the way it was all going down.

We watched the band for a few minutes. The girl who allegedly looked like Munger's daughter had pulled out a pennywhistle and was blowing a duet with the guy on guitar. Munger's chin was in his hand. I had no idea where his thoughts were. When the song ended, I dragged Munger back to our topic.

"You say that Arthur was definitely not murdered tonight? Or even today for that matter? Arthur disappeared last Friday. Could he have been dead since then?"

Munger seemed reluctant to get back to business. "Could. They should be able to determine that," he said. "Or some reasonable time frame."

"But at least he wasn't killed tonight," I said. "That's good." The comment won me a funny look from Munger. Or maybe he was trying to raise an eyebrow.

"Why is that good?"

I told him that I had it "on good authority" that Lucy Taylor had returned to Baltimore this evening from "an undisclosed location" out of town. Munger noted that I was using a lot of safety phrases.

"If Arthur had been killed today, I'd hate to think what the police would conclude, Lucy's coming back to town the same day," I said.

Munger floated his hands, palms up. "What's the difference? Instead of thinking she came back to town and killed him, they have her killing him first and then leaving town."

"Oh. Right. I guess they would."

"After killing Shrimp, of course."

"Of course. Lucy is a homicidal maniac. Everyone knows that. Common knowledge."

"Look," Munger said. "Two people are dead. She knew them both. She shot one of them. That's the direction I'd be sending my dogs."

I took a slow pull on my Guinness and watched as the fiddler who looked like Munger's daughter put a big sloppy kiss on the mandolin player. Munger didn't look like he was too happy about it.

"They take requests," I said to him.

Munger grumbled. "I wish they'd just stick to the music."

"You know that I don't think Lucy killed either of these guys, right?"

"I know that."

"And I'm assuming that this will eventually come out."

"If she didn't do it, the odds are in your favor. But it could take time."

"Exactly. I'd like to accelerate the process. For Lucy's sake. I've seen enough prison movies. I don't want her going through any of that. I was wondering . . . What would I be looking at to hire you to help me find out who actually killed Shrimp? And Arthur?"

"You want to hire me?"

"That's right."

"I don't do that."

"Don't do what?"

"I don't investigate murders."

"I thought you were a private eye."

"I've mainly worked domestics. Run-around husbands, run-around wives. Missing persons. Like Arthur Wisner. I snoop through phone records and bank statements. There's a lot of desk work, really."

"Why don't you do murders?" I asked. "You're in Baltimore. Fantastic murder rate here. You'd have great pickings."

Munger's gaze sat on me a moment before he answered. "I guess I'm not interested in doing something where I might get killed."

"But you carry a gun," I noted.

"Shit happens. You've got to be ready."

"Have you ever used it? I mean, in the line of duty."

Munger took up his glass again. It half-hid his face, but he was looking directly at me. "Shit happens," he said again. He said it with a great big period at the end. Subject closed.

Munger downed his beer and ordered another. I joined him. Hate to see a man drink alone. We sat back and listened to the music for a while. I had planned to tell the detective everything about Lucy, about her having gone off with Julia to Rehoboth to lay low for several days, and about how she had taken the bus back to Baltimore. But I couldn't see the point now. The details, that is. Especially if he wasn't going to take on an investigation. Munger and I had both located our missing persons. The only difference was, his was dead and mine was a suspect in the death.

A thought occurred to me. I waved a hand out in front of Munger's gaze. He was looking tired. Cranky.

"What?"

"I've got a question for you," I said. "If Lucy Taylor turns out to still be missing, if she didn't turn herself in after all, maybe you'd consider looking for her. That's not a murder case."

Munger frowned. "I thought you had it 'on good authority' that she was going to turn herself in to the police."

"But if."

"Fact is," he said, "this isn't really such a good time for me. I'm closing shop."

"Closing shop? You mean you're leaving the detective business?"

"You know the name of my company? Munger and Associates? You're looking at the associates. I had two people working for me. I just let them both go. I make my own coffee now. I'm getting out of this line of work. Who knows, I might even be getting out of Baltimore." He took a sip of his beer. "The truth is, I really don't know what the hell I'm doing. It's like I told you. Someone ripped out half the pages in my brain. Nothing that made sense is making sense anymore."

"But you're still a detective. You took on the Arthur Wisner case."

"That was a thing. A favor for Eleanor Wisner." He corrected himself. "Martin. I owe her. She was in a real panic about her son and she came to me. Shrimp had been murdered and now Arthur was missing. I told her I'd look into it. I guess I started looking a little too late."

He looked off in the direction of the band. One of the Cat's Eye regulars—a bow-legged shorty in a Greek fisherman's cap—was standing next to a pole, mimicking the mandolin player and having a good old time of it. Air mandolin. Munger returned his gaze to me. The pulleys failed to haul much of an expression into place. "What I guess I'm in is 'a transitional phase,' " he said heavily. "That's what they're calling it now. I guess it's supposed to sound better than 'my life's shot to shit.' " He picked up his beer. "Why the hell am I telling you this?"

"I'm in a listening profession," I said.

This got a small chuckle out of him. "For a listener, you do your share of gabbing, you know." He finished off his beer and landed the mug on the table. He had taken the thing down in about three pulls.

"I guess I'll be going." He stood up from the table. "It was a pleasure meeting you. Who knows, you might turn out to be the last person I ever pull a gun on."

"That is a distinction I will definitely ponder," I said. "Don't forget to apologize to your wife for me."

"My wife?"

"My phone call. I woke her up. She wasn't happy."

"Oh. That. Yeah. I'll be sure to tell her."

The subtitles right under his weary face read: Don't count on it. Before I could stop him he pulled out his wallet and slapped a ten-dollar bill down on the table. Then he picked it back up and shook it in my direction.

"One thing. If you're going to stick your nose in this thing? Rule number one in almost any investigation. It's just like in that Watergate movie. Did you see that one? Follow the money." He set the bill back down on the table.

I asked, "What money?"

He gestured vaguely to the ceiling. "There's always money. It's not always the prime thing, but it's always there. Might just be credit card receipts. Gas stations. Bills. Purchases. Whatever. It's different in every case. It's just a tip. Take it or leave it."

He put his wallet back in his pocket and moved toward the door. He paused there, right next to the stage, and watched for a few seconds as the fiddler was working her way through a wretchedly sad waltz. Then he pushed through the door and was gone.

CHAPTER 9

First thing in the morning I took out the phone book and worked my way through the "Cromwell, L." listings until I found Lee Cromwell. Her voice wasn't exactly crisp and clear.

"Did I wake you?" I asked.

"That's okay. I had to get up anyway to answer the phone."

I laughed. "I've always wanted to use that line."

"Well, it was great fun, let me tell you."

"Sorry. I didn't mean to wake you."

Lee answered, "Girl can't sleep her life away. What's up? Are you calling to invite me to a funeral?"

"I wanted to see if I could get some information from you." I told her what I was trying to find out. It was no state secret, and Lee was able to give me what I was looking for. I thanked her for the dope. Before we hung up she told me where the Edgar Jonz Experience could be experienced.

"The place is a pretty big yawn, but it's work."

I told her I'd try to catch the act then I thanked her again and hung up. I showered, ran a cold blade around my face and called Billie to tell her that I was back from the beach. I asked her if we had any new customers on ice. We didn't. I told her that I was going to be out and about for the day. She said that she had already enjoyed a morning promenade with Alcatraz and that she'd be happy to look after him for as long as necessary. Next I dialed Julia's number. To my surprise she answered on the first ring.

"Good morning star shine," I said. "The earth says hello."

"The hell with that. Lucy's been arrested. Come get me."

Click.

The damn woman hung up on me.

Lucy Taylor was arrested and formally charged with the murder of Shrimp Martin. In addition, she was charged with aggravated assault with intent to kill, for her shooting Shrimp in the belly earlier in the day. For the moment, charges in the murder of Arthur Wisner were being withheld, pending autopsy results. The general sniff, however, was that if Lucy Taylor stank for the one murder, she probably stank for the other.

Lucy was refusing to say where she had been the past several days or if she had been with any particular person or persons. In fact, she was still refusing to say much of anything. Too much time had passed since Saturday to declare that Lucy was still in shock over the events that had transpired that afternoon and evening. It looked like shock, but it wasn't. Lucy was simply overwhelmed. She appeared to be operating at roughly half the speed that events around her were operating.

"She looks disoriented," Julia commented as Lucy was being brought into the windowless courtroom for her arraignment. The State of Maryland had decided to swap Lucy's colorful beachwear for a set of pea green coveralls that appeared to be at least two sizes too big. Lucy spotted Julia and me sitting a few benches from the rear as she was being escorted to the front of the courtroom and she squeezed off a small smile that was not nearly so brave as it was bewildered. My heart flattened like a deflated tire.

"Oh honey," Julia crooned, barely audibly. "We'll get you out of here." She turned to me. "Can the police seriously believe that that little waif would sneak into someone's hospital room and stab him to death? Look at her, Hitch. She looks like a child."

Indeed, especially in the loose-fitting coveralls, that was exactly what

Lucy looked like. As Lucy and her lawyer moved to their place in front of the judge, the lawyer's hip knocked lightly against the small table where the representative from the District Attorney's Office was seated. A good-looking geek in tortoiseshell glasses. The lawyer's pen fell to the floor. Instinctively, Lucy bent and retrieved the pen, wincing a timid smile to the prosecutor as she placed the pen back onto the table. Seconds later the prosecutor was asking the judge that the defendant be denied bail and that she remain in custody pending trial. Lucy wheeled around as he spoke. Her expression was heartbreaking. Was *everyone* her enemy?

Julia hissed, "Hitch, I'm going to say something."

"There's nothing you can do right now, Jules," I said. "For your own good you'd be smart to keep your head down."

Julia had found Lucy's lawyer for her. A guy named Al Murray. Julia told me that she and Al "had worked on some briefs together once." A remark that I refused to dignify. Al was a strong-jawed, no-nonsense, three-piece fellow and he pitched a worthy fit in front of the bench, but he failed to convince the judge to set bail. The tortoiseshelled prosecutor made the argument that Lucy was a flight risk, and it was apparently a good argument. Gavel smash. Bail denied. Hoosegow time for Miss Lucy Taylor. Lucy lowered her head as she was escorted through a side door. A few minutes later Julia and I came down the steps in front of the courthouse and paused on the sidewalk.

"What now?" Julia asked.

I told her I had a few ideas. I was lying. I only had one.

"Did you talk to your detective?" Julia wanted to know.

"He's getting out of the game. Besides, he doesn't do murders."

"Is that like not doing windows?"

"He's going through a midlife crisis."

Julia wrinkled her nose. "People still do that?"

Al the lawyer had just stepped out of the courthouse and paused at the top of the steps, chin tipped in the air, aluminum briefcase catching the late-morning sun. A gentle breeze was blowing. If the guy had been wearing a cape . . .

Julia's cheeks went as rosy as a blushing baby's bottom.

"Why don't you go discuss the case," I suggested.

A little squeal. She was off. Scampering up the steps like a gazelle.

Ten minutes later I was on the fifteenth floor of an office building on St. Paul Street. The receptionist was giving me a very happenin' scowl.

"Do you have an appointment, Mr. Sewell?"

"No ma'am, I don't."

"Mr. Fisher is very busy. You would need to make an appointment."

I handed her a provocative phrase, which she related over her intercom.

"Yes sir. I'll tell him."

I was to be rewarded with five minutes. But I would have to wait ten minutes to get them. I ended up waiting twenty. I passed the time reading the news of the week from a month ago. Hard to get excited. The receptionist returned to her *Vogue*. For a while I tried turning the pages of my magazine in tandem with her . . . but she didn't seem to notice.

Barry Fisher reiterated the five-minute rule as I entered his office.

"I'm in the middle of a hundred things," he explained, standing up to lean over his great big egg-shaped desk to shake my hand. The desk was nearly empty. Wherever the hundred things were, I sure couldn't see them. A photograph of two chubby teenagers and one of Mr. and Mrs. Fisher on a sailboat, tanned and smiling like lottery winners, were about it.

"I appreciate your squeezing me in," I said.

The man was wearing silver cuff links. Had the grip of a bear. The eyes of a snake. He motioned for me to have a seat as he dropped back into his ergonomic chair. It looked like something developed by NASA. He was ready for liftoff.

"So what can I do for you, Mr. Sewell? When an undertaker says 'life or death,' I guess it's worth a listen."

That had been the idea. My provocative phrase.

"I was wondering if maybe your life was in danger," I said. Damn, but I liked that as an opening line. I had worked it up while reading last month's news. Unfortunately, Barry Fisher seemed less than wowed by it.

He steepled his fingers and set his chin atop the steeple. The steeple wasn't exactly quaking.

"Not the last time I checked," he said blandly. "But thank you for asking."

Barry Fisher was not a complete stranger to me. I had seen him exactly twice to this point. He was the man in the different pinstripe suits who had attended Shrimp Martin's wake and funeral. He was back in the blue pinstripe suit today. He was around forty-five. He had a power tan and a power haircut. The smell of Bay Rum lifted from his collar, along with an air of confidence and general business acumen. Myself, I had decided to play the in-the-good-old-summertime card, and was wearing cream slacks and a seersucker jacket. Blue tie, loosely knotted. White muslin shirt. Slightly wrinkled. Moccasins. No socks. Like no catalog page you'll ever find. I looked damn better than I had a right to. My opinion.

Fisher asked me politely just what it was I was referring to. I told him what he already knew, and what Lee Cromwell had told me on the phone.

"You were Shrimp Martin's partner in the club."

Fisher rocked back in his chair. "That's right. Technically."

"Technically?"

"The club was Mr. Martin's," Fisher said. "I'm not a club owner. Mr. Martin came to me with a business proposition. He was looking for some capital. It's what I do. I invest. I liked what I heard. Mr. Martin had a vision and a lot of energy. I was his partner in the sense that I helped him in the arranging of some loans to get things up and running."

"I understand that things weren't always up and running all that well," I said.

"Is that so?"

I liked his question, so I repeated it back to him. "Is that so?"

Stupid thing to do. Fisher blanched, then recovered smoothly. But his tone cooled noticeably.

"Mr. Martin's enterprise was experiencing its ups and downs. I suppose you could call them growing pains. The club hasn't been open all that long, after all. One needs to be willing to weather the rough patches in this sort of endeavor."

"Was the club in danger of going under?"

Fisher spread his hands like a pair of wings and looked down his nose at me. I realized that my chair was considerably lower than his. Old business trick. He rocked back farther in his ergonomic throne. "There's risk involved in ventures like this. Mr. Martin knew that going in, of course. As did I. Have you been to the club?"

I told him that I had.

"Well then, you've seen it. Shrimp did a top-notch job of putting the place together. Very classy. First-rate. The money shows. Shrimp was very shrewd, I thought. The Canton area is really breaking out. People are starting to head down there. Personally, I hate the word 'buzz,' but I think Shrimp's was starting to get it."

"I hear Cal Ripken even made the scene."

Fisher smiled. In his way. "That was a coup."

"What did Shrimp do, promise the guy all the free milk he could drink?"

"Shrimp knows this is a sports town. He worked that angle strongly. Smart move on his part."

"I notice that Kit Grady made an appearance at the wake," I said.

"I saw that, too. Shrimp would have been pleased."

"Was Shrimp in money trouble?" I asked bluntly. "Was he in debt?"

Fisher delivered a slow grin. "We're all in debt if we're in business. It's all about leveraging."

"Serious debt? Was Shrimp losing his leverage?"

Fisher paused and gave me a long look over before answering. "Suppose you tell me why this is actually any of your business. What does this have to do with life or death?"

"Two people intimately connected to the club have been murdered. You're one of Shrimp's business partners. I think it's not unreasonable to wonder if the murders might have been related to problems with the club. If they are, it's possible that you could be in some danger as well."

Fisher came forward in his chair. "Two people?"

"Arthur Wisner was found murdered last night."

Fisher blinked slowly. "I hadn't heard that." I believed him. You can't easily fake a cheek flush. "Where was he killed?"

"They found him out near Loch Raven. He was stabbed. Just like Shrimp."

"That's horrible."

"Yeah, I'm sure Arthur thought so, too. So you see my point. First Shrimp and then Arthur. Or maybe even Arthur first. He's been missing for almost a week. Either way, aside from their being stepbrothers, the club is their other obvious connection. So like I said, if they ran into some trouble related to the club, isn't there a chance that you could be in some danger as well?"

Fisher swiveled in his chair like a postulating shrink. "This would mean, of course, that I was aware of who it is who had this . . . problem with Mr. Martin and his stepbrother."

"I guess it would."

"And if I was aware of something like that, don't you suppose I would have gone to the police immediately with this information?"

"I suppose. That is, unless it were something illegal."

Fisher had returned to the steepled fingers. He was tapping his fingertips against his chin. "Illegal? Such as?"

"I've heard that there was some gambling going on at the club."

"Gambling?"

"Yes. Drugs as well."

"I'm afraid I can't help you with that."

"You have no firsthand knowledge of that?"

"Nor secondhand. You're bringing me new information. Or I suppose I should say speculation." His eyes narrowed. The look was decidedly reptilian. Maybe I was reading too much into it, but the man's iron grip on being cool and controlled was seeming decidedly forced, like the gentle quivering of a bent metal bar just before it snaps. "Your interest in all this, Mr. Sewell?" he said snidely. "Should I be honored that you have taken the time out of your busy day to come warn a complete stranger that he might be on some crazed killer's hit list?"

I considered letting him know that my day wasn't particularly busy. But his withering tone was working its magic. I was feeling oddly unhinged by the sarcasm. Must have been the power tan and the egg-shaped desk. These power guys have got handbooks on how to intimidate.

"A friend of mine is under suspicion in Shrimp's murder. I'm just trying to help her out," I said.

Fisher swiveled to look out the window behind him. His view was no great shakes, unless you like looking at other tall buildings. I noted that his mouse brown hair was thinly veiling a bald spot on the back of his head. It lost him a power point.

"I fail to see how you think you are helping out your friend by asking me questions about Mr. Martin's financial situation," Fisher said to the window.

"I'm just following the money," I said. I scribbled a mental Post-it to thank Pete Munger for the nifty advice. "I don't buy the so-called motives for my friend killing Shrimp. I'm trying to find someone else with a better motive."

Fisher swiveled back from the window. "And what is your friend's supposed motive?" he asked.

"Jealousy? Revenge?"

"Those sound good to me."

"You don't know my friend."

"I didn't mean to insult." He checked his watch. He checked it like a person who would gladly trigger a trap door under my chair had there been one. "We're going to have to wrap this up," he said.

"I thought I had five minutes."

"I really don't see the point in these questions."

"I'm just trying—"

He cut me off. "Look, Mr. Sewell, I am sorry about your friend. Honestly. Sometimes it is hard to accept that we don't really know people as well as we thought we did. I'm not saying that your friend murdered Mr. Martin. But let me give you some advice. You're not going to make any new friends if you start poking about in people's financial affairs in some effort to play the hero."

"I just thought—"

"We have police who are paid and trained to do this sort of thing for us. Correct me if I'm wrong, but you are not a policeman, are you?"

"I'm an undertaker."

"Exactly. You get to bury them. Someone else gets to figure out how they died. We all have our job, don't we?" That sounded a bit nasty.

Barry Fisher stood up and leaned across his desk to offer his hand. I rose from my inferior chair and took the hand. We played the eye game. To a draw.

Had Fisher left things right where they were, there's a chance I would have left his office feeling slightly sheepish and a trifle peeved, and that's all. But he didn't. He tagged on one more sentence, ratcheting up his power grip as he said it.

"Do I make myself clear?"

And that, ladies and gentlemen, is a threat.

After leaving Fisher's office I stood on the curb and raised a finger to see which way the wind was blowing. A taxi screeched to a halt. It's enough sometimes to make you feel like a wizard. I gave an address and a few minutes later I was dropped in front of the Medical Examiner's office on Penn Street. I told the fellow at the front desk I was there to see Arthur Wisner. The fellow was new to the job. He ran his finger down his laminated sheet then looked back up at me.

"I don't see an Arthur Wisner here. Does he work here?"

A dozen retorts collided . . . and nullified one another. I asked simply about Morris Kiefaber.

"Dr. Kiefaber? Sure. Hold on. Your name?"

I gave him an easier name to handle than mine. One I knew Kiefaber would recognize. The guy punched a button on his phone and reported the name. "No sir, he's not," he said into the phone. "He's standing right here." He looked up at me. "Mr. Kingman, Dr. Kiefaber says you're dead."

I went for the top card. "And he calls himself a medical examiner."

Morris Kiefaber came through the double doors a moment later. Plastic apron. Paper face mask dangling around his neck.

"Sewell. I should have guessed. That was cute."

"Hey there, Sweeney," I sang out. "What's cooking?"

"Your goose if I could get ahold of it. What brings you here, Hitch? Finally decided to donate your organs?"

"To the third lucky caller," I quipped.

The guy at the desk was looking concerned. Kiefaber addressed him.

"Steve, this specimen of bad one-liners is Hitchcock Sewell. Mr. Sewell is a local mortician. You can safely dispense with at least three quarters of whatever you hear him say. But we humor him." He looked back over at me. "Much more than he humors us."

"That's a bald lie, Kiefaber."

"So what is it, Hitch?" Morris said. "Business slow? You're looking for customers?"

"Could be."

Morris pushed open one of the double doors. "Come on in. Let's see what we can find."

As I followed Kiefaber into the sanctum of formaldehyde I told him the reason why I had dropped in. Kiefaber took a left into an examining room. I followed after him and stopped just inside the room. Twenty feet away stood a metal table holding a sight no mother should ever see. It didn't exactly make my day either. I took a few steps closer to the table. Morris took hold of the hanging microphone used for recording the autopsies and swiveled it out of the way, in case I really felt like getting in close. I didn't. Kiefaber had an amused look on his face as he watched me.

"You might want to consider another line of work, Hitch. You're look-ing like a chef who can't stand the sight of food."

"I maintain my humanity by remaining shocked at the sight of a corpse that's been sliced and diced." I took another step forward—saw the face, as well as a whole lot more—then took two steps back. Two thirds of the hokeypokey.

"So that's Arthur," I said.

"You've not made his acquaintance?"

"Not officially," I said. "I knew his stepbrother. Casually."

"I understand he's singing with the angels, too."

"More like chasing them around the Pearly Gates."

Kiefaber crossed his arms and squared off in front of me. "Okay, Hitch. Dance over. I don't know your involvement in this, but I know you know the rules. Autopsy results are not a matter of watercooler chat until the proper authorities have been notified. And that ain't you, babe."

He stepped to the wall and flipped a switch, apparently turning off the room's recording equipment. "So what do you want to know?"

"Dazzle me, Morris."

The medical examiner bored me with a brief biochemistry lecture. Time of death, he said, was difficult to determine with any great degree of accuracy. The body had been slowly rotting in the warm sun for a sufficient length of time to make any guesses concerning time of death open to argument. Kiefaber easily conceded, when I asked, that the previous Friday worked well enough for him.

"That boy has been mulching for a while. I've got no problem in calling it a week."

"And he was stabbed in the heart, right?"

"Right between the tick and the tock."

"Have you got anything on the weapon?"

"I'm not sure what you're asking."

"Yes you are. Was it the same weapon that was used to kill Shrimp Martin?"

Kiefaber chuckled. "Well, Sherlock, that hasn't been precisely determined yet."

"How about imprecisely?"

"Looks like the same weapon to me. A knife, most likely. Four- to five-inch blade. Folding knife. Like a pocketknife. There are indications around both victims' wounds of a pinching of the skin, like you might get from the grooves where the base of the blade attaches to the body of the knife. I'm speaking superficially, of course."

"The only way, Morris."

"Methodology appears to match as well."

"Translation?"

"The killer pushed the blade into the heart and then twisted it. Clockwise."

"Clockwise."

"The direction that the hands move on—"

"I know 'clockwise,' Morris. Something tells me that you find this detail significant."

"Could be. Depending on whether the killer held the knife like this"—Kiefaber demonstrated by taking a penlight from his pocket and holding it with the service end protruding from the crook of his thumb and index finger—"or like this"—he flipped the penlight around the other way and made a downward stabbing motion—"can give you pretty strong probabilities as to whether the murderer was left-handed or right-handed."

"How would you determine if it was a forward thrust or a downward stab?"

Morris shrugged. "Well, you'd have to ask the person who did the stabbing."

"You go to school to learn this?"

Before I left, Morris told me that he believed the body had not been killed where it was found.

"So he was taken there and dumped off," I said.

"Elementary."

"That's interesting. Any suggestions where he might have been murdered?"

Morris shrugged. "That's forensics. I just pass on the findings. And good luck getting that crowd to chew the fat with you."

I thought for a moment. "Any drugs in his system?"

"Nope."

"Any signs of a struggle?"

"Hitch, what difference could that possibly make to you?"

I conceded. "None. That's just one of those questions you hear being asked."

"Well, you've asked it. Good for you. And yes, there are indications that he struggled. Of course, someone's coming at your heart with a sharp object you'd expect that, wouldn't you?"

"That might rule out a surprise attack."

Morris thought on it. "Might. Might not."

I sat with the information for a minute. "Anything else?" I asked.

Kiefaber floated his palms upward. "Big Mac and a Coke?"

"Thanks," I said. "But I'm not especially hungry."

"No, not you. Arthur Wisner's last meal."

"Did he have fries with that?"

CHAPTER 10

I had some undertaking business to attend to. Billie and I had recently decided to have some shelving units built as a display case for cremation urns. These things come in all shapes and colors, as you can maybe imagine. Not to mention the ridiculous designer urns, the ones that pay tribute to the deceased's hobby or their vocation or their obsession. Or all-three-in-one, if a person has been so lucky. We live in an idiosyncratic world. We die in one as well. Billie and I have had spouses of golf freaks who'll spend hundreds of unnecessary extra dollars for an urn in the shape of a miniature golf bag. We once had a widower from Rodgers Forge by the name of Clifford Tuttle who opted to entomb the ashes of his deceased wife (she had been a librarian) in an urn in the shape of a book complete with the title "A Life" and his wife's name embossed on the spine. Apparently the urn sits on the bookshelf in Mr. Tuttle's study, right between Anthony Trollope and Anne Tyler. Some of these designer urns look like little jewelry boxes. Others look like humidors. There is even one that is a hollowed-out stone, like those things where you hide the extra house key. We can offer miniature castles, urns in the shape of any number of makes of automobiles, hollowed-out bowling pins, lovebird figurines, praying hands, even an urn in the likeness of Elvis Presley (the young Elvis) with the inscription: "Return to Sender."

You can't make this stuff up.

Billie and I had debated the issue of pushing these oddball things for quite a while, and then finally decided to go ahead and give it a shot. It's our job to facilitate the wishes of the bereft, not to steer them in one direction over another. The problem though was that our new urn display was looking more like a trophy shelf. It needed something. We considered draping the shelves with black material, but neither of us is too terribly keen on overstressing the somber. Billie had finally come up with a novel solution and I swung by the funeral home to see how it had worked out. I liked it. We had our woodworker give a nice deep cherry glaze to the shelving and then directed him to fashion a folksy-looking wooden sign to hang on the wall above the shelf:

IF YOU WILL . . .

Billie's touch. It's what makes us who we are.

Arthur Wisner's remains were released by the Medical Examiner's office late in the afternoon, along with the preliminary autopsy report. I got a courtesy call at the office from Morris Kiefaber. The remains were going to one of my competitors, which was fine by me. Eleanor Martin wanted the folks who had handled the funeral of her first husband—Arthur's dad—to handle the disposition of her son. Makes sense. Arthur was to be buried next to his father out at Druid Ridge. The funeral was slated for ten o'clock Saturday morning. The forecast called for rain. I can tell you, nothing beats a funeral in a downpour. I made a note in my mental calendar for Saturday: sleep in.

There was nothing scintillating in the preliminary autopsy report. Fatal stab wound to the heart. Exact date of death, indeterminable. Victim not killed where victim was found.

The report didn't even mention the Big Mac.

The day was a scorcher. I took Alcatraz and went home. I took a shower and a short nap, followed by a long nap and then another shower. I came out of it, feeling wistful. A little dreamy. I get this way sometimes—wistful—it just comes over me. Especially after a couple of naps. I wandered back to the funeral home and dropped into my chair. Up went my feet, onto the desk. Following the general rules of wistfulness, I allowed my gaze to track randomly about the room and out the window to my left while my mind scanned for the kernel, the nub, the specific source of the particular mood. Of course it eluded me. I thought about Lucy's being in jail. Her first night behind bars. Bad thought. Depressing thought. But not a source of wistfulness. It occurred to me how suddenly very still and silent it was, both in my office and outside on the street. As if someone had slipped in and turned off the volume. Curious. I recrossed my legs, just to make a sound. Of course there's not much sound in the crossing of legs. I glanced over at the Magritte on the wall. Same old mysterious whimsy there, of course. What did I expect? I tracked over to the window again, in its way a painting. A view within a frame, I mused. I noted a soft ringing in my ears.

Pin drop. Clock tick. Grass grow . . .

I went outside. The feeling held. I went down the street to John Stevens Pub and ordered a plate of mussels and a beer. I drank half the beer while I waited for the mussels, then the other half as I ate them. Naturally, the world wasn't silent anymore. The place was bang-clanging with bar noise. I took my mussels and beer at a table off near the pool table. Two girls and a guy were playing cutthroat. Here's what happened. I got up halfway through my mussels and put four quarters on the edge of the table. "Winner," I said, then returned to my table. One of the girls won. She racked the balls for eight-ball and gave me the break. I pulverized the break. A solid dropped. I went down close to the table to line up the one ball and I found myself in one of those hot staring contests with my opponent, who was standing at the pocket I was aiming for. I didn't want a hot staring contest, so I broke it with a polite smile. I guess this had some sort of appeal in itself, for my opponent's eyes were all over me as I slowly worked the table. The two. The five. The four. The seven. The world seemed to have gone silent again. I ran the table. First time in my life. I couldn't miss if I tried. I *did* try once in fact; it seemed sort of obnoxious to knock the balls all down at once. But I couldn't even screw up. The seven dropped . . . the five . . . and then—three bumper shot—eight ball, corner pocket. Ta-da. A cheer went up from the people who were watching. My opponent came up to me and said, "That wasn't fair." But she had a big smile on her face as she said it. Then she drew me down and whispered something very complimentary into my ear. I tried out my polite smile again and turned to leave. She wanted me to stay. She wanted a rematch. She dared me to run the table two times in a row.

I declined. "Then just stay," she said. She was dressed like Daisy Mae in "Lil' Abner" and was wearing a cowboy hat. Wispy blond hair. Even so . . . I left. As I headed up the street to my place, God bent down and whispered in my ear, "You're a good boy." It wasn't quite the compliment the girl in the cowboy hat had given me. But then you've got to consider the source.

When I got to my place, Mary Childs was standing there.

A crack of thunder sounded in the near distance.

Mary Childs didn't want to talk about her stalker. "I don't want to talk about it," she said. But she did have to bring up the subject in order to explain why she was talking to me and not to the police.

"I hate them. They screwed over my father."

"I thought you said your father was a cop," I said.

"He was. A good one. He put in twenty-three years. Then they screwed him."

"How did they do that?"

"Daddy shot the psycho who was stalking me."

"You told me that."

"The cops . . . Daddy's *people* . . . said he ambushed the guy. They said he set him up so that he could shoot him."

"Did he?"

The none-too-friendly blue eyes of Mary Childs took out a renewed lease on chilling frost. "The bastard was stalking me. He carried a gun. My father did what he thought was right."

"Let me guess. They canned him."

We were in my apartment, in my front room. Mary on the couch. Me in the fat armchair. Alcatraz on the floor. The distance between the three of us was noticeable. Outside, lightning was flashing and rain was falling hard, like in a bad monster movie. Or I guess a good monster movie, depending on how you look at it. Mary Childs was seated directly in the middle of the couch, arms and legs crossed (seemed to me this was the woman's posture of choice), glowering at my dog, the rain, her story, you name it.

"I don't like the police," she said again. "They turned their back on my father and got rid of him as quietly and quickly as they could. They cut a deal with him in return for not putting him up on charges. Some deal."

My teakettle began to sing. Mary had asked for tea when I offered her a drink. I popped into the kitchen and put the tea together. Alcatraz followed me into the kitchen. He *never* leaves a woman alone in the front room. This was a first.

I brought Mary her tea. Her skin was a rich copper from her week at the beach. Her hair was, I think, a bit lighter. She was wearing white shorts and a blue tank top. I caught myself staring as I handed her the tea. To my surprise, she didn't comment. I retreated to my chair across the room. Suddenly I felt like Sigmund Freud. *So now, my dear, why don't you tell me exactly what it is that is gnawing at you? As I recall, you said that when you were young, your mother had this habit of . . .*

"How do you know Mary Ann?" I asked.

Mary was blowing on her tea. "I needed a place, cheap," she said. "And quick. The place I'd been living, things weren't really working out. There was this guy . . . It wasn't working out." She shrugged. "It was a dump anyway, I was glad to get away from it. So anyway, I'd just started at Shrimp's and I—"

"Wait. What do mean you had just 'started at Shrimp's'? You *worked* there?"

"Sure I worked there. You didn't know that?"

Dr. Freud's spine tingled. His fingers made a ball. "Well . . . no. I mean . . . no, I didn't."

Mary set her cup down. "That's how I got hooked up with Mary Ann. Shrimp knew I was kind of strapped for cash and that I needed a place and he suggested his sister. Said she had a big house over by Montebello and there was plenty of room. Turned out to be true. It's way too big for one person. I basically have an entire floor to myself. And cheap, too. Mary Ann's doing all right for herself at the bakery. She doesn't have to charge me an arm and a leg."

"I didn't know."

"You thought, what? That I'm a friend of Mary Ann's or something?"

"I admit, it seemed like an odd couple."

"Well, I'll tell you this much, I'm not the odd part. Mary Ann's a nice person and everything. But she's not exactly setting the world on fire, if you know what I mean."

"No. What do you mean?"

Mary shrugged. "She doesn't *do* anything. I mean, that matinee at The Mechanic, that's just about her only big-ticket event. She's got this real nice income from that job, she's got this big house, but she doesn't go on big vacations or anything like that. She doesn't buy herself a lot of stuff or go out on the town or . . . I don't know. I'd be doing a lot more than going to plays on Saturday afternoons you give me that kind of money."

"She has simple tastes," I suggested.

Mary picked up her cup and took a simple sip. "I guess. So do I, really. But that's only because I can't afford anything else."

"So you worked at Shrimp's. As what?"

"Bartending. I'm a good bartender."

"You must've made good money there?"

She nodded. "Yeah, I did. Doesn't it figure? I don't think the place is going to reopen."

"I'm sure you can get another bartending job," I said.

"I can. I just . . . well, it gets old after awhile. I should be doing something else."

"Like what?"

"I don't know." She laughed. "Maybe I can go work in Mary Ann's father's factory. Make bread all day long. Truth is, who wants to work all the time?" She took a sip of her tea. "Maybe I can do what you do. You look like you're making out okay for yourself."

"It's a lot of dealing with people."

"Hell, I'm a bartender. Half of what I do is listen to sob stories. We're practically in the same line of work."

I wasn't sure how to respond to that so I didn't. "So, Mary, I'm guessing that you didn't just suddenly find yourself in the neighborhood and decide to drop in on your old pal, Hitch. Am I right?"

She gave me a wary smile. "I'm glad you don't think you're just too damned irresistible."

"I didn't say that."

"You're not."

"I wasn't asking your opinion on that. But thank you so much."

She uncrossed her legs and leaned forward. "Lucy Taylor is getting railroaded. She didn't kill those guys. That's ridiculous. I can't believe they actually arrested her."

"They actually did," I said. "I actually saw the arraignment."

"It's ridiculous," she said again. "She couldn't hurt a flea. That girl's in the clouds half the time. She didn't kill them."

"Do you know who did?"

Not much drama from the couch. Mary said, "No." Then she added, "But let me tell you something that happened last week. See what you think. First, you know about the thing on Monday, right? The TV reporter?"

"I do keep hearing about this. Greg Snyder, right? Some sort of fight?"

"Some sort of fight is right. He came out to the club to do one of those at-the-scene reports—"

"Wait. At the scene of what? Shrimp wasn't even dead yet. Snyder got into a fight *with* Shrimp."

"The coed thing," Mary said. "What's your story, don't you keep up with the news?"

"Mary, what 'coed thing'?"

She affected patience. Poorly. "The dead coed. Hopkins coed? Murdered last winter? They were announcing the verdict in the trial that Tuesday."

Now I knew what she was referring to. It had been a big deal in the papers and on the local television news. National, too, for a while. A senior, I think, at Johns Hopkins had been found murdered. Strangled. One of her professors had been arrested and put on trial. I remembered that the trial had ended not long ago. A couple of weeks, I guess. The guy had gone free. No more arrests had been made as far as I knew.

"Okay, I know what you're talking about," I said. "But what does that have to do with Shrimp?"

"That's where the killer dumped the body. Out back, behind the club. God, I guess you really don't keep up with the news. The girl and that professor had been in the club earlier that night. That's why the police picked him up."

"I guess that detail didn't jump out at me at the time," I said.

"I guess it didn't. Anyway, it sure jumped out at Shrimp. That isn't the kind of publicity a person wants for their nightclub. Come on down for a good time, ladies, end up dead in the trash can."

"So then what's the deal with the reporter you're talking about?" I asked.

"It's that Greg Snyder guy. I guess word got out that the jury was coming in with a verdict, so Snyder came out to do one of those reports. You know, 'the body was found here' kind of thing. He and the camera guy were out back. Shrimp saw them there and he just went ballistic. He went after the guy with a shovel. Practically took his whole head off. I mean literally. It was a mess."

"A shovel?"

"That's right. I was inside the club at the time. But I went outside right after it happened. That reporter's face was a complete bloody mess. You couldn't even . . . his mouth . . . It was ugly, trust me. That idiot Arthur, he was snapping pictures of the whole thing. Someone called an ambulance. There was a gash where the shovel caught Snyder right across the forehead. A little lower and he could have lost an eye."

"That's a lovely story, Mary."

"Yeah, well, I figured you'd already heard about that. But that's not the story I was going to tell you."

"Does this one also involve a shovel?"

"No, it doesn't. This is last Thursday now. The place was so-so. Decent-sized crowd for a Thursday. I was working the happy hour crowd. Around six, Arthur took off. What you've got to know about Arthur is that he was *always* at the club. He was *obsessed* with it. It was pretty sad, really. It was all about impressing his older brother. Or stepbrother. Whatever. I don't know what Shrimp paid him, but I'll bet it wasn't enough. Shrimp had a great deal, this guy who did all the detail work, all the ordering, the payroll, the bookkeeping. Shrimp totally relied on Arthur for all the crap work, while he just got to walk around schmoozing. He'd snap his fingers and Arthur'd run over with that damn camera of his and take everybody's pictures. So anyway, that's the point. Arthur taking off like that? Very unusual. But still, I probably wouldn't have noticed it too much except that Shrimp got all weird."

"How so? Weird what?"

"Fidgety. Nervous. He didn't say anything, but I could tell he was keeping an eye on the door. Normally Shrimp is down on the floor doing his kiss-up thing. I hardly ever see him around the bar." She corrected herself. "Saw him."

"So what happened?"

"Arthur came back, I guess it was around seven-thirty, eight o'clock maybe? I wasn't paying attention to the time. The minute he came in the door, Shrimp was all over him. He literally ran over to the door. Arthur was carrying a bag. Like a shopping bag. Shrimp grabbed it out of his hand and practically dragged him by the collar. They went off into Shrimp's office. It's just catty-corner from the bar. Later on that night, I had to go in to Shrimp's office and ask him something. I forget what. He was sitting there at his desk with the shopping bag on the floor right next to him. And I could see what was in it. Money. Lots of it. In bundles. Shrimp had one of them on his desk when I came in. He slid it off the desk, but I saw it."

"Money. Any idea how much?"

She shook her head. "A lot. That's for damn sure. I couldn't begin to guess. But the bag was filled. It was one of those large shopping bags. I mean, it was definitely a lot of money."

"Did Shrimp say anything?"

"No. It was an awkward vibe. No question about it."

I wasn't sure how to respond. I thought about Pete Munger's advice. *Follow the money*. Well sir . . . here was certainly some money. Mary went on.

"So the next night. Friday. I'm working again. No Arthur. I get a phone call from him at around six-thirty. He wants to speak with Shrimp, but Shrimp hasn't come in yet. Nothing unusual about that. So Arthur left a message with me. 'Something has come up. I'm going to be running late. I've got to meet someone. It can't wait. Tell Shrimp it's real important, but not to worry. He'll know what it's about.' " Mary made one of those wash-my-hands-of-the-whole-affair slaps with her hands. "That's it."

"He never showed up, right?"

"Nope. Never saw him again. Nobody did. And forget that part about 'tell Shrimp not to worry.' Believe me, he worried. Big time. The guy was a wreck. Shrimp kept asking me all night if Arthur had called again. He made me repeat the message a couple of times, which is how I know it by heart. He kept asking if there was anything else Arthur had said. I mean, okay, by itself, it's not all that strange. But you throw in a bag of money and the two of them getting killed . . ." She trailed off.

"And I take it you didn't tell any of this to the police when they spoke with you at the hospital."

"I talked to them as little as I could," she said flatly.

"Well, so why exactly are you here? Why are you telling all this to me?"

"I told you. Lucy Taylor's being set up. Something about that money is what got those guys killed. I'll bet anything. It's not Lucy. I'll bet if you can find that money, you can get Lucy set free."

"And how would you propose I go about finding this money?"

The woman shrugged. "You got me. That's your problem. I'm just doing my good deed for the day."

"For Lucy."

"Girls got to stick together."

"So, would you like me to take your story to the police? Is that what this is about?"

"That's up to you. I'm sure not going to talk to them, I'm telling you that. My father got the bum's rush because he protected his daughter from a psycho creep. I sure as hell don't owe the police any favors." She stood up suddenly. "Thanks for the tea."

I stood as well. I knew about her exits by now. Thunder boomed outside. "My pleasure," I said. "Do you want an umbrella? Or a hat or something?"

"I'll manage. So I get a little wet." She shrugged. "It's summer. It's not like I'm wearing a lot of clothes or anything." She stepped over to the door. "Speaking of which, what's your deal? You're looking pretty spiffy compared to the last couple of times I've seen you. I thought only little kids and old men wore seersucker jackets."

"You're right. Those are the two extremes I'm torn between. What do you think?"

I gave a little wing-spread of my duds. Mary cocked her head and gave me a sideways head-to-toe.

"Not bad, I guess. You're a pretty good clotheshorse."

"Mary, that's a compliment."

"What, you think I can't give a compliment?"

"I am still under the impression that you don't like me much."

"You asked me how you look. What does it matter whether I like you or not. You look good. Take the compliment." She looked down at my feet. "Lose the moccasins, though."

"Thank you. I'll keep that in mind."

"And maybe comb your hair."

"Now you're getting personal."

She took a beat. "Now I'm leaving."

I dipped down to the S.O.S. to get topped off. Friday night; both Sally and Frank were working the bar. Frank's end of the bar was the one with available stools so I dropped onto one and asked him for a whiskey. There were no traces of my earlier wistfulness. It was Lucy I was thinking about. I wondered if Lucy had been at the club on either of the two nights that Mary Childs had just been telling me about. If she had, it makes sense to assume that she would have observed these same fidgety behaviors from Shrimp that Mary Childs had observed. Maybe Lucy would have an idea as to what might have been causing Shrimp his anxieties. Maybe he had even talked to her about the bag of money. I tossed the whiskey back in a single gulp. At the exact instant that my glass landed on the bar, a loud cry came up from what sounded like half the patrons in the place. The cry was being directed at the television up over the bar. One of the basketball play-off games was on. Though at the moment, the game was on hold and a bench-clearing brawl was under way. A dozen or so millionaires in baggy shorts throwing bad punches at each other. I recognized Kit Grady right in the thick of it. He looked like an angry stork. He was being restrained by two of his teammates—they had him by the arms— but before they could pull him clear he was still able to land a solid kick to the thigh of one of the referees. My fellow bar mates were throwing their opinions up toward the screen, like balls toward a hoop.

"He's nuts!"

"What the hell does he think he's—"

"Did you see—"

"There goes the first damn—"

"Totally lost it—"

"Dirtbag!"

The referee who had been kicked jerked his thumb in the air. Grady was being booted from the game. I turned to the guy sitting next to me. "What happened?"

"Grady," he said. "This guy is out of control. Out of nowhere, he just starts . . . There. Look."

Up on the TV, a replay was being run. Grady had just stuffed a basket and was trotting backwards on defense, settling into his zone, when the player he was defending against took a pass and faked a run for the basket. Grady had him easily blocked. The player pulled up and was looking to pass the ball. Grady's arms were pinwheeling in his face when suddenly Grady brought his right arm up and delivered a karate chop–style blow against his opponent's neck, hitting him with his entire forearm. The force of the hit threw his opponent off-balance, and Grady finished him with a hard shove, sending him crashing to the floor.

A renewed chorus of boos rose up from the bar. Onscreen, the guy who had been knocked down scrambled up off the floor and took a swing at Grady, and the melee began. Once again Grady landed a kick to the referee. The television cut to a commercial. A businessman on a push-scooter drinking a beer and talking on a cell phone.

The guy next to me was incensed. Not about the commercial. "Did you see that! That was insane! What the hell is that kid thinking? Man, that was so damn bogus! In a *play-off* game. Do you know how much we paid for this guy?"

I shrugged. "But we're in the play-offs."

"Right. With a frigging misfit leading the way. Man . . . one hundred percent *amateur*."

I caught Frank's eye and ordered a Guinness. Something slow to draw, slow to drink. I left the basketball game to the angry fans. It's just not my sport. I wanted to lay out my scraps and see if any of them fit together. I had to admit, I didn't have much. Or rather, I didn't know much about what little I had. Arthur makes an uncharacteristic exit from the club last Thursday night. Shrimp is antsy the whole time he's gone. Arthur returns with a shopping bag full of money. The next night Arthur phones in to report that he'll be running late and that he has to meet someone, it's important, blah, blah, blah . . . *Shrimp will know what it's about.* Mary Childs is probably right. My guess, too, is that it's somehow about the bag of money. One way or another. My other guess is that Arthur is killed that night and his body is dumped out by the reservoir. The next day, Saturday, Shrimp introduces a pistol into an argument he's having with Lucy. I'm guessing—still just guessing, mind you—that Shrimp sure isn't packing heat in order to defend himself from big bad Lucy Taylor. He is obviously anxious about something. About Arthur? Lucy had described to Julia at the beach an exceptionally volatile and ill-tempered Shrimp the morning that she ended up shooting him in the stomach. The scraps I was putting together showed a nervous and pissy Shrimp Thursday night and Friday night. And then Saturday morning, pissy Shrimp with a gun. Didn't our mothers always warn us to stay away from pissy Shrimps with guns? If they didn't, they should have.

My Guinness arrived. (I told you it was a slow draw.) I dipped down and applied the mustache, licked it off, thanked the Irish. Up on the television, the game had recommenced. A few of the Oyster patrons were still snarling about the brawl. The camera cut away for a moment to track Kit Grady, towel over his head like a prizefighter, marching off beneath the stands toward the locker room. A man in a hat, an older guy, was walking alongside him. He appeared to be yelling at him. Sally caught my eye from the happy end of the bar and she waved at me. I lifted my mug and gave her a silent hi-ho. Tony Marino was at his usual place at the end of the bar. For some reason, sad Tony anchors Sally's side, never Frank's. It's a contrary fit. Tony saw me saluting Sally, thought I was saluting him, and he raised his glass solemnly in brotherhood.

I returned to my scraps. A man is seen by the EMS guys, hanging around Shrimp's place when they respond to the 911. What else? Dope at the club. Gambling. A guy with hands the size of toasters. God, these were miserable scraps. I had only two remaining scraps to look at. One showed Shrimp being murdered in the hospital early Saturday evening. And the other . . .

I took a long slow sip of my creamy brew. Barry Fisher. The man had not been happy with my questions to him about Shrimp's financial situation. He had reminded me that it was none of my business. He was correct; it wasn't. But why get steamy? Why threaten? My fingers were tapping against the side of my mug. I pushed two of my scraps together to see if there was a way they might fit. Barry Fisher's curtness about questions relating to his business partner's finances . . . a big bag of money coming into nervous Shrimp's possession.

I paid for my drinks, gathered up my scraps and left the bar.

The Edgar Jonz Experience, homeless with the temporary closing of Shrimp's, had snagged a several-night gig at a place called Junior's, in Federal Hill. It was a pretty routine joint, small bar, less than a dozen tables, a matchbox-sized riser for the band. According to the chalkboard marquee out front, the place ran comedy nights, jazz nights, bluegrass nights, rock nights and folk nights. Unless Edgar Jonz and his gang were planning to stand up and tell a bunch of jokes, tonight was jazz night. It being the early set, the crowd was sparse. Very sparse. I had my pick of six tables out of the possible ten when I arrived. I took a table near the small stage. Truth be told, they were all near the stage.

Edgar Jonz was in full cool cat mode, which is to say he was aping Miles Davis with a slick vengeance. As I was giving the waitress my order, Edgar turned away from a conference with his drummer and inserted a muffler into the business end of his horn. He bowed his head and squibbled silently on his trumpet in the direction of the floor. His fingers moved like lightning. Mr. Jonz was in black bell bottoms, a dark shimmery shirt that looked like it had been dragged through an oil slick and a Panama hat with a red bandanna knotted around it. His shades were the size and shape of small television sets. Edgar finished with his silent fiddling, then gave a slow three-beat count as the drummer picked up his brushes. Edgar lifted the muffled horn to his lips. The feel of a wet city street at night came squeezing out of Edgar's trumpet for several bars, then Lee Cromwell came forward into the light and began to sing.

> *My pulse begins to quicken*
> *When I'm caught up in the thick and thin of our love.*
> *There's nothing else that matters*
> *I'm as mad as any hatter*
> *For our love*

Lee and Edgar worked well together. Lee's voice was clear and full but she wasn't flaunting it. Half-throttled, she basically was taking the song out for a walk. Edgar Jonz, along with his bassist and drummer, shuffled along beside her. The power of restraint. Lee didn't even have to work at displaying any overt sultriness. She was in a simple red dress that slinked over her hips and came down to below her knees, high heels (I would later hear her refer to them as "high hells") and a pair of sunglasses up on her head, keeping her hair pulled back off her face. Unlike some singers, Lee didn't use her hands for expression. Mostly she held them behind her back as if she were reciting a poem by heart. She gave a direct, simple delivery to the microphone. The few occasions that she did bring one hand around to set it against the mike, or chase a strand of hair from her face, it was to great effect. Languorous. Several tunes into the set, Lee pulled her sunglasses down onto her face and took a campy run through "I'm Not Supposed to Be Blue Blues." It was midway through this tune that a retiring private eye with life issues dropped into the chair opposite mine.

"Some dame," Munger cracked, jerking his head in the direction of the stage. At least I hoped he was cracking.

"How's it going, Mr. Pete?" I asked.

Munger shrugged. "You pulled me away from *Nash Bridges*. I might never be able to forgive you."

"I told you on the phone it could wait."

"I'd seen it already. Bridges gets his man. Almost wrecks his car. I'll live." He raised his hand to get the waitress's attention. "Do I get anything with the ten-dollar cover?" he asked me.

"You get the music."

"Ten bucks I can get a CD and listen to it over and over."

"Pete, you need to get out more."

He grumbled. "I don't know what I need." The waitress came over. Munger ordered a beer. "She doesn't even look old enough to drink," he said after the waitress shuffled off. He let off a large sigh. "Don't listen to me."

I cupped a hand to my ear. "What?"

"I said—" Munger stopped himself and pointed a finger at me. "Funny man."

I pointed right back at him. "Grumpy man."

So. We got that established.

Munger and I settled back and listened to Lee and the boys. The drummer gazed up at the ceiling as he worked his skins. The bassist looked at his toes. And Edgar, with those TV-shaped sunspecs of his, you couldn't tell what the funky cat was eyeballing. I had already gotten the acknowledging nod from Lee between her first song and her second. She went ahead and served up another—this one more obvious—as she started in on some Gershwin.

"I guess this lady likes seersucker," Munger smirked.

"Best-kept secret, Pete? They all do." Munger gave me a don't-shit-me look across the table. I conceded. "Okay. I know her."

We settled in for the rest of the set. The crowd—what there was of it—applauded politely after each tune. But the room was flat. The Edgar Jonz Experience was working hard for the money. When they finally took their first break, Lee came down off the riser and over to our table.

"An undertaker is what this joint needs. Mind if I join you?"

Pete Munger rose halfway to his feet as Lee was dropping into the other chair at our table. Lee pulled out a cigarette, but the bartender called over, "No smoking, Miss." Lee snapped her cigarette in two and dropped the pieces onto the table. "Welcome to the gig from hell."

"You were good," I said to her.

"Thanks." She looked around the place. "God, I thought my itinerant days were over." She turned to Munger and held out a hand. "Hi, I'm Lee Cromwell."

Munger took her hand and gave it a shake. "Pete Munger."

"Tell her she was good, Pete," I said.

"You were," he said, tossing a glare over at me.

"Thanks," said Lee. "What you just heard was basically our sound check. They had some sort of plumbing disaster and we couldn't even set up until right before the set. There was water all over the place. I was half expecting I'd step in a puddle somewhere and go up in smoke."

"Sparks," I corrected.

Munger grunted. "I thought you sounded good." Lee shot me a quick look. Yes, he did already say that.

"Pete here was looking into Arthur Wisner's disappearance," I said to Lee. "I guess you've heard they found him?"

"Yes. Poor Arthur." She turned to Munger. "Do you have any idea who did it?"

"Nothing yet."

"God, it's awful. He was a decent kid," Lee said.

"How long is your break?" I asked her.

"Not long. Fifteen minutes or so. That's long enough for a cigarette. Care to join me outside?"

Munger was frowning. "Isn't smoking bad for your voice?"

Lee's eyebrows arched beautifully. "Mr. Munger, you just told me you liked my singing. Twice, in fact."

"I do. I just . . ." He trailed off.

Munger stayed put while Lee and I popped outside. She got her cigarette lit and took a grateful draw. "What's up with your friend?" Lee asked. Across the street, a large man was yelling at a small dog.

"Oh, he's just trying to figure out how the world goes together," I said.

"Seems to be having a little trouble with it."

"I guess so. I don't really know him." I told Lee how Pete Munger and I had made our acquaintance.

"Well I guess his job's done," Lee said. "Arthur's been found."

"You were at the club last Friday, right?" I asked.

"Sure."

"How about Thursday?"

"Thursday? We were there. Why?"

"I'm wondering if you noticed anything peculiar about Shrimp on either of those nights."

Lee laughed. "You mean more peculiar than usual? Let me think. No. Nothing pops to mind. What kind of peculiar are you talking about?"

"Mary Childs told me that Shrimp was practically jumping out of his skin both nights. She said that it had to do each time with Arthur being gone from the club."

"When did you speak with Mary Childs?"

"A couple of hours ago. She dropped by my place to fill me in on some of this stuff."

Lee's eyebrows went up at that. Her voice went up, too. "Oh, really?"

"Yes, really. Why do you say it like that?"

"Mary Childs is one odd little cookie."

"I can go with that assessment."

"It's a funny thing about getting older, Hitch. All the kids seem so much bolder. I mean, they seem to mature quicker than we did. Or I did, anyway. Maybe it's just me. When I was Mary Childs's age I didn't have a clue about how the world really operated. It just seems to me that the kids now are a lot savvier a lot earlier."

"You think Mary Childs is savvy?"

Lee waved her cigarette hand. "Savvy's the wrong word. I don't know what it is. Brazen? Fearless?"

"The word I keep coming up with is 'irritating.' "

Lee looked at me a few seconds, then broke into laughter. "She's wrapped you around her little finger, hasn't she?" I pointed out that all of Mary Childs's fingers were little. "You know what I mean. She's a regular vixen, isn't she? I've seen her at the club. Girl doesn't even have to crack a smile and the guys are stumbling all over themselves. In fact, I don't think I've ever really seen her crack a smile. Maybe that's her secret."

"I tried out a few jokes first time I met her. All she did was tell me she hates tall guys. Very sweet girl."

"Don't take that too personally, Hitch. You know Kit Grady?"

"Sure. Throws ball in hoop. Makes a zillion dollars." Or in some cases, throws punches, gets tossed out of million-dollar games.

"Well, you know how Shrimp loves to . . . loved to push the celebrity thing. Kit Grady was one of his big deals. He was in the club pretty regularly. Shrimp would give him the red-carpet treatment. Anyway, Grady and Mary Childs had a thing going for a while. A couple months, maybe. I couldn't tell you much about it, except that it ended about a month ago. But before they broke it off I saw them together a few times, outside the club. You know, when Mary was taking a break. Hitch, don't you go believing for an instant that Mary Childs hates tall men. She and Grady were getting along just fine, thank you. If she said that to you about tall guys, it's just backlash."

"Well, good. Now I'll be able to sleep nights."

The man across the street was still yelling at his dog. He had gotten considerably louder and more agitated. I've noticed some people are like this; they can't pull it together with people so they go ballistic on their pets. This one was demanding some answers from the pooch. I could have told him he wasn't going to get them. Dogs don't work that way.

"As far as last week is concerned," Lee was saying, "I can't really say I remember anything different about Shrimp. But yeah, Arthur not being there on Friday night was definitely unusual. That I do remember."

"And anything else about that night? Anything else out of the ordinary?"

"I don't think so. I remember Solly Biggs was there. He was his usual obnoxious self. What a cluck. He wanted to get onstage with us and sing along. Shrimp dragged him away. Must've booted him. I didn't see him again." Lee chuckled. "Ah yes, I do miss the good old days." She dropped her cigarette to the sidewalk and ground it under her heel. "Are you and your friend staying for the next set?"

"I'm not sure. I need to talk to Pete about a few things. This place is so small our table's practically in your lap. I think we might cut out."

"Sorry to hear that. I was going to dedicate a song to you."

"No kidding. What song?"

" 'St. James Infirmary.' Seems like a decent undertaker's song."

"Kind of grim, isn't it?"

"Well, you're not exactly in the clown business."

Edgar Jonz popped his head out of the club. His face lit up when he saw me. "Hey. Mr. Funeral Man. What's the deal, brother chenille?"

"Mr. Jonz. Nice tunes tonight."

"Yeah. How about our Lee, huh? White girl can sing."

Lee scoffed. "Jesus Edgar, don't 'white girl' me. It's white boys wrote most of these songs."

"Sorry, baby." He turned to me. "You got any more funeral gigs for me, man? I dug that."

"Sorry, Edgar. Nothing on the horizon."

"How about Arthur, man?"

"I'm not handling that one."

"Check." He addressed Lee. "You think you screwed up your pipes enough now, baby, we can get back to work?"

I followed them back inside. It's possible that Pete Munger had not moved a single muscle the entire time I was gone.

"We'll go in a few minutes," I told him as I sat back down. "I have a little mild basking first."

The Edgar Jonz Experience returned to the stage. Lee and Edgar had a brief tête-à-tête, then Edgar cued the other musicians as Lee stepped back up to the microphone.

"I would like to dedicate this next tune to a friend of mine who could bury every one of you in this room . . . and probably make you enjoy the experience." Lee lowered her head as Edgar counted off the beat.

Munger whispered to me over the table. "You got a thing going with that lady?"

I shook my head. "She's old enough to be my older sister."

Munger grumbled, "I should have shot you when I had the chance," then sat back in his chair and turned his full attention to the stage. Halfway through the song, Lee fumbled and lost the words. Edgar Jonz stepped right up with his horn and took over. Covered her beautifully. He gave the mournful tune an exceptional ride. Lee stood off to the side and blushed beautifully. I wouldn't swear to it, but I don't think Munger took his eyes off her the entire time.

"Let's go," I said as the tune wrapped up. We dropped some bills on the table and quit the joint. As we reached the door, Lee's husky voice ushered us out. "Bye, boys."

The downpour earlier had cooled things off. We decided just to walk. We headed up Federal Hill. A rehearsal for a free outdoor Shakespeare production was wrapping up. *The Taming of the Shrew.* We stood watching the Petruchio throw the Kate over his shoulder and stride offstage about six times. It didn't look to be a terrifically inspired production. You want inspired? Ask around about the Gypsy Players production of *Shrew* of several years ago. I played Petruchio. Julia was Kate. Zippity doo dah.

Munger and I wandered off to the north side of the hill, the side overlooking the harbor and Baltimore's ever-more-clustering skyline. I told Munger what I had learned so far. I told him about my meeting with

Barry Fisher and about how evasive the man had been. I recounted for him what Mary Childs had told me concerning Arthur and Shrimp at the club the previous Thursday and Friday nights. An eyebrow went up when I mentioned the shopping bag full of money, but he didn't say anything. Munger listened without interrupting. His gaze was carrying out over the harbor. When I was finished he asked me, "So what do you want from me?"

"I want to know more about the financial arrangement between Shrimp and Barry Fisher. Something in that partnership isn't right. But I have no idea how you go about looking into something like that."

"And I do."

"What you told me before, that most of what you do is desk work. Work the phones and all that. I figure you must know this sort of thing."

"And what if I do?" Munger said. He was still looking off at the distant lights. "I told you already, I don't investigate murders. I'm not really investigating anything right now. I'm out of service, bub."

"Do you believe Lucy Taylor murdered Arthur Wisner?"

"No."

"You said you were an old friend of Eleanor Martin's."

He nodded. "I said that."

"Wouldn't an old friend want to do what he could to help track down the killer of the old friend's only son?"

Munger's head whipped around so fast I thought his nose would fly off.

"You want to be a little more careful there, friend," he said.

"I was just asking a question."

Munger didn't look particularly happy. I got the definite sense that this was a place I shouldn't push too hard. I waited.

"I can make a few calls," he finally muttered. "It'd have to be next week. Nothing you can really do on a weekend."

"That's fair. Honestly, that's fine, Pete. I'm just curious to see if there's anything peculiar in any of the deals between those two guys. You're the one who said 'follow the money.' If you come up empty, no harm done. And I'll pay you."

He waved me off. "Keep your money. It's a favor."

"You don't exactly owe me a favor, Pete."

He turned to leave. "Not for you, big guy."

We headed back down the steps on the west side of the hill. Before we split up, Munger asked me if I liked crabs.

"Of course I like crabs. They run you out of this town if you don't like crabs."

Munger said, "Some people are coming over tomorrow in the afternoon for some crabs. You want to come out that's fine."

"That sounds good to me, Pete. Thank you."

He pulled out a small notebook and scribbled down the address for me.

"Your wife will be there, I assume," I said.

"Sure. Why?"

"I can apologize for waking her up the other night."

Munger shook his head. "Skip that. I tried it already."

"You did? Well, thanks."

"I said I tried."

The girl who pulled open the front door didn't look a thing like the fiddler at the Cat's Eye. Sixteen. Blond. Pleasant face. Bored. She said nothing.

"Hi, I'm Hitchcock Sewell."

Nothing.

"And you are?"

"Melissa."

"Pete's Melissa."

The lip smack of irritation. I took that to be "yes."

"Everybody's out back," Melissa Munger said. "You can go around."

I'm sure she didn't mean to make it sound as if I was unworthy of crossing the threshold of the Munger domicile. Then again, she had only opened the door partway and her body was securely filling the space. So maybe she did mean it. Either way, I went around.

Munger's backyard wasn't large and it wasn't small. Goldilocks would have found it just right. Two picnic tables had been pushed together end-to-end in the middle of the grass. They were covered with pages from the *Baltimore Sun*. (Note: Don't go hammering crabs in Baltimore on the *New York Times* or even the *Washington Post*. Lore calls for the *Sun*. Respect lore.) A small mountain of crabs was piled atop the picnic tables. About ten people were seated on the benches, busily hammering, snapping, picking, sucking, scraping. We're genetically predisposed in the

Chesapeake Bay region to know the means of extracting our ounce of flesh from our quarter pound of crab. It's a messy business, with shockingly low return for the effort. But it's as much about the effort. That and the Old Bay seasoning. Nothing makes a cold beer taste better than Old Bay on the lips. Carrie Nation herself would have been compelled to pop a cold one under the circumstances of a Baltimore crab feast.

Munger was coming out of the back door with a batch of steaming dead ones in a bushel basket. He was wearing a full apron over a tennis shirt and a pair of shorts, so it looked a little like a dress. The jokey slogan on the apron read: Crab of the Day. Munger's expression was looking the part as he came out onto the grass. It loosened up as he approached the picnic table; broke into a workable smile when he saw me standing off to the side.

"Hi there! Welcome."

Munger dumped the fresh batch of crabs atop the old batch. The action broke the spell at the table. Everyone snapped out of their crabbing rhythms and Munger introduced me. "Everyone, this is Hitch Sewell. Friend of mine."

The folks at the table, six men and four women, called out their names for me. I botched the moment and didn't land any of them, except one. And his name I already knew. As well as his face. Not a week previous in fact, our faces had been as close together as two faces can be and not be smooching.

"Well hey," Roger cried out. "How's the bicuspid?"

Pete turned to me. "You know Roger?"

"He filled in for my dentist," I muttered. To Roger I announced, "The tooth is fine. Good as new. I'm back to chewing on rocks already."

Room was made for me at one of the tables. "I want to talk to you," Pete murmured as I sat down. Apparently he didn't mean now, as he turned and headed back into the house.

"Don't you go trying to bite through the shells," Roger warned from the far end of the table. "Use your mallet. You're not as young as you used to be."

Who ever is, I wondered, grabbing up a mallet and a steamy crab.

• • •

Susan Munger was sleeping with Roger. That's what Pete told me as he was showing me through the house later.

"You're kidding," I said. "Roger the dentist?"

"Roger the asshole."

"Are you sure?"

"That he's an asshole?"

"About him and your wife."

"It's not a serious thing," Pete said.

We were walking down a hallway that led off from the kitchen. I stopped. "What do you mean, it's not a serious thing? Your wife is sleeping with your dentist and it's not a serious thing?"

"He's not my dentist."

"Whatever he is."

"He's a friend of mine and Susan's."

"More Susan's from the sound of it."

"What I mean is, Susan's not going to go running off with him or anything like that. It's not that kind of serious. For one thing, Roger's married."

"And that's apropos of what? You're married, too," I pointed out. "So is Susan. I fail to see where this is your safety feature."

"I mean that Roger won't leave Alison. It's complicated, Hitch."

"It had better be complicated. The guy is sitting out in your backyard eating crabs. Is that his wife that's sitting next to him?"

"Yes."

"Pete, what are they doing here?"

"I told you, they're friends of ours. Alison doesn't know about Roger and Susan. If we didn't invite them it would be awkward."

I scratched my head. "You folks out here in the burbs sure do things different. I'd have figured that inviting the guy would be awkward."

"I guess that shows what you know," Pete said.

I followed Pete through a door. We were in the family room. Got to love the symbolism. Pete's gaze fell on a framed photograph on one of the bookshelves. His two children when they were both much younger. Pete grimaced.

"Susan is unhappy. Things have been getting sour around here for a long time now. I don't want to go into it, but let's just say I haven't exactly been— I haven't been what you call 'present' for Susan."

"You mean you've been neglecting your wife."

"Don't be a wise guy."

"I'm just trying to help."

Pete sighed heavily. "There's a lot of repression and sexual projection going around these days."

"Huh?"

He turned red. "It's just something I read in one of those books." He looked over at me with a strange expression. "I should burn those stupid books, shouldn't I?"

"Not if they're actually helping."

His gaze trailed out the window. "They give me all sorts of fancy ways to say that everything stinks."

"You don't really strike me as the touchy-feely type, Pete."

His eyes narrowed. "I touchy-feely like going out there and giving Roger the asshole a broken nose," he said.

"Pete, your whole aura just lit up when you said that."

"I've got a lot of anger in me, Hitch," Munger said solemnly.

"Then I think it's incumbent that you go kick someone's ass. Let it out, Pete. Breathe. Land a perfect blow."

Munger laughed. "Maybe you want to help me burn those books."

We finished the house tour. It was an okay tour; I wouldn't go putting it on your list of must-do's if you're visiting Baltimore. I encountered Melissa Munger a second time. She and her boyfriend were sitting together on the couch, watching tennis on TV in the living room.

"It's nice outside," Munger said to them. His daughter responded without looking away from the TV. "We know."

"You two could actually *play* tennis."

"We know."

Munger and I headed back out to the yard. "Kids think they know everything," Munger said as we crossed through the kitchen. I held my tongue. With great effort in this case.

Susan Munger was perfectly pleasant to me. She was forty-five-ish, with short dark hair and a more seasoned, more pronounced version of her daughter's face. Attractive. An autopilot of gracious hostessing expressions, but at rest a little storm-cloudy. She and Pete interacted with ease as far as my eagle eye could discern. I watched for any particular eye contact between Susan and Roger, but I saw none. I had taken Munger's cue and not identified myself to Susan as the guy who woke her up the other night with the phone. But she pegged me anyway. In fact, she apologized to me for her curtness.

"I'm not normally rude like that," she said to me. We were standing over at the far end of the lawn, where there was a flower garden and vegetable garden that ran along the wooden fence separating the Mungers' property from their neighbors. Susan Munger told me that Pete was the big farmer. The vegetables were his.

"You're the flower child?" I joked.

She pocketed my joke. "Right. That's me."

Pete's garden was flourishing. I saw zucchini the size of my arm, green beans galore, numerous plump, bruise-colored eggplants lolling among the vines. He had staked out a half dozen wire trees for his tomato plants. His lettuce was as green as lime Jell-O. At the far end of the garden was a dirt patch containing a dozen or so tufted sprigs. Herbs. Basil. Dill. Rosemary. Chervil. I asked Susan Munger if Pete liked to cook.

"We share." She said it a little brusquely. "I'm sorry. I'm being rude again. Yes, Pete does like to cook. More than I do, in fact." She gave a small laugh that was more for her own benefit than mine. "It's probably role reversal. Sometimes I think I'd be happy being out there snooping into other people's business like he does. I guess the grass is always greener."

"Not always," I said. "I've yet to meet a gal who wants to do what I do for a living."

"I'm sorry. I don't even know what you do for a living."

"I'm an undertaker."

Susan Munger took "the pause." I am very accustomed to "the pause." She asked, "How do you know my husband again? Pete didn't really say."

I've no way of knowing how it is that the brain can do what it does as fast as it does. But it does. It's an amazing organ. In this case, it brought up the true answer to Susan Munger's question. *Your husband and I are both trying to figure out who murdered Arthur Wisner.* And then it snagged a fragment from one of my conversations with Munger. *I'm doing this for Eleanor Wisner . . . Eleanor Martin. She's an old friend of mine. I owe her.*

The result?

"Business," I muttered.

My hostess asked, "What business would Pete have with an undertaker?" When I didn't answer immediately (the amazing brain thing is not a constant, you realize), she added, "Did he kill someone and just forget to tell me?" It was a joke she was making, of course. But her delivery could have used some work.

She erased an invisible blackboard. "Never mind. Pete and I rarely discuss his business. I shouldn't be grilling you."

I took the out. I pointed to a small spiral of stones that were laid out next to the patch of herbs. "Did aliens do that?"

Susan Munger looked down at the stones with a mixture of bemusement and forbearance. "That's Pete," she said flatly. "Pete and his stones."

She excused herself and headed back to the party. Her step was heavy in the short grass. The eye contact I hadn't discerned between Susan Munger and Roger? As Susan returned to her guests, I discerned it.

During the grand tour I had seen some photographs of Pete and Susan's eighteen-year-old son, Kevin. He showed up in the flesh just as the last of the crabs were being dumped onto the table. Tall, rangy redhead who looked like neither of his parents. Nice kid. Gave me an authentic smile and a solid handshake. It wasn't until Kevin showed up that I was made aware of the occasion. Munger, too, for that matter.

"Happy birthday, Dad," Kevin called out, producing a small giftwrapped package from behind his back. Susan Munger came out the back door carrying several shopping bags. They were filled with wrapped presents.

"Surprise!"

I turned to Munger. "You didn't tell me it was your birthday."

His face had gone red. "It isn't. It's tomorrow. I told Susan I didn't want to make a big deal out of it." Roger's wife, Alison, was coming out of the kitchen carrying a cake. Susan Munger was setting the presents out on the glass patio table. "She shanghaied me," Munger muttered.

"Pete, I think it's supposed to be a good thing."

Munger threw me an anger-look. "I say no, she does it anyway. That's good?"

What could I say. "Pete, maybe we want to hold off on the book burning."

Roger stepped over and took hold of the birthday boy's hand. "Hey buddy, you don't look a day over fifty."

"I'm not," Munger grumbled. "I'm a day under."

I turned to Munger. "Fifty? You didn't want to celebrate the big Five Oh?"

"No, I did not," Munger said. But he wasn't looking at me when he said it. Susan Munger turned on her heel and marched back into the house.

Since I was out in the county, I finally fetched my car. Munger offered to drive me up to Hunt Valley to pick it up, but I convinced him that he shouldn't run out on his own party. He sorely wanted to.

Kevin Munger offered to take me instead. On the drive, he told me that he was attending Columbia University, in New York. He was studying architecture. His plans were to go into historic preservation. He got going on the topic of cornices and his face literally lit up. I asked him how he liked living in New York City. He thought a moment, then he said it was like being in a really really long movie that nobody had remembered to edit. The boy was all over the road as we sped along. I told him to slow down a little and he did. A little. A few minutes later Kevin jerked the wheel and took a speedy left into the lot of Hunt Valley Motors. He skidded to a stop on the gravel lot. "Good to meet you, Mr. Sewell," he said, pumping my arm like he was trying to get water to come gushing out from my nose. I got out of the car. He peeled a semicircle and headed back from whence he came.

My little green spaceship was parked in the back lot. I paid my small fortune and went down to the lot and slid behind the wheel. Driving back into town, she hummed, she sang, she crooned. So did I. To no one's pleasure but my own.

Lucy was rubbing her index finger absently back and forth along the little scar above her eye as she listened to me. From the look on her face, one could've guessed either that she was hanging on my every word or that she was completely entranced by her own daydreams and was hearing my voice as if it were low thunder sounding from the far shores of a distant river in an unreliable memory. We were in a pale green room at the city jail, seated opposite each other at a long table, separated by a three-foot-high mesh screen. We weren't alone; a half dozen other inmates were also receiving visitors. In order to hear and be heard, as well as to conjure a semblance of privacy, all of us—prisoners and visitors alike—were leaning forward, some nearly touching our heads on the screen and murmuring in low voices. The place had the feel and look of a group confessional.

Lucy looked tired. When she was led in from her cell she moved as if she had just read a pamphlet on how a person performs the tricks called walking, taking a seat, setting your hands on a tabletop, giving a smile to your visitor. When I asked her how she was doing she had answered me in a small voice that she was "fine." When I asked her if there was any-thing that she needed she had answered, "I need to go home."

I had only fifteen minutes with Lucy. I asked her if she was happy with her lawyer and she assured me that she was. "Do you feel comfortable telling him anything he asks? It's important, Lucy. Don't hold back, even if something feels embarrassing. You need to give him as much informa-tion as you can, especially about you and Shrimp. Don't try to protect Shrimp. Or his memory. I know you feel bad about shooting him, but you weren't trying to kill him, okay? That's important to remember. I don't want you thinking that you owe him something. It was a moment of panic and you wish it hadn't happened. And you didn't kill him, Lucy. Shrimp was involved in some things that weren't all on the level. That's no big secret. So if you know something, or if Shrimp told you something in confidence, or if you overheard something that sounded a little fishy, you've got to spill it all out. Do you understand that?"

Lucy continued rubbing her scar. I continued wishing she wouldn't. She wasn't doing it to irk me, it was just a habit, the way a man absently strokes his beard. Still, it irked me. The day I hit Lucy with that rock was the day that my parents and my unborn sister had been buried (that's where I got the rocks; from the grave dirt) so it's not among the fondest days of my memory. I elicited from Lucy a promise that she would coop-erate fully with her lawyer. I promised her that we would clear this whole matter up. I told her that I had a private investigator looking into things.

"It's just a matter of putting together a list of Shrimp's enemies and then seeing which ones we can't eliminate."

"What about Arthur?" Lucy asked in a small voice.

"What about him?"

"Arthur didn't have any enemies. He was just a nice guy, Hitch. No one wanted to kill him."

"Unfortunately, not true," I said.

"He's just a victim," Lucy said, tapping her finger unconsciously against her scar. "Wrong place, wrong time, that must be it." She leaned closer to the screen. "Arthur got caught up in something, Hitch. I know it. I'm sure he was just on the sidelines. He got pulled in."

"Lucy, you sound more concerned about Arthur's death than about Shrimp's?"

She didn't answer right away. Through the mesh I saw tears welling up in her eyes. In a voice so soft I might have sworn I didn't really hear it, she whispered:

"I am."

Shrimp had been dead for a week. Most likely Arthur, too. Lucy had not been charged with the murder of Arthur Wisner, since unlike the case with Shrimp Martin, there was no record of Lucy's having made a homicidal move on the young man some time previous to his deadly encounter with a very sharp object. To this point, then, the two murders were linked only by the extreme coincidence of timing and family relationship, as well as Morris Kiefaber's preliminary hunch concerning the knife that was used in each instance. This isn't to say that you could find anyone crawling out from under a rock declaring that the two murders were indisputably unrelated, only that the evidence so far was not setting the opposite conclusion in stone.

Am I being clear?

The weekend passed with no nuclear wars anywhere, at least none that I could discern. Locally, I didn't bury one damn soul. Not one. I did some home repair, some grouting around the bathtub. Replaced a hinge on a kitchen cabinet door. Theorized about cleaning my front windows by simply staring at them really really hard.

Saturday night I tried out a new Caribbean place I had been hearing about that was just up Broadway. I went for the curried goat . . . I can tell you that now I know what curried goat tastes like. Back home I flipped on the tube and found myself watching the second half of the play-off game between the Blues and the Pistons. Kit Grady wasn't in the lineup. The announcer made mention numerous times during the game of Grady's having been suspended for the game, as well as fined, for his "unsportsmanlike conduct" the night before. The phrase seemed awfully tame to me. But I guess you can't go fining and suspending people for being an all-out spoiled brat jerk. Though I'm not sure why not. The Blues ended up pulling out a squeaker. I have to admit, I got caught up in the thing by the time it was all over. The victory put Baltimore into the championship series, against the Indiana Pacers, kicking off in Baltimore the following week. We were being dubbed "the Cinderella team." No mention of how Indiana felt about being the wicked stepsisters.

Sunday afternoon I fetched Tony Marino from the Oyster and had him and Sam help me get one of Julia's paintings out of her studio and down to the street. It was a commission job for a new restaurant that was opening up downtown. Julia's larger canvases have to come out through the balcony-style double doors that she had installed when she renovated the place, then brought down by two people on two parallel ladders. It's not a terrifically difficult maneuver. We do it all the time. Tony and I man the ladders. Sam just stands on the ground, in the middle. If the painting should happen to slip from our grip and fall, it won't likely get past Sam. None have yet. On weekends we'll sometimes draw a small crowd of onlookers—we did on this particular day. Julia and Chinese Sue circulated with bottles of champagne and sparkling cider, to give the occasion some zest. Julia looked ravishingly frisky, with a red bandanna in her hair, a snug white T-shirt with a target design on the front and blue silk boxers.

Afterward, I drove Aunt Billie out to Dickeyville where a blind woman named Edith Frugh runs a small recaning business out of her home. Billie had a small antique rocker that Miss Frugh had recaned for her. The woman's little cottage is immaculate and as charming as something you'd find in a fairy tale. She collects colored bottles. God knows why. They were on every windowsill. Billie and I chewed the fat with Miss Frugh for a half hour then fetched the chair and took off back into town. We ordered pizza for dinner and Billie got onto her story about vandalizing Mr. Scott's bee boxes back when she was a ten-year-old terror in Charleston. I've got this story memorized. She laughed so hard she nearly choked on a piece of pepperoni. We knocked around some Grand Marnier as a chaser to the pizza then I left Billie to her PBS. I lingered just long enough—through the Gorey—to see Diana Rigg's cat eyes and that conspiratorial little smile of hers. "Tonight we meet a vicar with blood on his cloth . . ." I went home and managed to get through three years of *Seven Years in Tibet*. I wasn't sure I'd be hanging in there for the full tour. My eye was already wandering in the direction of a W. C. Fields biography over on my bookcase. Seven years of Fields was at the very least going to include a lot more pretty girls. I killed the lights and was just drifting off when a name suddenly flashed across my brain in large capital letters, and I let out a groan.

Clarissa.

I had totally forgotten our Saturday night repair date. I did a quick calculation; I had been chewing on goat about the time that Clarissa would have been expecting me to pull up at her door. With flowers, probably. And humility. I'd have to call her. Naturally I couldn't tell her about the goat. I had no idea what I would tell her. Or if I would even have the opportunity to tell her anything. The Hitchcock Sewell voodoo doll might at that very moment be undergoing some serious acupuncture over in the Clarissa household. "Alcatraz, think of something!" I called out into the darkness. Pooch didn't stir.

At some point during the night, Clarissa made an entrance in one of my dreams. It was an imperious entrance. She looked very very sexy and very very angry. All I remember of the dream was that Clarissa strode in and looked all around. But she never looked up. Where I was clinging to the ceiling.

The next day I had to pop up to Greenmount Cemetery for an exhumation. You probably don't want the details on that. Afterward, I was back at the office, noodling around at my desk, when a call came in from Pete Munger.

"How's the birthday boy?" I asked.

"One day older."

"If you start doing that every day you're going to regret it," I said. I told him I had had a good time at his sort-of-surprise birthday party crab feast.

"Susan said she thought you were charming," he said.

"She's an observant woman," chirped I.

"She wants us to go into counseling."

The tone of voice he was using made it sound as if his wife had suggested that the two of them step slowly down into a flooded basement stocked with piranha and loose electrical wires.

"Isn't that a good sign, Pete? She wants to work on things?"

"I think she just wants a trained professional to tell me I'm screwed up."

"But you're not screwed up. You're confused. Besides, your wife's the one having an affair. Maybe the trained professional will note that as a somewhat aberrant behavior for a spouse."

"Maybe."

"Okay, Gloomy Gus, have it your way. I'm just trying to keep to the sunny side of the street."

Munger changed the subject. Here's how he did it. "I've got some information about Fisher and Martin," he said. "I've done some digging."

I was all ears. Munger told me that what he had learned so far was that Barry Fisher had arranged a start-up loan of $500,000 for Shrimp Martin to get his club up and running. The loan had been made through the pension fund of a local union. Munger told me the rate.

"That's not exactly a bargain basement rate," Munger noted. "It's okay, but in the market at the time, it wasn't anything great." In addition to the loan, Munger said that Barry Fisher also kicked in a nice chunk of change of his own.

"How much did Fisher put in of his own money?"

"Well, the figure is $300,000," Munger said. "But hold off on calling it 'his own money.' None of these deals are really done with anyone's own money. It's all Peter-to-Paul crap."

"That's economics lingo?"

"Apparently Fisher took out a loan from the same pension fund. That's where his contribution came from."

"Nothing strange about that, I guess," I said. Sam had just come into the office. Effectively reducing the size of the room by half. "Hold on," I said to Munger. I cupped the phone. "What's up, Sam?"

"I got a dead body for you."

"You do?"

"Yes."

"Do you have him with you?"

Sam shook his head. "He's in the morgue. I was working over at Puppy's last night. This guy from Essex went down in the middle of the dance floor. Stony cold. Heart attack. I gave his girlfriend one of your cards."

"Quick thinking, Sam. Look, I'm on the phone. I'll get the details when I get off."

"Okay."

"Thanks, Sam. Good work."

His bashful smile could have blown me out of my chair. The human wall pivoted and went back out the door.

"Sorry, Pete," I said into the phone. "Go on. Where were we?"

"Fisher."

"Right. He's taken a loan as well."

"This is where it wrinkles a little," Munger said. "The loan to Fisher? It's at a much better rate than the one he arranged for Munger."

"Is that so? That seems odd."

"I think so, too."

"Is that legal?"

"Well, yeah, I'm pretty sure it is. But it's still strange. Martin's so-called business partner cuts himself a better deal than the one he does Shrimp."

"And why? Whose gain is that?"

"Technically, the pension fund's. They get a higher spike on the loan to Martin."

I thought about it a moment. Barry Fisher goes out of his way to have Shrimp kick a little extra back to this pension fund. Why would he do that? I rolled back in my chair and swung my legs up onto the desk. "Does Fisher stand to profit somehow by that?" I asked.

"I can't give you an answer on that. He shouldn't," Munger said. "Let me dig a little more. There's definitely something fishy here."

"Fisher," I said.

"Huh?"

"Fishy. Fisher. I'm just pointing that out."

There was a pause on the other end of the line. At its conclusion, Munger said, "Thank you for pointing that out." He hung up.

I chewed a few minutes on the information Munger had given me. I'm no wizard with numbers, so why I even bothered to scribble them down on a piece of paper is anybody's guess. I balled the paper, tossed it at the spittoon and missed by the old country mile. I brought my feet back to earth and popped upstairs to inform Billie that Sam was bringing us a new customer. Billie had just finished applying a cucumber mud pack. She looked like a colorized Al Jolson. "Ah, the secret to supple and pliant," I remarked. We pulled out one of her cribbage boards and played to the death. *For* the death, I should say. I was a little distracted thinking about what Munger had told me on the phone and Billie got a good lead on me. Then the cards began falling my way. I made some shrewd choices, got some good cuts, had some decent peggings and cruised to the finish line with my mud-packed associate far behind. In the end, it's all in the pegging.

"You get the stiff."

"There's no need to rub it in," Billie sniffed.

Back down in my office I planted my chin in my hands. I remained this way for nearly twenty minutes. I knew I should call Clarissa. I searched (dug, excavated, spelunked) for a rationale to justify my not calling her. She wouldn't want to hear from me anyway? Let dead dogs lie? Say it with flowers? Turn everything around and somehow make my screw-up *her* fault? In front of me stood an imaginary six-foot-three, decent-looking schmuck, arms crossed, drilling holes through me with the frankness of his penetrating glare. The good Hitch wasn't buying the bail-outs of the bad Hitch.

I squibbled through some papers for a phone number and picked up the phone and dialed. When the woman answered, I asked her if she would like to go out with me that night. There was a pause . . . and then she said, "Okay, why not." Her enthusiasm didn't exactly blow me off my chair. We set a time for me to pick her up and we hung up. The good Hitch had drifted over to the window during the phone call and was gazing out onto the street. He was clearly disgusted with me. *That was one of the most shameless and inappropriate stall tactics I think I have ever witnessed.*

Good Hitch was just jealous. And he knew that if he wasn't careful he was not going to be invited along on my date with Mary Childs.

● ● ●

Solomon Biggs had possession of a portion of a floor in a five-story warehouse down along the Jones Falls, just north of the train station. Four of the floors—the top four—were used for storing fabrics and muslins for a mill and dye factory that was located out Falls Road near the beltway. The bottom floor was leased to the Lyric Opera Company and was used by them to store various sets and props that the company kept and recycled for their opera productions, both main stage and educational touring shows. Solomon Biggs had ingratiated himself with the opera company many years ago, prior to his felony, first by donating his services in the form of a massive Biggs original, a canvas that served as the garish backdrop to an amusingly muddled production of Mozart's *The Magic Flute*, and then, and more important, by seeing to it that the production's star attraction actually made it to the stage. The story goes that during the rehearsal period, Biggs had been playing extracurriculars with the production's petite Papageno, a rising star in the opera world who was shagging top honors that year at all of the major competitions. Three quarters of the way through rehearsals, Solly dumped her and took up with the production's Queen of the Night, this one an aging diva with an imperious contempt for all creatures whose best professional days were still ahead of them . . . a clan of which the zaftig soprano herself was clearly no longer a member. Nevertheless, the hissy diva happened to be the big ticket in this production; she had name recognition that sold gobs of tickets in the burgh of Baltimore. Solly's dalliance with Her Loftiness, if you believe the dish on things like this, was allegedly masterminded—encouraged, at the very least—by Lyric management in the hopes of helping to placate the soprano's volatile ego. The singer (if I named her, you'd recognize her) had been gaining a reputation of late as "a walker," one who suddenly balks—walks off—at the eleventh hour, dribbling some lame excuse that nobody for a single moment is expected to really buy for her "inability" to go on. It's just a way of getting attention. Lots of it. The story runs that Solly Biggs, still a big deal painter at the time, was prevailed upon to kiss up to the diva, who, like everyone else in the company, was fully aware of the affair that Solly was conducting with the young up-and-comer. So long as the imperious soprano (I really do want to give you her name) could conclude that she had snatched a lover away from "that little tramp" then the risk of "a walk" was considerably minimized.

Anyway, that's the rough outline of the offstage drama. Most of the story I got from Julia, who is a fairly dependable source. Julia and I attended opening night. And like I said, the production was an amusing muddle. We both agreed that the Biggs backdrop looked like a Technicolor Rorschach. We weren't even being catty. It really did. It was a sloppy mess. The petite Papageno, however, was a stunning delight. I was quite smitten, and I don't even give much of a ho-hum for opera. (I managed to finagle a backstage introduction afterward.) As for the Queen of the Night, she descended a gold-flaked stairway worthy of Busby Berkeley and slammed the notorious high notes of her aria like the trouper she was. Brought the crowd to their feet. She held center stage for a full two minutes, taking in the cries of "Brava! Brava!" with all the coyness of Mae West at a men's club. Management had to be very very pleased.

Upon his release from prison, Solly had quietly finagled a pity-deal with the production department of the opera company to allow him to set up shop in an unused portion of their warehouse floor. This was where Solly now resided, surrounded by the columns and parapets and wooden horses and castle doors and various medieval whatnot that make up the melodramatic world of the opera stage. There were no facilities for cooking, of course—beyond a hot plate that Solly had stolen from the Salvation Army—but this posed no real problem for Solly, who swiftly mastered the art of cadging free food and drink from his numerous "patrons," Shrimp Martin having certainly been one of these. As for hygiene in his rigged-up digs . . . invention no doubt followed necessity. Solly managed.

Solly Biggs pulled open the warehouse door and I entered the criminal painter's lair. The first thing that struck my eye—wrong phrase . . . *shrieked* at me—was the very same gold-flaked stairway from *The Magic Flute* production. It stood about thirty feet in from the warehouse entrance, approximately where you would expect such a grand staircase in the front hall of a millionaire's mansion. But of course, this one was in the middle of a musty brown warehouse. Without the full wattage of the opera stage's spotlights, the thing looked pretty dingy, sort of like a petri-fied slice of wedding cake. Solly had dragged out various other props and pieces from the production department's inventory as well, in order to give some form to his living space. An eight-foot plaster statue of the Madonna stood off in a corner. She was holding an umbrella. The ceil-ing over her head was waterstained. Solly invited me to have a seat in what looked like the sort of carnival carriage that might trundle you along through a Tunnel of Love. It was basically a booth in the shape of a swan. *Flying Dutchman,* Solly muttered by way of explanation as I settled uncomfortably into the breast of the bird. The swan was pulled up in front of a large table in a black-and-white-checked design. Solly pulled an anvil (looked heavy; weighed about a pound) up to the table and took his perch atop it.

"I feel like Alice in Wonderland," I commented. Solly was pulling a silver flask from his jacket pocket. He looked at the flask, then across the checkered table at me.

"By God, it says 'drink me'!"

I waved off his offer. He took a bite and then set the flask down gingerly on one of the squares, as if he were making a chess move.

"Solly, I want to talk to you about Shrimp."

He nodded. "Still dead, is he?"

"I want to know who killed him."

Solly's expression held for a few seconds, then he exploded into laugh-ter, which was almost immediately replaced with a bilious coughing fit. Solly slapped his pockets for a cigarette, found one and plugged up the coughing fit with it.

"I'll be more delicate in my questioning," I said, as soon as the crimson began to fade from the painter's cheeks. He swiped his hand through the air like he was chasing a fly.

"Christ's sake, Sewell. What's delicate? Bloody fellow was shot and stabbed all in one day, lost his bloody kidney in the bargain. There's noth-ing delicate about any of it. But I don't bloody know who butchered him."

"What do you know about Barry Fisher?" I asked.

"Barry Fisher."

"That's right."

Solly worked his jaw. "That's the money man, isn't it. Shrimp's patron?"

"I don't think 'patron' is quite the right word in this case. Fisher and Shrimp were business partners."

"I know the King's bloody English, Sewell. What, you think just because I'm beautiful I'm dumb, too?" We shared a carefree laugh over his delightful little joke. I really *was* feeling Alice in Wonderlandish here. The stairway to nowhere, the swan seat and the checkerboard table. Solomon Biggs himself was working a pretty mean Mad Hatter in his own right.

"I spoke with Fisher the other day," I said, adjusting myself on the seat. This swan wasn't built for comfort. Or for such a tall drink of water as I. "He wasn't exactly evasive. But I seemed to strike a nerve when I brought up the issue of money."

"Strikes a nerve in a lot of people. Root of all evil. Can't say I'm upset to be rid of it myself."

"Was Shrimp in some sort of financial trouble that you knew about?"

Solly had taken hold of his flask. He didn't take a sip, however. He lifted it up and set it back down on a different square.

"Couldn't tell you, mate. I didn't discuss business with the man." He kept his eyes on his stubby fingers.

"What did you two talk about?"

Solly grinned. "Girls." Now he took his sip. I held my tongue. It's a fact that most people feel compelled to fill a silence. Solly capped his flask and smacked his lips. "Something *was* chewing at our friend, last couple of times I saw him. Chap couldn't sit still. Fidgety, you know? Hundred miles away."

"What about the night before he was killed? That Friday night?"

"What about it?"

"Was he fidgety that night?"

"Bloody well almost took my head off."

"Really? Why was that?"

The felony painter gave me a sheepish grin. "Solly boy thought he'd take a crack at the microphone. I've got pipes, Hitchcock. Just wanted to try 'em out."

"I heard about that."

"Ah, I'm going to miss that place."

"Solly, do you remember anything else Shrimp might've said that night? Was he in some kind of a jam?"

"My memory's not what it used to be, friend," Solly said, sighing. "Ever since the war—"

"Solly . . ."

"Don't bully me."

"Solly, can you think of *anything* Shrimp might have said or implied about being in a jam? Did he ever even mention Barry Fisher to you, even in passing?"

Solly thought on it a moment. Or pretended to. It was hard to tell. He took a stubby finger and scraped it thoughtfully against his cheek.

"They weren't bosom buddies, I know this. On that money part, I do happen to know there were times my good Mr. Shrimp was dealing out blanks."

"What do you mean?"

"Dead checks. Bouncers. Shrimp told me a few times. About the bloody rent on that place for one thing. Not cheap, you know. Shrimp was on about how envious he was about my arrangement here. Can you imagine? This mansion comes to me rent-free, you know."

"It's a wonder."

"It's a liberation, I can tell you. It's all low overhead living for me now, here on in, ever since my taste of the rent-free accommodations of the good State of Maryland. Land of Pleasant Living, just like they say. I tell you, Hitchcock, living free, I'm all for it. Like that Thoreau chap, up there by the lake."

"It was a pond. Walden Pond."

"That one. Live off the landowners, by God. Simplify, simplify, simplify. Best thing that could have happened to me, being put in that cage for a spell. Set my head straight. Simplify. Not like our poor dead Shrimp now. Ah, Christ. Poor stupid boy." He wagged his head sadly. "Here. Let me show you something. You've come all this way. Let me show you how stupid our dead friend was."

Solly got up from his anvil. I quit my swan and followed him to the spiral staircase. We went behind it, where it was nothing but plywood framing. The backsides of the wide stairs were exposed, all except for one. About eye-level with Solly, one of the curved stairs had been boxed off. A rectangular hinged door was secured into place.

"Here," Solly said. "They built this piece here to hold some of their props."

Solly lifted the hinged door and pulled from the sizable little storage space a black-and-white Hecht's shopping bag.

"You'd think a man who owes money would be happy to have one of these," Solly said, handing the bag to me.

The paper bag was bulging. And heavy. I set it down on the floor and pulled the carry-handles apart. Even in the shadow of the gilded stairway, I could see that the bag was stuffed with packets of hundred-dollar bills.

"How much is in here?"

"Haven't even counted it all, mate," Solly said. "I never hit bottom. Got to a hundred thousand and just stopped there. Bloody hell. That was about halfway."

"So around two hundred grand then."

"Likely as much. Wouldn't you think that would make someone happy?"

"Shrimp gave this to you?"

"He did, mate. Night before he was killed."

I lifted out one of the bundles. Ben Franklin stared blandly back at me. "What did he say when he gave it to you?"

"Not bloody much, I'll tell you. It was late. Past midnight to be sure. Pale as a ghost. Called me into his office and asked me to hold on to this for him. I took one look and told him no way on granny's good green earth, but he near begged me. Said it was wicked important. Said I had no idea, which was right enough. I still don't. He said for me to just sit on it. Said depending on how things worked out, could be I could bloody well keep it for myself."

I bounced the bundle in my hand. "Looks like things worked out."

Solly grimaced. "If I had that pond handy, I'd be smart to toss this all in it. I know the stench of trouble, mister. That's a whole sack of it right there."

I returned the bundle to the bag. "Have you mentioned this to the police, Solly?"

He sighed. "I thought about that."

I drove over to Pulaski Highway to the main factory of Mabel's Bakeries and asked if I could see Mary Ann Martin. Ten minutes later I was standing with Shrimp's sister in front of several industrial-sized vats of oyster-colored bread dough, thick pastes being churned in slow figure-eight patterns by shiny mechanical arms. The place smelled great. You've got to give bakeries all-tens when it comes to their smell. Mary Ann Martin was doing a commendably so-so job of explaining to me how things worked here at the bread factory. Even so, she lacked the conviction and pep of a seasoned tour guide. Then again, she had recently attended the funerals of her two brothers. So we can maybe forgive the absence of pep.

I was glad when a fellow with a clipboard appeared and beckoned her over for a little conference. He was dressed pretty much like a pharmacist. The fellow appeared to be recounting a problem of some sort. Mary Ann appeared to be having difficulties comprehending the problem. The more she frowned and peered earnestly at the fellow, the more obvious it seemed to me that the poor gal was helpless to the task of assisting him.

I turned back to the big vats. The movement of the large metal arms was hypnotic. In almost no time I was imagining one of those chrome arms suddenly going *bang!* and stuttering against a foreign object at the bottom of one of the vats, an object that when fished out would prove to be a dead body. The wishful-thinking portion of my brain immediately deduced that the body was that of Shrimp Martin's and Arthur Wisner's killer, that some sort of Divinely sanctioned poetic justice had prevailed in landing the perpetrator of the two killings in a vat of unswimmable pastry dough here at Mabel's Bakeries. The eager-beaver portion of my brain was anxious to wipe away the mudlike dough and reveal the killer's identity. I tried. In my mind's eye, I watched the gummy substance being smeared away. A nose. A cheek. A chin . . .

"Hi. Sorry about that."

I jumped partway out of my skin. Mary Ann Martin was right at my elbow. I saw the pharmacist-looking fellow walking off.

"Problem?" I asked.

Mary Ann's cheeks were as pink as those on Mrs. Santa Claus. "A problem with the turnovers," she said.

I was tempted to ask if they have a lot of turnover here. But I didn't. Instead I said, "There must be a lot to learn in running this place."

"Yes, there is." She added defensively, "One person couldn't possibly know it all."

"Of course not."

"There's a lot involved."

"I can see that. I baked a loaf of bread from scratch exactly once in my entire life," I told her. "It was a daylong event. You'd have thought the Three Stooges had taken over the kitchen."

"How did the bread turn out?"

"It had the consistency of stew and it tasted like pencil shavings."

"Too much yeast," Mary Ann said solemnly.

"Well, you're the pro."

I followed the pro out of the factory and along a drab hallway to her office. Mary Ann took a seat behind her desk and proceeded to turn even brighter pink. She set her palms down on her desk as if afraid that it might suddenly begin to float off toward the ceiling. I dropped into a small, black, uncomfortable couch.

"This would have been Shrimp's office," Mary Ann declared. She glanced around the place as if this were her first time ever seeing it. I did the same, except of course it *was* my first time. The walls were decorated with framed posters of photographs of Baltimore locales. It felt a little like a tourist bureau. Mary Ann looked over at me with a great sad look on her face.

"You're here about Shrimp and Arthur," she said. This wasn't clairvoyance on Mary Ann's part. This was an almost direct quote of what I had told her when she came out to greet me in the reception area.

I told her again how sorry I was about Arthur.

"His funeral wasn't as good as Shrimp's," she said. She failed to make much of her attempt to smile. "I preferred yours."

"It's nice out there at Druid Ridge," I said, hoping to deflect the peculiar compliment. "Were the swans around?"

"Daddy hit one."

"He what?"

"With his car. They were crossing the road on the way to the pond and he hit one of them."

I wanted to ask if her father had done it on purpose, but I didn't. "He wasn't riding in the limo?"

"Daddy didn't want to. He said one limo was enough for one week."

"What about your stepmother?"

"She did. I was riding with her." She fidgeted. "I preferred your limo."

I thought of about a dozen places I would rather be at that very minute. And not all of them were too terribly pleasant. I shifted on the couch.

"Let me get straight to it, Mary Ann. Did Shrimp ever talk to you about his financial arrangements with Barry Fisher? Or even just in general? How the club was doing? That sort of thing?"

Mary Ann blinked a few times before she answered. "Not really." She placed her hands in her lap. I guess she had determined that the desk was secure. "Sometimes. I mean, a little. You know. It was kind of stressful sometimes. Do you mean— Are you talking about specifically?"

I said nothing. I knew from experience that Mary Ann Martin liked to talk. I gave her a vacuum to abhor.

She started to cry. Not what I had in mind. I didn't even notice at first; her face was already as pink as it was going to get. But then I saw the glistening in her eyes. And then she inhaled noisily. Wetly.

"I'm sorry . . . I just . . ." She went into a drawer and came up with a tissue and went to work on it. I waited. A woman with a beehive hairdo paused by the open door and took in the tableau. Man on couch. Woman at desk, crying. She frowned at me—I scowled back—and she carried on down the hall.

"I'm sorry," Mary Ann said again, sniffling back the tears. She fisted the tissue like it was some small animal she had just caught. "Shrimp tried so hard. He really did. Daddy . . ." she trailed off.

I coaxed. "Daddy what?"

"Could you close the door, please?"

I was able to reach over half-standing and flip the door closed. Mary Ann sighed largely. "Daddy wanted Shrimp to fail. I know that's terrible. He was so angry with Shrimp for turning his back on the company the way he did. Daddy would have nothing to do with him after that. Shrimp and I were close and Daddy was always pumping me for information. He wanted to hear that the club was struggling."

"That's very mean."

Mary Ann's voice dropped to nearly a whisper. "Yes, it was."

"Was it?" I asked. "I mean, the club. Was Shrimp really having a tough time of it?"

"I don't know. I think so. Shrimp knew that Daddy was always trying to use me to find out how things were going, so he kept pretty vague about it all. He liked to brag about all the celebrities he was getting to come into the club. He was a real promoter, you know. But somehow . . . I guess it wasn't all coming together the way he'd hoped."

"Let me ask you something else," I said. "Do you know how your brother felt about Barry Fisher?"

Mary Ann answered immediately. "Shrimp didn't like him. They were partners and everything, but that was as far as it went. Shrimp resented that Barry Fisher didn't have to sweat any of the debts the way Shrimp had to. Shrimp was . . . he was always behind on things like paying his rent on the property and stuff like that. I don't think he was really ready for all the expenses a place like that brings on. He piled a ton of money into the décor. Maybe too much. The cash flow wasn't working. It really bugged him that Barry Fisher wasn't helping him out more. He used to call the guy 'the partner from hell.' " She dabbed at her eyes with a tissue. "If I told any of this to Daddy, Shrimp would kill me."

I passed right over the logistical improbability of this scenario. "So your brother was really behind the eight ball."

Mary Ann said in a quavering voice, "Shrimp was being sued."

"Sued. By who?"

"Greg Snyder."

"The TV reporter. I heard about what happened," I said. "I understand your brother hit the guy with a shovel?"

Mary Ann's mouth formed a grim line. "He broke his nose and he knocked out a couple of teeth."

"Any idea what the problem was?"

She sighed heavily. "Gosh, that whole week just started off crazy."

"How do you mean?"

Mary Ann lowered her voice, as if the walls might be listening. She leaned forward in her chair. "Shrimp called me up that Monday morning," she said. "First thing in the morning. He sounded terrible. Even over the phone I could tell he was jumpy. He . . . he said he hated to do it . . . but he asked me if I could loan him some money. He said it was really important."

"How much did he ask for?"

"A hundred thousand dollars."

"That's a hefty chunk of change. Had he ever asked you for something like that before?"

"Never. No."

"Did he tell you why he needed it?"

Mary Ann shook her head. "I didn't ask him. I didn't want to know. He just said it was very important and I believed him. He said that he hated to ask and all, but that he was in a bind. 'Bad timing,' I remember he said. He said he was behind on a debt and that it would make his life a whole lot easier if he could just get it paid off. He . . . he was trying to make it sound casual, but I could tell he was anxious. I mean, Shrimp would never want Daddy to know he was doing this kind of thing."

"So then you'd say he sounded kind of desperate?"

"I guess so. I thought so."

"And did you lend him the money?"

"I was going to. I told him that I would. I needed a couple of days to pull it together. I was going to sell some stocks I have. And dip into savings. Maybe even arrange a loan through the company, though I hoped I wouldn't have to do that. But then Shrimp called me the next day and told me to forget about it. He said he was fine. He said something was coming in and he'd be okay. He thanked me and everything. Made sure I hadn't told Daddy or anything like that. Which of course I hadn't."

"And that was Tuesday?"

"Yes. The very next day. Tuesday afternoon. I didn't even find out until later that he had gotten into that fight with Greg Snyder the night before. Shrimp never even mentioned it. He just sounded so relieved. I mean, about not needing to borrow money from me or anything. He even made a joke about it. He sounded like himself again."

"And you didn't ask him how come everything was suddenly okay?"

"No, I didn't."

I pictured the Hecht's bag that Solly Biggs had just showed me. The bag that Arthur Wisner had strolled into the club carrying on that Thursday night. I did the math. Two plus two equals the strong likelihood of the shopping bag's contents supplanting Shrimp's need to call on his sister for a helping handout. When Shrimp phoned his sister on Tuesday, he must have known that help was on the way.

I came off the couch and moved over to the desk as smoothly as a salamander. Mary Ann edged back perceptibly as I lowered into her visitor's chair, placing my arms on the edge of her desk and leaning forward, never once letting the woman break free of my piercing blues. Body Language 101. Space Invasion.

"You haven't told this to the police," I said. Gently. But firmly.

Her whispered response was disembodied from her lips. "No."

"Because you don't want your father to know how screwed up Shrimp was with his finances and his debts."

A nod.

I leaned even closer. "Mary Ann, you think your brother was murdered because of his money troubles, don't you? You don't think that Lucy Taylor did it."

"They arrested her," she said weakly. "She shot him."

"You don't think Lucy stabbed your brother in the hospital though, do you? I mean really. Do you?"

She wavered. Before she could answer, the door to her office banged open and Sid Martin stormed into the room. For a little man he could make a big storm.

"What the hell is going on here?" The man threw a withering look at the two of us. I suppose it looked peculiar, me folded halfway onto the table. Mary Ann sitting bolt upright in her chair. "What's going on here?" Martin demanded again. "What are you doing to her?"

As I came off the desk and stood up, Mary Ann tried to answer. "Daddy, I—"

"I asked *him*!" Martin snapped. "I asked you. What are you doing here?"

I turned to face the bakery scion. He looked as if he was perfectly willing to sink a fist into my stomach. Or a loafer into my crotch, for that matter. In the hallway behind him I caught a glimpse of the beehived woman. Face pinched like a pickle-doll. Nobody likes a tattletale.

"It's personal," I said.

Sid Martin batted the notion aside. "What does that mean?"

"It means it's personal," I said again, in a deliberately calm voice. "Which means, since you ask, that it is really none of your business."

A crimson flame roared across his face. "What the hell kind of personal business you got with my daughter? Why was she crying?" I was deliberately blocking his direct view of Mary Ann. He jutted to his left to address her directly. "Mary Ann! What's going on here?"

I answered before she could. "I was just in the neighborhood and I thought I'd swing by to see if Mary Ann wanted to go out to lunch." I added pointedly, "Since you ask."

"Lunch?" Mary Ann's father barked out the word as if it were a hairball. He made no attempt to conceal his opinion that the very idea was ludicrous. I turned back to Mary Ann.

"I'm sorry you can't join me, Mary Ann," I said. I was trying to give her eye-signals to have her just play along, but I couldn't tell if she was receiving them.

Sid Martin was still popping gaskets. "Why was she crying?" he demanded again. "What the hell is going on here?"

I let his question hang in the air for a few seconds while I fashioned my answer.

"Both of her brothers have been murdered," I said simply. "It's the kind of thing a person cries about." I turned back to Mary Ann. "We'll take a rain date." Poor girl. She was deer-in-headlights. She nodded mechanically.

"Nice to see you again," I said blandly to Sid Martin. "Please give my condolences to your wife for the loss of her son." He growled. I stepped past him and left the office. In the hallway I backed up the beehive with a laser shot. She fired back. But it wasn't much.

I found my own way out.

CHAPTER 13

I got word that Lucy's lawyer had managed to get Lucy released on bail after all. Lucy was pleading no contest to the various charges resulting from her shooting of Shrimp. Her lawyer was able to go back to the judge and reargue the case for Lucy's release, using Lucy's cooperation as one of his bargaining chips. As to the issue of Lucy's being a flight risk, one of Baltimore's upstanding citizens had promised to take full responsibility for seeing to it that Lucy stayed put in the city. I can well imagine that this citizen rose up like Venus on the half shell and worked the judge over shamelessly . . . and as we see, effectively. Julia told me over the phone that she wore a little black number for the occasion.

"Isn't it kind of hot for black?" I asked.

"Yes, it is," she giggled.

"Let me guess. The judge melted."

"It was over in two shakes of a fanny."

I didn't have to bother to ask whose.

Julia was calling me from her cell phone. The burbly quality of her voice told me so. "Where are you?" I asked.

"At the Chadwick. I brought Lucy over for some pampering. We're getting a pedicure, manicure, a facial, massage—the full treatment."

"That was nice of you."

"It's wonderful, Hitch. My feet are covered with some sort of warm jelly as we speak. You should try it."

"Jelly."

"Warm. Yes."

"I'll need some convincing."

I left Julia and Lucy to their jelly feet and hung up. No sooner had my hand left the receiver than the phone rang. I figured it was Julia calling right back.

"What now?" I said into the phone. "Peanut butter on your face?"

The pause told me that the caller wasn't Julia. Julia is always quick with a comeback.

"Hello?" I said into the silence.

"That's more like it." It was Kruk.

I switched ears. "Sorry about that. I thought you were someone else."

"I'm not," he said flatly.

"What can I do for you, Detective?"

"I understand that Lucy Taylor has been released on bail."

"I just heard that myself."

"Your ex-wife posted."

Julia hadn't mentioned that part. But it didn't surprise me. "Okay," I said. "Well, thanks for calling."

Kruk didn't even bother to blurt out "wait." He knew I wasn't hanging up. "I have a bone to pick with your ex-wife."

"Detective Kruk, I cannot in good conscience give a reply to what you just said."

"I believe Miss Finney was knowingly harboring a wanted murder suspect. I have the same bone to pick with you."

"Detective. Stop."

"I have talked to you before about interfering with an official police investigation."

"Yes sir, you have."

"You're an undertaker. I'm a detective."

"Yes sir."

"You don't see me putting people in the ground, do you, Mr. Sewell?"

"No sir."

"Everyone has their part to play," Kruk said.

"Who said that? Shakespeare?"

"I did. And I am reminding you that your part is to bury the dead. If they were murdered, my part is to figure out who done it. It's pretty simple, isn't it?"

"Does this conclude your bone picking, Detective?"

"I could have both you and Miss Finney brought in for questioning. You know that."

Yes, I did know that. "I don't know your thoughts on Miss Finney, but I can't imagine you really want to clog up your day questioning me."

"Let me do my job, Mr. Sewell."

"Lucy Taylor didn't kill those two," I said.

"She shot one of them and she was sleeping with both of them."

This got my attention. But I had to wait a few seconds until Kruk finished barking something out to someone nearby. He came back on the phone. "Sorry."

"Who told you that?" I blurted. "Who told you Lucy was sleeping with Arthur Wisner? That's not true. Whoever told you that is lying."

"You know every intimate detail of Miss Taylor's life?"

"Lucy is a friend of mine."

"Have you ever had intimate relations with Miss Taylor, Mr. Sewell?"

"What difference does it make whether or not I've had 'intimate relations' with Lucy?"

"Your alibi for last Saturday is rock solid? You told me something about a dance program?"

"Okay, Kruk, stop it right there. I had nothing to do with killing Shrimp Martin and you know it."

"You were with Miss Taylor immediately after she shot Mr. Martin. Or at least we have your word that it was afterward. You conveniently 'forgot' to inform the police that Miss Taylor was at your aunt's until she happened to wander off and disappear for six days. Your ex-wife seems to have been out of town those same six days. And now she has posted Miss Taylor's bail."

"But—"

"Mr. Sewell. My perspective? Lucy Taylor either killed those two on her own or with the help of someone else. I have no real reason to believe that person was you. But I can't help noticing that when I look at this case, there you are."

"I'm trying to help out a friend."

"Then here's how you do that: You cooperate with the police. You keep clear of this investigation unless your assistance is officially requested. And you keep yourself from getting killed. One way or another, there is a murderer out there. Now, I *know* I've told you this before."

He had. "I'm a big easy target."

"I could shoot you with my eyes closed," Kruk said. He added, "Don't tempt me." And that was his way of saying good-bye. He hung up.

Alcatraz sat on the floor with his big chin on the seat of my armchair as I got ready for my date with Mary Childs. He looked like a drunk who had tumbled to the floor and couldn't get back up. His dopey wet eyes traveled left and right, tracking my movements as I showered, shaved, put on some music, buffed my hair dry with a towel, jumped in and out of several sets of clothes, tried out my singing voice, spruced the place up (I have a lot of throw pillows and "sprucing" for me is largely a matter of throwing the pillows into new locations), ran a surprise tango with a broom, made faces in the mirror and brushed my teeth with uncommon vigor. Twice. My canine Greek chorus watched it all. Could he speak, he would no doubt have pronounced the obvious:

Big man, big plans.

I swung by the Oyster for a bracer. It worked well, so I went for a second. Sally sensed something in the air.

"You have the look of love about you, Hitchcock. Who's the lucky target?"

I told her that I had a date with a short, irritable woman who didn't much care for tall men in general and who didn't seem all too wowed by me in particular.

"Sounds like an enchanting evening," Sally said. "I expect you'll be back on that stool later tonight grousing like a pissy old bear."

"You don't think I can overcome a few little obstacles?"

"A short crabby woman who hates tall men? I think your idea of a good time is getting seriously warped."

I had to admit she was kind of right. I took a third bracer. The circumstances seemed to call for it. I leaned over the bar and planted a kiss on Sally's forehead, took a sturdy handshake from an unsturdy Tony Marino and set forth into the night.

Mary Childs dressed up well. Maybe it was because she had brushed her hair, which seemed more full, more bronze. Maybe it was the simple yellow-print dress that looked as if it could be removed with a simple tug. Her skin each time I saw her seemed to be more and more tanned. She was looking like a piece of amber chocolate. A thin gold chain glistened from her left ankle. She was wearing sandals and her toenails had been painted a pale blue, not unlike the color of her eyes, which she had taken the time to gussy up with mascara and whatever else it is that women use to deepen the windows to their souls. The dress was sleeveless and pretty damned short. The irony here is that even though this was the most dressed I had seen Mary Childs, there was an implicit near-nakedness about the whole presentation that gave my heart a hippety-hop as she stood in the doorway watching me stare at her.

"Nice ankle bracelet," I said, not wanting to give away the entire farm with one jaw-dropping "Wow!"

"Thanks," she said curtly. "Where are we going?"

Ah, that's my Mary.

I reeled off a list of possibilities. Dinner, dancing, a movie, the planetarium (she winced at that one), night racing at Pimlico (she winced at that one, too), something highbrow like the symphony, something lowbrow like Hammerjacks. She rejected them all. The Timonium State Fair was under way, I said. We could ride out there and look at the prize cows. Buy some apple butter. Nope. I wasn't sure if the Orioles were in town or not, but if they were we could take in a game. I mentioned the Oyster as a swell place to get plastered and chitchat but that I thought she looked too awfully good to run off to a semiseedy bar. I tossed out the possibility of suffering through a potentially disappointing production of *Taming of the Shrew* up at the summer stage on Federal Hill. The idea of Shakespeare made her pout. I started to propose that we catch the Edgar Jonz Experience at Junior's, but then I remembered that Mary had bartended at Shrimp's and had probably had her fill of that Experience already. Just for the hell of it I tossed out one of my specialties, a tour of famous gravesites in the Baltimore Metropolitan region. Poe. Mencken. Francis Scott Key. It was staying light late these days; it's a tour best done at dusk in any case. Mary shook her head. My well was getting dry. Hmmmm . . . There was Annapolis, I suggested. Maybe something fun was shaking down there. There was pedal-boating in the Inner Harbor. Going for crabs at Obrecki's. God knows what sort of nonsense at the Theater Project. Irish music at the Cat's Eye. Maybe some free grain and tempeh over at the Krishna House. Mary Childs's steady and dubious gaze was shooting down one idea after another. Finally she uncrossed her arms and invited me inside.

I was right. The little yellow dress disintegrated with a single touch.

Mary Childs was no hypocrite. Which is to say an ungodly romp in the hay such as that which had just shaken the floorboards of Mary Ann Martin's spare bedroom did not transform the piquant woman into a post-coital soft and cuddly pussycat. No way. Were I to describe a moist warm body tucked into my arms and little fingers playing tippy-toe on my chest, I would be describing a lie. When Mary Childs peeled herself off me—I half expected to hear a sound like ripping Velcro—she took a two-minute shower, wrapped a flimsy cotton robe around herself and plopped into a white wicker chair over by the window, tucking her feet up under herself, and asked, "So, what do you want to do now?"

We went out for dinner.

Which—correct me if I'm wrong—had been my first suggestion.

The woman looked like a bird but ate like a horse. So did I. The horse part. We ripped through a pair of T-bones at the Prime Rib on Calvert Street like they were finger food. Mary asked for a second little bucket of sour cream for her baked potato, then she asked for a second baked potato. The waiter had suggested a particularly thick red wine, which, mixed in with my three predate bracers and the subsequent capillary extravaganza with Miss Childs, was leading me to a world-class pounder. I should have switched to water. But what a wimpy thing to do.

Mary and I didn't talk much during the early and middle innings of our dinner. We were each too concentrated on replenishing our depleted nutrients. We finally reined in the fork-fest as our waiter was topping off our glasses with the last of the wine. He asked if we wanted a second bottle. Mary said she was switching to water. I had missed my chance to take the lead.

"I've got to start looking for a job," Mary said as she was mashing up the final third of her potato. "I've already coasted too long. It doesn't look like the club's going to reopen."

"It seems such a waste to just shut it down," I said. "If Barry Fisher wanted to make a go of it, he could hire someone to manage the place."

"I guess it's not worth his while."

"I guess you're right. I spoke with him the other day. I can't say he showed a whole lot of gung-ho about the place. It's a money pit."

Mary shifted in her chair. "Speaking of money, what I'd like to know is what ever happened to that bag of cash that Shrimp had in his office. That could sure tide a person over."

"I know what happened to it," I said. This just popped right out; I regretted it the moment I said it. Mary's face took a turn for the interested.

"You're kidding. You know where it is?"

"Shrimp handed it off to someone the night before he was killed, for safekeeping."

"No kidding," Mary said again. "Who?"

I hesitated. "It might be better if I didn't tell you. I mean, for your own safety."

"Was it Lucy Taylor?"

"No, it definitely wasn't Lucy."

"Then who?"

"Mary, I haven't even told the police."

She gave me her warmest smile yet. "Now you're sounding like me. So how come you haven't told them?"

"It's a good question. I guess I'm just waiting to see how things shake out. I only found out about it this afternoon."

"That still doesn't explain why you're protecting whoever it is who's got it." Mary's chin suddenly tipped up—just a little—almost as if she were sniffing something in the air. Her eyes narrowed. "Unless of course you've got your own plans."

"My own plans?"

"For the money. Maybe a little fifty-fifty with whoever has it?"

"Hold on, wait a minute. It's nothing like that."

Her voice was laced with sarcasm. "You've got a pretty decent do-gooder act going on. But I think we both know you're not the complete Boy Scout."

"Look, I'm just stepping slowly. Shrimp handed the money off for safekeeping. And frankly, the person he gave it to could use it."

Mary scoffed. "Who couldn't?"

"This person more than others," I said. "Look, I might not be a Boy Scout, but I hold on to a confidence. I think you can understand that."

"So what you're saying is that you can keep a secret."

"That's what I'm saying."

She looked at me a moment. "So what if I told you a secret? Would you keep it?"

"If you asked me to, yes," I said. I took a bite of steak. "Maybe."

"That's not much of a promise."

"Well, I haven't heard the secret. Some are easier to keep than others. I mean, if you were to tell me that you knew who killed Shrimp and Arthur for example, I might find it a little tough to carry that one to my grave."

"Well, I don't know who killed them, so you won't have to worry about that."

"Okay then. You talk, I'll listen."

She made pouty lips. "Let's drop it, okay?"

"You're not going to tell me your secret?"

"I changed my mind. I don't think I can trust you."

"You never know until you try."

Her elbows were up on the table and she made a bridge of her hands, fingers lacing; her chin rested lightly atop it.

"Tell you what, you tell me your secret, I'll tell you mine."

"I don't know what yours deals with," I said. I set my knife and fork down and mimicked her pose. "Mine's worth around two hundred thousand dollars. What's yours worth?"

She closed her eyes; slowly they opened. "More."

"Do tell."

"You first."

"Mary, I'm not biting. I'm sorry. Chances are this money is what got Shrimp and Arthur killed. Now what kind of friend would I be if I were to put your life at risk by telling you who has it?"

"I wasn't aware that we had moved on to being friends," she said. The candlelight twinkled in her eyes. Like light off a knife.

I lowered my voice to a loud whisper. Leaned forward. "Mary, we kissed on the first date."

She whispered back, "Look, don't let sex confuse you." She added, "A lot of men seem to have that problem."

"Did our current Great White Hope have that problem?"

She gave me a patented Mary Childs look. "I guess I could have figured a nosy guy like you would be snooping around asking questions."

"I've been figuring I have Mr. Grady to blame for your no longer liking tall men."

"Kit is taller than you."

"So maybe your issue with me would be proportionally reduced."

"Somehow I doubt it."

"So what happened with you and Kit Grady, anyway? If I might ask."

"What happened? What inevitably happens?"

"Tell me."

Her tiny shoulders shrugged. "Someone falls in love and someone else doesn't."

"Let me take a stab here. You were not the one who fell in love."

"You've got me pegged for a hard case, don't you?"

"I think you're a person who knows what she wants and then goes after it."

"And then tosses it aside?"

"Is that what happened with Kit Grady?"

"I'll tell you what happened with Kit. That guy has got his head screwed on backwards, that's what. Here he comes, fresh off the farm, straight out of Ohio, and he gets handed everything at North Carolina, then the next thing you know he's on the cover of *Sports Illustrated*, he's not finishing college, the pros are knocking down his door and he's an overnight millionaire. He's got people hanging all over him telling him what to do, what not to do."

"And where do you fit into all that?"

"I don't. That's just the thing. Kit comes into the club last winter. November, I guess. He had one of those slinky amazon girls on his arm. You know the type."

"Tall, bored, anorexic."

"Right. One of those. And he looked miserable. I mean, really, really bad. He starts chatting me up. Now the thing is, I don't follow basketball. I don't really give a damn about all that stuff. So I'm just giving him the usual bar talk. And do you know what he sees in me? He told me. Freckles."

"Freckles."

"That's right. Between freckles and the way I'm always keeping my hair short, I've gotten that tomboy rap all my life. And Kit . . . he leans over the bar and tells me that he can't stand this bulimic bimbo he's with and that he's going to come back in tomorrow without her."

"So you started dating."

"Whatever. I told him right up front, I'm not looking for a serious thing. I just want to have some fun. Which we did, for a while, anyway. I mean, this guy has a serious rowdy streak. He could be a lot of fun."

"So what happened?"

"I told you. The guy fell for me. I'm serious, it was the freckles. That and the fact that I didn't give a damn one way or another about all this basketball crap. He *loved* that. This whole fast-lane game he was playing . . . I think Kit decided I was just the farm girl next door and *that's* what he fell in love with."

"He was homesick?"

"You tell me. He'd been getting in all sorts of trouble. The team was bailing him out. Then he totaled his car. That was right before I met him. Did you know about that? Almost killed him."

I remembered hearing about this. "His car got hit by a train, right?"

"Yeah. The idiot was stopped on the tracks and he passed out. It's a miracle he came to enough to jump out. Totally nuts. Anyway, they got his high school coach on the payroll after that. The Blues did. It's sad, really. They brought his old coach out here to hold Kit's hand. Kit's just not handling it. He's immature is what it is. Did you hear about his fight in the game the other night?"

"He got tossed out."

"Exactly. First big game against the whatevers, and Kit loses it. I'm not surprised though. Kit's on self-destruct."

The waiter came by and cleared our plates. We ordered coffee and agreed to split a Chocolate Disaster. I think that's what it was called. They're all the same. Big oversized slice of brownie, vanilla ice cream and rivers of chocolate syrup. We hacked away at it pretty good, but we didn't finish it.

In the car driving back to her place, we picked back up on the conversation about the club and the likelihood that it would not be reopening.

"It's got a curse now," Mary said. "Too much murder for one place."

"You're talking about that coed thing?"

"Big time. Shrimp really got bent out of shape when that girl turned up dead out back. You can't blame him. You don't want your club to be known as 'the place where that dead girl was found.'"

"Were you there the night it happened?"

"At the club? No, I was off that night. But I saw it on the news the next day. The next morning. I was just getting up and suddenly Mary Ann let out this huge scream. I went downstairs to see what was going on. She had the TV set on. There it was. Coed found dead behind local nightclub. Yeah. Real happy day for Shrimp, you can bet."

"Doesn't sound so nifty for the girl either," I said.

"Hey, you got to be careful out there."

"I understand Greg Snyder was suing Shrimp."

"Oh, you'd better believe it. Big time. He'd have won, too. The camera guy who was with him? He got the whole thing on tape. While we were waiting for the ambulance to get there he invited me over to the van to watch the tape. It is brutal. You've got to see this tape. Shrimp really went nuts. I don't know what got into him."

We were traveling up Charles Street. The tinted streetlights were working a slow strobe on my passenger. Flashes of amber. As we turned onto 33rd Street, Mary asked me one more time about the bag of cash.

"Forget it, Mary. Stay uninvolved."

A tiny sort of laughter came from the passenger side. "Look who's talking."

"I'm trying to help out a friend," I said.

"Such loyalty."

"Don't knock it until you've tried it," I said, which pretty much wrapped up the old conversation until we were pulling up in front of Mary Ann's house. I had already guessed that I wasn't going to be given a second invitation to come inside. I had also already concluded that if I was wrong about that, I was going to respectfully decline. I wasn't wrong. The lights were on.

"Mary Ann is home," Mary noted.

"Say hi for me," I said.

She ignored what I'd said and turned to face me. She brought one leg up onto the seat, scissored at the knee. "I'm going to tell you anyway."

"Tell me what?"

"What I was going to tell you earlier. It's about Kit. He told me once that Shrimp was pressuring him to control some of his games."

"Control his games. What does that mean?"

"It means cheat. Control the point spread. Shrimp even tried to get him to throw a game but Kit wouldn't do it."

"That's crazy . . . Why in the world would Grady want to do a thing like that?"

"Well, he didn't want to do it. Exactly. Shrimp told him there could be a lot of money in it."

I scoffed. "The guy's a millionaire. How much more money does he need?"

"Well, I don't think he ever did it. But it really got him frustrated one night. Real angry, too. That's when he started to tell me about it."

"That's crazy," I said again.

"I agree." She shoved the door open with her shoulder and scooted out of the car. "Hold on," she said as she closed the door. I sat behind the wheel and watched as she crossed in front of the car. I hadn't killed the headlights. They hit her about waist high. Mary came around to my window and without a word she ducked her head inside and put a big sloppy kiss on me.

"Thanks for dinner," she said, pulling back out the window.

"My pleasure, Miss Mary."

She stiffened. "Don't call me that," she said coldly.

"Sorry."

"Shrimp used to call me that. I don't like it."

"I didn't know. I won't do it again."

She took a few seconds to look down at me. "Don't go thinking something's going to happen just because we slept together tonight," she said.

"Mary, can I say that you are a confounding woman?"

She turned without a word and headed for the house. She didn't turn around, but the hem of her little yellow dress waved good-bye as she hopped up the front steps. I watched until she was safely inside then I drove on over to the Oyster and reclaimed my spot on the same barstool where my evening had begun.

"It's not what you think," I said to Sally as she slid a tumbler toward me. "What is it then?'

Gratefully, I took up the tumbler. "Well, now that part, I don't know."

Ten minutes and two tumblers later Kit Grady came in through the front door of the bar, stepped immediately over to me and took a swing. It connected. Shortest fight I'd ever been in.

CHAPTER 14

Billie thought I should press charges.

"He could've hurt you."

"He did hurt me," I pointed out. I lowered my Ray-Bans to show her my shiner.

"This is why you press charges. What in the world got into him?"

I explained. "I was out on a date with a woman he had been seeing. She told me that he hadn't gotten over it. I didn't realize it was a warning. I didn't know that it meant he'd follow us and then come ambush me."

"That's what you think? That he followed the two of you?"

"Had to. He must have been hanging around Mary's place and saw me come pick her up."

"Have you called the girl?" Billie asked. "To let her know?"

I had. No one had answered, so I had left my message on Mary Childs's machine. "*I had a little run-in with Kit Grady last night after I dropped you off. A real sweetheart. If his fist feels like my eye, then I guess it was a draw.*"

Billie and I were down in the basement having this conversation. Billie was wearing rubber gloves and a gray smock. A cup of tea sat on the metal swing-tray alongside the clamps and tubes of our profession. The Porti-San was humming on the floor. The unfortunate soul Sam had sent our way was stretched out on the metal table. Quiet as a mouse. Dead as a doornail. Not longed for this earth. Billie can embalm with her eyes closed. She's a real pro. Her little hands flickered about on autopilot, puncturing, poking, prodding, unpopping stoppers, measuring and mixing. Out with the old, in with the new. Billie has a demure and delicate, yet assured touch. It's much like the one she uses when she's mixing drinks, come to think of it.

Billie finished up her work and patted the dead guy on the head.

"*Bon soir,*" she crooned. She snapped off her gloves and took up her teacup. "Shall we?"

We went upstairs and had some breakfast. Homemade biscuits and gravy. Smithfield ham. Fried tomatoes with sugar. Embalming does something to the appetite. That's an established fact.

"Y'all feeling a Dixie pang?" I drawled, running my knife around a not-ripe peach.

Billie was rolling a piece of ham up into a cone to feed to Alcatraz. She wasn't in the mood for verbal Ping-Pong.

"I don't like you getting beaten up in bars, Hitchcock." She dropped the ham cleanly down my dog's gullet, wiped her hands and picked up a knife.

"Hey, I don't like it either, Billie. It's not like it happens every day."

Billie made no move to use the knife for anything. There was a basket of biscuits on the table right in front of her, and a butter dish next to it, but she ignored them. She turned the knife in her hand and gazed at the handle.

"Hitchcock, do you ever think about what you might be doing with your life if your parents hadn't died?"

"No," I lied. "I can't really see the point in that."

"Well, you wouldn't be here. We know that much. You wouldn't be helping me run this place."

"Billie, we don't know that."

"I do." She set the knife down. "Honey, you're only here because your uncle and I raised you. Most children go out and mow the lawn or wash the car. We had you washing corpses, for goodness sake."

"I washed the hearse," I pointed out. "That's a car."

"Not exactly a conventional upbringing, was it?"

"You don't hear me complaining." I leaned forward on the table. "What's this all about, anyway, Billie? I love working with you, you know that. This is a great setup. Flexible schedule. I get outside a lot. Meet a lot of people. Some of them still alive." I took a flaky biscuit and flipped it open as if it were a snuff box.

Billie chuckled softly. "You're just not going to let me get myself all worked up, are you?"

"If that's really what you want, by all means. I'm not accustomed to seeing you do it, but you go right ahead. I'm just curious where this is coming from."

Billie stood up from the table and gathered our plates. I wasn't actually finished with mine, but I didn't point that out. Alcatraz leaped to his feet. Compost time. "You're always getting yourself in some sort of trouble," Billie said. "And it's not something that just comes to you. You go looking for it."

"Billie, I was sitting at the Oyster minding my own business," I reminded her. "Man walks into a bar. How can you say I was looking for that?"

Billie paused at the entrance to her kitchen. "Hitchcock, I'm certain that you can explain away everything on a case-by-case basis. You're clever. All I'm noting is that it seems to me that you tend to collect rather a lot of trouble to explain away."

"And you're blaming that on my being an undertaker?"

Billie thought a moment. "Yes."

"May I point out that that is ridiculous?"

"You may."

"That is ridiculous. You're an undertaker. I don't see you getting into bar brawls."

"Don't be silly, Hitchcock. I'm not saying it comes with the profession."

"Well then, Billie, what are you saying?"

"Oh, never mind me. I shouldn't embalm before breakfast. It puts me in a strange—Hitchcock, I see you running around trying to track down a killer. Which is sweet of you, I know. You're trying to help out Lucy. Everyone appreciates that. But then I see you getting beat up in a bar and then, I don't know, we're down in the basement draining the blood out of a dead man and I find myself thinking, 'Where did I go wrong?' "

I got up from the table and stepped over to my aunt and placed a kiss on her forehead. Her eyes rolled up to look at me.

"You think you can buy me off with a kiss?"

"I have just so many tools."

"Well, I'm not as easy as some of the girls you go chasing after."

"Billie, I want to go on record right now. Trust me. Easy just isn't what it used to be. At least not in the women I seem to be meeting lately." My aunt slowly shook her head. "Billie, exactly when did you start popping these worry pills? I don't want you to concern yourself, okay? I'll be fine. A little fisticuffs is good now and then. The world is getting too damned cerebral as it is. Don't you think?"

"Ha ha."

Billie went into the kitchen and put the dishes in the sink. Alcatraz and I followed. Alcatraz stopped the precise moment I did. Sometimes I think we're attached by a string. Billie looked out the window over the sink, down onto the street.

"There's a man down there," she said.

I reached into my smart-ass arsenal. "Last census, there were three hundred billion of them."

Billie turned around slowly. She crossed her arms and cocked an eyebrow way, way, way high. Little woman had an arsenal of her own.

"Why don't you go join them?"

"Can I help you?" I asked.

The man on the front step hesitated before answering. He was clearly a little uncomfortable. But then this is not terribly unusual. Funeral parlors give people the heebie-jeebies, in case you didn't know. This guy was somewhere in his early fifties, I'd say. About my height. He was wearing a lightweight madras jacket, khakis, a tie and a hat. I don't really know how to describe one hat from another. I'd call it a fedora, except that might suggest something a little classier than the snot-green Irish-tweedy thing this guy was wearing. Anyway, his face was etched with permanent worry lines—at least they looked permanent to me—and his skin looked either like sandpaper or its recent victim. Ruddy. Weathered. Sand-blasted.

There was an entreating look to his eyes that reminded me a little of Alcatraz, who had just joined me at the door. In fact, when the man glanced down at my pooch, the ridiculous thought shot through my brain that he was here to see the dog.

"Mr. Sewell?" he said. (Well, technically, that *is* Alcatraz's last name.)

"Yes."

"I'm Hank Mackey." He was giving me a peculiar look. The sunglasses. I had forgotten that I was wearing my Ray-Bans. Wearing a pair of sunglasses is *not* the way to answer a knock on the door at a mortuary. You'll find that in any handbook. "Can we talk?"

"Sure," I said. "Would you like to come inside?"

He glanced uncertainly past my shoulder.

"Is this about a recently deceased?" I asked. Mr. Mackey wasn't carrying a valise; it didn't seem he was here to sell me something. And I didn't see one of those five-foot-long checks for a million dollars under his arm either. Damn it all.

"It's about Kit Grady," he said. "About . . . um, about what happened last night." Mr. Mackey's worry lines deepened. Dark canals transversing his face. It occurred to me that what with the conversation I had just had with Billie upstairs, perhaps a chat about Kit Grady and "what happened last night" would just as well be conducted off-premises than on.

"Why don't we go down to the water," I suggested. "This isn't about a funeral, I'd as soon take it out of the office."

As we strolled down the several blocks to the water Alcatraz trotted slightly ahead of us. Scouting. Clearing the way. Rendering fire hydrants and lampposts momentarily stunned. Once Hank Mackey began talking, I had a context for him. This was the fellow Mary Childs had alluded to. Kit Grady's old high school coach, from back in Cleveland. Coach Mackey warmed up slowly to the main topic. First he presented me with a not-so-brief synopsis of Kit Grady's high school basketball success, a litany of semis and finals to which Kit Grady had led his high school team, the Wildcats. Mackey seemed to feel the need so intently to establish Kit Grady's credentials for me that I began to wonder if he was leading up to something along the lines of: "And so, as you can now see, it is quite an honor for you to have gotten popped in the eyeball by such a natural talent. I just hope that you appreciate the distinction that will always be yours, and that years from now, when you tell your grandchildren about . . ."

We reached the harbor about the time that Kit Grady was being bombarded with offers from colleges. Every scholarship under the sun. Goodies. Cars. Off-campus housing . . . Alcatraz lumbered off after a cat that he would never catch (six years and he has never captured the cat; same cat) and Hank Mackey and I strolled out to the end of the Brown's Wharf pier and looked out over the harbor. The water was remarkably blue today, deepening its reflection of the cloudless sky. It was a Tuesday, so the water taxis were not out in force as they are on weekends. Only one was out, less than half full, going slowly against the current on its way to the Harborplace complex about a mile to the west. Hank Mackey was concluding his biography lecture as we reached the end of the pier. He told me that of all the offers from all of the colleges, Grady had decided— as I and anyone within shouting distance of the sports world knew—on North Carolina, where he had gone on to become the basketball team's undisputed alpha dog. Mackey had monitored his protégé's success from his home back in Cleveland.

"Kit was the biggest thing that would ever happen to me as a basketball coach. Of course I knew that. A player with Kit's natural abilities comes along just a handful of times. The fact that I managed to get him and to coach him in high school was a gift from God."

The coach and his former player had stayed in touch during Grady's ultimately truncated college career. Mackey and his wife attended games whenever North Carolina traveled to the Midwest, and he was given tickets by Grady when the young phenom led his team to the so-called Sweet Sixteen and then to the finals. It's not exactly a unique story, player and coach. And it became clear to me as Hank Mackey rambled on that he had essentially served as a second father to the young ballplayer during Grady's high school years. Mackey gave me the clear implication that Grady's own father, a real-life honest-to-God farmer, hadn't exactly been a sideline cheerleader to his son's successes—"Work, not play" was Russell Grady's motto—and Kit's mother was dead. She died when the boy was eight years old. Mackey and his wife were childless, so okay, let's run the numbers. Of course. Mackey came right out and said it to me. "Kit is like a son to me."

I pocketed the sentimental cliché and wondered if this somber but affable-enough fellow was ever going to arrive at a point that would explain why he was gently chewing my ear on a Tuesday morning. He did. But not until he rounded out his story. His voice was flat and without much inflection. I scanned the harbor for signs of enemy submarines as I listened.

"When Kit was bombarded with offers to leave college and turn pro, naturally he asked my advice. I told him to stay in school. But it became pretty obvious that he wasn't going to listen to me. Distance'll do that. Kit's plans all along were to become a professional basketball player. College was always just a stepping-stone toward that goal anyway. But his performance at North Carolina . . . it was so superb, the pros weren't going to sit around waiting for the boy to graduate. The offers they were making him— You simply cannot ignore this sort of pressure. I don't care who you are, you just can't. I helped Kit sort through all of this. That wasn't an easy time for me. Dottie, that's my wife, she was . . . well, she wasn't responding too good to her treatments."

His mouth formed a grim line. He nodded to my unasked question. "Cancer," he said. "She was a brave girl about it. She really was."

"I'm sorry."

"Yes. Well . . . there it is. It tore Kit up, too. Dottie really loved that boy." He cleared his throat. "So. In the end, we went with Baltimore, which surprised a lot of people, new team and all that. That was my call. I pushed for Kit to go with the Blues. Frankly, I didn't want to see him thrown onto a super team right out of the gate. Kit is a thoughtful young man. I'm sure you just see him as a spoiled young millionaire basketball player, but I know the boy. I didn't want to see him in Los Angeles, for example, or New York. He's a young man. He has a long career in front of him. I wanted to see him grow into it as best he could. If that meant putting him with a team where he could grow with the team and where his own leadership skills could develop and mature, then to my mind, that's the better direction to take. Kit was getting plenty of the spotlight already. And I don't know that it was serving him so well. My thinking was to slow things down a little. This sounds old-fashioned to you, I'm sure. But slow things down. Take a nice solid offer with a team that's building and don't burn out too quickly. Of course . . . look what happened."

Mackey looked out over the harbor, as if he actually *was* looking at what had happened. "Who would have figured? Kit has helped to take a brand-new team all the way to the top in just a single season. My 'great vision' of how this might work certainly hasn't proven to be true."

"Is that really so bad?" I asked.

"It has come at some cost. After his accident, I came out here last fall to see if I could keep Kit focused on what's important. Dottie was gone and I didn't . . . well, I came out here." Mackey pursed his lips; his eyes narrowed. Like he was trying to solve a math problem in his head. "I feel like I left home a hundred years ago," he said wistfully. "If I had had any damn idea what all this . . ." He trailed off. He cleared his throat and squared his shoulders. "Are you thinking of taking action against Kit, Mr. Sewell?" Mackey asked. The question came suddenly. Even after that hell-and-back preamble.

"Action?"

"Kit told me about what happened last evening."

I took a beat. I couldn't tell if the man meant that Grady had told him that this undertaker guy from Fell's Point had mixed it up with his former girlfriend, or simply that for reasons he was keeping to himself, he had walked into a bar around midnight and knocked me off a barstool.

"You mean my eye," I said.

"Kit showed up at my door this morning with two broken fingers." He added pointedly, "On his shooting hand."

"He broke his fingers hitting me?"

"Yes, he did."

This last sentence, Mackey delivered exactly like a disappointed, irritated father figure. Which I guess is pretty much what he was.

"No shit?" I removed my sunglasses for the first time so that Hank Mackey could see his protégé's autograph. He blanched.

"I'm sorry," he said.

I said, "Well, I'm sorry, too. But you didn't do it. The millionaire spoiled brat did it."

This got a reaction from the man. "Kit is not a millionaire spoiled brat. I'm sure he might seem that way to you. He is under a lot of pressure and maybe he isn't handling it as best he could, but—"

I interrupted him. The majority of my storehouse of patience had been emptied already. The man shouldn't have rambled on so long.

"This had nothing to do with Kit Grady and his basketball games," I said flatly. I gestured with my sunglasses at my eye. "This is very simple, very old-fashioned stuff, Mr. Mackey. This has to do with a girl. It has to do with your young friend's jealousy. The girl dumped him recently and he took it badly. Apparently he was spying on her and he saw me take her out on a date. A mature man would go home and beat up a pillow. Your boy walked into my local bar and popped me in the face."

Mackey was shaking his head. "He shouldn't have done that."

"No sir, he shouldn't have."

"Kit . . . Kit is probably not going to be able to play tomorrow. We open against the Pacers."

"Are you blaming me?"

"No, no. Of course not. I just— The media is going to find out today about Kit's fingers. Obviously we can't keep that from them. They're going to be swarming to find out what happened."

The sun was already out in full force, so any additional illumination put out by the lightbulb going off over my head likely went unnoticed by Mr. Hank Mackey.

"*That's* what this is all about? This is all about my keeping my *mouth* shut about why the Great White Hope broke his lousy knuckles?" Mackey tried to head me off, but my adrenaline pump had kicked in. "You have got to be kidding. Is this what 'personal assistants' do? Run around patching leaks that their prima donnas have sprung?"

"It's not—"

"Where the hell is Mr. Big Shot himself? How come he's not standing out here with me? Nothing personal, Mr. Mackey, but to use the parlance of your profession, you're second-string, aren't you? What did Grady do, come to your door and tell you to come down here and unruffle my feathers? He needs you to fight his battles for him?"

"Kit doesn't even know I'm here," Mackey said. Gravity was sucking his face nearly to the wood of the pier. He was clearly distressed that he wasn't handling this situation as well as he had thought he could. I had kicked into piss-and-vinegar mode.

"What exactly are you afraid I'll do, call the sports desk at the *Sun* and tell them that Grady got ditched by a woman and then went after someone who happened to take her out to dinner?"

The guy looked like he was going to cry. "So much is riding on all this, and Kit's been way off his game as it is. He's not performing at all to his abilities lately. If we get . . . oh Lord, if we start getting stories about sex and bar fights and all the rest of it . . . you know how the media can blow something like this way out of proportion, Mr. Sewell. Besides, do you really want that kind of publicity? You seem like a stand-up guy."

"Don't they say any publicity is good publicity?"

Mackey answered gravely, "Don't believe them." Suddenly he was pulling a handful of cash out of his pocket. A woman had just come onto the pier. She was pushing a stroller in our direction. "Please," Mackey whispered. "I know Kit regrets what he did. He's been under a lot of pressure since the play-offs began. He knows he made a mistake."

"Put that money away," I hissed.

"But I—"

"Now!"

The woman with the stroller was close enough to hear me snap. Lord knows what she thought as she watched the man in the Irish-tweed hat and madras jacket reluctantly stuffing a wad of cash into his pocket. I shot her an it's-not-whatever-in-the-world-you-think-it-is smile, but she wasn't buying it. She and her stroller performed an abrupt about-face and headed back down the pier.

"Let me tell you something, Mr. Mackey," I said. The tremor of anger in my voice was clear. "I'm sure, in your own way, you mean well. I'm sure this whole basketball thing is loaded with stress and pressure. You've made it clear that you are doing what you can to look after the welfare of young Mr. Grady. But you know what? He is old enough to take care of himself. He got involved with a woman, it didn't work out, he got jealous and he lost his temper. It happens."

"But—"

"And just so you know, I have no intention of doing anything about all of this. Certainly not going to the media and making a big noise. That's not how I get even, if getting even was what I had in mind. Which it isn't. So you and Wonder Boy can go right ahead and make up any story you'd like to about how he got his fingers broken. That's what you came down here to hear. Be as inventive as you like. I won't suddenly pop up with a lurid tale of sex and revenge."

"Thank you," Mackey mumbled.

"Well . . . you're welcome." As we headed back down the pier I added, "*This* might sound terribly old-fashioned, but why don't you consider asking your boy to give me a call sometime and, oh . . . apologize?" I couldn't help adding, "If you're supposed to be keeping the guy's head on straight, I don't think your running off to me to buy my silence and clean up his mess is really the best lesson you could be giving him. You cover someone's ass when they screw up, they're going to think they can keep on screwing up."

"I think Kit is about finished with me and my lessons," Mackey said heavily. "I've tried . . ." Abruptly he stopped walking. "You're right, you know. I do have to stop holding Kit's hand. It's been a total— It really hasn't worked. I'm not doing the boy any good anymore. I'm really not. I would have done anything to help Kit. But . . ." He looked up at me. His eyes narrowed and his jaw went a little slack. He aged a few years right before my eyes. "I wish I had never left Ohio," he said simply. Then he added, "At this point, frankly, I wish I'd never even met Kit Grady."

He grabbed my hand—awkwardly—and gave it a hard tug. I stood and watched as he moved up Broadway. I felt rotten. And I felt rotten that I felt rotten. I hate these layering kinds of things. I was all of ten steps from the Oyster and I thought about popping in for a so-called pick-me-up. But I didn't. Fate tossed me a bone. A very familiar cat suddenly streaked by me, racing along the cobbled stones of Thames Street. It was followed by a very familiar dog bounding helplessly after it. His coat shone beautifully. Alcatraz glanced at me as he rumbled past and let out a wonderful baying. He was as happy as a clam. I downshifted and peeled out after them myself. Three can play this game.

Television Hill rises above the Jones Falls Expressway like a miniature Mount Olympus. Both of my parents worked there, as on-air talent (weather, hosting bowling shows, kids' cartoon shows . . .) and doing scores of voice-overs. My father was a radio and television veteran. After he met my mother — at the time a struggling New York actress — and married her, he brought her up to the Hill and got her plenty of work there as well. Up to the point when I lost my parents to the beer truck, I spent a lot of time on Television Hill myself. The stories I could tell you could fill a book. Radio and TV people are nuts. I don't suppose that comes as any real surprise, does it? Fun nuts, for a kid growing up. Memorable nuts. Venerable nuts. Outrageous nuts. But still nuts. You've no idea the sort of mayhem that takes place just off-camera or just prior to going on the air, or in some supposedly deserted corner of an empty studio. You have to keep in mind here the measure of vanity and ego that goes along with some of the people who choose these professions (I exempt my parents from this charge because I am totally biased and I love their memory). The place was chock-full of God's gifts to *something*. It was unavoidable. And I don't mean to sound derisive. I have great fondness for most of those people. Maybe even especially for the truly self-deluded among them.

I parked my car in the slot designated for visitors — twenty-some years ago I would have dumped my bike onto the grass — and went inside. Even with the changes made over the years, the reception area still feels vaguely old-fashioned to me, endearingly behind the times. The faces in the photographs up on the Wall of Fame are all different, of course, than in my parents' era, but the general earnestness on the faces harkens right back to days of yore. The tradition continues. The receptionist raised a finger to signal me to hang on as she directed the call she had taken. As I waited, I squared my shoulders and took a few deep breaths. I felt like a child star who has come back to where it all started . . . and then realizes that he isn't recognized on sight. I tried to remember where in the photo display my own parents' head shots had been located. I shouldn't have done that. What I ended up recalling was the first time I had visited the station after their deaths and discovered that their photographs had been removed from the wall. I had been shown a plaque dedicated to their memory in the station's Green Room, but that hardly made up for their removal from the wall. I didn't want my parents dipped in bronze. I wanted them back. I wanted to go on with the show. The premature cancellation . . . it will gall me to my own grave.

Do I digress? Can't help it.

The receptionist took my name with a blankness that, well, asked me to have a seat. I did. A few minutes later a large bearlike man with a bushy red beard and prematurely disappearing reddish hair came around a corner.

"Are you Mr. Sewell?"

"Hitch." I stood up. The guy clamped a vice grip on me.

"Kenny Rogers."

"I loved your chicken," I said.

He laughed. "I haven't heard that one."

"I'll bet you've heard all the rest."

"You picked a fine time to leave me, Lucille?"

"Nearly a perfect song," I remarked.

"The boy went downhill from there, didn't he?"

"Christmas specials," I said. "They can kill you."

Bonded, we headed back through one of the studios to an editing room. I explained to Kenny that I was wearing the sunglasses because of a black eye.

"How does the other guy look?"

"Oh," I joked. "She's fine. Not a scratch."

Kenny was editing a piece he had shot on the U.S.S. *Constellation*, the small wooden war boat permanently docked in the Inner Harbor.

"Can you give me five minutes?" he said.

"Take six."

While I sat twiddling my thumbs I saw a vision of crisp loveliness passing by the open door. I hurried out into the hallway and hailed her.

"Miss Nash, could I have your autograph, please?"

The smile was all smirked up even as the blond head swiveled back to face me.

"Hitchcock Sewell? Is that you behind those Foster Grants?"

" 'Tis I. Winner of five daytime Emmies and a Bonnie."

She pretended to scowl. "Who's Emmy?" She came forward and kissed me on the cheek.

"How's the hard-news game going?" I asked. Bonnie Nash and I had met and parted when she was still doing weather. Soon after, she had managed to chuck the barometers and make the leap.

"Not so hard," she said. "How are the corpses doing?"

"Still can't get a word out of them."

Bonnie rolled her beautiful blue eyes. "Do you ever change?"

"I mature."

Bonnie clucked. "Hitch, don't feed me a line like that. So what's with the shades?"

"Unscheduled run-in with a fist."

"Jealous husband?"

"I don't swim in those waters, Bonnie. You know that."

"People can change."

"Not this fish."

"So what are you doing here?"

I jerked a thumb in the direction of the editing room. "I came to see Kenny."

From inside the room, Kenny called out, "Hello, Bonnie!"

"Hi, Lucille!" she called back. To me she said, "Look, Hitch, I'm sorry, but I've got to run."

"Big breaking news story?"

"Oh, right. An alleged weeping Madonna in Govans."

"You do mean a statue, don't you? Not a pop star in her underwear?"

"It's in someone's garage. What the hell a religious statue is doing in someone's garage is what I want to know."

"Well then, you go dig for the truth, girl reporter," I said.

Bonnie slipped a hip. "You're still a patronizing sexist, aren't you, Hitch?"

"Only with you, I swear. You bring it out in me, Bonnie."

She reached up and tapped me on the nose with her finger. "Well, put it back. Look. Really got to run."

"You go ahead," I said. "I'll watch."

Bonnie nodded largely. "Uh-huh? Very mature."

We kissed cheek to cheek (I suddenly felt like Yves Montand) and she went on her way. Yes, I did watch. She flipped me the bird over her shoulder just before she rounded the corner. Kenny appeared in the doorway.

"Bonnie Nash. Man, I'll bet she's a terror in the sack."

I told no tales.

I followed Kenny back into the editing room.

"So your dad knew my dad," Kenny said as he slotted a new tape into the editing machine.

"Couple of old-timers."

"Pop said your dad was real special."

"I go with that," I said. "Look, thanks for doing this for me."

"No problem," Kenny said. "Pop called and said could I do a favor for the son of an old friend. Why the hell not? Give me just another second here."

Kenny fiddled with a few knobs as a video screen came alive in a flash of horizontal squiggles.

"So let me get this," I said. "You and Greg Snyder were doing a stand-up behind Shrimp's nightclub, right? I'm guessing you didn't call ahead?"

"We sure didn't. Yeah, the word came in that the jury on that coed thing was going to deliver the verdict the next day. The professor, up or down. Snyder thought a stand-up back out at the scene of the crime would be a good idea. He worked it out in the van on the way over. You know how it goes. This is where the body was found. We'll find out tomorrow if the case is closed or if the killer is still out there. Blah, blah, blah. Real standard stuff. Nothing Pulitzer going on. Here. Look."

Kenny got the tape rolling. The image did one more seasick move, then I was looking at a still shot of a group of cheerleaders stacked into a human pyramid. Some sort of furry orange creature stood just off to the side. A mascot.

"Shit," Kenny muttered. "Hang tight."

"What's that?" I asked, even as the image was replaced by a tighter shot of the same thing, this one showing only the top three people in the pyramid. The two cheerleaders who constituted the next to the last row had been dimmed out in gray; the one on the very top was electronically highlighted within a circle. Kenny hit the pause button.

"That's the girl," Kenny said. "Kelly Bishop."

"The girl."

"The coed. The one that was killed. We were going to lead in with this."

"Oh. Right. Got you." Kenny started to forward the tape. "Hold on," I said. "Just a sec."

If I hadn't known any better I would have sworn I was looking at a picture of Olivia Newton-John from her *Grease* era. Kelly Bishop was fresh from Central Casting. Blond hair pulled back in a perky ponytail, large lively eyes, hundred-gigawatt smile. School colors appeared to be red and gold. Kelly Bishop couldn't have looked more comfortable and natural there atop a pyramid of her peers. Even as I looked at the image, it struck a vague chord. I'd seen this photograph. This was the picture that had been widely used last winter when the girl was found murdered. I remembered it now. You couldn't have asked for a more languishingly perfect photograph of a pretty, well-scrubbed All-American girl. People in the news game die for a photo like this.

"She was pretty," I said. I was stating the obvious, but there are certain times when that's about all you can do.

"Million-dollar shot," Kenny agreed. "Some survey they did about ten years ago had the white, blond female as the most sympathetic of all crime victims."

"That's pretty grim."

"You got that. You want to go on?"

I nodded, and Kenny hit the play button. Smiling Kelly Bishop remained on the screen for a few more seconds and was then abruptly replaced by the image of Greg Snyder the way I had seen him on TV dozens of times before. Clean-cut guy, preppy handsome, too-serious demeanor. His handheld microphone bobbed just at the bottom of the screen. In the background, I recognized the area behind Shrimp's. In fact, over the newsman's shoulder was the very spot where Pete Munger had poked a pistol into my neck. Now *that* would have made compelling viewing.

"What a clown," Kenny muttered. Apropos of nothing particular except, I'm sure, a history of having to aim his camera at Greg Snyder.

Snyder did a little throat clearing and intoned sonorously, "The boy stood on the burning deck, test, test, one, two, three." He broke character and asked, "How's that?" Kenny must have given him the thumbs-up. Snyder cleared his throat again and took a three count . . . nodded, then locked his ponderous gaze onto the camera.

"It all started here last November. Then again, for Kelly Bishop, this is where it all . . . ended. Next to that garbage bin just visible behind me. It was—"

He bit off his sentence and an expression of irritation came across his face. "What?" He lowered the microphone.

Kenny said to me, "The jerk was blocking the garbage bin."

On-screen, Snyder made his adjustment, the camera bobbled a bit . . . the garbage bin in question appeared, and the newsman went right back into his spiel.

"It all started here last November. Right behind where I am standing. Then again, for Kelly Bishop, this is where it all—"

The image suddenly tipped sideways, simultaneous with a new voice—off camera—yelling, "Hey!"

"That was the guy," Kenny said. "The club owner. Came around the corner. First thing he did was shove me."

The image on the monitor remained scrambled for several more seconds, then leveled off again, showing slightly more of the area behind Shrimp's than in the original shot. Kenny had moved back a bit. Shrimp Martin appeared on the screen. He was wearing his white tux and was standing toe to toe with Greg Snyder, who was shoving the microphone in Shrimp's face and attempting to work in an impromptu interview.

"You're Shrimp Martin. Owner of the club where Kelly Bishop's body was found, brutally—"

"Turn that fucking thing off!" Shrimp snarled.

"Please don't swear on-camera," Snyder said peevishly. He cleared his throat. "Mr. Martin . . . I'm sure you've heard that the jury has finished its deliberations and will be delivering its verdict on Robert Kincaid's guilt or innocence to—"

"I said turn the fucking thing *off!*" Shrimp wheeled around to the camera and drew his finger across his neck. Beside me, Kenny Rogers chuckled.

"Right. Now he's my director."

On-screen, Shrimp had turned back to Greg Snyder, who once more made an attempt to get a usable sound bite from Shrimp.

"Mr. Martin, with the trial concluded, would you care to speculate? Do you believe Kincaid will be found guilty of this crime? Or do you think—"

"Why don't you try minding your own fucking business?"

"I asked you to please not—"

"Get off my property. I have a business to run here."

Snyder persisted. "You actually saw Kincaid with the victim when they—"

Shrimp suddenly reared back with both arms and, landing cleanly on Snyder's shoulders, shoved the newsman as hard as he could. Snyder backpedaled a few steps and then stumbled to the ground. Shrimp yelled something else at him, but his words were out of range of the microphone. In fact, the noise that came from the speaker was a sort of *huffing* noise, the friction sound of the microphone dragging along the ground. Snyder got back to his feet. He was standing about eight feet from Shrimp. Snyder whipped the microphone to his chin, touched his hair, and barked, "Shrimp Martin, owner of the Canton nightclub where the Hopkins coed's body was discovered last fall, is clearly upset with what must be—"

Shrimp bent partway down. It was too dark to tell what he was doing, but Kenny told me.

"Watch this. The guy grabbed the mike cord."

Greg Snyder's hand, the one holding the microphone, suddenly jerked away from his face, taking the mike with it, and obscuring the rest of the newsman's sentence. Snyder grabbed hold of the mike with his other hand and pulled. Shrimp had straightened now, and the two engaged in several seconds of a tug-of-war with the microphone cord. It was almost laughable, except that Shrimp, with the strength that comes from being the more agitated, swiftly hauled the newsman in as if he were a fish on a line, and as soon as he was within striking distance, delivered a punch to the side of Snyder's face. Shrimp snatched the microphone free and inexplicably held it up to his mouth as he shrieked at the newsman, "Leave me alone, you god damn bloodsucker! This is none of your fucking business!" Snyder, who had doubled over to protect himself from getting hit a second time, straightened and took a paltry stab at Shrimp. His fist grazed Shrimp's bowtie. Shrimp dropped the mike and turned to the camera. Even without the direct volume, it was obvious what he was saying.

Turn that off!

The camera didn't go off. All that happened was that the image jostled and expanded.

"The hell with him. I just stepped back a few more feet," Kenny explained to me. "You don't turn a camera off when this kind of shit's going down."

Meanwhile, Greg Snyder had recovered enough to pick the microphone up from the ground. He, too, took several steps away from Shrimp, and then he did the foolish thing. He once more turned in the direction of the camera. His perfect face and hair were smeared up now. A trickle of something dark—blood—was visible below his nose. With his other hand, he made the circular gesture—keep the camera rolling—and spoke once more into the microphone. "For reasons that are not at all clear to this reporter, Mr. Shrimp Martin's reactions to the impending verdict in this trial is far from what—"

And that, folks, was all she wrote. Or in this case, all he said. A shovel was in Shrimp Martin's hands, and with a perfect Babe Ruth/Boog Powell/ Mark McGwire swing, the blade of the shovel landed with devastating accuracy, square in the middle of Greg Snyder's face. It is impossible to describe the sound, which was picked up close range by the microphone. Metal. Flesh. Bone. *Crunch.*

"Watch this," Kenny said. He froze the image, ran it backwards a few seconds, then replayed the moment, this time in slow motion. It was grisly. Snyder's face seemed to expand like pancake batter hitting a griddle . . . and then Kenny stopped the frame.

"Is that a tooth?" I asked. I knew it was. A little white projectile rocketing from the mothership.

Kenny simply said, "He messed that guy up big time." He returned the tape to full speed. Shrimp cocked the shovel and then hit Snyder again, nearly as hard. Snyder went down on one knee, and Shrimp raised the shovel one more time, holding it now more like a spear, and he brought the blade down directly across the side of Snyder's face. The image on-screen immediately scrambled, a few seconds later freezing on the back wall of the nightclub.

"I couldn't keep filming this," Kenny said to me. "The guy was apeshit. I swear he would have killed him. He totally lost it."

I could hear muffled sounds. Yelling. Snarling. Nothing intelligible, except for the sound of Kenny's voice. "Are you fucking crazy?"

"Nice sound bite," I said to the cameraman.

"Dude was out of control. I mean, look at me. I'm a big guy. This guy was a weasel. But I had a hell of a time controlling him. He was ready to take me on, too."

On-screen, a door suddenly opened from the back of the club and a figure darted out.

"Who's that?" I asked.

"That was Martin's brother. He must have heard all the noise and he came running out to help. Wasn't much damn help. Came running out of the place with this camera. I thought, what the hell's he going to do, start taking pictures? But he just stood there screaming at everybody."

Indeed, a new voice was audible now. I could make out only a few words. *Stop! Please! Leave him alone!*

Kenny said, "I finally got my arms around the guy and just squeezed. I held on to him until he began to cool off. This other dude, this brother? He was almost just as nuts. He was actually crying. And Snyder . . . What a wreck. Everybody started coming out of the club at that point. Someone called an ambulance. Martin cooled off enough that I felt okay letting him go. He jerked away from me. You know, big macho. He was still plenty pissed. He was calling Snyder and me all sorts of names. Mainly bloodsuckers. He seemed to like that one. His brother tried to cool him off, but he was useless. It was weird, man. I mean, can anyone say 'over-reaction'? Snyder was just doing his job for Christ's sake. How big a deal was it, after all? A one-minute stand-up."

Kenny reached over and killed the video. "Show's over. Makes you want to throw up, doesn't it?"

He was right. It did.

"So, Snyder was suing Shrimp?"

"You betcha. I would, too. With footage like this?"

"I'm surprised this hasn't made it onto the six o'clock news," I said. "It has that certain *je ne sais* Rodney King quality going for it."

"Evidence, if it comes to trial. The station's lawyers immediately put the clamp on it, just to be safe. Besides, Snyder stands to get tagged as the guy who got all fucked up with the shovel. There's a good chance something like this could taint him as an on-air. A career boost or a career killer. This could fall either way. Though it won't matter if his face doesn't get patched up good enough. You should see him. He looks like a truck hit him head-on."

I thanked Kenny for the big show. He chuckled grimly.

"Next time maybe you'll just rent *Psycho*."

Before I left I asked him about Mary Childs.

"Who's that?"

"She was bartending that night. She told me you showed her this tape back in the van."

"Oh, her. Yeah."

"How did she react to it?" I asked. I realized I was steeling myself for the answer. I hoped he didn't tell me she had asked to see it twice.

"Oh. She threw up right there, man. She called me an asshole for showing it to her in the first place." He made a sheepish face. "I thought I might've had a chance with her. She was all right. Cute little package. Blew that one big time."

"Tough luck, Kenny."

"Yeah," he said. And then for the second time in fifteen minutes, he said, "I'll bet she's a terror in the sack."

Zipper-lip Sewell left the station.

I met Pete Munger for lunch at the Women's Industrial Exchange on Charles Street. Munger had gotten there first. He was seated at a table for two in the small restaurant area at the rear of the place. He didn't look exactly like a bull in a china shop, simply a rough-hewn middle-aged man in a room filled with Dolley Madisons.

"What is this place?" he asked.

"It's one of the best places for lunch in the city," I said. "You saw all that artsy-craftsy stuff in the front? Women on hard times make that. They get the proceeds." I took the seat opposite Munger. I'm taller than Pete by a good five inches. He's broader. Between us, the little table was like a TV tray.

"I feel like I'm in some kid's dollhouse," Munger grumbled. "How come you're always patronizing these places that give their profits to some cause?" When I drew a blank he reminded me. "The Irish place. One pint of beer and you've bought somebody in Belfast a god damn fuse."

I sat back in my chair. "So what you're telling me is that you're bright and chipper today, is that it? Did you get up on the wrong side of the bed this morning?"

Munger glared. "Wrong side of the couch."

"Ouch. Sorry."

"Tell me about it."

Our waitress came over. Slight limp. Hair like pink cotton candy. She set down two glasses of ice water and produced an order pad. Pete and I each ordered chicken salad sandwiches. Pete asked for his on wheat. As the waitress moved off, Pete asked me about the sunglasses. "Are you feeling famous?"

I lowered the specs to my nose. "You want to look at this all through lunch?"

His lower lip rolled out. "Impressive."

"I'm glad you like it."

"What happened?"

"I was trying to help a little old lady cross the street. But she didn't want to go."

Munger scanned the geriatrics in the room. "So you choose to have lunch here?"

"Confront your demons, Pete. Don't your books tell you that?"

"Don't start on that."

I gave Munger the quick version of what had happened. Mary Childs. Kit Grady. Sore loser. Me victim.

"So Grady's not good for tomorrow's opener?" Pete asked.

"Doubtful."

"Well shit. That's just great. The Blues don't stand a chance without Grady."

"Hey, don't say it like it's my fault. The guy didn't have to take a poke at me. I was minding my own business."

Munger smirked. "You want to try that again?"

"I was. Didn't you hear what I just said? Those two broke up. Mary dumped him something like a month ago. In the lingo Grady would understand, it's free agent time. Besides, I wasn't expecting anything to happen between the two of us. The woman doesn't even like me."

Munger had to chuckle at that. "She sure found a strange way of showing it."

"That she did."

Pete had started fiddling with his silverware. Absently moving it around. Placing the fork next to the spoon. Placing the knife where the fork had been. He looked up.

"Here's a thought: What if she did it on purpose?"

"Did what on purpose?"

"Took you to bed."

"Pete, she did. Didn't you just hear me?"

"That's not what I mean. I mean, what if she knew that Grady was lurking around. Hell, you even said the two of you stood at her door forever while she shot down all of your ideas. What if she saw him hanging out there in the shadows?"

"Meaning what? That she took me inside specifically to get Grady jealous?"

"It's just a thought."

"You've been a detective too long. You're too accustomed to motives."

"I'm just looking for the angle on a girl who you say doesn't really like you dragging you inside all of a sudden like that."

"You can't just settle for an overwhelming inability to keep her hot little hands off hot little me?"

"Well, now, if it makes you feel better . . ."

"Damn it, Munger, you're trying to mess up a perfectly legitimate seduction here. Not fair."

"I'm just saying, if the girl didn't really like you—"

"Oh hell, Pete, I don't like her either. But you'll notice I managed to find a way around that."

The bastard across the table was grinning from ear to ear. "You amuse me, son."

I glowered. "Don't call me son, old man."

"You're telling me you don't like that girl? Well, I'm telling you, you're lying."

"Mary Childs? Pete, come on. You don't know what you're talking about. She's too short for me, for one thing. She's one of the snidest people I think I've ever met. She carries more chips on her shoulders than you can imagine. She's abrupt. She's harsh and I suspect that her regard for her fellow man is about as minimal as the law allows."

"But you went to bed with her." Munger snapped his fingers. "You dropped like that, am I right?"

"It was no contest."

I retreated behind my water glass while Munger chuckled up his sleeve. Damn it. The man made a good case. Now that I thought about it, Mary Childs seemed perfectly capable of the sort of jerking around that Pete was suggesting. Little woman with all these tall guys on a string. I hate to judge, but some people do choose peculiar ways to get attention. Though in this case, it wouldn't even be so much a desire to get attention on Mary Childs's part. If Kit Grady were still mooning for her, then she already had the attention. So then what else would she be gaining in drawing me inside knowing that Grady was out there watching? Revenge? That makes no sense. She was the one who dumped him. In that case, it would simply be cruelty. Salt in the wound. Rubbing it in. Or did she want to provoke him? Maybe she knew that the guy would come after me the way he did. Maybe it was as perverse as that.

I set my water glass back down.

"You're looking kind of grim," Pete noted.

"I feel used."

"You'll live. Listen, let me change the subject. I've got some more information on this business arrangement between Martin and Barry Fisher."

"Let's hear it."

"This Martin guy was an idiot," Munger pronounced. "I told you how Fisher arranged two separate loans to help get the nightclub up and running? The low rate for his loan, the higher rate for Martin? Well, it gets even worse. It seems that just a couple of weeks ago Fisher turned around with his money and lent Martin a hundred thousand dollars himself. Same rate as Martin's other loan."

"Wait. So Shrimp was borrowing money from Barry Fisher as well?"

"That's right."

"Would you like to give a speculative why-the-hell?"

Munger shrugged. "I can't. I mean, the interest on the pension fund loan is going right back to the pension fund. But now you take Fisher's loan. He's got his money at the bargain rate. He ratchets up the interest rate on his loan to Martin, it's his own little old profit to pocket. Basically,

Fisher becomes the middle man. Takes his low-interest loan, marks it up, peddles it to Martin for a gain."

"Swell partnership."

"We're not really talking about a lot of profit here though," Munger said. "You've got to keep that in mind. A few points on a hundred grand. It's just the sleaziness of it that's worth noting."

"That and the fact that Shrimp needed to borrow that kind of cash," I said. I was thinking about Mary Ann's story. About Shrimp's suddenly calling off his loan from her. I told Pete the story about Mary Ann and the almost-loan, and then about Solomon Biggs. Pete was especially interested in the shopping bag filled with two hundred thousand dollars that Shrimp Martin had entrusted to Solomon Biggs. Shopping bags full of money usually do draw one's interest.

"I've been under the impression that it was this shopping bag of cash that bailed Shrimp out," I said. "But now, with what you just told me, I wonder if it was the loan from Fisher instead?"

Munger was shaking his head. "Why 'instead,' Hitch? Think bigger. Maybe Martin had to pull out all sorts of stops. Maybe a hundred grand from Fisher was just part of it. Maybe he still needed more. Could be the bag of cash was the rest of what he needed, not the whole thing itself."

"So a very big debt."

"Two people are dead. People don't always get murdered for peanuts, you know."

Suddenly I was feeling queasy. I thought about Aunt Billie. Maybe she was right. What the hell was I doing nosing around in all of this anyway? Was it really all just to help Lucy? I pictured Lucy sitting in my office that day, sliding the pistol onto my desk, looking so forlorn. Am I really such a sucker for the pretty and helpless? It wasn't a question I really felt like asking. Or rather, answering.

"How'd you find all this out, Pete?"

"I'm good at what I do," he said flatly.

"You might want to beef up on the humility part," I told him.

Munger ignored me. "There's something else I found out that you might find interesting."

"You're the busiest man in Baltimore."

Pete asked, "Do you know what a 'key-man policy' is?"

"All my guesses would sound stupid."

"I'm glad you see that. It's an insurance policy. It's structured to protect people who are in partnership from incurring losses on debts incurred by their partner in the event of death or default."

"Translation?"

"You and I go into business. Then you die. Woe is me, I've lost my partner. With a key-man policy, I collect."

"Like life insurance?"

"Exactly like life insurance. In fact, it is life insurance. It's just that it's between business partners, not loved ones."

"And from what I've been hearing, Martin and Fisher were certainly not loved ones in any remote sense of the term."

"Interesting, no?"

"Interesting, yes. That would certainly be a murder motive," I said.

"It would," Munger said. "But you know, Hitch, I was able to get all this information without a hell of a lot of trouble. You can be sure that the police have nosed around in Martin's business affairs as well. If we know this, they know this."

"That's fine with me, Pete. I'm not in competition with the police. I'd just as soon they track down the killer and do the arresting. I'm just not convinced that they're working all the angles. Not so long as Lucy is their prime suspect."

"I just wanted to remind you that this insurance thing is pretty transparent. Barry Fisher would have to be a whole lot stupider than I think he is if he figured no one would be looking into something like this."

"I suppose."

"I'm not saying he might not be involved. But you can bet he's aware of how this one would look and I'm sure he's got his defenses in place. Key-man policy is smart business. It's legit."

"And that loan thing. Between Fisher and Shrimp. That's legal, too, right?

Munger nodded. "Perfectly legal. Still, a business partner pulling something like that? It's all legal, but it's still bullshit."

"Legal bullshit. Careers are made on that," I said.

"Don't I know it?" Munger made a wincing face. "I had me one of those careers once."

"What's that?"

"Lawyer."

"No kidding. You were a lawyer?"

"In my former life."

"Before you became Sherlock Holmes?"

"Hung out a shingle and everything."

"What happened? I mean, how come you went into the private-eye biz?"

"Long story."

"Hey, I don't think our sandwiches are coming out until Christmas."

"Some other time." He took a sip of water. "Or not." He set his glass down. And crossed his arms. Shifting in his chair, his knees bumped the table. The guy suddenly looked terrifically forlorn.

"This fucking place is a metaphor for my life," Munger grumbled. I wasn't precisely sure where he was going with that, so I passed on commenting. He worked his hand over the back of his neck. "You were married once. Did you ever spend a night on the couch?"

"Not alone."

Munger grumbled, "I'm fifty. That's well past the midlife point. Shouldn't I have had my crisis a long time ago?"

"Break it down for me, Pete. You and your wife are having troubles. She's sleeping with a jerk who is sort of your friend. You've decided that you no longer want to make your living doing what you're doing. Have I touched all the major points?"

"Isn't that enough?"

"Don't get defensive. I didn't say they weren't. I'm just trying to get the general picture. Are those the major points or are there any other big-ticket items?"

"Like what?"

"I don't know. What's your position on dressing up in women's clothes, for example?"

"Well, I haven't tried that one, Doc," he said snidely. "Would that be a cure or another problem?"

"Hey, I'm just kidding with you."

"Yeah, I know you are. I'm sitting over here with a knot in the middle of my back, a crick in my neck, three hours' sleep and a life that suddenly doesn't make any god damn sense anymore. And I've got Bob Hope shooting zingers at me."

"I'm sorry."

"Oh, don't apologize. Christ's sake. Life's too long, that's all."

"No, I meant I'm sorry you chose Bob Hope."

But Munger wasn't listening to me now. He was listening to his freshly minted demons. "Christ . . . I've gotten through fifty years. I got a wife, a house and a couple of kids with all their limbs. I've done all right. But . . . what next? If I don't get run over by a bus, I've got a lot of years still to go."

"That's a problem?"

"Somewhere here I just started waking up every day and thinking, 'Munger, what the hell are you going to do *now*?' It's like I can't wait for the years to just be done already." He rubbed his hand along his jaw. "I don't know what I'm supposed to do with them."

Our sandwiches arrived. The waitress asked if we would like to hear about the desserts. "Later, darling," Munger said. The woman's face sagged and she walked away. Pete watched her disappear into the kitchen. "I hurt her feelings." He pulled the tasseled toothpicks out of his sandwich.

"Pete, she'll get over it."

As we ate our lunch, Pete brought me back to my story about Solomon Biggs. "Let me make sure I've got this straight. Eleanor's boy brought the bag into the club on Thursday night. Then on Friday he left the club presumably to go meet up with someone. That same night, Shrimp handed the money off to this Biggs character for safekeeping."

I nodded. "And he indicated to Solly that there was a chance that Solly could keep the money."

"Which I assume means that Martin knew he might be killed," Munger said.

"That's how I see it."

"Which I'm also guessing means that Martin suspected the worst about Arthur when he didn't show up back at the club on Friday night." Munger mused a moment. "The camera."

"Camera. You mean Arthur's camera?"

"It was found next to the body. What if Arthur's killer used the camera to take a picture of Arthur? You see where I'm going here? The guy snuffs out Arthur, takes his photograph, then delivers it to Martin sometime that same night. You can bet something like that is going to freak you out."

"But why go to the trouble of giving Shrimp a picture of his murdered stepbrother?"

"To scare him, obviously," Pete said. "To show Martin that whoever it was, they meant business."

"And then they kill him the next day?"

"Whoever did this must have wanted something from those boys," Munger said. "Wanted it real bad. Either they were hoping to get it from Arthur and when they didn't they killed him. Or they killed Arthur so they could turn up the heat on his stepbrother."

"And when they didn't get it from Shrimp, they went ahead and killed him?"

Pete's head was shaking almost imperceptibly. "Not necessarily. Could be they got what they wanted and then killed him anyway. We can't know that."

"Was it the money?"

"It's got to factor in here somehow. The timing is too obvious. Arthur picks up the cash on Thursday night and on Friday he's killed. Whoever killed Arthur knew about the money. I think that's fair to assume."

"So then maybe it was the same person who gave it to him in the first place," I said. "Maybe the person had a change of heart then got so pissed that Arthur didn't return the money that he killed him. Maybe Shrimp refused and he met the same fate."

Pete had taken a mouthful of his sandwich; he held up a hand to silence me while he chewed and swallowed. Mother Munger must've instilled good manners in her little Pete. He took a sip of water. "Something doesn't work there. How is Shrimp going to see a photograph of his own stepbrother murdered over some god damn money and then decide to hide the cash with this painter guy? Would you take that kind of a risk?"

"We don't know that he saw a picture of Arthur," I reminded him. "That's just your crapshoot guess."

"Doesn't matter. He still went out of his way to hide the money, even when we're guessing he knew his life was in danger."

"Well, I suppose that could mean his life was also in danger if he didn't keep the money. Maybe he owed it to someone who was sure as hell going to come after him if he didn't deliver."

Munger nodded. "I like that. Catch-22. Damned either way. I like that, Sewell."

"Well then, what about what you just told me . . . that Shrimp took a big loan from Barry Fisher. According to Mary Ann, her brother was in a pinch to cough up some money P.D.Q., then something happened that he chilled out and canceled his loan from Mary Ann. What if it was just a payback? What if Fisher was calling in his mark?"

Munger looked across the small table at me and chuckled. " 'Calling in his mark,' eh? Listen to you. You're going detective on me. Are we going to have to get you one of those offices with the glass door and the venetian blinds?"

"Do I get Lauren Bacall teaching me how to whistle?"

"You must know how to whistle—"

"No! Pete. Not you. God, don't *you* tell me."

"Hitch, the problem with the whole Fisher thing is that it's too above-board. It was a legal loan. Out in the open. Plus, you sure as hell don't think Martin was afraid for his life if he didn't pay back his own business partner. That doesn't add up. Even if Martin was feeling the squeeze from Fisher and he started to borrow money from his sister . . . and then this bag of cash pops up and he earmarks it to pay back Fisher, so what? If suddenly your life is being threatened by someone, you just tell your partner that something's come up. That's business. That's life."

"What about gamblers?" I said.

"What about them?"

"Lee Cromwell told me that Shrimp was pretty heavily into gambling. Seems it was sort of a side business out there. Mary Childs mentioned it, too. What if Shrimp got in a little too deep with some gambling-thug types? They demand payment. Shrimp borrows some of it from Fisher. He also gets this bag of money from points unknown."

"When did Lee mention gambling to you? Wasn't the other night, was it?"

"No. It was after Shrimp's funeral."

"Why didn't you tell me this before?" Pete said.

I shrugged. "I thought I had. Or I just didn't think about it."

Pete gave it a little thought, then shrugged his shoulders. "Interesting. That's something we'll have to look into."

"Here's another thing while you're at it," I said, and I related what Mary Childs had told me, about the possibility that Kit Grady was being pressured to throw some basketball games. Pete perked up at this bit of news.

"Just how hard did the guy hit you last night, Hitch? Do you have any memory of actually hearing bones breaking?"

"I heard me hit the floor, Pete. That was about it."

"Interesting," Pete said again. That was all. We finished our sandwiches and passed on the desserts. Munger insisted on paying.

"You're a cheap date, Sewell."

"Hey, if I had known . . ."

Outside, Munger stood on the corner with his hands in his pockets and stared up the street in the direction of the Washington Monument, several blocks away. He seemed to have gone into a trance. Finally, I tapped him on the shoulder and pointed at the statue on the top of the monument.

"His name is George."

Munger ignored me. "That other thing," he said distantly. "Shrimp and the news guy."

"Greg Snyder."

"I'd like to see that tape."

"I can probably arrange that," I said. "Why?"

Munger's lips were pursed. "I don't know. The way you described it, sounds like Martin overreacted."

"He did. No question. Big time."

"Why?"

I trotted out Mary Childs's assumption. And Lee Cromwell's, for that matter. "Bad publicity for the club?"

Munger didn't buy it. "So instead he makes hamburger of a newsman? With a camera running? What kind of publicity is that?"

"The tape has never been shown."

"But at the time he couldn't have known it wouldn't be. The smart thing in a situation like that is to defuse it. He ignited it."

The smart thing. I reminded him that no one was exactly passing out Phi Beta Kappa keys to Shrimp Martin.

"Doesn't matter," Munger said. "Here's what I see. A girl gets killed and dumped off behind this club. Maybe she's even killed there. The guy who goes to trial for the murder is found not guilty. Shrimp Martin pulverizes a reporter who is only trying to do his job. Five days later, Martin is killed." Munger added, "Plus, there's a bag of money floating around. That's what I see."

"You think that Shrimp and Arthur's murders are connected to the coed?"

"Hitch, let me give you the word that will keep you moving forward in any criminal investigation. The word is 'maybe.' "

"But then what about Barry Fisher and these weird financial arrangements? And the fact that he clearly didn't like me asking questions?"

"What about it?"

"Does that fit in?"

Pete Munger gave me a patronizing smile. "Try out your new word."

"Maybe."

He patted me with a hammy hand on the shoulder.

"That's my good little undertaker."

We found a pay phone that worked and I got a hold of Kenny Rogers at the television station. I put Pete on the line and let the two arrange a time when Munger could swing by and view the gruesome videotape. I popped back into the Women's Industrial Exchange and purchased a knitted tea cozy stitched up in the colors and likeness of a Black-Eyed Susan. The Maryland state flower. It was a gift for Aunt Billie. Something to maybe help siphon off her mood.

"What's that?" Pete asked me when I returned to the sidewalk.

"Hat for my dog."

"You're kidding, right?"

"Have you ever known me to kid?"

Pete took off for parts unknown. I decided to walk a bit. I think better on my feet. At least I think I do. I headed up Charles Street, past the Walters Art Gallery and up the marble steps to the base of the Washington Monument. I craned my neck to look up at the statue of the Father of Our Country some several hundred feet above me. The ongoing debate in this town is whether it was a fluke or a devilishly inspired decision on the part of the sculptor who forged the statue of old George to depict him in the act of handing over some sort of document (one day I'll have to dig up what the thing is supposed to be) at a particular angle such that the combination of Washington's arm and the rolled-up document he is holding form a seamless unit, extending out from the waist and tilted ever so slightly down, just below the belt (if, in fact, people actually wore belts in those days) a good foot or so. The image, especially best when viewed from the east—Calvert Street is your prime spot—is unavoidable. Our boy George is hung like a horse. Father of Our Country indeed. It's really quite something, and once you've seen it, you can never delete the idea from your mind.

"Hitchcock?"

My head was still tipped back. If not for the monument rising up in front of me, I might have looked like I was staving off a bloody nose. Among the three thoughts that surged through my brain at the sound of the voice was in fact the thought that I might indeed be receiving a bloody nose any second now. This was actually the third of the three thoughts. The second was the recollection that the Washington Monument stands only a few blocks away from Read Street. Thought number one was, in fact, not a thought at all. It was a recognition. Of the voice calling my name. I lowered my gaze from the dead president with the super duper to the dance instructor with the great big grudge.

"Hello, Clarissa," I said, smiling widely.

I didn't even see the PBS tote bag until it was a foot from my face and closing fast.

I quit asking people if I looked like John Lennon after the third person in a row told me no, not a bit. My new wire-rimmed sunglasses were perfectly round, like the late Beatle's. But true, they sported a bright blue tint. Also, I have darker hair than Lennon. Wavier hair. Broader face. Better chin. A much gentler nose. Not to mention no accent, no fame and fortune and no avant-garde wife who drew me away from my Liverpuddlian mates to the dismay of millions.

Newly rigged with my blue specs (Clarissa failed to apologize for the obliteration of my Ray-Bans), I circled back to my car in time to see the fat derriere of the cop who had just ticketed it round the corner on Cathedral Street. I never feed meters. I get away with it more often than not, so my thinking is that it all balances out in the end. I waited until the cop had moseyed along, then I crumpled the ticket and sunk a two-pointer in the trash bin on the corner. Hell, I thought, maybe I could stand in for the injured Kit Grady. As I slid behind the wheel, I wondered what story Grady and his protector, Hank Mackey, had come up with to explain away his double-digit deficit. I started up the car and looked for one of those all-sports stations. I found one, but the talk was all about the Orioles and the drubbing they had given the Yanks the night before. Spun the dial — my car is a '63, the dial actually spins — and landed on an oldies station. I pulled out into traffic as Petula Clark was crying out her exuberance over "Dowwwn . . . town!" I thought of Pete Munger and his violent reaction to the Dusty Springfield tune at the Mexican place in Canton. I wondered if Petula Clark pissed him off as well. Funny guy, this Munger. It appeared he had arrived at a real crossroads in his life and was having a hell of a time getting himself through the intersection. I took a right on Saratoga. Munger had told me that he was getting out of the private-eye business, yet even after Arthur Wisner had been located, Pete had been awfully easy to cajole into jumping in on the investigation of who killed Arthur and Shrimp.

Eleanor Martin. This was the key, of course. I knew that. It was for Eleanor Martin that he was snooping about. Pete's "old friend." Of course, none of that was my business. Whatever Pete Munger's reasons for looking into this matter, it was all the same to me. Hell, I had a trained professional on the job and it was costing me nothing. Besides, I was liking the guy. A little cranky, true, but there's nothing really wrong with that.

I took a right on Howard then got onto Mt. Royal and headed east. Why the hell was I musing on Pete Munger, I wondered. My own midlife crisis wasn't scheduled to take place for another ten years or so. Maybe I was just hoping to pick up a few early clues and pointers from watching old Munger flounder about. Hard to say. I decided it must be the damn oldies station on the radio. Petula Clark had faded away in a slicker of tenor saxes when I hit Mt. Royal and had been replaced by Percy Sledge. *"When a Man Loves a Woman."*

I pulled over and dialed Information. I got a number from the operator and I made a call. It took almost no effort to wrangle an invite. I hopped back into my car and got onto the expressway, got off at Northern Parkway and went up the steep hill and across Roland Avenue, across Charles Street. As I reached the intersection of Northern Parkway and York Road, my car radio was pumping out the Henry Mancini theme for "Peter Gunn." I glanced to my right. The Senator was showing the newly rere-leased print of *Touch of Evil.* The glass bricks of the old deco theater, the wraparound marquee, the miniature skyscraper facade . . . I felt positively noir as I glided through a yellow light and made a smooth left turn onto York. I scanned the sidewalk for Lisbeth Scott. Or maybe Barbara Stan-wyck. Anything in nylon.

Nine minutes later I pulled up at the curb and killed the engine. The front door of the house was open, and the woman of the house was stand-ing in the doorway. She wasn't Lisbeth Scott. And she didn't smile as I approached. Not even warily. Her eyes, however, were wet with fresh tears.

Eleanor Martin took a step back and opened the door further. "I'm all alone," she said. I gathered that my arrival hadn't really altered that basic fact.

CHAPTER 15

Eleanor Martin came out of the house holding a tray. I stood up to help but she smiled me away.

"I'm fine. Thank you." She set the tray down on the glass table. "It's still warm. I put the kettle on right after you called. You'll want a lot of ice."

She took a seat opposite me. Daintily. Perched on the edge of the cast-iron chair. I hadn't really taken notice at either Shrimp's wake or his funeral how porcelain and almost frail his stepmother was. Delicate, perhaps, is the better way of putting it. She looked tired and she seemed disinclined to blink, lest fatigue immediately make its move. Mrs. Martin was wearing a white dress with a large collar. A narrow tortoiseshell horseshoe had the job of holding down her hair. I suspected the woman had let her hairdresser-day slip by this week. Her fingernails were bitten back; several of her fingertips were slightly splotched from the nibbling. Through the glass table, a pair of thin legs scissored at the knees.

The Martins' backyard caught a lot of afternoon sun; I didn't feel the need to explain my sunglasses. I loaded a glass with ice—as instructed— and poured freshly brewed tea from the pitcher. The ice in the glass made cracking noises. I slid the glass across the table to my hostess then repeated the process for myself. "Sugar?" she asked. I declined. She dumped three hefty spoonfuls into her glass. Slowly. Deliberately. As if she were memorizing them.

"I want to tell you how sorry I am about your son," I said. Eleanor Martin was running a spoon in gentle circles in her glass. She stopped circling and looked wistfully over at me.

"Arthur was only twenty-three."

"It's a terrible tragedy."

She stopped stirring, but kept hold of the spoon. Didn't lift it from the glass. "Did you know Arthur, Mr. Sewell?"

I lied. "I met him a few times. At the club. He seemed like an awfully good guy."

"He was my baby," she said softly, lifting the wet spoon from the glass and setting it down gently on her napkin. It dawned on me, then: The woman was heavily medicated.

"Mrs. Martin, I know you said on the phone that it was okay if I drop by. But if you would rather just be left alone, I understand."

"No. It's fine, really. I'm sure you know this. It's these first several days after the funeral. Everyone is getting back to business as usual. But it will never be business as usual for me. I've lost my only son."

She picked up her glass. Before I could stop myself, I heard myself asking, "How about for your husband? Is it business as usual for him?" Eleanor Martin paused before answering. I wished I had paused before asking. "I shouldn't have asked that," I said. "I'm sorry." There was a large elm in the middle of the backyard. Its shade was covering nearly three quarters of the yard, including the stone patio where we were seated. Eleanor Martin's gaze traveled off in the direction of the elm, then it ran a gentle roller coaster back over to where I was sitting. She set the glass back down without taking a sip.

"Sidney has his own way of handling his grief," she said. She spoke as if she were reading from a handbook. "It would be unreasonable of me to expect that we would handle what has happened in the same way." She looked back out at the elm again, as if the effort of exposing herself directly to my gaze for more than a few seconds was more than she could manage. "People are funny, aren't they?" she said.

"I'm sorry. Funny? How so?"

"Shrimp and his father. Sidney wanted his son to follow in his footsteps, but Shrimp had a whole different set of ideas of what he wanted to do with his life. Sidney disapproved, of course. Yet in some sense, they were very alike. I mean, their temperaments. Their stubbornness. I think that if they had truly been different sorts of people, not so alike at their core, then Sidney wouldn't have let himself become so worked up over the way Shrimp was leading his life." She reined herself in from the elm once more, forcing herself to look across the glass table at me. "Arthur, for example. Sidney hadn't a care in the world one way or the other concerning Arthur. Not one damn care." She looked down at her hands. "Arthur's father— Dan was certainly more dynamic than Arthur. Perhaps Arthur would have blossomed more fully had Dan not died."

"May I ask how your husband died, Mrs. Martin?"

She set her hands gently, palms down, on the glass tabletop. "No," she said simply.

"I'm sorry. It's none of my business. Forget that I asked."

The woman recrossed her legs. She picked up her glass and took a small sip of her iced tea. When she set the glass back down, she placed it at nearly the precise spot that broke my view of her knees through the glass. A jetliner was passing overhead. Or had already passed. Its faint rumble was lagging after. I looked up into the cloudless sky, but I couldn't see the plane. When I looked back down, Eleanor Martin was staring at me.

"Why are you here, Mr. Sewell?" She brought forth a seasoned fake smile. No attempt to pretend it was anything else. "To what do I owe the pleasure of your visit?"

"I'm working with Pete Munger to try to find out who killed your son, Mrs. Martin," I said. "I don't know if you knew that."

She blinked slowly. "I have asked Peter to please stop investigating Arthur's murder."

"Why? Why would you want him to stop?"

"Well, I suppose that's my business," she said coolly.

Bordering one side of the patio was a thicket of ivy. At a point where the ivy touched the stone stood a cast-iron frog, on one leg, holding a small bug torch. The frog was laughing.

"Of course," I said. "I'm sorry."

Eleanor Martin's face had gone completely red. "Don't apologize, Mr. Sewell. *I'm* the one who should apologize. That was terribly rude of me."

"It was stupid of me to come over. I really shouldn't have." I skidded my chair back and stood up. "I can find my way out."

She was flustered. "No, please. Don't go. I'm sorry. Stay. I'm . . . I'm not like this normally. I've been doing nothing but wandering around this house and this yard for three days now. I've friends who want to come over and distract me, but I haven't let them. Please. I apologize. Sit back down."

I lowered myself back into the chair. Eleanor Martin leaned forward on the table. Her eyes had taken on the look of dark glass.

"I can understand someone murdering Shrimp," she said evenly. "Shrimp enjoyed taking risks. He could be abrasive. I am sure that he made enemies along the way. People who are like Shrimp—who are like Sidney for that matter—I can see it." Her eyes fell to her hands, which had balled together into a single fist. When she looked back up at me, I detected a flicker of fire. "I can tell you this much, Mr. Sewell. Shrimp is the reason why Arthur is dead. I have no idea what went on, but this much I'm certain of. It is Shrimp's fault that my son is dead. And . . ." She glanced back at the sliding door into the house, as if checking to see if anyone was listening. But there was nobody else on the premises except the two of us. "And it's my fault. That's how I'm feeling."

"How is it possibly your fault?"

She answered immediately. "For marrying Sidney Martin in the first place," she said. "Granted, that was well over ten years ago, but I can't help saying it. My baby is gone. I married Sidney because I wanted Arthur to have the security of a father. Dan's death was . . . it was such a shock. Suddenly it was just Arthur and myself. I didn't choose well, Mr. Sewell. Arthur felt Sidney's indifference from the very start, so immediately he latched on to Shrimp. Arthur would do anything Shrimp told him to do. I can't overstate that. Anything. And Shrimp had no problem with abusing Arthur's devotion. That's what this is all about, Mr. Sewell. That's what got Arthur killed. Shrimp was up to something. I have no idea what, but whatever it was he got my son involved in it and it got him killed. I blame Shrimp. And I also blame my husband. If Sidney had been a real father to Arthur . . ." She bit off her sentence. Tears had welled up in her eyes. This time she didn't turn away.

"Arthur was a good boy, Mr. Sewell. He was a nice young man. Maybe he wasn't exactly setting the world on fire. But you know what?" She paused. "Not everyone has to."

We fell silent. Rather, Eleanor Martin fell silent. I was already muzzled. She sniffed back her tears and took up her glass. She sat back in her chair and started to take a sip of her iced tea. The next thing I knew the glass was gone. She had cocked her thin arm awkwardly and thrown it. The ice and liquid splayed out briefly; the glass landed just to the right of the laughing frog, landed in the ivy without breaking.

"Damn."

She pushed herself effortlessly out of the chair and strode across the flagstones in prim crisp steps, lifted her shoe and brought it down on the glass. *Crunch*. She came back to the table and dropped back into her chair. She picked up the napkin and leaned over to dab at a thin zigzag of blood high on her ankle.

"Are you all right?" I asked.

"How stupid am I?" she said peevishly. "I'm fine. It's just a little cut."

"Do you need a Band-Aid?"

She stopped her dabbing at the cut—she was right, it appeared pretty insignificant—and looked up at me. "What I need, Mr. Sewell, is a drink."

An hour later, I left. I had nursed one drink to Eleanor Martin's three. Midway through the second one, she had started to cry again. This time she'd been unable to sniff back the tears. She had gotten again onto the topic of her first husband, Arthur's father. Dan Wisner had been a building contractor, she told me. A pretty successful one with a solid reputation. Then she said he made a mistake. It was in the installation of an air-conditioning and heating unit in a pool house for a doctor over in Green Spring Valley. Something about a valve. A manufacturer's recall. The valve had a tendency under certain conditions to stick. The thing shouldn't have even been lying around her husband's workshop. According to Eleanor Martin, Dan Wisner had wrapped up his job on a Friday. She told me that the doctor's son had had a friend over for the night and that he and the friend had been told that they could spend the night out in the new pool house. Eleanor Martin's tears didn't come when she described how the two boys had been found dead of asphyxiation in their beds the following morning, or even how her husband had been arrested later that day and charged with negligent homicide in the boys' deaths. The tears didn't even come as she recounted the trial and her husband's public and private misery at what he had done.

The tears finally came—along with the third drink—when Eleanor Martin recounted listening in from her son's bedroom one evening as the trial was nearing completion . . . listening in as her husband's lawyer, who also happened to be his best friend, read him the riot act out in the living room over the unconscionable lapse that had allowed him to use the faulty valve during his installation of the air-conditioning and heating unit. Her husband's lawyer had done a masterful job in the trial of high-lighting so-called mitigating circumstances. He had managed to shift the focus of the blame largely over to the company that had manufactured the valve in the first place and had, it was implied, failed to institute a suf-ficient recall plan once the facts of the valves' failings had surfaced. Chances were pretty good that Dan Wisner was going to get off with the lightest possible slap on the wrist the law would afford. Unintentional manslaughter. A fine. Short jail time. A very rough patch in his life, but something that in time he could manage to put behind him. Eleanor Martin told me that she was in her son's room that night because she didn't want the boy to hear what was going on out in the living room. The passions of the two men were way too high for her to intervene, and so she had gone into Arthur's room and climbed into bed with him and pulled him close to her in an effort to protect him from hearing what was going on, or at the very least panicking about it. For the lawyer was ferocious. Ballistic, from the sound of it. He told Dan Wisner that even though he was about to escape the full wrath of the law, he was sure as hell guilty of the deaths of those two boys and that he sure as hell had better never ever forget that fact for as long as he lived. Eleanor Martin told me that her husband's lawyer was feeling horribly guilty himself. He had discovered late in the trial that it had in fact been pure negligence on his client's part. Dan Wisner had been aware that he was using a corrupted part. He had confessed to his friend, told him that he had had every intention of replacing the valve as soon as its replacement arrived by U.P.S., but that he had wanted to complete the job on schedule. What harm could a few days make? The weather forecast was for moderate temperatures. Nobody would be swimming. There would be no need to even flip the unit on.

U.P.S. was expected Monday. He would pop back out to the Valley and fix things up then.

Dan Wisner's lawyer was furious. He was screaming at his client in the living room, asking Wisner to come up with one good reason why he shouldn't remove himself from the case and tell the judge this final and obviously fatal fact of Wisner's negligence. *What harm could a few days make?* Wisner could not come up with one good reason. All he could do was appeal to his friend's loyalty. Eleanor Martin's tears began in earnest as she had described to me how her husband had begged his friend for mercy and how his pleas had been met with a rage of accusation. In the end, Wisner's lawyer relented. He had extracted his pound of flesh. His many, many pounds. The lawyer had done what he could to ease his own conscience. He left, and soon after, so did Dan Wisner. Eleanor Wisner fell asleep in her son's bed. She was wakened the next morning by a visit from her husband's lawyer. Dan, he told her, had gone out to Green Spring Valley during the night. He had brought his toolbox along with him and jimmied with the replacement valve in the air-conditioning and heating unit. He had then turned on the unit, broken into the pool house, lain down on the floor between the two single beds, and gone to sleep. He never woke up. The lawyer was in a state of shock. "I killed him, Ellie. I killed Dan." Eleanor Martin told me that he just kept saying this over and over. *I killed your husband. I killed my own best friend.*

Which was nonsense of course.

But try convincing Pete Munger of that.

Sam and I brought our latest customer up from the basement and positioned him in Parlor One, in the place of honor. The viewing was scheduled to begin at five. That's a little early, but the dead man's girlfriend insisted. She had told Billie that the man had absolutely lived for two things. Happy Hour and dancing. As it happened, of course, it was the latter that had killed him. The least we could do, the girlfriend had said to Billie, was to give him one more Happy Hour before he went. Billie explained that we couldn't serve drinks at the viewing. She did, however, offer to put out some chicken wings and platters of baby back ribs. I was to swing by The Horse You Came In On Saloon and pick them up.

Normally, Sam doesn't help out with this part of the game, getting the body in place for the big show. He'll sometimes stand in if a pallbearer is needed—though as big as he is, he usually looks as if he could shoulder the casket all by himself—but generally, he's the hearse guy. The driver. But Sam was feeling a certain propriety about this particular corpse. Sam had brought him in. There was a flush of pride. He couldn't stop fussing with the corpse, straightening the fellow's tie, poking and tucking at his hair. I started to call him off, but instead Billie called *me* off. She led me by the elbow over to the parlor doorway.

"This one's Sam's," she whispered to me as we stood watching the human wall preening and fussing the corpse. "Let him be."

I fetched Alcatraz for the walk over to the Horse. I sat down for a beer while I waited for the kitchen to finish prepping the wings and ribs. I lifted my sunglasses and looked deep into my doggy's eyes and guessed that he was in the mood for a Virgin Mary. I was right. The bartender poured out a bowl of V-8 for the hound and Alcatraz lapped happily.

What happened next happens a lot in movies and on television, and I'm always one to grouse about it. So when it happens in real life, I've got to take my slice of humble pie and be a man about it. The Horse is a bit of a sports bar. Certainly the Ravens and the Orioles and the Blues are well represented there, logo-wise. Banners and all that stuff. The television set up by the ceiling is always tuned to ESPN. As I sipped my beer, I found myself gazing up at none other than Kit Grady. (That's the part that happens in movies; that achingly poignant coincidence.) Grady was sitting with a bank of microphones all duct-taped together in front of him, like an ugly bouquet. He was wearing a Blues baseball cap and was holding up his right hand for all the world to see. What the world was seeing was that Grady's middle finger and his ring finger were each taped and splinted. I asked the bartender to turn up the volume, which he did. What the world was learning was that Kit Grady had slipped in the bathtub while taking a shower and had broken the two fingers as he tried to catch himself.

"How bogus," the bartender sneered, tossing the remote back onto the bar like it had just nipped him. I was curious what he meant. I inverted his statement.

"Bogus how?"

"That pile of crap. 'Slipped in the shower.' How lame can you get? That went out with 'my dog ate my homework.' "

"You think he's making that up?"

He was still looking up at the television. Grady was answering questions. Flashbulbs were popping. He seemed very subdued. Practically mumbling. The sound of cameras clicking in the background sounded like an orgy of grasshoppers. Grady was looking vaguely bored and vaguely irritated. In other words, like an overpaid superstar.

"Of course he's making it up," the bartender said. "When was the last time you slipped in the shower and seriously hurt yourself?"

"I guess it happens," I said.

He snorted. "Have you ever known anyone it happened to? It's like the banana peel. Who really ever slips on a banana peel? People in the movies, that's it. That guy didn't slip in any god damn shower any more than I did."

I was intrigued. It hadn't even occurred to me until this minute that the real facts behind Kit Grady's bungled knuckles might have leaked out anyway. Hank Mackey had elicited my silence on the matter. But Grady hadn't exactly assaulted me in private. Kit Grady was definitely high profile, not to mention extremely tall profile. Recognizable from a hundred feet away. Presuming that at least some of the S.O.S. clientele the previous night were on the starboard side of comatose, there had certainly been witnesses to Grady's unceremonious punch. There was no way that Hank Mackey would have been able to track down the Oyster's late-night customers and draw them into his conspiracy of silence.

I asked the bartender, "Did you hear something or something?" Besides an echo in my question.

"I heard he got 'em slammed in a car door by a prostitute."

A guy a few stools down the bar looked up from his beer. "A *prostitute?* You talking about Grady? Weren't no prostitute. Shit. He was scoring drugs, man. Got a major rush and, you know, put his hand right through a window."

"You're both wrong." This was the guy next to the guy. I had thought he was sleeping. He raised his head from the bar. "Gamblers. Game fixers. They wanted the kid to throw the game tomorrow, like he did last week. But he wouldn't do it. Won't have to now. Fixed *him*."

The cook was coming in from the kitchen, carrying a tray of chicken wings. "You're talking about Kit Grady? Acupuncture. Damn fool went to a hack. Take off those bandages, you'll see. Bunch of pinpricks all over the place."

From one of the tables behind me: "Cybersex, man. Dude's a total perv."

The bartender scoffed. "He hurt himself *typing*?"

"I said *total* perv, man."

"You're a total perv."

From elsewhere; I couldn't even tell from where: "Frying pan fell on his hand."

A guy at the jukebox: "Mud wrestling."

I suddenly felt like I was in a bad musical. Through the trap door behind the bar, a bald man was coming up from the basement carrying a case of beer on each shoulder.

"Grady? Hell's Angels smacked him with a pool cue, man."

"Cybersex!"

"Gamblers!"

"Pool cue!"

"Whore and a door!"

"Frying pan!"

The cook left and came right back with the baby back ribs. I nudged Alcatraz with my foot. Dog had a V-8 mustache. Vamoose. He reached the door before I did. I glanced back at the television. Kit Grady was straining to hear a reporter's question. Either that or he was simply sitting there looking pained. Or was somehow tuning in to the fictions that were still flying about the bar below him.

"Hell's Angels."

"Whore!"

"Gamblers!"

"Cybersex!"

Off to the side, on the television, I saw a familiar face. Hank Mackey, standing mutely with his arms crossed. His expression was every bit as strained as Grady's. Maybe more.

· · ·

"Ribs 'n' stuff," I announced as I came through the front door. Some of the mourners had already arrived. They turned to me as a single unit. Big smiles as I plucked off the tin foil. "All *right!*" They surrounded me and began picking.

Sam emerged from Parlor One, hands folded, head tilted as if in prayer. Poor guy was taking it hard.

CHAPTER 16 I suppose I should tire of reporting how sexy my ex-wife can look, but you try describing a woman like Julia when she is wearing one of those little French maid outfits and see if *you* don't slip in the fact that the creature looks like a libidinous lollipop. Go ahead. Prove me wrong.

Julia Finney looked like a libidinous lollipop.

The thing about Julia is that notwithstanding the hips, the breasts, the legs, the unforced perfection of her Aphrodite parts, the woman could be wearing an oversized sweatshirt and a pair of baggy khakis and she could still make hearts seize up. And all of that is still simply a prelude to a face that simply defies description. Something remarkable and inevitably devilish happens in Julia's large brown eyes. She produces her own light; it sifts and pulses just below the surface of her skin. High cheekbones (there is a member of the Cherokee nation rumored to be galloping through Julia's genes), a melt-in-your-mouth mouth and all sorts of funny things she does with her jet black hair, and there you have it: a woman who would make Eve herself plop down onto a rock and pout.

By the way, I don't want to give the impression, what with this French maid's getup that Julia was wearing, that she is an exhibitionist. She's not. Around her shoulders was a half-cloak/half-coat sort of thing, something suggestive of the jackets of the old gendarme. I don't know where she goes to dress up like this, but the combination of the two French motifs on this barefoot woman was electrifying. One could almost detect an honest to God breeze whipped up by the heads that turned—they *all* turned—as Julia Finney crossed the floor of the large restaurant and stepped up onto the makeshift stage that had been set up against the rear wall. The little half-length cloak fluttered as she stepped onto the stage, inexplicably lifted as if drawn on strings. Discretion has kept me from deconstructing my ex-wife's beautiful bottom. Suffice that I heard one gentleman sitting near me gasp, another utter, "Oh my God" and yet another sniff back actual tears. And I'm not exaggerating here.

I was seated at a table with Lucy Taylor and her lawyer. I glanced at Al's face. That look. I've seen it before. A knowing look. What it was knowing was that this remarkable episode in his life—pretzling with Julia Finney—could not, would not and really should not last. Al looked over at me, began to say something, then realized the full futility of words and remained mute.

Lucy, of course, didn't have any of the hang-ups of the stricken male population in the room.

"God, she's gorgeous," Lucy declared.

Lucy herself wasn't looking too gorgeous, I have to say. For one thing, she looked awfully tired. There were dark rings under her eyes, which were themselves a little bloodshot, a little unfocused. Julia had told me that Lucy wasn't sleeping much and that even when she was, she was having bad dreams. Mainly about her shooting Shrimp. We had agreed for this evening not to talk about Shrimp's murder and Lucy's problems and all the rest of it, at least for as long as we could manage. Lucy sat next to me in a drab dress with her shoulders slightly hunched and tried to pretend she was having a good time. But her spark was gone. It killed me to see that. When I placed my hand on top of hers at one point, atop the table, she was actually trembling.

Applause!

The dinner guests made a joyous noise for Emile DeBussey, who had just joined Julia on the little stage. Le Fromagerie, the name of the restaurant, was Emile DeBussey's newest baby. The guy was already a huge hit with his French hash houses in New York, Los Angeles, Dallas, Atlanta and Miami. Now Baltimore was getting a shot. Or, as I noticed in gold embossing at le bottom of le menu, Baltimore/D.C. Emile

DeBussey also had one of the more popular cooking shows on cable TV. I had seen it a few times; the guy was very entertaining. I suspected he had a lot better command of English than he put out, as well as the ability to haul in some of his "theeze"es and "eez"es. But hey, that French *merde* sells.

I already knew what the painting behind the drop cloth looked like. It was the one that Tony Marino and the others had helped me carry out the French (!) doors of Julia's studio several days earlier. The central motif was a cooked goose. In a myriad of colors. All about the goose were a series of half-rendered faces, different expressions registering various degrees of delight, curiosity, anticipation and just a few of disdain. Slathered throughout the rest of the canvas were simply a bunch of nifty color swirls and energetic brushstrokes. Here and there an onion, a carrot, a head of garlic, a sprig of herb. One of the more fully realized faces bore a striking resemblance to one Wilomena Sewell. I hadn't told this to Billie yet; I wanted to surprise her with it by bringing her by sometime for dinner. A glance at the prices on the menu, though, told me that I'd be having to go at my silver fillings with a screwdriver if I was going to finance a meal in this joint.

Tonight, however, was a freebie. Grande opening. Lucy and lawyer Al and I were Julia's invited guests. So far we had shared a sampler appetizer plate of all sorts of stuff I couldn't begin to identify. Mostly it tasted like chicken. I'm kidding. It tasted novel and damned good, whatever it all was. A lot of Emile DeBussey's shtick was also presentation, so everything arrived like a little package put together by Salvador Dali. Or, maybe, torn apart by Salvador Dali. I had never before seen a beet laced and tied into a half-hitch knot, or a mushroom hacked into the shape of a bird's nest. The three of us small-talked (mainly it was Al and I) and noshed on the various unknowns.

The unveiling of Julia's painting was taking place during the pause between appetizers and the main event. The chef made a little promotional speech for his restaurant then a little promotional speech for Julia. He and Julia made a showy thing of kissing each other on both cheeks, then Emile cried out "Voilà!" as Julia yanked on the cord that released the drop cloth. The goose was revealed and the restaurant exploded in applause. *Applause, applause, applause.* Julia and Emile grinned like a couple of dope fiends, then Emile took my ex-wife into a hug that was the envy of every man in the room. Poor Al. He was as pale as the tablecloth.

An army of snotty waiters swept through the room and delivered . . . guess what? Cooked goose. Clever boy, that Emile. Expressions of delight, curiosity, anticipation and just a few of disdain floated above the tables. Mine was one of the ones of curiosity. My goose tasted exactly like sea bass. I wanted to know how the hell he had done that.

My swollen eye had gone down considerably—there was just a small bruising to the side—and I had chucked the sun specs. My head was pounding. It had started up soon after I left Eleanor Martin. I put it down to the heat, to my minor drubbing the night before, a drink here a beer there, and to the general winds of whim. It was mainly a temple headache. Though my left eye, the one that had tasted Kit Grady's knuckles, was undergoing a second wave of throbbing as well. My predinner cocktail had probably been a mistake. Certainly the second one had been foolhardy. The problem with afterthoughts, of course, is where they're located. Not much good they do you there.

Julia was dining at a table with several other guests of honor. And guess what again? One of them was Cal Ripken, along with his wife. So really, how much difference was there between the celebrated international chef Emile DeBussey and the late Baltimore club owner Shrimp Martin? Everyone wants a celebrity. I watched Julia jabbering away with the Ripkens. Julia is big on the Orioles. She's met Cal and his wife on numerous occasions. She had the Iron Man in stitches with her stories. Also seated at Julia's table was what could pass for the love child of Clark Gable and Tallulah Bankhead, John Waters, the movie director. He was seated alongside a woman who looked like Cleopatra. Waters and the Empress of Egypt were erupting into giggling fits every few minutes. I recognized—by face, not name—several power couples also seated at Julia's table. One of them was in real estate. The other was simply old money.

There was one other person at the main table who I also recognized. He sat head and shoulders above the others. Literally. I had watched as he attempted to cut his food with his left hand—clearly not his dominant—and then finally he had prevailed upon Cleopatra to cut up his food for him. The two bandaged fingers on his right hand didn't keep him from taking hold of the handle of his fork in sort of a caveman style. It gave his eating a shoveling appearance.

I could see the injured basketball player, but it was difficult for me to tell whether or not he had spotted me. My table was near the front door, about as far from the table of honor as possible. Not that it mattered to me one way or the other. Surely the spoiled kid from Ohio wasn't going to take another poke at me in this setting. And if he did, I was more than ready to sacrifice a few knuckles of my own. Generally, I'm a pacifist, but I'm not an idiot. And I know how to throw a punch if I have to. I know how to throw a lot of them for that matter. One right after another. In my experience, this tends to be the most effective.

Dessert came. I have no idea what in hell it was. It was blue and yellow and it jiggled on the plate as if it were battery-operated. It tasted like jelly beans. It was vile.

I was keeping my eye on Kit Grady, and when he made what I interpreted to be the beginning of his exit move, I was ready. He made tall and nice with the people at his table, including a kissy-face with my ex-wife, and then he came down off the little riser and headed for the front door. Which means he was headed toward my table. Al was babbling on with a story about a judge who had experienced some sort of panty-hose trauma (I hadn't even caught the sex of the judge, which very likely was the point of the story) when I blurted "Excuse me" and popped up from my chair. Grady saw me pop up—he was about twenty feet away and closing—and he indeed recognized me.

"Hello, Kit," I said as he got within striking distance. "I don't know that we've formerly met. Hitchcock Sewell."

I offered my right hand, and then made a big show of pulling it back and offering my left instead. Grady hesitated, then took my hand and gave it a bounce.

"Sorry about your hand," I said. "I understand that you might not be able to play ball tomorrow." I said all this with a straight face. Neutral tone. Nothing provocative.

"Look, I'm sorry," Grady muttered. "That was really dumb."

"It was dumb," I agreed. "What exactly were you trying to prove?"

"Nothing. I told you, I'm sorry I hit you."

He tried to step past me, but I moved with him. He stiffened. "Do you know what happened to the last person who stalked Mary Childs?" I asked.

The ballplayer scowled. "I'm not stalking anybody."

"Her father shot him with his service revolver. In the head, as I understand it. The guy couldn't find his way out of kindergarten now if he tried."

"What are you telling me for?"

"Look, what you do about your ex-girlfriends is your own business, Kit," I said. "But if you want my advice, Mary Childs is the kind of girl you'd do well to forget. As quickly as you can. She's sure as hell no girl next door."

"I don't recall asking for your advice," Grady said snottily.

"No, you didn't. I'm giving it to you as a bonus."

"Well, I don't need your damn bonus," Grady said. He started forward.

"Wait."

I placed a hand on his chest to stop him. Without thinking, Grady swiped my hand free. He used his right hand. "Well, that didn't seem to hurt much," I observed. "I was under the impression that broken fingers are kind of fragile."

Grady sneered. "What do you want?"

"Did you send Hank Mackey down to see me this morning, or was that his idea?"

"I don't know what you're talking about."

"Hank Mackey. Your high school coach."

"I know who the hell Hank is," Grady said. "Why would I send him to see you?"

"To buy my compliance with your brilliant fell-in-the-shower story. Who came up with that, anyway?"

Grady gave me a skewed look. "Hank talked to you?"

"First thing this morning. It must be nice to have someone so willing to cover your tracks."

From the expression on Grady's face, he didn't appear to agree with me. He brought in his lower lip for a nibble. "I didn't tell Hank to do a damn thing. Fact, I told him *not* to do anything. He's got to stay out of my . . ." He trailed off. "Look, whatever Hank said to you, forget it. He's not my mother. I'm sorry about your eye, man. I was just upset. Stupid thing to do. Hey, you got doctor's costs or anything like that, just let me know. I'm good for it, no problem."

"Let me ask you something, Kit. Are you throwing basketball games?"

He answered without hesitation. "Fuck off."

"Do you know anything about Shrimp Martin's murder that maybe the police would like to know?"

He sneered. "Like what?"

"Like who killed him? Like who he was in such heavy debt to? And why?"

"How would I know shit like that?" he asked.

"Because you're the Great White Hope."

His eyes narrowed. He looked like he wanted to hit me again, but there was little chance that he would. Besides, this time I was ready. Maybe I'm not a killing machine, but I hit high and I hit low when I have to. I had never hit a millionaire, but I was willing if I had to.

I didn't have to. The front door opened and several people came noisily into the restaurant. Before the door had closed behind them, Kit Grady was on the sidewalk. Good moves for a big man. I sat back down at my table.

"What was that all about?" Al asked.

I rubbed my hand along my jaw. "Al, I'm clueless." I picked up a thin-stemmed glass of some sort of potion that had come with the mysterious dessert. My temples were sending tom-tom signals to each other. I downed the potion anyway. Mmmm. It was the best thing I had tasted all night. Tart yet sweet. Rough yet velvety. I saw that Lucy hadn't touched hers. "May I?" I asked. She nodded her assent. I emptied her tiny glass. "This stuff is good," I said. "What is it?"

Al was sniffing his glass. "I think it's yak piss." He set his glass down. "You want mine?"

I reached across the table for his glass. Already the stuff was taking the pressure away from my head. The drumbeat in my temples was subsiding. My beaten-up eye was buzzing warmly and comfortably. Tingles moved into my cheek. "Yak piss. Where have you been all my life?"

I did finally speak with Lucy about Shrimp and the events leading up to his fatal day. We were seated on a cartoon-looking couch in the restaurant's bar area. The decor bore a definite resemblance to the presentation of the food. At least this was how I was seeing it. I can't say I had full trust in my vision at that point. My headache, however, was long forgotten. Julia had gotten a small crowd to join her over at the bar for a game called Ali Baba and the Forty Thieves. It was a noisy game of copycatting and drinking. She had removed her cloak for more freedom of movement.

Lucy and I had the entire couch area to ourselves.

Unfortunately, Lucy couldn't give me a whole lot that I didn't already know. Because of her grandmother's death and taking care of the details, Lucy had not been at Shrimp's on either the Thursday or the Friday that Mary Childs had described to me. She told me that she had spoken to Shrimp briefly on the phone on Friday night. Early. Around eight o'clock. He had mentioned that Arthur was not at the club.

"How did he sound?" I asked. "Did he sound worried?"

"A little."

"Frantic?"

"No. But we didn't talk real long. He said he wanted to keep the phone free in case Arthur called."

"No call waiting?"

"His private line. I guess not."

"What's this about Shrimp accusing you and Arthur of having an affair?" I asked.

"That's nothing, really. Shrimp knew better. It's just that Arthur and I had gotten closer lately. We were just friends. He was a nice guy. Shrimp was just being all weird and paranoid."

"Is it possible he accused you of having an affair because maybe he was having one himself?" I asked. "I've heard a rumor that Shrimp was seeing another woman." An explosion of laughter from the bar area drew our attention. Julia was slapping her fanny like she was a racehorse. A dozen or more other fannies were summarily being hit. I turned back to Lucy. She was looking a little fuzzy. It wasn't her fault. It was the yak piss. It seemed to have a time-release factor built in. The entire restaurant had gone kind of soft.

"It's not a rumor," Lucy said simply. "He was. That was part of our argument that Saturday. I was calling him on it."

"Did you tell that to Julia when you two were down in Rehoboth?"

"No."

"Why not?"

"Hitch, it's always the same story with me, that's why. I always screw up. I just— It's embarrassing after a while. I felt like such a loser. I just didn't want to tell her."

I understood. Or I thought I did. "Lucy, is it possible that the woman Shrimp was seeing . . . is it possible that she could have had something to do with Shrimp's murder? Maybe it was someone she knew? Is she married? Maybe an irate husband?"

"No. She's definitely single."

"So you know who she is?" I scooted up on the cartoon couch. Tried to, anyway. It was some sort of chamois. Slippery.

"Sure, I know who she is," Lucy said. "It's that little slut. Mary Childs."

CHAPTER 17

"Mary Childs?"

I corrected. "That little slut, Mary Childs."

"Well, I suppose it's possible. She certainly struck me as the type who might sleep with anyone."

I hoped the low lighting in Junior's masked whatever blushing I did. Lee Cromwell didn't need to see whether I was blushing or not. Her radar was more finely tuned. She reached out and patted my hand atop the bar. "Don't sweat it, Hitchcock. She's a cute kid. It happens."

"That's not the point," I said. Though when I tried to articulate to myself what exactly *was* the point, I drew a blank. It wasn't the first blank of the evening either. My memory of the drive over here from Le Fromagerie, for example. That was already dark and porous.

The Tuesday night crowd at Junior's had practically doubled when I walked into the place. Lee Cromwell was finished singing for the night. She and I were at the bar. I was drinking a good night whiskey for no good reason. Lee was knocking back a cranberry juice and soda. She looked damn good in profile, I have to say. There's a movie actress she was reminding me of—not Ida Lupino this time, a living one—but I wasn't coming up with the name. She was in that movie about the guy and the car and the money and the double-cross and the goofy best friend who gets killed? You know the one. At first the man and woman don't get along? There's that hit pop song playing when the two make love the first time? I just can't remember the name right now.

Some people simply look tired when they're tired. Lee Cromwell looked sexy. Or maybe she looked sexy when *I* was tired. The cigarette didn't hurt, the blue smoke curling up past her ear. When the bartender had reminded Lee that there was no smoking in the club, Lee had eye-balled the slender crowd remaining in the place and answered him in a husky voice, "I think they'll live."

Lee couldn't help me out much concerning Mary Childs.

"I'll give her this much. If she was sleeping with Shrimp she was at least being discreet about it," Lee said.

"Wouldn't that stand to reason? Shrimp and Lucy were an item," I said. "It's a time-honored tradition when you're fooling around on the side to try to keep a low profile."

"So I hear," Lee said. She took a long drag on her cigarette. She was forcing the question out of me.

"You've never fooled around on the side?"

Lee chuckled. "The side of what?" She stubbed her cigarette out and shifted on the stool to face me. "My life in a nutshell. Ready? I always wanted to be a singer. That's where I met my husband. Ben. Ben saw me singing in a club when I was not yet twenty and he started chasing after me. We dated, we got engaged, we got married on my twenty-first birth-day. Ben was so thrilled to have a singer for a wife. But he also wanted to begin a family, and when I got pregnant the first time, it began. The singing career . . . you've got to really stick with it. You've got to push it and prioritize it, or it goes away. There are too many others ready to bump you out of the way. The next thing I knew I had two kids I was rais-ing, and the singing career . . ."

She made a sweeping gesture with her hand. Off and out.

"Ben didn't mind at all that I was no longer a singer. Not by that point. Wife and kids, that's what he wanted. I wore the apron for almost twenty years. God, it's hard to believe."

"I guess it happens," I said.

Lee picked up her glass of cranberry juice and soda and tap-tap-tapped a red talon against it. "What happened was that someone poisoned me." When I remained silent, she added, "It was me."

TIM COCKEY

238

"This is none of my business, Lee."

"I know it's not. Doesn't matter. I don't have any reason to be keeping an old secret. Believe me, I spent a lot of my energy keeping that a secret for a lot of years. You have no idea the relief of letting that go."

She pulled out another cigarette and she saw me looking at it. "These are another story," she said. She lit the cigarette, shook out the match but kept it in her fingers. "So here's the joke. I'm drinking too much. I'm unhappy. My kids are grown and heading out on their own. And Ben? Guess what he does?"

"Tell me."

"He starts sleeping with a god damn singer." Lee tossed the match onto the counter and cackled a good one. "Son of a bitch. Some little lounge Lucy down in Orlando, which is where Ben went a lot on business. Can you beat that? That son of a bitch pulls me off the stage to get a family going, then he goes running after what I *used* to be."

"That's pretty twisted."

"I'll say. And you know what? It was the best thing that could have happened to me. I sobered up. Literally. Wised up, too. I left him. I read him the riot act like you wouldn't believe and I walked out the door and climbed back on that silly stage and I really don't care much after that, so long as I can scrape by. Which I do. And to answer your question: No. I have never fooled around on the side. I was loyal to Ben all those years. I guess I'm a very old-fashioned girl."

"When did you leave him?"

"Oh, it's been almost three years now. He made an attempt to patch things up between us, but I wouldn't let him fool me a second time. He said we could go back to the way it was before the kids and everything came along." She laughed. "Can you believe that?"

"So let me be nosy. Has there been anyone in your life since . . . well, in your new life? Or your new old life. Or whatever you're calling this?"

"Nope."

"No one?"

"No one. Zero. Zilch." She took a pull on her cigarette. "Maybe I'm gun-shy, I don't know. Or smart. It's not like I haven't had the opportunities."

"Oh, I'm sure you've had those."

"I just . . . I don't know. I guess I don't need it. Who the hell knows. I'm just so grateful that I was able to save myself," she said. "Praise God these pipes hadn't rusted out completely."

"Lee, you sound fantastic up there. I'm not kidding."

"Thank you, Hitchcock."

"The truth is easy." I clicked my glass to hers.

She tipped her chin at my glass. "So how are you about that stuff?" I paused with the glass midway to my lips.

"This? Oh, I'm fine. I'd say we have an understanding."

Lee frowned. "Don't let me preach. But that sounds awfully close to a relationship."

"Not to worry then. I have solid commitment issues."

She pointed at me with her cigarette hand. "Don't dance with the devil, Hitchcock. Trust me. He'll insist on leading."

"Noted." I put the glass back down. It landed harder than I had intended. I dipped a finger into it, and licked the finger clean. "The end."

Lee pushed a hand through her hair. "I'm beat." She stubbed out her cigarette. "I'm sorry I couldn't help you more about little Miss Mary."

"Don't worry about it."

Lee had a small handbag with her. Little square thing on a leash. She pulled a compact out and flicked it open. She glanced at her face in the compact mirror and snapped it shut without judgment. "I've got to get home. I can't go running around till all hours like you youngsters." She slid heavily off the stool.

I asked, "Can I give you a lift?"

Lee's eyebrows rose like a pair of stretching cats. "If either of us needs a chaperone, Mr. Undertaker, it's not me. Would *you* like a ride? I've got a car."

"I'm fine," I said. "Home is a hop and a skip."

"Then you'd better hop along. Good night then."

Lee flipped her little handbag over her shoulder and stepped past me and down the bar toward the front door. Some people when they're tired, they walk tired. Not Lee Cromwell. There was a kind of indolent swagger. As she reached the door, she gave me one of those over-the-shoulder waves, without looking back.

See? Julia's right. They do always know we're looking.

What the hell. I finished off my drink. The end.

It was nearing one o'clock, but I was too antsy to just go home and crawl into the sack. I was also too loaded with cocktails to locate my chariot. Either that or evil forces were busily moving the car from location to location just in advance of me. I wandered over to Federal Hill and the next thing I knew, I was running up the steps to the top of the hill and back down. I was miserably out of shape. But the oxygen tasted good. I did the run a second time. I continued to feel miserably out of shape. Maybe even more so. I took about five minutes to catch my breath, then I did the jog one more time, slower this time. With feeling. Heavy feeling. My legs were turning to lead. It was like trying to run in a dream. When I reached the bottom of the steps this time there was a uniformed cop standing there with his hands on his hips and the same look on his face that the cop gives Gene Kelly when he's singin' in the rain. It's the look that says, "I could either remain bemused or I could clunk you on the head with my nightstick, what's it gonna be?"

"What do you think you're doing?" he asked.

"I'm running . . . up and down those stairs," I said. I said it somewhat breathlessly. I leaned over and put my hands on my thighs. "There are one hundred and . . . sixty-three of them."

"Okay, why are you doing it?"

I straightened. Somewhat. Best I could manage. "I need the exercise."

"At one in the morning?"

"No time like the future."

"Let me see some ID, please."

(Note: What you're supposed to do when a cop asks you for some ID is give him some ID. It's very very simple.)

"Why?" I asked. Even I could hear the belligerence in my tone.

"ID, please."

"Is there a problem? I'm just running up and down some steps in a public park. Is the park closed?"

He held his hand out. "I'm not going to ask again."

God help me, I always jump on that line. "Well, good." And here's the not-smart move that I added. His hand was still out. I slapped him five.

"Have you been drinking?" the cop asked.

"Yes sir."

"I'm going to ask you again. Let me see some identification."

He had taken a few steps away from me. I guess he was getting himself out of my reach, in case I went nutso on him. I can't say exactly why I was being so uncooperative. I think the Moon was simply rising in my Be-a-Pain-in-the-Ass House. That happens sometimes.

"I don't think I have any."

"What's your name?"

"John D. Rockefeller."

I didn't even see him go for his cuffs. But suddenly they were glinting off the light from the nearest streetlight. "Okay, Mr. Rockefeller, I've got some jewelry for you. Turn around, please."

I did hard time until about eight in the morning. I didn't meet any lifers, just a gaggle of slowly sobering fools like myself. A guy named Jim and I entertained ourselves discussing a jailbreak. We decided that if one of us could slip a spoon from the cafeteria up our sleeve and we started shoveling, we'd have a tunnel out to Calvert Street in about a decade. Jim solved the age-old problem of where to hide the dirt. "We'll eat it as we go." We didn't have any posters of Rita Hayworth handy to hide our escape tunnel, so we volunteered a fat Hispanic man who was snoring in the corner. We'd prop him up against the opening of the hole while we were working on it. Once we were out we would promise to meet every ten years in some tree house bar in the Caribbean and split evenly whatever worldly assets the both of us had amassed to that point. It sounded mostly sound. Among the problems with our plan, though, were that we were not likely to ever make it to any cafeteria to get a spoon—we were going to be released first thing in the morning. We simply didn't have an entire decade to play with.

I came out of prison with a mighty hangover, and with no life skills except those I had gone in with, a facility with putting dead people into the ground. What kind of system is this that will spit a tall, hungover undertaker out onto the street to bury again! Can't something be done about this?

I had a public drunkenness fine of a hundred dollars to pay but only thirty-two dollars and seventy-eight cents in the envelope I was handed upon being sprung. My watch was also in the envelope. It was a pretty cheap watch. Not worth the sixty-seven dollars and twenty-two cents I still needed in order to buy my freedom. I ran a hand over my stubbly jaw. I just couldn't spend another night in stir. Not without that spoon to at least give me some glimmer of hope. I'd go nuts in there. I'd be the tall guy they call Shorty. I'd grow simple and daft. Bookish and docile. A wan Gregory Peck kind of fellow with a colossal potential for greatness and good simply balled up and tamped down and wasted.

Well, I'd have none of that. I ran the roulette wheel of my friends and cohorts . . . and it came up Munger. I was allowed a single phone call.

"Pete? This is Hitchcock. Yeah, look. I'm in the big house but I'm getting sprung if I can scrounge up a hundred bucks. Can you help me out?"

He allowed as how he could.

"Great," I said. "Have Suzie and the baby meet me at the front gate, will ya? Ah begosh, and I've never even laid eyes on the little pipper."

"Are you all right?" Pete wanted to know. A cop nearby was looking at me weirdly as well. I allowed as how I was just keeping my spirits up.

"See you in a bit."

Pete looked like *he* was the one who had spent the night in jail. His jaw was comic-strip blue. He was wearing a light gray suit with mostly horizontal wrinkles. A few diagonals. My jacket was also a mess, since I'd scrunched it up to sit on the holding tank floor while Jim and I had passed our time until dawn. I hadn't slept, so I sort of knew how my face looked. It probably looked like Pete's. A fine pair we made.

"Pete, you and I ought to just go on over to the tracks and hop a damn boxcar. We've got hobo written all over us."

Pete paid the hundred dollars. Free at last.

We went over to Sammy's diner for an oil change and a pile of eggs.

"You look like shit," I told my dining companion.

"Then I look like I feel," Munger mumbled.

THE HEARSE CASE SCENARIO

"Bad night?"

He looked across the table at me as if I had just sprouted aluminum tubes from my ears. "No, Hitch. I spent a most pleasant evening. I dined with the fucking Queen of England and then slept on a feather bed."

"Sounds downright fairy taleish," I said. I refused to be baited.

He grumbled. "It is. I slept in my car."

"Front seat or back?"

"Fuck you."

"Hey, Pete. Tell you what. I'm going to sit over here and work up a big apology for you. But you know what? In the meantime, I'm going to remind you that I just spent the night in *jail*. I feel like an anvil has been dropped on my head. A car seat would've been exactly like a feather bed compared to that place."

Pete grunted. The man was mightily unimpressed.

Our coffees arrived. This was not necessarily a good thing. Mine had a blue-green paisley pattern across the surface. I milked it. Pete took his black (and bruised, too, if it looked like mine). He made a face.

"Christ."

"I'll bet it tastes like you look," I said.

Pete's cup rattled as it landed on the saucer. Cups and saucers. Sammy's touch of class.

"Sewell, is it a death wish, is that it? Do you go out and bait Dobermans for fun? You don't really know me that well. You don't know I won't shove this table down your throat if you say one more god damn smart-ass word."

I took a beat. "Word."

Damned if he didn't mean it. Munger grabbed hold of the little table and shoved it neatly aside and lunged at me.

"*Pete!*"

Munger got me by the lapels and the momentum of his lunge took the two of us to the floor. The table toppled next to us. I immediately grabbed hold of the insane man's wrists and clamped on. Our faces were about three inches apart. A volatile cocktail was coming off the retiring private eye. He was seething.

"What the *hell* are you doing?" I cried. He tried to free his hands, but I wouldn't let him.

"Let go!" he snarled.

"No chance." I thought my eyes were going to burst out of my head, roll across the floor and get swatted by the resident tomcat who was watching us from the door. Sammy had stepped over to us; his greasy black shoes were inches from my nose. I looked up and saw the toothpick dangling from his chapped lips. I also had a sideways view of the dozen or so other diners all pausing to take in the show.

"Let go," Pete growled again.

"Are you going to go for my carotid?"

"Just let go. This is ridiculous."

"I didn't put us here, Pete."

"Sewell." It was less a growl now. It was plaintive. Or would pass for plaintive. I let go of his wrists. My finger marks were tattooed there in white. Sammy stepped back a few steps as Munger and I slowly got up off the floor. Two stubbled bums in nice wrinkled clothes. Plus Pete's shirt was stained from coffee that had tumbled to the floor with him.

"No fighting," Sammy snapped. A little late, I'd say.

"Sorry," Pete murmured as he bent over and righted the table by himself. Our waitress had come over. She and Pete picked up the forks and knives and sugar bowl and everything and put them back on the table. I was busy grooming. The waitress had a wet rag, which she took after the spilled coffee.

"We'll tip generously," I said to Sammy. "My apologies."

"No fighting," Sammy said again. I looked to Pete. He nodded tersely. I turned back to Sammy.

"We're with you." I righted my chair and sat back down. "Could you get us some fresh coffees, please?" I asked the waitress. I added, "New pot? We didn't react too well to that last one."

Like an ocean wave on the ebb flow, the place returned to what passed for normal. Pete sat back down.

"Sorry about that," he muttered.

"Hey, don't mention it. Next time, though, let me know you've got a psychotemper. I'll sit farther away."

"I said I'm sorry."

"And I accept your apology. Doesn't mean what you just did wasn't nuts."

He swatted vainly at the coffee stain on his shirt.

"Susan and I saw a marriage counselor last night," he said, pulling out a cigarette. I shook my head. He placed the cigarette on the table.

"The suit?" I asked.

"I thought I should look respectable." He paused. I think he was waiting for me to bring up a wisecrack. I didn't. "It was a total disaster," he added.

"Do you want to talk about it?"

Munger ran a paw over the back of his neck. He massaged it a little. I knew exactly how he felt. My neck was not the happiest of campers either.

"There isn't much to talk about," he said finally. "Susan told the counselor why she was unhappy with our marriage. She took some of the blame. But she mostly put it on me. She said I was mopey and surly and I didn't pay much attention to her anymore and that I don't seem very interested in what Kevin and Melissa are doing with their lives."

"Mopey and surly? My Pete?"

"Funny. She said I used to put all of my focus into my work, but now I didn't care about my work anymore and that I'm putting all my focus into my vegetable garden." He sneered. "And my rock garden. You should have heard the tone of voice she used for that one."

I had heard it, at his birthday party. Or at least a version of it.

"So what did you say?"

Pete shrugged. He picked up the cigarette and played with it. "I said basically she was right."

"Did you happen to mention to the marriage counselor that your wife was sleeping with someone else?"

"I didn't get to that."

Our new coffees arrived. Some measure of hope showed in their blank black surface. I poured in some creamer and hope vanished. Came up like soiled desert camouflage.

"Pete, how come this whole thing is your fault?"

He gave a large sigh. "Maybe if all that other crap wasn't happening, Susan wouldn't be sleeping with that asshole Roger."

"There are other ways to deal with problems." God, now *I* was sounding like a marriage counselor. "Look, this is none of my business. If it helps at all to talk about it, go ahead. Otherwise we can clam up."

Munger lifted his coffee cup. "Clam up. That's what men do. We don't let out our feelings."

I groaned. "Pete, we're going to have to have that bonfire."

"I didn't get that from a book. The counselor said that."

"Then we'll toss him on the flames."

He corrected me. "Her."

"Her? Pete, they're ganging up on you."

He lowered the cup without having taken a sip. "I know. They beat up on me for an hour and a half. Then I wrote a check for a hundred and fifty bucks for the privilege of having them do it."

"Then what did you do?"

"Then I went out and got stinking drunk. I woke up about five this morning in the front seat of my car. I was parked in front of the place I went to high school."

"Ouch. Pete, that's bad."

"I know."

"Well, I guess you've got to go through it, though."

"Stinks. What the hell is a guy my age doing going through this kind of shit? You don't see everybody else waking up hung over in their car in front of their damn high school. How ridiculous is that? Everyone else is in their home like a normal person."

"Or curled up on a jailhouse floor."

"You don't count."

"Aw thanks, Pete. It's good to know you care."

"You know what I mean."

"Point of fact, Sherlock, I don't."

"I mean I'm talking about a fifty-year-old married man doing the crap I'm doing lately. I didn't see a line of god damn cars outside my high school filled with old men sitting there scratching their heads and wondering what the hell is wrong with them."

"Come on, Pete, we don't know a damn thing about what other people are doing. Don't start being the only guy in the world who's got problems."

"Have you got my kind of problems?"

"Hell, I'm thirty-four. You've got a fifty-year-old's problems."

He scoffed. "Right. I forgot."

"So what are you going to do, Pete? I mean about your marriage? Are you going to try that counselor again?"

"I don't know. Maybe. Right now I'm not even sure if I feel like going back home."

"I can put you up for a while if you need it," I said.

"Thanks." He toasted me with his coffee cup. "I don't think so, though." He managed a grin. "Might land my ass in jail, hanging around with a nut like you."

"Just offering, old man."

"Appreciate it." He took a sip of his coffee. Made a face. "I guess I got to keep on working it out with Susan one way or another."

"Can I make a suggestion?"

"Can I stop you?"

"Tell her to stop sleeping with Roger. Don't ask her, Pete. Tell her. Lay down the law."

He set down his cup and looked at me across the table. "You know why I don't? I figured this out the other day. It's this. I'm screwing up. I'm letting everyone down. At least that's how I'm feeling. My wife and I got no romance. I'm thinking of changing professions but I've got no idea to what. No plan. No prospects. I can't work up any excitement about the future. So I don't know. I guess a part of me thinks I've taken all this shit away from Susan, it's not my place to tell her she can't go out and try to find a little happiness on her own."

I didn't say anything. I let Pete's words sort of hang there. Our breakfast arrived. Our waitress set the plates down warily, as if afraid that one wrong move and we'd send them skittering to the floor. She left, and I smacked the ketchup bottle around until it gave up the goods. I wasn't sure if I had the stomach to stomach my breakfast. I looked over at Munger. He hadn't even picked up his fork.

"I'm totally back-asswards bullshit, aren't I?" he said.

"I didn't want to say."

We got through breakfast without any further fisticuffs. Sammy drifted over to our table about halfway through our meal. He asked, "Everything okay?" I growled under my breath. Pete said everything was fine.

"I went by the TV station yesterday, after we split up," Pete said after Sammy drifted off. "I saw that videotape."

"America's Most Gruesome, wasn't it?"

Munger agreed. "My first thought was to stick that reporter right at the top of the list."

"Of possible killers?"

"That little prick Martin hit me with a shovel like that? Just might ignite my famous psychotemper." He followed this with a smile, though one frighteningly devoid of mirth.

"But you're not actually serious, right? You don't think Greg Snyder had anything to do with killing Shrimp?"

"I don't. It doesn't hurt to keep an open mind, though."

"The infamous 'maybe.' "

Munger nodded like a sage, stubbly, sleep-deprived Buddha.

"Well, speaking of maybes, let me fill you in," I said. I sketched out my scenarios from the night before. Munger didn't get the full Julia-in-French-maid's-outfit treatment. I knew I couldn't do it justice. I trotted pretty quickly to the part where Lucy told me that she knew that Shrimp had been having an affair while they were together.

"You want to guess who?" I asked.

"The Queen of England, I don't know."

"Well, it was someone who worked at the club."

What with the blue jaw and the ghostly pallor, it would be difficult to report that Munger literally paled. But his face definitely went a little slack.

"Lee? Was it Lee Cromwell?"

"Well, in fact, I did see Lee Cromwell last night as well," I said. "I swung by Junior's. But no. It was Mary Childs."

The wavering private eye seemed relieved. "That's your little girl-friend."

"Did you hear what I said? I said that she was sleeping with Shrimp."

"You're not picking the most discriminating women in the world, are you, bub?"

"This isn't about me. You're missing the point."

"I wasn't aware you were making one, Hitch."

"Pete, listen to me, okay? Look at this. Mary Childs is seeing Kit

Grady. Right? He is gaga for her. Thinks she's the girl next door and all that. Which is no great advertisement for the guy's judgment skills, but that's another story. Meanwhile, the girl next store is screwing around with her boss. Mary breaks it off with Grady. Tells him to grow up or buzz off, something kind and gentle like that, I'm sure. Grady doesn't take too kindly to it. He's got all this craziness going on in his life and he's decided that sweet little Mary Childs is his Rock of Gibraltar. She's the steadying influence that he needs. She's Miss Normal." I paused. A portion of the tape of Miss Normal and myself the other evening was playing in my head. God, I thought, if that little gyroscope qualifies as normal, I've got to look the word up again.

Munger was leaning forward on the table. I had his interest. Either that, or his head was too heavy for him to hold up without some help. "Go on."

I continued. "Mary dumps him. Either after she dumps him or maybe before, I don't know which, Kit discovers that his sweet little thing has been boffing Shrimp Martin."

"And so he kills him."

"Hell. There goes my punch line."

Pete sat back in his chair and took a hand to his jaw. I started to say something but he silenced me. "Hold on. Let me run through this a minute."

While Pete pondered, the image of Eleanor Martin popped into my head, and I took the time-out to consider the story that she had told me about Pete and her husband. The horrific chain of events that had left two young boys dead, Dan Wisner dead and Pete Munger devastated. I assumed, though Mrs. Martin had not expressly said so, that this was what had triggered Pete's decision to quit being a lawyer. I didn't know Pete Munger too terribly well, but I'd had glimpses already of his temper. I could well imagine a dark rage from this guy, especially in the sort of morally ambiguous no-win situation that Eleanor Martin had described. Two dead boys and a best friend who was not only responsible for the deaths but for whose best legal defense Munger himself was responsible. I could well imagine Pete's anguish on learning that his best friend had made a calculated gamble in installing that faulty part. The trial was nearly over, and Munger had already done his level best to defend his old buddy. His only recourse had been to mete out his own punishment on Dan Wisner, to read him the riot act of all riot acts and essentially give him no avenue of escape from the despair he was already feeling for what he had done to those two boys. Basically, to hound him into taking his own life.

Pete was giving me a funny look. If mind reading was among his private-eye skills, then we were in for an awfully uncomfortable conversation.

"It's a thought," Pete said at last.

"What's a thought?"

The funny look had a sequel. "Your thought, Einstein. That Kit Grady killed Martin."

Oh, *that* thought. "It's a thought," I said.

"I just said that," Munger grumbled. "You know, you can be a pain in the ass to talk to sometimes."

I corrected him. "Talk with."

Good Lord, I thought he was going for his gun. Turned out to be his wallet. "Let's get the hell out of here." We paid up for our scrumptious crap, left the big tip I had promised and vamoosed. Outside, we paused on the sidewalk.

"Why don't we grab an empty bottle of Irish Rose and find a corner and put out a hat," I suggested. "Rack up some quarters while we've got the look."

Pete shook his head. "Something else."

My car was still parked somewhere in Federal Hill. I couldn't immediately recall where I had left it. It was probably festooned with parking tickets by now. We sauntered off to Pete's car. It turned out to be an old Impala. White. Not a speck of rust that I could see. Immaculate. Clearly the product of extraordinary care and buffing.

"Time capsule?" I asked.

"Get in."

"Let me do the talking," Munger said as we waited for the elevator. I nodded. Munger gave me a dubious squint, adding, "I guess that's expecting an awful lot."

"You tell me to shut up, I'll shut up."

The elevator arrived. "Shut up," Munger chuckled and stepped into the elevator. I smiled, gave him the finger and followed.

We got off on the ninth floor. The place looked like it hadn't seen upkeep since the days of Eisenhower. Faded red carpeting. Dingy shark-skin wallpaper. Conical wall sconces giving off small wedges of yellowish light. Pockmarked stucco for a ceiling. The window at the far end of the hallway was frosted and crisscrossed with chicken wire. A smell like stale peppermint—or flesh grown old—permeated the air. In all, it felt like a nice place to come hang yourself.

We stopped at a door marked 9-F. The miniature colonial knocker was actually a buzzer. Or to be more specific, a grinder. That was the sound it made when Pete lifted the little handle. Pete placed his thumb over the view hole. He told me later that there was no specific reason he did that. It was just a habit he had picked up.

I heard sounds from within the apartment, and then the door opened a crack, only as far as the inside chain would allow it. The midslice of a man's face filled the crack. Dirty blond mustache. Dark, deep-set eyes.

The mustache moved. "What is it?"

Munger answered. "Mr. Kincaid?"

"What do you want?"

Pete had produced his wallet, which he opened and held up to the crack for the man to inspect.

"I'm Pete Munger. Munger and Associates. We're a private investigating firm. I was wondering if you would give us a few minutes."

The man peered at Pete's wallet, then at Pete. I got the one-second glance.

"What about?" His question was directed at Pete.

"The matter of Kelly Bishop," Munger said.

"I'm through with that matter," the man said sharply. There was a definite snideness in the way he said "that matter." Pete continued on in a polite, even manner.

"Yes sir, I'm aware of that, of course. And I'm terribly sorry to be bothering you. I'm sure that the last thing you want to do is talk about this. But it's very important."

The man hesitated. This time he gave me a longer consideration. Maybe he felt he was being ganged up on.

"This is Mr. Sewell," Pete said. "My associate. We really do apologize for the intrusion. This will only take a few minutes."

I wondered whether Pete was trying on purpose to sound like a TV cop. Maybe the thinking is that people like to hear something familiar. Or maybe there's just no better way to say this stuff.

The man was remaining wary. "I really have nothing to say. It's all on records and transcripts. You can go read them yourself. I'd really just as soon be left alone if you don't mind." He started to close the door, but a scuffed brown shoe was wedged in the doorway. Attached to the shoe was Pete Munger. "*Do* you mind?" the man asked testily.

"I'm trying to locate Kelly Bishop's killer, Mr. Kincaid," Pete said. "I'd really appreciate your help."

This brought a laugh from the man. Or rather, a snort. "Is that right? You mean the guy who got a six months' head start to cover his tracks while they dragged *me* through the mud? That's the killer you're looking for?"

Pete nodded. "Yes sir."

The man made a show of looking over his shoulder, back into the apartment, then he turned back to Munger. "Well, he's not here. That's one place you can cross off your list. Good luck."

Deftly, he kicked the toe of Munger's shoe, knocking it out of the way, and swiftly closed the door. Pete's move was not as deft, but was no less swift. Before the guy had a chance to drop the deadbolt, Munger grabbed hold of the doorknob, twisted it and simultaneously slammed his other hand against the door as hard as he could. The door flew open and Munger stepped inside. The man had reeled backwards; he was catching his balance against a small table in his entryway.

"What the hell do you think you're doing!"

Munger barked over his shoulder at me, "Get in." I did, and I closed the door behind me. Pete turned back to the man. "I asked politely."

The man's voice rose an octave. "I'm calling the police! You can't just break in here like this!"

"Wrong on the second count and I don't really give a damn about the first," Pete said matter-of-factly.

"What do you want?"

"I told you that already, Mr. Kincaid. I'm trying to get some information about Kelly Bishop. You're the last known person to have seen her alive. I thought I'd start with you."

The man's eyes had gone to hard red beads. "The last person who saw Kelly Bishop alive was the person who killed her."

"Correct. I said you are the last *known* person. That's why you were arrested in the first place."

The man relented at that point. His anger dropped, along with his shoulders. At least I thought his anger had dropped. But suddenly his arm jerked and he took a swipe at a tasseled lamp that was on the small table. Clean hit. The thing flew off the table and into the living room, landing sideways on the rug. The lightbulb burst in a *pop*! *Now* his anger softened. Kincaid's lamp-swatting move had left his arm in one of those walk-this-way gestures. He played it, turning an unpleasant sneer on his two guests.

"Won't you please come in?"

• • •

Once upon a time, five months ago to be exact, Robert Kincaid had been professor of political science at Johns Hopkins University. Tenure-track. Trusting his own assessment, my report is that the guy had been a good professor, popular with his peers, well liked by most of his students (graded on a curve; students always like that). Kincaid was only in his late thirties, a nice-enough-looking man, wavy blond hair, prominent nose, Sundance Kid kind of mustache, intelligent eyes. There was a touch of adenoids in his voice; it gave his speech a slightly affected sound, a trace of intellectual smugness. Even so, when relaxed and in his element I could imagine the man bringing forth a quite pleasant smile from behind his mustache, and an engaging and likable demeanor.

However, sitting in the living room of apartment 9-F, discussing his relationship with the late Kelly Bishop, Robert Kincaid was not in his element. The dingy apartment aside (Kincaid's more spacious university apartment had been taken back concurrent with the professor's strongly encouraged "voluntary" leave of absence so that he could concentrate on his trial), the former professor was not really accustomed to lecturing on the matter of his involvement with young murder victims. Kincaid's eyes had remained dark and wary for quite a while as he spoke. His habit of running his thumb and forefinger down his mustache suggested a calculation and caution. He had appeared to be choosing his words carefully. Like a lecturer working without his notes. Better still, a former murder suspect who has sussed out the importance of planting one foot firmly before even considering lifting the other. As he moved farther along in his story he began to relax somewhat. His shoulders loosened, his hands became more expressive, he went less often to the mustache. I gradually got the feeling that in a way, Kincaid was working out the lecture that he now knew he would be giving for years to come; not to a classroom anymore, but to whatever audience might appear in front of him at any particular moment with an interest in "Hey, so just what *did* happen back then with that coed, anyway?" Like it or not, this was to be Robert Kincaid's story for life. Accused of murder. Set free after a difficult trial. Career decimated. Kincaid would likely never be lecturing in front of a classroom again. Still, lecturing was his skill. Stacking point upon point. Forming his narrative. Holding off on questions until the end.

Translation: Once he had gotten started, the guy wanted to talk.

Munger had warmed him up. After the violence of Pete's slamming open the door and then Kincaid's frustrated swipe at the table lamp, the two seemed to have achieved some sort of common ground. I was clearly odd man out. Munger's crackdown in the lobby that I "shut up" was bearing fruit. I was a six-foot-three fly on the wall.

And what I heard—or at least what I thought I heard at first—was that Robert Kincaid was only human after all. Flesh and blood. Male variety. Flawed like the rest of us. Accustomed in his teaching career to the excessive attentions of some of his female students, Kincaid admitted to several times allowing himself to cross that line. He freely admitted that he flirted with his students. Mildly, he insisted. Well within "the accepted norm," whatever the hell that was supposed to mean. Teaching is a matter of forming relationships, he explained. The look, the laugh, the innuendo . . . these are all a part of what can go into a relationship. As well, it would seem, as the occasional bump-and-boff back at the Kincaid bachelor pad. The passionate educator driving home a point to one of his more earnest charges.

"We're all adults at this juncture," Kincaid said. He was relaxed now, pretty much in lecture mode. Munger and I were sitting in twin chairs in front of him, hanging on his words. "I was teaching graduate as well as undergraduate level and I was strict about my boundaries with the under-grads. It's highly inappropriate to feed on these kids who are fresh from high school. It's wrong. Plain and simple. Plenty of other professors ignore that fact, mind you. But I was never one of them. My several . . . involvements with my female students were always with those on the graduate level. Consenting adults. That's why . . . that's why this thing with Kelly was so *stupid*." He emphasized its stupidity by slamming his fist into his palm. Pete and I registered the same thought; I could tell just by the slight shift Munger made in his posture. Kincaid's fist-slamming move was a fake. A cheap theatric intended to give weight to his bogus self-criticism. He didn't feel that it was stupid. He simply had not gotten away with it.

"This was my single transgression," Kincaid continued. "I broke my own rule. Kelly was a senior, mind you. She was twenty-one. Legally her own person, of course. An adult. Responsible for her own decisions. But I know we're not talking legality here. We're talking boundaries and we're talking ethics. And I freely admit, in this case, I ignored them both."

He paused at this point and let his gaze travel around the apartment. The place was no great shakes. Dim. It shared that same stale smell with the hallway. "It doesn't matter that they didn't find me guilty of murder. She's dead, and I was in court testifying to sleeping with her. One of my students. It rubs off on you. I could make a big stink and hire some more lawyers who I can't afford and sue to get my position back. But I don't have the fight in me. I'm tainted. I slept with the cheerleader and the cheerleader got herself killed. That's as far as people want to see it. Now I'm an evil man. Give me a break . . . the *cheerleader*."

He paused, stroking his mustache slowly again and traveling, it seemed, a rather bumpy trip back down memory lane. Munger and I rode out the silence, which Robert Kincaid finally ended with a large sigh.

"You've seen pictures of Kelly, right?" he asked. Munger spoke for the both of us.

"Why?"

Robert Kincaid had suddenly abandoned his steady lecturer's tone. In fact, this was when I got my glimpse of the smile behind the mustache. At once pleasant and not so pleasant. He rose from his chair and went for his desk in the corner. "She was fucking amazing," he said, pulling open a drawer. "Here. Look."

Munger and I left Robert Kincaid's apartment roughly a half hour after our brusque entrance. I had muttered five words the entire time. Right there at the end. They were, "You're a piece of work." Five and a half if you count the contraction.

Munger and I said nothing to each other in the elevator. Pete's call. I could see in his expression that he would have silenced me if I had opened my mouth. Once we got back outside, Pete stopped at the bottom step to the apartment building and looked back up at it, seeking Robert Kincaid's window.

"That is one sick puppy," he said heavily.

"Do you think he killed her?"

Pete was still scanning the windows. "I don't know. I don't think so."

"But those photographs," I said.

Pete quit the building and looked over at me. "A lot of people take dirty pictures, Hitch. Believe me. I've been in this business long enough. I've seen all that before. It's just what some people do. It doesn't make the guy a killer."

"I know it doesn't. But he didn't have to show them to us. I mean, how creepy was that?"

Munger agreed. "That was plenty creepy."

"It was like he was dying to show them to someone."

"He was." Munger reached into his pocket and pulled out a pack of cigarettes. He fumbled one from the pack. "I don't know how he managed to deep-six those pictures from the D.A. Snapshots like that would've sure as hell jazzed up that guy's trial, you can count on that." Pete lit his cigarette and took a great big pleasurable drag. "He's free now. He can't be tried again. My take? I think you're right. He's been *dying* to show those photos to someone."

"You're going to brag about your big conquest right after you've been acquitted of her *murder*? You're going to flash her picture around like that?"

"Well, you're not going to do it before you're acquitted."

"But why at all? Jesus."

We went over to the curb and got into Pete's car. He rolled his window partway down. I was trying to square the photographs I had just seen with the squeaky clean cheerleader snapshot that had been the murder story's popular visual. I was having a difficult time of it.

"I hope that girl's parents never get a look at those," Pete muttered. "Send your girl off to college and she ends up sleeping with her professor and posing for pictures like that?"

"Ends up dead," I reminded him.

"That, too."

"Maybe it's blame-the-victim syndrome," I said. "I mean, the pictures. That girl's murder has ruined Kincaid's life. You heard him. He's finished as a teacher. Like it or not, Kelly Bishop's always going to be the most important thing that ever happened to him. Maybe he needs those damn pictures to remind him how this all came to pass."

Munger sent a stream of smoke out the window. "Sick pup."

"Like you said."

"Like I said."

"But you don't think he killed her," I said again.

"What do you think?"

"If you believe his story, he and Kelly went to Shrimp's to celebrate her birthday, they got in a small fight, your basic lover's quarrel, and then they made up and went back to his place. They rolled in the hay for a while, and the last he saw her was when she left. About an hour later, he says."

"My question is, do you buy it?"

I shrugged. "The jury did."

"The jury was confronted with evidence of Kelly Bishop's having struggled with her assailant. The blood type and the DNA from the skin they found under her fingernails didn't match Kincaid's. They had to hold to the evidence. And she was seen leaving by a neighbor in Kincaid's building. Alone."

"He could have chased after her," I said.

"The neighbor said he didn't. A classic busybody."

"According to Kincaid."

Pete sighed. "According to trial testimony, too." Pete stuck the key into the ignition, but he didn't turn it. He sat there, tapping his fingers on the steering wheel.

"What were you hoping for, Pete?" I asked.

Pete leaned forward slightly and looked up again at Kincaid's building. "I don't know. I'm still thinking about Martin taking that TV guy apart. You learn not to like coincidence in this job. Four days after Martin beat the crap out of that guy with a shovel, Martin was dead. I still want to know why."

A thought suddenly occurred to me. The moment it hit me I realized that it should have occurred to me earlier, but it hadn't. All of a sudden there it was, floating in front of me like a helium billboard, complete with bells and whistles and flashing neon. I turned to Munger.

"Pete, do you think *Shrimp Martin* killed that girl?" Hearing the words out loud, especially coming from my own mouth, nearly took my next breath away. "Jesus Christ, is *that* what's going on here? Was Shrimp murdered because he killed Kelly Bishop?"

Pete turned to me with a rueful look. He held a steady gaze before he answered.

"Maybe."

I sat back in my seat. "Holy shit. A *revenge* killing? That would mean that someone had figured out that Shrimp killed the girl."

"More than that," Pete said.

"What do you mean?"

He tossed his cigarette out the window. "It would mean not just that someone figured out that Martin killed her. It would mean that whoever it was, it was someone who cared a lot. A whole hell of a lot."

Had there been a third person in the car with us, I have to assume they would've laughed. Not at what Munger or I had just said. There was nothing at all funny about that. But they'd have laughed at what we did next. With a precision you couldn't get if you practiced for weeks, my head and Munger's head swiveled perfectly in synch, as if on a single neck . . . and we both looked back up at Robert Kincaid's building.

CHAPTER 19

Pete and I drove over to the campus of Johns Hopkins University. We parked near the tennis courts and walked down along the main campus drive to the administration building. "This one's going to be female," Munger had said to me as we took the turn off University Parkway. "I won't make you shut up this time. I know how much that would kill you."

The woman manning the desk at the administration building didn't want to cooperate at first. Pete finally asked to see someone a little higher up the administrative food chain, and a Mr. Rodriguez came out from his office. Munger and Rodriguez shadowboxed a little, and Pete came away with the information he needed. Rodriguez disappeared into his office, then reemerged a minute later and scribbled down something on a piece of paper and handed it to Pete, who thanked him and shook his hand.

"Did he give you a hall pass?" I asked as we came out of the building.

Munger looked up in the direction of the sun. "I could use a drink."

"And I could use an all-expense-paid trip to Tahiti. Now back to our regular programming. What exactly are we doing?"

"We're going to see if we can find out if the Bishop girl knew Shrimp Martin." Pete pointed off to the left. "Let's go."

It's an established fact that college students get younger in direct proportion to the number of years elapsed since a person has left college themselves. My Frostburg days ended more than a dozen years ago. The formula was about right. The boys and girls tossing Frisbees on the main quad at Hopkins or sitting pensively off by themselves reading in the grass looked to me easily a decade younger than I know I must have looked when I was a student back in Cumberland. Everyone here was clean cut and well groomed. Not an exotic in the bunch. No bohemian wanna-bes. What, I ask, is the problem with kids today?

I followed Munger to Gilman Hall. It was a brick building with white columns. Rodriguez must have given him detailed directions. To have simply said, "It's the brick building with white columns" on the Hopkins campus would have been like saying, "The person you're looking for is the one with the two ears and the nose." We entered the building, the hallway was markedly cooler than the outside. Pete and I parked ourselves outside a classroom on the first floor. We could see the lecturer through the door's glass. A short man with hair like Larry of the Three Stooges and a terrifically thick pair of glasses. He was ranging back and forth in front of his desk like an animal in a cage at the zoo. He was apparently soliciting feedback from his students. The gesture he made to call on them was identical to the one he would use if he were trying to fetch something down from a high shelf.

"Medieval lit," Munger muttered to me. "Whatever that is."

We waited another five minutes and the class broke up. Munger was through the door before I knew it. He went directly to the professor and showed him the note from Rodriguez. The man nodded, shoved his glasses back up on his nose and called out above the din of skidding chairs and chattering students.

"Tricia Novack!"

I came into the room and joined the two. Seconds later, a young girl joined us, clutching her books and notebook to her chest, her eyes darting from face to face to face. She was large-boned (okay, she was slightly overweight), olive-skinned, with dark eyes, heavy eyebrows and black hair in a thick braid that ran down nearly to her waist. T-shirt, plaid vest and jeans. Munger introduced himself and introduced me. Mr. Munger. Mr. Sewell.

"Is there a place we could talk?" he asked her.

"This is about Kelly, isn't it?" the girl said.

"Yes, it is."

Her mouth drew a grim line. "You're never more popular than when you're dead," she said with an air of resignation. "Let's just go outside."

The three of us went outside and arranged ourselves on the front steps.

"You were Kelly Bishop's roommate, isn't that right?" Munger started off.

"Yes."

"You were her roommate at the time she was murdered?"

"Yes."

"I know that you've answered most of these questions a hundred times already, Miss Novack. I'm sorry to have to repeat them. I just want to make sure I have everything clear."

She nodded that she understood. Munger glanced at me. I got his message. She was clamming up. He didn't want that. My turn.

"Can I call you Trish?" I asked. "I'm Hitch, by the way. The 'Mister' thing doesn't work too well with me."

"Sure," she said. "Why not."

"Trish, I'm sure you know that Robert Kincaid was acquitted a few weeks ago in the murder of your roommate."

"Of course I know that."

"Would it be rude of me to ask you if you think Kincaid did— If he killed Kelly?"

She didn't answer immediately. I'm certain that she had an instant opinion on the subject; she was simply deciding if she felt like sharing it. She did. "I don't think he did it," she said.

"Was that your opinion before the verdict?" I waved my hand. "No. Forget that. Before the trial? Have you felt all along that Kincaid was the wrong guy?"

She had taken hold of her braid—brought it around front just above her waist—and was absently brushing her fingertips with it. "Kelly was really into him," she said. "I mean, she wasn't in love or anything. She wasn't stupid. Bob Kincaid was . . . well, you know, he's kind of sexy. At least, a lot of the girls think so. Kelly knew she sure wasn't the first student to sleep with him or anything, but you know, she liked it. She said he was a lot of fun."

"Did you know that she posed for him?" I asked. "Photographs?"

Munger blurted, "Don't talk about that."

"Too late," I said. Munger made an effort, only somewhat successful, to swallow his anger. I turned back to Trish. Maybe she saw the trace of mirth on my face. Red-letter day for Mr. Sewell. I had just learned good cop bad cop.

Trish shook her head. It looked a little like she was controlling her head electronically, via her braid. "I don't know anything about that." She paused, looked down at the grass, over toward a tree, then back at me. "But it doesn't surprise me."

Munger nudged me with his foot. "Why not?" I asked.

"I liked Kelly, okay?" Trish said defensively. "That's important. I want you to know that. We were good friends, especially junior year. That's when we decided to be roommates senior year. I really liked her. She was always a lot of fun. She was always wanting to do things. Have fun. Find a party. Get in a car and just drive. And she was also a great student. I don't know how she did it. Well, she was smart is how she did it. Kelly could be out all night and raise all sorts of hell and still pull off a big exam the next day."

"A party girl," Munger said.

"She was a cheerleader in high school. I mean, head cheerleader. I'm sure you've seen that picture. Top of the pyramid." Trish looked down at her hands and released her braid. She looked back up at us, scanned both Munger and me. "That's what she used to always say about her high school days and her cheerleading. 'Top of the fucking pyramid.' "

"I take it that's a direct quote," I said.

Trish flicked her head. "Yes."

"Did she do any cheerleading here?" Munger asked.

"At Hopkins? I don't think so." She laughed. "That might be cool in Ohio and in high school and everything, but when you get to college? Different story. Listen, a lot of people change when they get to college. That's part of what it's all about, right?"

"You're saying that Kelly changed once she started here?" Pete asked.

Trish looked at the detective as if she were trying to spot the leak. "I didn't know her back in Ohio, but yeah, I think it's safe to say. That photograph they blasted everywhere when she was killed? Old news. Kelly cut her hair halfway through freshman year. She bagged that whole cutesy look. I mean, she was still real pretty, she could get any guy she wanted."

"Did she?" Pete asked.

"Did she what?"

"What you just said. Was Miss Bishop promiscuous?"

I felt embarrassed for Pete. He was clearly uncomfortable. Trish looked at me as if wanting to know if she had to answer the question. "We're not asking you to name names," I said. "Nothing like that. We're just trying to come up to speed."

"People really love to blame the victim," Trish said. "Especially when they're not around to defend themselves."

"It's nothing like—"

"Then what is it? Sure, Kelly liked to have fun. Big deal. Did she sleep around? Is that what you're trying to find out? You've got one name. Bob Kincaid. You're the ones who say you've got dirty pictures of her. I guess you've already made up your own minds."

"Trish—"

Pete cut me off. "We're trying to get a bead on this girl," he said wearily. "According to trial testimony, Kelly Bishop was portrayed as the girl next door. Cheerleader. Bright and bubbly. Good student."

Trish scrambled up off the step. "A girl likes to have a good time, decides she's not going to be tied down to one boyfriend . . . then what? She's asking for it? She deserved to be killed?"

Pete said, "Of course not."

"So then what's this all about? Kincaid was let off. The killer's still out there. I've told all this shit to the police a long time ago. What are you two looking for?" She spun on Munger. "And so what if Kelly liked to have a good time? I mean, come on."

Munger snapped back. "You think sleeping with your professor and posing for nude pictures constitutes having a 'good time'? Is that what it takes these days to have a good time? Did it ever—"

"Pete!"

"—occur to you that you might—"

"*Pete!*"

Munger glowered. "What?"

"Shut up," I said. He opened his mouth to protest, but I already had my warning finger in the air. "Miss Novack doesn't need to waste her time talking to us at all. She has been kind enough as it is. Let me just get to the point."

Munger made no effort to disguise his desire to remove my head from my neck. Without surgery. Blood rose up in his face. But he held his tongue. I turned back to the dead girl's roommate. "Your friend's body was found behind a nightclub called Shrimp's. That's the name of the guy who owned the club," I said to her. "Shrimp Martin. This guy Shrimp . . . how do I put this. He fancied himself something of a swinger himself. A party guy, I guess. A lot of fun, if you happen to like that kind of fun. Which, you've just told us, your roommate did."

Trish nodded. I went on.

"Trish, do you have any knowledge of, or even any maybes, about whether or not Kelly ever knew this Shrimp character? Had she ever been to the club before, to your knowledge? Or mentioned him at all? Anything?"

"No."

"You sound awfully certain," I said.

"I am. I remember real clear the night Kelly was killed. I've gone over it in my head a hundred times. It was her birthday. She told me that Kincaid was taking her out for her birthday. She was really looking forward to it. She said he was taking her to this club down in Canton. This jazz place. She'd heard about it, but she had never been there."

"She said that. Specifically."

"Yes. For a fact. That was her first time ever down there." She made a grim face. "First and last."

I thanked her for talking with us. As she gathered up her books I asked her, "Any wild guesses, Trish?" The girl pursed her lips. She looked down at Munger and me.

"It was someone she knew," she said. "I'm positive of that."

"And why are you so positive?"

"No reason. But I just know it. Kelly knew a lot of people. Somehow . . . somehow I just know it wasn't random. You run around with as many people as Kelly did, at some point one of them's going to turn out to be rotten. I guess those are the odds."

Pete got up off the steps. "Miss Novack, I'd like you to consider that perhaps if your friend had not insisted on always having so much 'fun,' she might be alive today."

The coed absorbed Pete's words, then looked past him and addressed me. "This guy's got a teenaged daughter, doesn't he?"

● ● ●

"I need to shower, die and be reborn," I said to Munger as we got back to his car. "Who knew that spending a night in jail could take so much out of you."

Of course Munger himself wasn't looking too terribly refreshed either. He also wasn't too terribly happy with me for having taken over the questioning of Kelly Bishop's roommate.

"Did you have fun just now?" he asked as he pulled out onto University Parkway.

"As a matter of fact, yes."

Munger hadn't expected that sort of answer and it seemed to shut him down. I thought over the chat that Munger and I had just had with Trish Novack. Our main purpose in seeking out Kelly Bishop's roommate had been to see if we could determine whether the late coed had at any time prior to her last night on earth been in contact with Shrimp Martin. It was a stretch we were making. Shrimp murders Kelly Bishop; Robert Kincaid gets arrested and put on trial; Kincaid is freed but his life is in a shambles; somehow he knows that the person responsible for all of this is Shrimp Martin, so he seeks him out and kills him. That was our fantasy.

"Why would Kincaid murder Shrimp?" I said out loud. Pete, guiding the car in a sort of autopilot, was in his own reverie.

"Huh?"

"Kincaid. Why in the world would he go to the trouble, not to mention the risk, of killing Shrimp? According to our little hunch, if Kincaid knew that Shrimp murdered Kelly, wouldn't he have been singing that song loud and long these past six months?"

"Maybe he knew he couldn't prove it. Maybe killing Martin was the only way he could set things right," Pete said.

"You buy that? I mean really? Especially after what this girl just told us?"

"All she said was that she wasn't aware of the Bishop girl's already knowing Martin. It's still possible that she did. Roommates don't know everything about each other."

"It's weak," I said. And when Munger made no response, I added, "Then there's Arthur. If Kincaid was getting back at Shrimp, why kill Arthur?"

Pete's eyes were glued to the road. Or maybe burning a hole right through it. A line of scorched pavement running off behind the impeccable white Impala. It was difficult to tell. "I know," he said heavily. "Then there's Arthur."

Pete cruised the streets of Federal Hill until we spotted my spiffy green car. He pulled over to the curb and I got out. "That's nice," Pete said, as I cleared the windshield of a parking ticket, a flyer for a moving company and an announcement of a blow-out sale. "Valiant. Sixty-three? Sixty-four?"

"Sixty-three," I said. "Push-button automatic."

"You're kidding. God, I remember those."

"Old man like you probably remembers the horse and buggy."

"If I weren't still hung over I'd make you eat those words."

"Didn't stop you trying earlier," I noted.

"Right. Look." He cleared his throat. "I'm sorry about that, really. I just . . . shit, I don't know what's going on. It's a total mess."

"Let me ask you something," I said, stepping over to his car. "Do you think what with all the pressure you're under right now that you really ought to be running around trying to track down a murderer? I mean, I know this was my idea, but . . ."

Munger squinted up at me. "Hell, I need the distraction." He had pulled out a cigarette. He lit it and tossed the match out the window. It landed next to my shoe.

"So now what?" I asked.

"If you think you can keep control of yourself, I'd suggest you go have a talk with your little girlfriend," he said.

"Mary?"

"She hasn't been straight with you. She didn't let on that she had been seeing Martin and that Kit Grady might've had that as a reason to be a little unreasonable about him. Or for that matter, whether she played you like a fiddle the other night. Girl didn't tell you any of that. I think it'd be a good idea to find out why not."

"Sounds sound."

He was grinning like Huck Finn. "That is, if you think you can control yourself."

"Pete, why is that really an issue one way or the other?"

"You're not thinking, are you?"

"What's that supposed to mean?"

"Mary Childs. Where was she when Shrimp Martin was killed?"

I had to give the question a few seconds of thought. "Hell. She was right there. She was at the hospital."

"Uh-huh . . ."

"You don't think *Mary* killed Shrimp? God damn, Pete, you're getting completely grassy-knolly on me here. Who *don't* you suspect?"

Munger answered, "I've had a little more experience than you with people who lie and cheat and sometimes kill. You're not used to watching your back. I'm just trying to get you to be a little more aware."

"Thank you, Pete."

"Don't mention it." He tossed his cigarette away. I was noticing that he only smoked his cigarettes less than halfway down. I've known that to be a quitting trick. Or rather, a prelude to the attempt.

"You didn't go home all last night," I said. "Is that going to be a problem with Susan?"

Munger thought a moment before answering. "I guess if it's not, then *that's* a problem."

I drove home and took a long hot shower, followed by half as long a cold one. Alcatraz was nearly all the way through his running-away-from-home letter, but like the loyal friend he is, he agreed to chuck it in exchange for half a can of SPAM and a pee-walk. There was a message on my phone machine from Hank Mackey. Mackey said that there would be a pair of tickets to the basketball game tonight at the Will Call window under my name if I wanted them. "It's not a bribe, Mr. Sewell. It's a thank you." I checked my social calendar for the evening. Lo and behold, a rare night off. The game started at nine. Late, I gathered, because of the television audience. I asked my dog what he thought of basketball. He chose not to share his opinion, so I phoned Pete's number. His wife answered.

"Is Pete there?" I asked.

There was a pause. "Who is this please?"

"This is Hitchcock Sewell. Is this Susan or Melissa?"

She laughed. "Very cute. It's Susan. And no, Pete isn't here. In fact, I haven't seen him all day. I have no idea where he is." She added, "Or if he's alive or dead."

"He's alive," I said. "I was just with him. He must still be on his way home." The fact was, since dropping me off, Pete had had more than enough time to get home. I didn't mention that. "Pete was good enough to help me out of a little trouble this morning," I explained.

"Pete is a kind man," Susan Munger said. I couldn't tell for certain, but she sounded pretty facetious. I went ahead and put my foot in it.

"Look, Pete's told me that you two are going through a rough patch," I said. "I'm sorry."

She laughed again. Sort of. Not exactly a needle-twitcher on the mirth meter. "Is that what he calls it? A rough patch?"

"That might be my term."

"Well, I think that would be an understatement. Pete stormed out of here last night. Not for the first time either. You didn't happen to be with him last night, did you?"

"We hooked up this morning."

"I see."

I wasn't certain what she saw, but I doubted that it was a vision of her husband curled up on the seat of his car drunkenly counting sheep. "Did you two by any chance meet in high school?" I asked.

"No we didn't. Why do you ask?"

"No reason." So much for Pete's Memory Lane being named after his wife. "Pete's been with me all day," I said. "We've been running around town questioning people."

"Oh? Well, that's interesting. Are you two working a case together? Because Pete told me that he was quitting the private-eye business. At least, that was the latest. But I know he's been working on something lately that he's decided not to share with me."

I didn't want to be a part of this conversation any longer, but I felt the need to defend Munger. "I think Pete is trying to work out some demons."

"Do any of them happen to look like me?" Before I could respond, she went on. "That was stupid. Look, I shouldn't go on like this. It's a two-way street, I know that. I haven't exactly been the angel wife in all this. It's very complicated."

I had an idea. "Listen," I said. "I've got two tickets to the Blues game for tonight. That's why I was calling, to see if Pete felt like going. But maybe the two of you should go."

"That's good of you to offer, but I think I'll pass on that. I could care less for basketball."

"I was actually just thinking of the two of you doing something together."

"Well . . . no. It would be too artificial. We'd have a miserable time. Thanks for the thought, though. You two go." She laughed. "God, maybe I've got this whole thing wrong for all I know. Maybe the two of you will be out there running after cheerleaders."

"I won't speak for myself," I said, "but I don't see your husband as the sis-boom-ba type."

"You can say that again."

I didn't. Instead, we hung up. I turned from the phone and addressed my dutiful dog.

"Bleh."

Alcatraz and I went out to do dog's business. I swung by the dress shop where Lucy works, but Dorothy Slinghoff told me that she had sent Lucy home already. "People were coming in just to look at her. It was too distracting." Dorothy also showed me one of the hideous blouses that Lucy had ordered. It had wing collars and a nasty pink floral print. I bought it. "You're too loyal to that girl, Hitchcock," Dorothy admonished me as she folded the shirt in tissue paper.

We stopped in at Julia's gallery. I dropped the blouse on the counter. My last glimpse of my ex-wife the night before had been a hazy one of Julia in her ooh-la-la outfit, standing atop one of the cartoon couches at La Fromagerie, brandishing her gendarme's cape matador-style while a small bald man in a Nehru jacket made horns of his pinkies and was charging the cape, either giggling unstoppably or suffering a severe case of hiccups. I suffered a minor panic as Alcatraz and I entered the gallery. A small hairless creature was that very instant sliding down the fireman's pole from Julia's studio and apartment upstairs. My blood iced; I thought it was the giggling man. Julia's business is her own business, but that doesn't preclude me from first-impressions-are-everything, knee-jerk value judgments. However, it wasn't the giggling bald man. It was Heather. Krishna Dave's girlfriend. She came down the pole and then stood beside it as Krishna Dave followed after. Krishnas were dropping from the sky.

"Hi, Hitch," said Dave.

Heather nodded solemnly.

"Hey kids, what brings you here?" I asked. "Where's Squeak?"

"Squeak's with me." This was Julia. Her face appeared in the pole hole. She was kneeling on the floor. She held the little Krishna baby aloft so that I could see it. "We'll be right down."

"After I saw you the other day, I realized how long it's been since I'd been back down here," Dave said. "Heather and I decided to take a sentimental journey." He allowed his gaze to travel the gallery walls. "Little Julia's doing some kind of okay for herself, isn't she. Man, have you checked out the prices she's got on this stuff?"

"Julia's grande fromage, Dave."

Dave's shiny head was spinning this way and that. "No shit, Sherlock. She's not just for breakfast anymore, that's for sure."

Julia and Squeak joined us. They had come down the spiral staircase. Seeing them make the descent, a thought occurred to me. I filed it away. In honor of her guests, I guessed, Julia was wearing a small parachute, a togalike collection of folds and tucks, tied off at the ankles with gold tassels. Squeak was naked, except for a tiny blue baseball cap that read FELL'S POINT in red script.

"We're touristos," Dave said, tugging lightly on the tiny brim of the kid's cap.

"Doesn't David look great?" Julia said to me. "Don't they all? Isn't Heather beautiful?" Beautiful Heather blushed. All the way up her temples and into her scalp. "They've agreed to pose for me, Hitch. Will they not make a fantastic family portrait? I can't wait."

Dave took Squeak from Julia's arms and, with an okay nod from me, placed the child on Alcatraz's back. "Mush." He kept a steadying hand on his child's head as Alcatraz gave a laconic loping tour of the gallery. Heather parked herself in front of Julia's huge canvas, *Three Ducks Light a Fire,* and levitated slightly as she gazed dreamily at it.

"I love these people," Julia said to me. "I am *this* close to shaving my head."

We retired to a corner by the window, where Julia keeps three butterfly chairs. A birthday gift from me one year. "They're canvases," I had told her when I gave them to her, and within twenty-four hours, one of the chairs was painted like a butterfly, one like a ladybug and the third like a butterfly with ladybug dots. She called the third chair "Baby Butterbug." You'd do a serious back flip and probably hurt yourself if I told you how much Julia made securing the concept and then selling it off for mass production. These baby butterbugs are all over the place now. You must've seen them.

Julia gave me a brief postmortem on the rest of her evening. The giggling bald man in the Nehru jacket turned out to have been the publisher of a magazine called *Whoa N'elle* who was down from New York at Emile DeBussey's invitation for the big restaurant opening. By evening's end, Julia told me, he had not only gotten down on his hands and knees and begged Julia to consider spearheading a project to revamp the entire look of the magazine ("You can fire anyone you want," he had promised. "Even me!") but in the end had curled up in fetal position and wrapped his little hands around her ankles and wept copiously. Julia was strongly considering the offer.

"What's this magazine about?" I asked.

"Hell, Hitch. It's three quarters advertisements, one quarter celebrity gossip and one quarter artsy-fartsy mishmash filler."

"That's five quarters," I pointed out.

"Well, you see. Hercules needs my help."

"The man is named *Hercules?*"

"Only temporarily. Last year it was Zeus. He's on a Greek thing."

"Interesting."

"Next year it's Agamemnon," Julia said. "I chose it for him last night at Emile's."

"I take it the guy is a nut case."

Julia nodded sagely. "Corn flake. One hundred percent."

I gave Julia a rundown on my activities since last we saw each other. She was impressed. "So my little Hitch has been in the Big House."

"Your little Hitch has been in the drunk tank. Doesn't quite qualify as a Sing Sing."

"It's a start, my dear."

Julia was also quite interested in the news that Shrimp Martin had been two-timing Lucy with Mary Childs. She was sad to hear that Lucy had withheld this information from her, but she sympathized with Lucy's explanation as to why she had kept the information to herself.

"I knew there was something about that girl the moment I laid eyes on her," Julia said, pulling her feet up under her. She was in the ladybug butterfly chair.

"About Mary? What was the something you thought?"

"Oh, no specifics. But there are some people who have a volatile spirit. You can just tell. I wouldn't trust that girl any farther than I could throw her."

"I have a confession to make," I said. I went ahead and let the cat out of the bag about my date with Mary Childs the other night. Rather, my predate entanglement in Mary's room. No sooner was the cat out of the bag than it yawned and lay right down in the sun.

"Oh, I guessed as much already," Julia said. "I could tell with one glance down at Rehoboth that you were being targeted."

"You might have warned me."

"The point being?"

"You might have warned me."

"Hitch, I could also tell what a waste of time any warning from me would have been."

"But we can barely manage a civil word to each other," I protested.

"Chemistry is not made up of words."

"Jules, Mary Childs and I do not have chemistry," I said flatly.

"The other night. What you just described for me. Before your date."

"What about it?"

"Was there an explosion?" When I didn't answer immediately, she made an explosion noise. "Chemistry."

"This is depressing."

Someone Julia recognized had just walked into the shop. Julia gave a toodle-ooh wave then turned back to me. "Of course there's always the other possibility."

"I'm not sure that I want to know. What's the other possibility?"

"She's using you," Julia said. "She wants something from you. She's playing you like a fiddle."

"Right. That. That's what Munger said, too. Same phrase. The fiddle thing." I sighed deeply and looked out the window. A clown in the square was making balloon animals. There was not a single kid in sight. Maybe he was just practicing, under real conditions. Taking in the wind factor and all that. I looked back at Julia. "That's what Pete wondered after

Grady came in and tattooed my eye, if Mary wasn't just trying to make him jealous. Though I don't understand why, but it's definitely a thought." I added, "You women do funny things."

Julia was doing a funny thing even as I spoke. She had taken hold of her left ankle and she was raising it steadily up toward her shoulder. She ignored my insightful jab. "I think it's something else, Hitch. Call it intuition. But I'd be very careful around that girl if I were you."

"What are you thinking?"

She took a deep breath, then with a final tug, hooked the heel of her foot around the far side of her neck. She now looked absurdly dislocated. Or like she was taking the wackiest way imaginable to walk out the window.

"My guess? I think that Grady *and* Miss Mary are somehow involved in these murders. That's what I think. With Grady you've got the motive of jealousy. I mean, look how he reacted when he found out that you and his ex-girlfriend were mixing it up. He blew."

"Fine. That's what Pete and I discussed. Kit finds out that Mary is sleeping with Shrimp so he loses his temper and he ups and kills him. Extreme, no question about it. But then when is murder not extreme?"

"Good point."

"But so where do you get Mary mixing in with it?"

"I don't know," Julia said. From my vantage point, it looked as if her left foot was sticking out of her right ear. "Maybe he did it in a rage, like you said, and now Mary is helping him cover it up."

"That doesn't add up. Nothing is showing that they're even on the same team."

"Well, if they're in cahoots, they're not exactly going to advertise the fact."

"What about Mary's drawing me into her lair? Where would that fit in? The result was a display for me of Grady's hot-headed temper. All that does is get me wondering about Grady as Shrimp's killer. Maybe she's trying to get me to look in that direction."

"To target Grady?"

"Something like that."

"Or so that you'll look away from her?"

"Ah, it's nuts, Jules. All signs point to Kit, not to Mary."

"Hitch, are you defending the girl?"

"No. I'm just looking at the facts."

Julia reached up with her hand and scratched either her ear or her foot. I couldn't tell which. "Mary knows you're nosing about. She probably knows you've got a private eye helping you. You might want to consider that she's trying to neutralize your suspicions by taking you to bed."

"Jules, that's exactly what's got me suspicious." I waved my hand irritably. "Stop that, will you? You're making my back hurt."

Julia unhitched her foot from her neck and brought her leg slowly back down.

"Hitchcock . . . I didn't say it was a *clever* tactic. Just a tactic. People tend to lead with their strengths. Would you say that sex is one of Mary Childs's strengths?"

"It's one of yours," I pointed out, deflecting the question.

Julia smiled. "Yes. But I never use it for evil, only for good." Her foot reached the floor. The sigh of relief came from me. I asked Julia what she thought of Shrimp being the one who killed Kelly Bishop. She found the idea plausible.

"I could see it."

"Pete is thinking that there's a connection between the Bishop girl and Shrimp and Arthur," I said.

"Shrimp kills the girl. The teacher kills Shrimp." Julia batted her big browns at me. "Who kills Arthur, honeybunch? Can we say, overkill? This professor of yours, is he a psychopath or simply a ruined human being?"

"I'd hate to judge."

"Here's one, Hitch. What if *Arthur* killed the girl? Chubby boy, sexy girl, must happen all the time."

"You're demented," I said.

She stuck out her tongue at me. "My theory's better than your theory. Arthur kills the girl. The teacher almost takes the rap. He gets his revenge on Arthur."

"And Shrimp? Now *your* theory has an overkill."

"Easy. Arthur always tells Shrimp everything. Shrimp knows that Arthur killed the girl. Somehow your professor is aware of this. He kills Shrimp because Shrimp would rat on him for snuffing Arthur. Lord, this is easy."

"And the money?"

Julia floated out of her chair. "Oh, you just want everything to fit neatly together," she sniffed. "I like my theory and I don't care about your silly old money. Forget the money."

"Ah!" I stood up. Led by my index finger.

Julia frowned. " 'Ah' what? Do I dare ask?"

"This: Kincaid kills Kelly. There's not sufficient evidence to convict him, but he's done it. Now, somehow, Shrimp and Arthur know that he did it. *They* have proof. Kincaid pays them off to keep their mouths shut." A low groaning was beginning to come from my ex-wife. I ignored it. "Then, the trial ends and Kincaid once again ponies up for their silence. The bag of money. He then changes his mind and tries to get the money back. When he can't, he—"

"He runs around slaughtering people. Hitch, how logical is it that a guy who has just been acquitted of a murder that he is in fact guilty of is then going to run out a few days later and start killing all these people? For what? Just to get some money back?"

"Maybe they were going to squeal on him after all," I said, knowing even as I said it that my tale sounded as lame to Julia as it did to me. She was ticktocking her head.

"Well, it's a theory," I protested.

"Sorry, pumpkin."

"No you're not."

Krishna Dave and Heather and Squeak were ready to go. Before they left, Julia grabbed a sketch pad and knocked off a pair of lightning quick pencil drawings of Squeak. In one, the child was in a delirium of delight; in the other, Squeak looked downright philosophical. Julia ran up to her studio and slid back down on the pole with a small glass frame—no backing—into which she slipped the two sketches. She located an eyehook, which she secured into the top of the frame, then she took one of the gold tassels that was anchoring her toga at her ankles and slid it through the eyehook. Voilà. Free hanging, the frame would rotate lazily in the air, a Squeak on either side. Julia and the Krishnas group-hugged and discussed plans for Julia to go out to the house soon and paint them.

After they left, Julia came up from behind and wrapped her arms around me to give me a big hug. Chinese Sue—silent this whole time behind the counter, lost in her book about the making of the atom bomb—looked up with a placid sneer.

Julia whispered in my ear, "You go and get yourself killed, you know I'll never speak to you again."

"You've said that to me before."

She hugged tighter. "Meant it then, mean it now. Be careful, crab-cake."

Twenty minutes later I felt like an idiot. It was the sight of Julia snaking her way down the spiral stairs from her studio that had made me think of Solomon Biggs. Specifically, it made me think of his gilded stairway to nowhere from *The Magic Flute* production. It had occurred to me that with a juicehead like Solly Biggs, entire portions of his brain probably flickered on and off regularly, like a loose lightbulb in a windstorm. Solly's recollection of the night that Shrimp had entrusted him with all that money . . . there was every possibility that the man's memory had huge holes in it. Temporary holes, perhaps. It seemed well worth the quick trip up to Solly's warehouse to see if perhaps he might have an additional recollection or two about this whole affair for me to add to my pile. Munger's very first tip to me, *follow the money* . . . It was worth a follow-up. Besides which, if Munger and I were correct, that one way or another this bag of cash was the common denominator in the two murders, then the idea of Solly's holding on to it was making less and less sense. If, in fact, it had ever made much sense in the first place.

Moot point.

What made me feel like an idiot was the sight of Solly's semiordered domicile in general disarray, various prop pieces overturned and torn apart and scattered about the warehouse floor as if a private tornado had found its way in and had its way with the place. Which in essence is exactly what had happened. Solly was seated on his anvil when I arrived. His checkerboard table was legless and in two sections on the floor. Solly, too, was legless, though strictly in the vernacular sense. I could practically see the booze fumes coming off him. Alcatraz plodded about the place sniffing with unbridled delight.

I don't know if Solly had any holes in his memory, but he had a brand-new one in his head. He showed it to me. I had to get past the clump of dried blood and hair that was in the way, but I saw it. A two-inch gash just above his right ear, riding high atop a tremendous lump.

"When did this happen, Solly?"

The man was stewed. "Lost track of the time, mate," he slurred. "What day've we got here?"

"Today's Wednesday."

He gave the matter some thought. There was dried blood on his collar. A crusted cake of it on the floor next to the anvil. And next to it, a juggling pin. Dried blood on the juggling pin as well. Solly saw me looking at the blood on the floor. "That's where I woke up," he muttered. "Must've been last night sometime. That's right. Woke up in the bloody dark."

"Last night?"

"Last night. This morning. Call it what you like." He held up his flask, turning it upside down. The lid was off. Nothing spilled out. He looked at me and worked to steady his gaze.

"What happened, Solly?"

"Someone cracked me open. That's plain enough. I come in from my rounds, you know. Early night. Nine o'clock. Ten. Never saw it coming. Bloody coldcocked me and left me on the floor. Woke up to this disaster." He lowered his head and swung his arm in the air, a gesture intended to take in the entire warehouse. "Root of all evil."

"The money," I said. I stepped over to the gilded stairway. It seemed intact. I ducked in behind it. The wooden door to the little prop-hide-away had been ripped off its hinges. The money was gone.

"They got what they came for, huh?" I called out. I looked back around the side of the staircase. Solomon Biggs had gotten to his feet. He was urinating on his anvil. He looked over at me with an expression of extreme sophistication. Then he went to make a bow. It got pretty ugly.

CHAPTER 20

Idiot.

I could kick myself. Mary Childs. At the restaurant the other night, Mary had tossed out a seemingly innocuous curiosity about the money and I had blithely told her that I knew where the bag of money had gone. I hadn't named Solomon Biggs directly. But Mary Childs was no fool. She knew who was at the club that Friday night. And if I'm not mistaken, I had made a reference to the fact that the person Shrimp entrusted the money to could've maybe needed it a little more than the next guy. If that wasn't throwing a spotlight on Solomon Biggs, I don't know what was.

Idiot!

I had no proof of course that dear Mary was the person who had broken into Solly's place and then whacked him on the head with a juggling pin when he came home early. But a sickening feeling came over me as I realized that I didn't have a whole lot of trouble imagining it. I ran over the several encounters I had had with the woman. Money. Somewhere in each of the times I had seen her, or so it now seemed, the topic of money had cropped up, and usually in a context of Mary's not having as much of it as she'd like. Unless there were other evil forces at work here, *my* money said that Mary Childs had found a way, at least short term, to solve that problem.

I convinced Solly to venture out into the light of day. I piled him into my car then drove him to my place and aimed him toward my bathroom. While Solly was showering, I popped down to one of the secondhand shops on Aliceanna Street and picked up a pair of lime green clam-diggers that looked as if they would fit him. I added a twenty-five-cent T-shirt and a two-dollar cream-colored V-neck sweater to my purchase and returned to my place. Solly was still in the shower. He was singing "Mona Lisa" in a voice so clear and pure I could barely believe it was Biggs. I pulled up a chair next to the bathroom door and sat and listened.

> Mona Lisa, Mona Lisa men have named you
> You're so like the lady with the mystic smile . . .

It was beautiful. Solly came out of the shower forty minutes after he went in. When he came out he was grumbling that the hot water had died on him. "You should look into that." Solly was impressed with the clothes I had gotten for him. He pulled on the clam-diggers and slipped the T-shirt and the loose-knit sweater over his head.

"I'm bloody J. Crew himself," Solly declared, turning this way and that before my full-length mirror. "How about we go find a sailboat? Gather up some little darlings in their swimmy suits. You don't go keeping a pisser like this in hiding, mate. Not in my green clammies. Let's go have a drink."

"Sorry, Solly. Other plans," I said.

"Let's drop in on Finney, then." The old letch fairly sang. "By Christ, that's an afternoon. If I were a woman I'd slit my throat I see that piece of work walking around on the planet. God all . . . I'd ask me what's the bloody point of even trying? God damn piece like that."

Solly continued singing the praises of my ex-wife in his tender loving terms as I steered him down the steps and back out to my car. It was a short trip up Broadway to Hopkins Hospital. Solly groused a bit, at least until his imagination began taking on a few of the nurses. "I ought to have my head examined," he crooned at the nurse who was looking him over. He asked her after she had poked and prodded, "What's the prognosis? Will I live to love again?"

"Afraid so," the nurse replied dryly. Solly waived the idea of stitches. Fifteen or so hours of healing had already begun closing the wound. He said he didn't want a bandage on his head to ruin his snappy new look. Solly was given a prescription for painkillers. I took it and threw it out when he wasn't looking. I knew how Solomon Biggs planned to handle the pain. His method wouldn't mix well with the Hopkins plan.

Next we drove over to Mary Ann Martin's house. Solly stood next to me as I pounded on the front door. I didn't expect anyone to answer it, and I was right. Mary Ann was likely at work. As for Mary Childs? If I was right about the money . . . pick a beach, any beach. Anywhere in the world.

Played like a fiddle.

I drove down to police headquarters. Solly wasn't thrilled about this. "I've had it with coppers," he grumbled. I asked to see Detective John Kruk. The man with the yellow hair was in. Always happy to see me. You can tell by the squint and the sneer and the general dubiousness he manages to put into his every gesture.

"Mr. Sewell, let me guess. You have a confession to make."

I bowed slightly from the waist. "It was I who shot Mr. Lincoln, Detective, not that Booth character."

"That's not my case," Kruk responded, his pan, as always, ever so dead. "What else have you got to say for yourself?"

I introduced Kruk to Solomon Biggs. It turned out that they had already met. Kruk and his men had interviewed everyone who had been at Shrimp's the night before Shrimp was murdered. This, of course, would have included Solly.

"How are you doing these days, Mr. Biggs?" Kruk asked, motioning Solly into the chair in front of his desk. "Keeping out of trouble, I trust."

Solly alighted like a cautious canary. "An honest day's wages for an honest day's work," he declared warily.

"Oh? You've located employment?"

"Cross that bridge when I come to it," Solly answered. Kruk looked up at me. I shrugged. The detective leaned forward on his desk.

"I'm assuming that Mr. Sewell hasn't brought you all the way down here for a social visit, Mr. Biggs."

Solly took a moment to gather his thoughts. He crossed his arms. "It's a long way to Tipperary."

"I see." Kruk sat back in his chair. He addressed me. "Your friend doesn't seem inclined to talk, Mr. Sewell. Perhaps you can explain your visit."

"What's wrong, Solly?" I asked. "Cat suddenly got your tongue?"

The painter was scowling like a juvenile delinquent. "In a pig's eye."

Kruk appealed to me. "Mr. Sewell?"

"I want to report an assault and a robbery," I said.

"I see. Were you by any chance the victim of this alleged robbery and assault?"

"No sir, I wasn't. It was Mr. Biggs here."

"The man who won't talk?"

"I have the right to an attorney," Solly blurted. "If I can't afford one, one will be provided for me."

"You're not under arrest, Mr. Biggs," Kruk pointed out. "Mr. Sewell, I have quite a lot to attend to here. Suppose you act as your friend's mouthpiece."

I paused, just long enough to give the detective time to follow up on his own straight line. But he didn't. So I launched into the account of Shrimp Martin's having given Solly the shopping bag full of money the night before Shrimp was murdered. I explained how Shrimp had alluded to the fact that there was a possibility Solly would be able to keep the money. I recounted what Solly had told me, about his coming home just the night before only to be knocked unconscious by an intruder. I said that a juggling pin appeared to be the weapon that had been used. The money, I concluded, was no longer where Solly had hidden it. Presumably, the intruder who coldcocked Solly had made off with the loot. I held back on my suspicion that the intruder and coldcocker might have been an infuriatingly caustic unemployed bartender named Mary Childs who had played yours truly like a fiddle. It wasn't so much that I wasn't looking to get her hauled in—assuming she was even within haul-in range at this point, but I didn't want to let on to Kruk the extent to which I had thoroughly ignored his warnings about keeping my nose out of this case. The man can get a little pompous when he starts in on his lectures and I just wasn't in the mood to volunteer for one of them just now. So I fudged the time line a little, not letting on that I had known about the money for nearly a week now. I knew Kruk well enough to know that he was not about to go arresting Solomon Biggs on charges of withholding evidence or withholding information. I couldn't be so sure that he wouldn't throw that book at me, however; so I played it safe with a couple of innocent fibs. Kruk appeared to buy it.

"Why didn't you inform my men of this money when you were first questioned?" Kruk asked Solly.

"Silence is golden," quoth Solly.

Kruk sighed. "Mr. Biggs apparently learned this little not-talking trick while he was in prison. I've seen it before." He leaned forward again on his desk. "It's not very original, Mr. Biggs."

"God save the Queen."

Kruk backhanded the air. "Please. Go."

When the announcement was made that the name of the new expansion team in town was to be the Baltimore Blues, speculation had taken either of two forks in the road. The one fork led down the path of Baltimore's being the birthplace of folks such as Billie Holiday, Eubie Blake and even Frank Zappa (whose musical notability might be that he dabbled in damn near every form *but* the straight-out blues). This fork held to the name of the new basketball team as being a nod to the musical heritage of the city. The other fork of speculation had been poked into the shell of the famous Chesapeake Bay blue crab. And since you're not exactly going to go name a major sports team the Crabs . . .

The second fork was the correct fork.

As the usher showed Munger and me to our nearly prime seats several rows behind the home team bench, we were confronted by a gigantic foam rubber crustacean, primarily blue with hot orange edgings. The thing had large bulbous cutesy fake eyes on a pair of springy antennae, monstrously large and clumsy-seeming foam claws and across its breastplate, in hot orange, the letters BB.

"Brigitte Bardot?" I speculated.

"Baltimore Blues," the usher said, happy to inform me of what I already knew.

Pete looked ready to pull out his weapon and pistol-whip the thing. It had stopped in front of Munger and was prancing from foot to foot as if the floor were too hot for it to stand still. Suddenly, from a small hole near the base of the eye-antennae, a stream of soap bubbles began spewing forth, accompanied by canned laughter, most definitely a mechanical noise, not a product of the person inside the foam suit. The bubbles engulfed Pete's head. He batted irritably at them, but a fresh stream spewed from the blowhole and engulfed him again. The canned laughter, I thought, bordered on the maniacal.

"He's Crabby," the usher said. I assumed that he meant the foam mascot and not my friend. I could have been wrong.

Crabby la-la-la'ed off to pester other ticket-holders and Pete and I made our way to our seats. The arena was already nearly filled to capacity (which looked to me to be about a zillion), the seats going up and up and up into a blackness where I was no longer able to make out individual people, just a shifting undulating mass. TV camera crews were roaming around the edges of the court. A giant screen hanging from the ceiling was flashing images nonstop. Out on the court itself, a cheerleading squad for the Baltimore Blues was bouncing around in a disco/aerobics meets the funky chicken frenzy. The girls were being tossed into the air and performing frantic leg splits while the boys were displaying a penchant for throwing themselves to the floor chest-first and then sliding along the slick surface on their bellies before exploding back onto their feet. There was no way in hell to make out the music that the kids were dancing and prancing and flinching to. The noise of the arena was an amalgamated echo, buzz, roar and cricket-chatter cranked to the max. As I took in the scene, I could well imagine going into a seizure.

A few minutes after we had settled in, the lights went out and a digitally programmed disco ball effect swirled a confetti of pinprick lights about the entire arena. Like the flushing of a giant toilet bowl of phosphorescent water. A low sustained note from a synthesizer started up and held steady through the introduction of the starting lineup for the Pacers. There were enough Indiana fans in attendance to give a worthy cheer as each of the players emerged from the tunnel beneath the grandstand into the moving spotlight. Naturally, the low sustained synthesizer note was in place as a momentum-builder for the home team. After the Pacers had all trotted onto the floor, the arena announcer suddenly came alive.

"Ladies and gentlemen . . . boys and girls . . . let's hear it for yyyyyyyyyyyyour *Baltimore B-L-U-E-S!!!!!*"

Crabby was poised right at the spot where the players emerged from the tunnel. The dancing crab was twitching and hopping around as if someone had loaded lit firecrackers into his back fin. As each of the starting players was announced and emerged into the follow-spot, Crabby went into his religious ecstasy routine and the crowd went bananas. A smoke cannon had gone off at some point and the smoky haze was picking up the colors of the swirling disco lights. I was amused, appalled, bored and excited. A panoply of indecision and open-mindedness. Pete cupped his hands at one point and yelled into my ear, "This is bullshit!" I turned and fired him a thumbs-up and a big grin, "Yes! You're right! Lots of fun!"

Finally the introductions were over and the house lights came back up. The two teams took to the court and commenced with their warm-up drills and shots.

"There's Grady."

Pete was pointing toward Crabby's position. Kit Grady, dressed in street clothes, had just emerged from the tunnel. Crabby patted him clumsily on the back as he passed. The roar went up from the crowd as he was spotted, interspersed with some boos and hisses. Grady ignored the crowd at first, then as he reached the Blues' bench he raised his hand in a nonchalant acknowledgment. It was his right hand, the bandaged one, the one that I knew intimately. The roar intensified. The gesture was so laconic he might have been giving the one zillion paying customers the finger. He sat down on the end of the bench and found something to stare at on the floor.

"Boy knows how to milk a crowd," Pete sniffed sarcastically. It occurred to me that Kit Grady was roughly the same age as Kevin Munger, Pete's boy. I thought of what Mary Childs had said to me— Hank Mackey, too, for that matter—about Grady's difficulties in handling all that had happened to him since leaving Ohio and coming east. No small wonder. The guy was *nineteen* for Christ's sake. An instant corporation unto himself. Suffering sycophants left and right. Grady sat on the bench looking out at his teammates warming up, dropping the ball through the hoop from amazing distances, high-fiving, working off their nerves, psyching up. He looked miserable. To be sidelined at his first ever championship game . . . it must have been killing him.

The game got under way and a lot of the adrenaline in the arena leveled off. Or rather transferred to the players on the court. Suddenly the arena had gone quiet enough to allow for our hearing the sounds of sneakers squeaking on the wood floor, the grunts of the players as they moved up and down the court and the exhortations of the coaches on the sidelines. The crowd fell into a rhythm along with the ballplayers, the cheers swelling and fading in synch with the action on the court. Rising with the fast breaks, peaking with the baskets, falling instantly to silence with the missed shots. The score remained close through most of the first quarter, though in the last several minutes of the quarter, the Blues went on a run, dropping a half dozen unanswered baskets. The Pacers were flat. They looked disorganized. The crowd noise seemed to be spooking them, keeping them off their game. The quarter ended with the Blues up by fourteen points. The crowd was loving it.

During the short break—as the television audience no doubt watched commercials for beer and sports utility vehicles and financial services—I bought two beers and two hot dogs, for Pete and myself. Paid a small fortune.

Just before the second quarter got under way, I recognized a bald spot that had been sitting two rows in front of me. I hadn't given it any notice before and only registered it now because it stood up from its seat and went over to where Kit Grady was now standing, and commenced a conversation with him that swiftly became animated. I couldn't make out what the two were saying, of course, but it seemed something other than "Gee, nice to see you, you're looking great." The bald spot was poking his finger into Grady's chest and Grady didn't appear too happy about it, even though he was putting up with it. Odd. I recalled how this same bald spot had stood in Parlor One during the wake for Shrimp Martin and similarly put up with someone's poking their finger into *his* chest. I turned to point out the exchange to Pete but saw that he was already watching it.

"Do you know who that is?" I asked him.

He nodded. "I do." His eyes narrowed. They didn't move from the two men. It almost looked as if he were trying to send them telepathic signals. *The mother ship will be in the parking lot at ten. Don't be late.*

"What are you thinking, Pete?"

His words came out slowly. "I'm thinking that the man is not happy with the boy."

I thought back again to Shrimp's wake. Had Barry Fisher and Grady even spoken with each other at the wake? Were they even there at the same time? Fisher's comings and goings I remembered less. But Kit Grady, I had watched him. Everyone had. He had remained no more than ten minutes. And no, he hadn't spoken with Barry Fisher. Not a word. Interesting, I thought. Shrimp's wake had taken place just over a week previous and the two certainly were talking together now. Chest-jabbing, hand-smacking buddies of the first order.

A wide man on his way back to his seat stepped in front of Pete, blocking his view for a few quick seconds. I thought that the retiring private eye would hurl the man aside. But he didn't. Pete continued squinting at Grady and the bald spot. As we watched, Grady lifted his right hand and shook his bandaged fingers in front of the man's face. The man angrily swatted the hand away—much like Grady had swatted my hand away just the night before. Grady didn't flinch.

"You see that?" I said to Pete.

Pete nodded. "Those fingers aren't broken." He finally broke his gaze and he looked over at me. A smirk was on his face. "Your head just isn't that hard, buster. Grady didn't break any damn fingers popping you in the eye."

"He purposefully took himself out of the game," I said.

"That's a fact."

"Why?"

Pete shrugged. He took a long sip of his beer. It appeared to be an immensely satisfying long sip. He smacked his lips. "That, my friend, might just be the two-hundred-thousand-dollar question."

The second quarter got under way. The Pacers turned up the heat and were able to cut Baltimore's lead in half before a pair of three-pointers by Chad Singleton, the Blues' second-string center and Grady's replacement, got the crowd, and the team, back into the game.

Barry Fisher didn't seem to be enjoying himself. Certainly he wasn't doing much rooting for the home team. He was seated slightly more toward the center of the court than where Pete and I were sitting, so I was able to get a partial-profile look at his face without much problem. He spent as much time talking to the guy seated next to him as he did watching the action on the court. Fisher's friend was around five-ten, wore black slacks and a too-tight polo shirt that gave a good reading of his iron-pumped torso. More than once the guy leapt to his feet to yell something out at the players, the referees, the coaches. One of those fans who'd have you believe they could do it all. He had a waist women would puke for, jet black hair worn seventies-style long, over the collar and flipped up in a ducktail, a square jaw and a complex nose, not pretty. Rearranged a few times was my guess. I figured him for around my age, give or take. And actually, I didn't really pay all that much attention to him at first. Every half minute or so the guy ran his hands over his hair; a redistribution of grease as far as I could tell. After maybe a dozen or so groomings it dawned on me. He had awfully large hands. His palms covered half his head. Rings covered half of his fingers. This was the guy Lee Cromwell had told me about. The one whose late-night visits to the club hadn't exactly caused Shrimp Martin to start turning somersaults of delight.

Toaster Hands.

The Pacers called a time-out. They had fallen behind now by eighteen points. The charged-up Blues were working absolute magic on the court, even without their superstar player. As the buzzer sounded for the time-out, Barry Fisher stood up, ostensibly to stretch, and locked eyes with Kit Grady, who was standing on the outer edge of the team huddle. My angle on their silent exchange was perfect. Pete's, too. Fisher's expression was, simply, one of absolute fury. Aimed directly at Grady. For his part, the young ballplayer was attempting a nonchalance, attempting to return the man a cocky, devil-may-care look. But Grady couldn't quite pull it off. The brave veneer was paper-thin. The expression just beneath the melting mask was easy to read. Even from where I was sitting. It was fear.

Pete was the first to say it.

"Fisher's got Kit Grady in his pocket."

"You think?"

Pete was making his sage face. He ran a palm over the blue bristle of his cheek, his lower lip extending in thought. "I do."

At halftime, the Baltimore Blues were enjoying a twenty-one-point lead. Chad Singleton was having the game of his career. He had already scored nineteen points as well as fed the ball cleanly for a good number of assists. His agent was probably this very minute scribbling in new clauses on the ballplayer's next contract. Called on in a tight situation, Singleton was coming through in spades. The Blues Arena was rocking. The cheerleading squad took to the floor . . . and the crowd actually paid *attention*.

Pete went off to use the bathroom. I lingered a few minutes then decided to stretch my legs. I hadn't seen Hank Mackey all night, which I thought was strange, and I wanted to thank him for the tickets. I crab-walked out of the row and had just started down the shallow steps toward the tunnel when suddenly I was face-to-face with Barry Fisher.

"Hello," I said.

He didn't seem to place me right away. Or maybe he just didn't want to.

"Hitchcock Sewell," I said.

Recognition flashed in his small blue eyes. "The undertaker. Yes."

"How are you enjoying the game?" I asked. "I thought I had good seats, but I see you're practically on the bench."

"The home team seems to be doing fine," Fisher said. He ignored my comment about his seats.

"Indeed. Even without their ace." When Fisher didn't respond, I went on. "I noticed you talking with Grady earlier. Friend of yours?"

"We've met."

"It looked to me like you two were pretty well acquainted," I said. "I can't imagine just anyone could wander down from the stands and start busting the guy's chops like that."

Fisher gave me a bored face. "I don't know. Why don't you try it?"

I tapped a finger next to my bruised eye. "Grady and I are having trouble locating a civil tone with each other."

"I'm sorry. I don't understand."

"The Great White Hope gave me his autograph the other night. In a manner of speaking." I tapped the side of my eye.

"Kit did that?"

"Beats the old slipped and fell in the shower story any day if you ask me."

"I don't suppose it's possible that you deserved it," Fisher said, smirking just a little. "You can be a bit of a smart-ass, you know."

"I didn't. But thank you for letting me know."

Fisher smirked again. "Well, it was nice running into you, Mr. Sewell." He made a move to go back to his seat. I halted him with mere words.

"Is Kit Grady on the take?"

Fisher stopped. His cheeks sank and then reinflated, pink. "I have no idea what you're talking about."

"Did you know that your recently departed business partner tried to pressure Grady into throwing some games?" I asked.

"If you mean Shrimp, the answer is no."

"So what exactly was it that you and Grady were arguing about earlier?"

I sensed someone behind me who wanted to squeeze by. I was right. It was the guy who had been sitting next to Fisher. Toaster Hands. He glanced at me, then at Fisher. "All right?"

"Fine, Jerry. I just ran into a friend."

Jerry drew in his bottom lip for a nibble, gave me a dulled look, then shrugged and moved off to his seat. Fisher swatted backhanded at something on his sleeve. Or pretended to.

"Grady's a good kid," Fisher said. "He's gotten himself some bad publicity, I know. Those are growing pains. We all go through them. It's just that most of us don't go through them under a national spotlight. Frankly, I think he has held up pretty well. And believe me, it's killing him not to play tonight. Kit's being extremely hard on himself. Too hard, in my opinion. I'm a competitive person myself. I know how difficult and frustrating this is for him. But whining isn't going to do Kit any good. That's what I was telling him earlier. Kit needs someone who will talk back to him. Everyone's too soft with him. That's not my style. I told him to snap out of it and act like a man."

"So you know nothing about Shrimp's leaning on Kit to throw any games."

"I told you, no."

"Shrimp was in a lot of money trouble, wasn't he?"

Fisher let out an exasperated sigh. "We've been over this, Mr. Sewell.

As I recall, I told you in my office that I see no reason why I should be discussing my former business associate's financial situation with you."

"In fact, what you told me was that I should mind my own business."

"I think that was good advice. I don't understand why you refuse to take it."

"Then I'll tell you why." I folded my arms on my chest. "Since the time I decided not to take your advice, I've learned that you were apparently a pretty lousy business partner for Shrimp Martin. I've learned that you arranged loans for him at rates that were higher than the rates that you managed to secure for yourself. I've learned that you even lent money to Shrimp out of your cut-rate loan and that he was pretty desperate to pay it back."

"You don't—"

"And tonight, I've learned that even though you and Kit Grady behaved like total strangers at Shrimp's wake, apparently you're so chummy chummy with the guy that you can waltz out onto the court and tell him to shape up and start acting like a man. At least that's what you say you were telling him. *That's* why I'm not taking your advice, Mr. Fisher. Because it's bad advice. So far I'm learning a lot more by ignoring it."

Fisher paused. And then . . . guess what? He jabbed a finger in my chest. I joined the club!

"You are way out of line," Fisher said, clenched teeth and all.

"I think not," I responded calmly, then stepped past him and went off in search of a beer line. I found one. I got an entire tray of beers. Four. And two more hot dogs. When I got back to the seats, Munger asked me who's having the party.

"We are," I said. "We're about to solve us a couple of murders, Munger old chap."

Five minutes later, Fisher and Jerry Toaster Hands took off. I looked around and noticed that Kit Grady had vanished. After Pete and I finished our dogs and beers, we left, too. The Blues looked like they had this one in the bag.

I never want to hear again that a forty-seven-year-old woman can't wear a miniskirt. Lee Cromwell pulled it off. Little plaid number, simple black top, hair piled atop her head in a sexy I-just-woke-up rat's nest. Pete literally stopped in his tracks on our way to our table. I had to backtrack a few steps and fetch him.

"God damn," he muttered, then followed me to the table and ordered a whiskey. I asked for the same. The Wednesday night crowd at Junior's was not half bad. At least you couldn't count them on one hand. A party of some sort seemed to be going on at one of the tables—rather, at three tables that had been pushed together. It looked like an office thing. Maybe a going-away party. Or a the-boss-is-having-open-heart-surgery party. It was a noisy bunch, paying more attention to themselves than to the Edgar Jonz Experience. The party was off to our right. Pete turned in his chair and glowered at them. His batteries must have been low; they continued making their noise.

"Don't sweat it, Pete, I said.

He muttered, "Assholes," then turned his attention back to the small stage.

> I'll be seeing you in all the old familiar places
> That this heart of mine embraces all day through . . .

The sleek and lithe Edgar Jonz had the mute on his trumpet, the big hat on his head, the sunglasses on his nose. He was facing away from Lee, away from the audience, too, his horn tipped up toward the bricks of the club's side wall . . . and ever so gently he was punctuating Lee's voice with soft *bap-bap-baps* from his horn. The drummer was stirring the skins with his brushes. The stand-up bass player was sitting on a stool, his buxom instrument tilted against his shoulder. He wasn't even playing.

> I'll be looking at the moon,
> But I'll be seeing . . . you.

Lee received warm applause. Even a few of the office partiers took a time-out to clap. Lee behaved like someone who has just come out of a trance . . . or someone who has just noticed that she is singing out loud and that people have been listening to her. "Thank you," she said shyly into the microphone. Edgar slithered over to her and whispered something into her ear. Lee shook her head and said something back to him. Edgar bobbed his head, then cued the other musicians. Lee stepped back up to the microphone.

"This next song starts off pretty quietly. If you could please . . ."

Some of the people at the party table took the cue. A few others continued to cackle and talk. Pete leaned back in his chair and put his thick finger to his lips. "Shhhhh."

Lee winced a smile into the lights, then brought her fingers to rest lightly against the base of the mike. The bass player thumbed a string four times. *Thum . . . thum . . . thum . . . thum . . .* Then the drummer fell in with his brushes. Lee tilted in toward the microphone, but just as she opened her mouth to begin to sing, one of the boneheads at the office party called out, "*I can't hear you!*" Lee froze.

Pete Munger sprang.

It took Munger maybe four seconds to reach the loudmouth and grab the front of his shirt with both hands. "Move!" Pete snarled at the woman who was seated next to the guy. She skidded out of the way, and Pete proceeded to lift the guy partway to his feet and drag him stumbling off along the bar and all the way to the front door. The guy was speechless. Less than fifteen seconds after his little outburst he was gone. Out the door with Mr. Munger. Like the earth had opened up and swallowed his smartass ass.

Up on the small stage, Lee stood wide-eyed. The bassist and the drummer were still laying down the tempo, but Lee wasn't singing. Her eyes, like those of the rest of the people in the club, were still on the front door as Pete stepped back inside just a short moment after he had stepped out. He stepped in alone. Pete always looks a little rumpled, so I won't push the issue too much. There was a definite cat-and-canary look about his face, even as the dark scowl remained.

Lee Cromwell's smile grew as Pete returned to his seat. It was a killer smile. Just remarkable. Pete settled back in at the table, turning ever so slightly red. Lee leaned in close to the microphone. Her voice came through the speakers like a happy growl.

"Wow."

•   •   •

"My man, Gentle Ben." Edgar chuckled at his own joke. "I should sign you on. What you tell that dude when you got him outside?"

Pete didn't much feel like discussing it. "I told him he could come back inside and die, or get lost and live."

"You're sweet work, brother."

Lee and Edgar had joined us on their break. Lee touched Pete lightly on the arm and thanked him for his chivalry. He growled it off. "Jerks. You can't get away from them."

Lee beamed. "But you can throw them out on their ass."

Pete reached across the table and clamped on to Edgar's thin wrist. "We need to talk to you."

Edgar bopped his head from face to face, mine, Pete's, Lee's. "That's what's happening, honey. We're jawing."

"About Shrimp," Pete said. "About gambling at the club. About all sorts of stuff, Edgar."

Edgar was still wearing his sunglasses, but I could see his eyes flitting about. Lee glanced at Pete's surly face, then over at me. The tension rose about chin-high. Pete turned to Lee.

"I think it'd be better if you— Don't you want to go have a cigarette?"

Lee locked eyes with him. I don't think she liked being asked to leave and she wanted Pete to know that. "Is Edgar in some kind of trouble?" She addressed Edgar. "Edgar, did you screw up?"

Mr. Jonz raised his hands. "Don't shoot me, I'm just the entertainment."

Lee looked over at me. "I'll be outside." She turned to Pete. "You got a cigarette? I'm all out." Pete pulled a pack from his jacket pocket. He handed it to her.

"You need matches?"

"Someone out on the sidewalk will have a match," Lee said, standing up from the table. Pete was going for his pocket. Lee stopped him. "If I can't manage a light I might as well give it up."

I was in a position to watch as Lee sauntered out of the bar in her plaid mini. Poor Pete. He wasn't. He was facing the wrong way. And I just knew he wanted to turn around.

Edgar looked from Munger to me to Munger. "What's the scrabble, ladies?"

We gave him the scrabble. Rather, we told *him* to give *us* the scrabble. Pete laid it out for him.

"There was gambling going on at the club. And drugs. There was a lot of money floating around. There's been something going on with these basketball play-offs. Maybe even stuff during the regular season. Something with Kit Grady. Barry Fisher is also in here somewhere. And this guy, Jerry. Certainly Shrimp was in on it. Maybe Arthur, too. This is very simple, Edgar. You're not getting back on that stage . . . you're not even getting out of that chair until you've told me everything you know and until I'm convinced that you've told me everything you know. I've got a gun, I've got a short temper, I'm having a very very crappy year. You can ask Hitchcock here if you don't believe me. I've got all the freedoms of just not giving a good god damn anymore. So sing to me, Edgar. Down and dirty. The whole ugly tune. Get started."

Edgar had slipped his sunglasses up onto the top of his head. "Man . . . you're flying."

Pete Munger leaned forward on the table. "Talk."

Edgar talked.

According to the lithe trumpet player, the deal had gone this way. Shrimp had, in fact, gotten to Kit Grady. Edgar didn't know the details of how. He suspected it had something to do with drugs. ("Farm boy might as well've been wearing a sign: EXPLOIT MY ASS.") It seemed that Shrimp was shrewd enough not to expect Grady to attempt to throw his first-ever set of professional championship games. That would be asking too much. The very thought was absurd, not to say awfully difficult to pull off. Grady couldn't very well control the flow of an entire series without enlisting the help of some of the other players. But it was reasonable to figure that the young phenom could manage to at least muck up one game. If Shrimp could offer up a decent guarantee that the *first* game of each of the championship series resulted in a Baltimore loss, and especially if Grady could manage to work the point spread, well, apparently there were those in Shrimp's gaming world who could run with an angle like that. With Baltimore favored to win, savvy wagers could see a fat return. According to Edgar, Shrimp set it all up. He was the one who floated the guarantees of a Baltimore loss in the first play-off game, which was against the Knicks. Shrimp pulled Grady's strings. But apparently he had not pulled them so deftly. Baltimore had fallen behind by a substantial number of points when Kit Grady had suddenly gone on a tear, dropping buckets from every corner, muscling in with his layup, going downright balletic with his hook shot and defending the other team like a man possessed. The Blues took that first game and, as Edgar Jonz tells it, Shrimp was in deep shit. He was feeling the heat. Munger and I did the math and we figured that Shrimp's frantic phone call to his sister asking for the loan of a cool hundred grand was one of his responses to the heat. So, too, possibly, was the "loan" from Fisher. Pete was the one who put this theory together. His guess was that Fisher had been in on the whole thing from the start, and that the "loan" was actually Fisher's kick-in on the game fixing. Covering his tail, Fisher had made the thing aboveboard, a loan. Even if he lost the bet, he would not lose his money. When Grady failed to deliver, Shrimp paid the price. Fisher then moved in and picked up the reins. He put Grady in his pocket and continued on with business as usual.

"That would explain Grady's asinine behavior in that opening game against the Pistons," Pete said. "Where he did everything he could to get thrown out. Baltimore was flat that night. They needed Grady in top form if they were going to beat Detroit. He gets himself tossed out, the team tanks . . . Fisher wins."

"It scares me you can put that together," I said to Pete. "You think like a world-class cheat."

He shrugged. "By-product of the job."

As for the bag of money—the two hundred thousand that Shrimp had handed off to Solly Biggs for safekeeping—it still wasn't exactly clear where it came from, unless possibly it was the money that Shrimp had collected from some people who were now very very angry that they had taken Shrimp's tip on the game. One angry person in particular came to mind.

Jerry Toaster Hands.

Edgar didn't know a lot about Jerry, or if he did he managed to convince us otherwise. Edgar pretty much repeated what Lee had said, that the guy started showing up about a month ago and that he was an unpleasant presence around the club. Edgar said that Jerry (he could give us no last name) was loud and volatile and cocky. Edgar had sat across the table from Jerry a number of times in an after-hours card game. He reported that Mr. Toaster Hands was nasty and rude and racist and full of himself. He bragged about the fights he had been in. He bragged about the people he had humiliated. He bragged about all the women he had slept with, and about his money, his cars, his iron-pumped physique.

"Dude's trouble," Edgar said.

Pete and I guessed that it was big, brash, pumped-up Jerry who had killed Arthur and Shrimp after Shrimp screwed up in his game fixing. We tried the idea out on Edgar. He liked it.

"The Blues won and Shrimp lost. Took fat little Arthur down with him. I'm there, girls."

Pete and I stayed until partway through the next set. Lee had taken the stage with one of Pete's cigarettes tucked behind her ear. It wasn't quite Billie Holiday's gardenia, but she managed to make it look sexy. When Lee tried to give the pack of cigarettes back to him as we were leaving, Pete told her to keep it. Lee insisted he take it and then she was finally forced to hold the thing up in front of his nose, so that he could see where she had tucked a scrap of paper in the cellophane. "What's that?" Pete asked. Lee literally rolled her eyes. I told Pete, sotto voce, "It's the woman's phone number, Romeo." Pete stammered to Lee that he was married. "Then smoke the cigarettes," Lee said. She was trying to sound tough. Casual. But what she had sounded was awfully sad.

Pete was silent as we headed for his car. It was after midnight. Whether Pete was processing what Edgar Jonz had just told us or was running a tape loop of Lee Cromwell in his mind, I couldn't tell. We reached his car without saying a word. But by then I could tell in which direction the man's thoughts had strayed. He rapped his hand—palm down—against the roof of his car. Not hard. Not in severe frustration. More like . . . futility.

"I'm a cliché, Hitch. I just turned fifty. My marriage is shaky. I'm all huffy about my wife's sleeping with a so-called friend of mine. And now . . ."

He didn't finish the thought. He didn't have to. Pete pulled the cigarette pack from his pocket, shook out a cigarette and stuck it between his lips. He turned the pack over in his hand and looked at the scrap of paper tucked into it.

"Who am I kidding?" He pulled the cigarette from his mouth and dropped it to the street, then tossed the cigarette pack to me. I told him I didn't smoke. "Then throw them out." He rapped his hand against the roof of the car again. "I've got to get home."

There was a trash can a few feet behind me. I turned and tossed the cigarette pack in a hook shot, right into the can.

"Two points."

Pete pulled open the car door. "Which reminds me." He reached in to turn on the radio and fiddled with the dial until he found a sports channel. He turned the volume up, then straightened and stood holding the open car door as we listened to the phone-in chatter. It only took about a minute to determine what we had already guessed; the Blues had won the opener against the Pacers. The buzz on Chad Singleton was huge. Thirty-four points.

"Fisher's out some money," Pete said. "Probably Jerry as well."

"I wouldn't want to be Kit Grady tonight."

Pete grimaced. "I'd never want to be Kit Grady. You get up there in the limelight, it only makes you an easier target."

"Kind of pessimistic, Pete."

"Kind of realistic." He added, "As we've seen."

He got into his car.

"I'll get a hold of Kruk and pass all of this on to him," Pete said. "It's their game, you know, not ours." I had no problem with that. Pete reached his arm out the window and we shook hands—an awkward sort of formality, I felt—then I headed off toward my car, which was parked over in the next block. As I rounded the corner I glanced over in time to see Pete getting back out of his car, stepping over to the trash can on the corner and fishing out the pack of cigarettes.

I parked at the corner at the end of my block, in front of St. Teresa's, directly across from the funeral home. The moon was rising just off the church spire. *Très* dramatic. I was bushed. I was dreaming of my bed, my late-night date with the pillows and all the silly meanderings of the subconscious. I noticed the shadow moving, but I was too tired to think what it meant. A few seconds later I learned what it meant, as a figure emerged from the alley next to St. Teresa's and stepped in front of me. It was wearing a watch cap and a scarf of some sort hiding most of its face. It said nothing, but immediately piston-punched me directly in the stomach. All of my air left me and I doubled over. Fists rained down on my head; I have no idea how many times I was hit, but it was a considerable number. If I hadn't fallen to the sidewalk, maybe I'd have been spared the kicking. But I did fall. I had the presence of mind—or simply the instinct—to keep my arms up over my head, so the kicks landed primarily on my back. I caught a few in the ass, too. My assailant didn't say a word. He grunted with his efforts, but that was about it. He was mean and efficient.

The guy wasn't after my money. He hadn't even made the request. He was after me. My pain was his gain. Simple formula. The whole attack lasted probably a minute. You'd be amazed at how many punches and kicks a person can land in the course of sixty seconds. I remained on the sidewalk, doubled up, as my attacker moved off. My head was buzzing, but the full pain of the blows and the kicks hadn't yet begun to register. I heard a strange noise behind me and I twisted to see the figure huddled over next to the front of my car. That old dramatic moonlight glinted off something shiny in his hand and as I watched, the guy appeared to take a punch at my front right tire. I heard the strange noise again. It was my tire being punctured. I watched as he continued around the car and punctured the remaining two tires. Then he picked up something from the sidewalk, raised it over his head and brought it down hard. *Crash!* I'd be needing a new windshield.

He took off, leaving me with nothing but the memory of our brief time together. I knew who it was, of course. Even with his face hidden. How many people do I know, after all, with hands the size of toasters.

CHAPTER 22

I woke up in severe need of an out-of-body experience. I lay in bed trying to focus on a particular portion of my left calf; this seemed to be about the only quadrant of my body that was pain-free. My head felt like chopped liver. My rib cage felt as if it had been rearranged. Poorly. My tailbone throbbed. My knees felt as if they were the size of softballs.

And my dog wanted to go outside to pee.

No amount of groaning on my part convinced Alcatraz to back off. No subsequent amount of groaning eased my pain as I slid off my bed and gingerly pulled on a pair of shorts and a sweatshirt. "I hope you know . . ." I didn't even bother to finish my sentence. Alcatraz was waiting at the door, panting with anticipation. Just the mere sight of my dog's get-up-and-go was painful to me. I moved at the speed of a stunned snail.

It was a scorcher. I was drenched with sweat by the time I was halfway down the block. The sunlight assaulted me; the light was attacking my head like driving spikes. I reached the harbor, where the water was nothing less than a thousand sharp glass chips. Either a tugboat sounded or I let out another long low groan. The Domino Sugar sign across the harbor—red neon at night—was as translucent as a ghost.

Alcatraz was merrily leaving his newsletter in all the usual places. I lumbered off past the Oyster and sat down, gingerly still, on the end of the pier. My legs dangled above the water. God, I thought, how simple to lean forward and simply tumble into the drink. The way I was feeling I doubted I'd have the energy, not to mention the strength, to haul myself back out. What would people make of that, I wondered. It was morbid, I know, but I played the scene out in my head anyway. I pictured Detective John Kruk arriving at the scene. "A floater," one of his men grunts to him. Then they fish me out. Kruk sneers. "You again. What have I been telling you, Mr. Sewell?" Off to Morris Kiefaber I go, where my various bruises and broken ribs are all noted and documented. "Victim was apparently assaulted and then thrown into the harbor." And so begins the fiction. The seemingly obvious scenario, the logical-seeming sequence, but still, the wrong one. Maybe Pete Munger checks into the scene. He can add two plus two. He aims Kruk in the direction of Jerry of the Manos Grande, who has no real alibi for this Thursday morning. Jerry is arrested and charged with my murder. Ha! He is outraged, denies vociferously. He is offended. Where is Justice? Yeah, yeah, I killed those other two punks but I didn't kill the undertaker. It's a setup. I'm being framed!

If not for my aching ribs, I'd have laughed out loud at the scenario. The look of outrage on Jerry's face as he is charged with a murder that he didn't . . .

Well, I decided not to sacrifice my life for the sake of pissing off Toaster Hands. I ordered my body to stand back up and I went off slowly in search of my dog. He was up to his old tricks, racing after the elusive alley cat. My thoughts drifted to Kit Grady. It occurred to me that he must know, or at the very least have awfully strong suspicions about, who killed Shrimp and Arthur. More than simply suspicions, the young ballplayer must also be harboring a fair measure of guilt. For whatever reason Grady allowed himself to get drawn into Shrimp's schemes (money, drugs . . . probably both; possibly, it occurred to me, even Mary Childs), he was indirectly responsible for the fate of the stepbrothers. It occurred to me that Grady needed to be brought in. Immediately. There was no telling what sort of fur was going to fly between Grady and Barry Fisher and my good buddy Jerry. It dawned on me that I should contact Hank Mackey immediately. Wasn't this his job, after all? Baby-sitting the new Great White Hope? Wasn't this why he had been summoned from

Ohio? As I came down off the pier, my mind was running through the little ditty—I have no idea where I picked it up—*Why-oh-why-oh-why-oh did I ever leave O-hi-o?*

Alcatraz bounded around the east corner of Thames and Broadway, his feline nemesis a safe distance in front of him, its tiny legs a blur. The cat crossed Thames and leapt onto one of the wooden barrels near the tug pier. Alcatraz pursued, hitting the brakes in a skid, and reared up, landing his front paws on the lip of the barrel. The mangy old cat let out a wild, maniacal shriek, then she took a clean swat at my dog's mug, catching him smack on the nose. Alcatraz immediately backed off from the barrel, looked up at the cat bewildered and barked at her. The cat let off a sharp hiss, and then once more, that wild shriek. She then leapt with remarkable grace right over the baying hound, back to the street. Something screwed up in her landing, though—and how often does that happen?—and the cat took a tumble. Still, her recovery was like that of a trained gymnast. The animal rolled with the momentum of her leap, then sprung into the air, landed on her feet and scampered off almost daintily.

Suddenly it hit me. My mistake. And I took off as well. At a dead run. Despite my aches and pains.

Why-oh-why-oh-why-oh . . .

My car was in as bad shape as I was in. All four tires were flat. A cinder block sat on the front seat, surrounded by windshield glass, thank you.

I took the hearse.

I double-parked in front of the Basilica, directly across from the Enoch Pratt Library. I turned on the emergency flashers. Most times I do this, I don't get a ticket. Looks like I'm there on business.

A reporter friend from the *Sun* had once told me that the newspaper's archives were kept on microfiche cards at the main branch of the library. Computers and all the attendant digital nonsense were likely to be phasing out the old microfiche machines before too much longer, but as yet hadn't made their entrance into the realm of the Sunpaper's archives. I was directed to the second floor and instructed on how to go snooping through back issues of the *Baltimore Sun*. Slip a microfiche card into the reader, scurry it about until you land on the page you're looking for. It took a few minutes before I had mastered the soft touch required to scan the cards without creating a nausea-provoking blur on the large plastic screen of the microfiche reader. The cards are being magnified about a thousand times their original size; the barest movement of the card and the screen goes nuts. Finally I sort of got the hang of it, and I was able to track down what I was looking for, the editions of the paper that included accounts of the murder of the Hopkins coed last November and the subsequent arrest of Robert Kincaid. I scanned. There was little of note in the several articles I read that I didn't already know in one fashion or another. Kelly Bishop and Robert Kincaid had spent several hours at the club, during which there had been a brief argument. By all accounts, it had amounted to little and an hour or so later, they had left. Early the next morning, Kelly Bishop's body had been discovered next to one of the green trash containers out behind the club. She had been strangled to death. The police were called. Within the hour they descended on Robert Kincaid's apartment and after brief questioning arrested him for the murder of Kelly Bishop. He was brought downtown to police headquarters to commence with his nightmare.

The newspaper account on the following day included a profile piece on Kelly Bishop. This was where the cheerleading photograph first surfaced. Just as with Kenny Rogers's video piece, the paper printed the photograph of the entire cheerleading squad in their pyramid formation alongside a close-up of the picture, highlighting the very pretty and now very dead Miss Bishop. Indeed, most of the article focused on Kelly's rah-rah days back in Westlake, a suburb of Cleveland. The story, along with the photograph of the peppy well-scrubbed girl beaming atop the backs and shoulders of her peers, made of her an exquisite victim. The bio-piece didn't spend nearly so much ink on Kelly's college years. There was a quote from Trish Novack, Kelly's roommate, but it wasn't the sort of quote that Trish had given to Pete Munger and myself. Nothing along the lines of, "She was always wanting to have fun . . . Kelly could be out all night raising hell and still pull off a big exam the next day."

I found one of the librarians and asked how I could print up some of the pages off the microfiche cards. I was directed to a separate machine, larger, but of the same basic design. Copies were a quarter apiece. I slipped in one of the cards. It turned out to be the one that was an edition of the paper that came out nearly a week after the murder. The follow-up story included a different photograph, not the cheerleader cheesecake shot. This one showed a somewhat older Kelly Bishop, her hair cropped short, her face looking a little broader. She was smiling in this photograph as well, but the smile was not so infectious, the effect was not that of a hundred-watt bulb. The two photographs were only taken, I calculated, four years apart. But those four years from the end of high school to the end of college (or as near the end as Kelly Bishop was to get) are, as Tricia Novack had astutely observed, ones in which people grow up fast. In this second photograph, a mature, self-possessed-looking Kelly Bishop was seated next to her political science professor, Robert Kincaid, shoulder to shoulder, pinching the stems of their martini glasses, and smiling moderate smiles for the camera. The caption identified the image as having been "caught by the club photographer." I recalled my first visit to Shrimp's that past spring, with Lucy and Julia. We had been "caught" by the club photographer as well. Arthur Wisner, as it turned out. In fact, our photograph was up on the wall, alongside the hundreds of others that Arthur had diligently taken and then tacked up there. My guess was that this photograph—the one of Kelly Bishop taken just hours before her murder—was one that never made it up on the wall. Provocative as it no doubt was, the photo could do nothing but remind patrons of the fate that had befallen one of the club's customers. Not good for business. It was probably in the evidence files: *Maryland vs. Kincaid.*

I slipped in a quarter and copied it up.

I went ahead and scanned the follow-up articles as well, though I wasn't sure why I was bothering. I had already seen what I wanted to see. Possibly I just needed a few minutes to allow my heart rate to settle back down. Pete and I were wrong. I was convinced. Or nearly convinced. Nobody looking at me sitting there at the clunky machine would have guessed that adrenaline was pumping through my poor beaten-up body, but it was. And it felt good. My aches were easing, or at least that's how it felt. I sat there and calmly scanned through the articles. I skimmed an article concerning Robert Kincaid. Born in Long Beach, California. Educated in the East. Published here, published there . . . I noted the subtle ways in which the not-yet-judged come off as the will-be-found-guilty in articles like these. Even the tamest quotations from former colleagues or neighbors ("always seemed pretty normal to me") manage to come off damning.

I slipped my original microfiche card back into the machine—the one with the first newspaper account of the coed's murder—and again slid it to the cheerleader photo. I used my next to last quarter and pushed the Copy button. Then I moved the card around in the machine, slowing down the blur enough to read the headlines of the other articles from the day's paper. When I found what I had suspected I would find, I used my last quarter and copied the page.

I don't care that it has power steering, muscling that hearse through traffic in my delicate condition was no walk in the park. I was absent my morning caffeine. However, the surges of adrenaline having their way with me were proving a worthy stand-in. Pleasure even while there was pain.

Sam convinced Billie and me several years ago to spring for a car phone for our hearse. It's not as if we're such a high-volume establishment that Sam is constantly zipping from one place to another, scooping up the dead as fast as they can drop. Nonetheless, the car phone has proved handy now and again, and now was one of those times. Gritting against the pain of my shifting ribs, I leaned forward and flipped the phone out of its holster and dialed Information.

"Mackey. Hank, Harry, Harold. Anything you've got with an H."

The first Mackey (Harold) had a British accent and a way too chipper phone style. Harry Mackey was either hard of hearing or he had never before in his life answered a wrong number. "What? Who? What'd you say? Here? Who?" I hung up and tried the number for "Mackey, Henry."

"Hank Mackey."

Pay dirt.

"Mr. Mackey. Hitchcock Sewell. How're you doing? I missed you at the game last night. I wanted to thank you for the tickets." I had steered the hearse onto the Jones Falls, headed north. I was sticking in the slow lane, keeping just under the flow of traffic.

"Don't mention it," Mackey said.

"Surprised you weren't there," I said. "Big game."

Our connection was so-so. Hank Mackey could have been on the moon. I couldn't make out his response. I was passing Television Hill, the two towering antennae that rise up so insanely high. It made me think again of the videotape, and the violent shovel-beating that Shrimp Martin had put on that TV reporter just days before his murder.

I fell in behind a slow-moving Datsun. I could see the driver nervously checking the mirror. "Listen, Mr. Mackey, I need you to meet me at Grady's house right away."

"Kit's house?"

"Yes. It's too much to explain on the phone, but I've got a feeling Kit is going to be needing you more than ever." There was a pause on the line, followed by static. I could barely make out Mackey's voice. "I'm sorry, what did you say? I'm on a car phone. Our connection's not good."

"I said— Never mind what I said. When do you want me to meet you?"

"Right now, Mr. Mackey."

There was another pause. More static. "Okay."

I got directions to Grady's house from him and I hung up. I phoned Pete's number. Susan Munger answered.

"Hi. It's Hitchcock Sewell. Is Pete around?"

"He just ran out to pick up some groceries. I expect him back in about fifteen, twenty minutes."

"I'm really sorry about this, but it's very important that Pete drop everything and meet me right away. Can I give you an address?"

"Hold on, let me get a pen . . . Okay. Let me have it."

Mackey had told me that Kit's was the ranch-style house at the dead end of Candlewick Lane, which proved to be a gravel road with only about a dozen houses on it, all set back behind sizable lawns. Nothing large or ostentatious. Old houses built in the fifties and sixties. Probably cost next to nothing back then. Now, especially with the hefty acreage each property enjoyed, I was looking at a bunch of low-key millionaires. Kit Grady's place was isolated from its neighbors. Trees squeezed in from both sides of the gravel drive for about thirty feet, they opened back up as I hit the property line. Grady's house was wood and glass. Like its neighbors, nothing fancy. Candlewick fed directly into a circular driveway. To the right of the house was a garage. I could see that a car was parked in it. Parked in front of the front door, maybe twenty feet from the garage, was a red Corvette. As I swung the hearse around to the left, so that I would be pulling up nose-to-nose with the Corvette, the front door opened and a man stepped out. I recognized him by his hands.

Jerry froze.

I didn't.

I hit the gas.

With a reluctant roar, the hearse lurched forward and took the Corvette right between the headlights. I wish that I could report a wonderful *crunch* of metal meeting metal, but the fact is Corvettes are three parts fiberglass. Plastic, basically. I can, however, report a shout from Jerry (*Hey!*) as I rammed his jewel, and at the same time a set of tiny explosions (*Pop! Pop!*) as the car's twin airbags deployed behind the windshield. The impact drove the sports car back about five or six feet. Clearly I had the upper hand here. Tank versus toy. I slipped the hearse into reverse and backed off a few feet, until I was alongside Jerry. His mouth had dropped open. For the life of me, I couldn't think of anything to say—certainly nothing that would hurt him as much as he had hurt me—so instead I simply gave him a little smile, along with the finger, then threw the car back into Drive and hit the gas again.

This time I drove the cheesy Corvette all the way to the garage. (What the hell . . . *Crash!*) I stayed on the accelerator; my speedometer said that I was nearing forty. Of course the tires were simply spinning, the car in front of me shifting occasionally, folding another inch, fiberglass bits flying off like sparks. I was in full adrenaline, my knuckles sheet-white on the steering wheel. The high roar of the hearse's straining engine filled my head and, God help me, I cried out like a man possessed. I wanted nothing less than to flatten the Corvette completely, fold it up like an accordion against the wall of the garage. I glimpsed Jerry in my sideview mirror, and the look of astonishment and outrage on his face was simply manna to my own fury. I bore down. When I glimpsed in the mirror again, it was to see Jerry bounding around the side of the house like a jack rabbit. A moment later, a heavy hand came in the open window and landed on my shoulder.

"Slow it down, cowboy." I let off the gas and threw the hearse into Park. I looked up at Pete Munger. "Nice parking job there," Pete said. "Whose car are you having fun with, Hitch?"

It took a few seconds to catch my breath. "Jerry's."

"Our Jerry?"

I nodded.

"Where is he?"

"He took off running. I guess you scared him."

Pete looked over at the crunched Corvette. "Buster, I doubt it was me." He stepped back as I shoved open the door and got slowly out of the hearse. Pete let out a slow whistle. "Did you get all banged up like that just now?"

I shook my head. "Last night. On my block."

"Let me guess who did this to you."

"Don't strain yourself, Pete. Come on."

Pete followed me into the house. We found Kit Grady sprawled on the floor in front of a large picture window. Visible through the window were two or three acres of backyard, then a row of untended bushes and behind that, a large field that stretched several hundred yards toward a stand of trees. Three quarters of the way to the trees was Jerry . . . letting no grass grow.

Grady's left leg was bent in a direction that legs don't normally bend. Same thing for his right arm, which fell across his back with the elbow pointed in the wrong direction. His head was turned toward Pete and me; his mouth looked like a burst tomato. It burbled.

He was alive.

Pete cleaned some of the blood out of Grady's mouth and saw to it that Grady wasn't swallowing his tongue. We slid him—groaning, gurgling— onto a rug and carried him out to the hearse. Company had arrived. Quite surprised me. It let out a small scream when it saw what was being loaded onto the back of the hearse.

"Is he dead?"

I made the introductions. "Pete. Mary Childs. Mary. Pete Munger."

"You're the girl," Munger said. Three words, but he managed to make a whole paragraph of it. Mary snapped off a look at me; it was easily deflected.

"Get in the car," I said.

"I'll follow you."

I shook my head. "You'll get in the hearse."

Mary tipped her chin. "You'll make me?"

I didn't have to answer. Pete stepped forward and lifted her at the waist with one arm, walked her around to the passenger side, pulled open the door and tossed her onto the front seat. He held up a warning finger as she began to protest. "Hitchcock is nuts today, Missy. And I'm always nuts. If you're smart you'll just sit tight and enjoy the ride."

Mary relented. "I'm going to ride in the back with Kit." And she crawled over the back of the seat. Grady was groaning softly. Mary sat cross-legged next to him and scooted forward, gently sliding his head up into her lap. She stroked his forehead and looked sadly down at his bloody face. Then she looked up at me. I was still standing at the rear door of the hearse.

"Well, let's get moving already," she said.

Pete had joined me behind the hearse. "G.B.M.C.?"

I nodded, "P.D.Q."

"I'll meet you there. I'm going to take a quick run along Hillside. See if I can't find me a Jerry." He glanced into the rear of the hearse. "You going to be okay with them?"

"Fine, Pete."

"You're lucky our friend Jerry didn't kill you."

"Jerry's not our killer," I said. "We got it wrong."

"Oh?"

"Oh," I repeated. I jerked a thumb at the couple in the back of the hearse. "Our killer's in there."

I nearly collided with a midsized something or other as I careened out of the woodsy entrance to Kit Grady's place. I recognized Hank Mackey behind the wheel. I slammed on the brakes and called out, "G.B.M.C.!" He nodded. I continued on.

The folks at the Greater Baltimore Medical Center were not accustomed to seeing hearses pull up to make a delivery. Mary scooted out from the back of the hearse and she and I watched as Grady was loaded onto a gurney and whisked inside.

"What happened?" I was asked by one of the attendants.

"Got the shit beat out of him."

"How about you?"

"Me?" I had forgotten that I wasn't looking my normally dapper self. "Same thing," I said. "There's a lot of that going around."

Mary and I went inside. Hospital. Fluorescent lighting. Plastic chairs. Sharp and sterile. I asked, "So, do you want to say it or should I?"

"Say what?"

"We've got to stop meeting like this."

"I've got something to show you," Mary said.

"I've got something to show you, too."

Mary and I wandered off to a waiting room. There were a few people there. We found a corner where, speaking low, nobody could hear us. We sat in a pair of facing chairs. I got right to it.

"Grady's a murderer."

Mary looked me directly in the eyes. Her smoky blue eyes were like stones. "I know."

"How long have you known?"

"I just found out this morning."

"You're lying."

"No, I'm not."

"Why should I believe you, Mary? My limited experience of you hardly tells me that you're anything but a self-serving manipulative liar and thief."

"Gee, you sure know how to charm a girl."

"I do. And I'm also chump-material in the hands of a pro like you."

"Would you like to stop insulting me already? I get your point."

"You played me like a fiddle." I felt duty-bound to get that on record. A hard grin tugged at the edges of her mouth.

"It takes two to fiddle."

I corrected her. "That's 'tango.' "

"You know what I'm saying. As I recall, I didn't exactly have to knock you over the head and drag you inside my place the other night."

Interesting choice of words, I thought, considering Solly Biggs and the juggling pin. I let it pass.

"So how long have you known that Kit's a killer?" I asked.

"I just told you. I found out this morning. That's why I came back."

"Where'd you go after stealing the money from Solly?"

She glowered at me. "I went back down to Rehoboth."

"Rehoboth? Mary, I figured you had your sights set on more exotic beaches than Rehoboth."

"I did. I wanted to see my parents. I wanted to find a way to give them some of the money."

"Find a way?"

"Without their being suspicious of where I got it."

"So you were cooking up a story."

She glowered at me. "I was working on it."

I checked her out, one eye at a time. The natural anger that seemed to be a part of the woman made it difficult to judge when she was and she wasn't lying.

"So tell me how you figured out what Kit had done," I said.

Mary squinted at me. "I don't know who you think you are that you can bully me."

I can squint, too. And I did. "Would you like me to tell you? For starters, I'm the guy who knows that you broke into Solomon Biggs's place, knocked him unconscious with a juggling pin and made off with a shopping bag full of money that Shrimp had entrusted to him. I know that I accidentally let you figure out where the money was. That's all you wanted me for in the first place. That's right, isn't it?"

She started to fold her skinny arms, but I reached over and interrupted the move. I had had enough of the woman's indignant poses. I took hold of her left arm and wouldn't let go. This sure as hell brought the fire into her blue eyes. "I'm tired of you folding up on me, Mary. Enough of the attitude. How about you try to convince me that you and Grady haven't been in cahoots all along?"

"How about you let go of my arm?"

I did. She began again to fold her arms, but then she slid her hands underneath her on the plastic chair. "Better?"

"Good girl."

"Screw you."

"We tried that already."

"And I didn't hear any complaints."

"I'll bet you never do."

Mary burst out laughing. "You guys . . . you're really nuts, you know that? You're always ready for a good time, then you're all ready to blame the girl who shows it to you. Nice double standard. You were buzzing all around me, mister, so don't go putting it all on me just because you regret it now. I'm a lot more honest than you are. I like to have fun. I think I missed the part where that's a crime." She pulled one of her hands from underneath her and wagged a finger at me. "You had fun, too. Remember, I was there. Don't go telling me that you didn't."

Sometimes the truth will set you free. Other times it locks all the doors and won't let you out. That's all I'm going to say on the subject.

Suddenly Mary relaxed. She even smiled. "Look, why don't you tell me what you know about Kit," she said, "then I'll tell you what I know. Deal?"

"Okay, deal." I reached into my pocket and pulled out the several articles that I had copied up at the library. "Show and tell." I handed her the photograph of Kelly Bishop and Robert Kincaid at Shrimp's. "Recognize this?" She nodded. "You told me that you weren't there that night," I said. "Truth or lie?"

"I wasn't there that night."

"This was in early November. Had you already met Kit by then?"

"No."

"How long after Kelly was killed did you meet Kit?"

"I don't remember exactly," she said. "Not long after. Like a week or something."

I pulled out the final article that I had copied and handed it to her. "Did you know that this happened the same night Kelly Bishop was murdered?"

Mary scanned the article, then looked up at me, her eyes a new blue. Darker. "This was the same night?"

"Yep."

"Get out." She looked down at the article again. "Kit never mentioned that."

"I don't suppose he would."

She looked again at the article. "This is insane."

"No it's not. It's panic. It wasn't an accident. Kit set it up."

"I don't follow."

I took the photocopy from her. The article was an account of Kit's run-in—literally—with a train, out in Hartford County. The article quoted the engineer of the train as saying that he had seen a car stalled on the tracks and that he went for the brakes, but there was no chance of stopping the train before it barreled into the car. He had also pulled on the train's whistle. Seconds before impact, the engineer reports having seen someone leap out of the car. The article reported that the driver of the stalled car had been drinking heavily and had given "an incoherent statement" to police concerning how his car came to be stalled on the train tracks. The car was destroyed of course. Gone to scrap. The headline read:

BLUES STAR ESCAPES INJURY
IN TRAIN MISHAP
KIT GRADY'S CAR HIT BY TRAIN

"Here's the picture, Mary," I said. "Kelly Bishop is strangled and then dumped off behind Shrimp's. Several hours later, Kit Grady's car is stalled on some remote railroad tracks and hit by a train."

"So what're you saying?"

"Kit's car. I'm saying that Kit followed Kelly Bishop and Kincaid when they left the club and went back to his place. Kit waited outside. You and I both know that Kit does this sort of thing. Kelly comes out of Kincaid's place, Kit gets her into his car. I've no idea exactly what took place at that point, but soon enough afterward, he strangled her and then dumped her off behind the club."

"And then arranged for his car to get smashed? That's ridiculous."

"That's where he killed her. In his car. I'm guessing he was as high as a kite. The papers say alcohol, but this wouldn't be the first time a little fudging was arranged with the police to protect a big shot. What I'm saying is that Kit was trying to obliterate any trace evidence that Kelly Bishop had been in his car."

"God, but . . . that's even supposing that the police ever thought of questioning him in the first place."

"Well, I guess our boy wasn't taking any chances. Of course, as it turned out, no one ever questioned him about it."

"How did you make that connection?"

I handed her the other article. The one with the cheerleader photograph.

"Yeah? So? I've seen this about a hundred times."

"Hank Mackey came and talked with me the day after Kit popped me in the eye. He was trying to see to it that I didn't make a big stink about it. You should thank me, by the way, Mary. A big stink would have included your name."

"Thank you," she said facetiously. "So what's with the picture?"

"Mackey mentioned that the name of the high school team where he had coached Grady was the Wildcats."

"Okay. Wildcats."

"Look at the picture. What's that thing standing off behind the cheerleaders?"

She squinted at the photograph. "Looks like a bear or something."

"It's a wildcat," I said. "It's the high school team mascot."

"That's a wildcat? God, it looks ridiculous."

"They normally do, but that's not the point. The point is Kelly Bishop was queen bee cheerleader for a team that has a wildcat as its mascot. The Westlake Wildcats. Westlake is a suburb of Cleveland."

Mary finally got it. "Which is where . . . that's where Kit's from."

Why-oh-why-oh . . .

"Bingo. I haven't had time to check this whole thing out, but it's my bet that Kit's Wildcats and Kelly Bishop's Wildcats—"

Mary finished off for me, "Are the same god damn cats."

I nodded largely. "Same damn cats."

Mary and I were silent for a moment as we processed the logic of it all—or perhaps not logic. Mary ran a hand through her hair. "Wow," she said at last.

"You're surprised? I thought you said you knew this morning that Kit had killed Kelly."

"I'm surprised that you figured it out. That's what."

"Well, how did you figure it out?" I asked. "Or did Kit tell you?"

"He didn't tell me. Are you kidding?" She reached into her rear pocket and pulled something out. It was a photograph. "I found this this morning. It was at the very bottom of that bag with all the money. It was the first time I had taken all the money out. This thing was tucked under the rubber band of the bundle on the very bottom."

"So Shrimp must have put it there," I said as Mary handed the photo to me.

"I guess."

I looked down at the picture. And I couldn't believe what I was seeing. I swore softly. "Holy shit."

I was looking at a Polaroid photograph that had been taken at night, using a flash. I recognized the photo as the type taken by Arthur Wisner in his role as club photographer, the type that were tacked up all over the walls of the club when you first entered. Only this photograph . . . no way in hell it would have ever made the wall. The edges of the photograph were dark. Even so, I was able to make out enough to tell me that the picture had been snapped out behind Shrimp's. A corner of the Dumpster was just visible. Smack dab in the center of the photograph, caught by the flash of Arthur Wisner's camera, was Kit Grady. He was hunched over, but he was looking directly at the camera. He was cradling a limp body. The feet were dragging along the ground. The look on Grady's face was one of pure astonishment. The look on the face of the body he was carrying . . . well, there was no look. But I recognized the face. The blood that less than an hour previous had been running so hotly through my system as I was crunching my hearse against the red Corvette . . . that same blood turned to cold cold cold *ice*.

Mary had on her grim face when I looked back up at her. "I told you, Kit gets all bent out of shape with these girl-next-door types."

"Madonna versus whore."

She sniffed. "Men better start getting that shit figured out."

I was still holding the photograph when Hank Mackey arrived about twenty minutes later. I was standing at the window at the end of the corridor, looking out at the parking lot. Mary had gone off to fetch some bad coffee in the hospital cafeteria. Grady was out of X-ray. His leg had been put into a temporary cast. It was going to require surgery. The knee was all messed up. An orthopedic surgeon had been called. Grady had been rolled into a room across the hall from X-ray where a cast was going to be put on his arm, which was apparently not quite as mangled as it had looked to me. Grady was heavily sedated. He had looked directly at me as he was rolled down the hall, and had not registered a thing.

Mackey approached me with the darkest of clouds over his head. Or over his hat. I turned from the window to face him.

"Grady killed the Hopkins girl," I said. I handed him the photograph. Mackey barely reacted. I gathered that his mood had probably gone as dark as it could already. He studied the photograph for a few seconds and then handed it back to me.

"Where did you get this?"

"Long story. I think Arthur Wisner took it. After hours at the club. He must have just been in the right place, right time. Or wrong place and time. Depending how you look at it. Certainly wrong for Grady. I think Arthur and Shrimp were blackmailing your boy. You'll have to get the details from Grady, but it looks like Shrimp had him over a severe barrel and decided to milk it for all it was worth. Money, of course. But I'd guess also Grady's frequenting the club and bringing along other teammates . . . that whole celebrity thing. Shrimp had him by the balls, plain and simple."

Mackey didn't say anything. He took the photo back from me and stared at it again.

"You knew about the game fixing, didn't you?" I asked.

Mackey looked up, expressionless. "I knew."

"Did you know why Kit was doing it? Did you know that Shrimp had this over him?"

Mackey looked confused for a moment. "You're asking me if I knew that Kit killed that girl?"

"Yes."

"Of course not."

"Did you know that Kit killed Shrimp and Arthur?"

Grady's high school coach took a deep breath and let it out before answering. "I had my suspicions about all of this. I knew that something complicated was going on between Kit and Martin. The first time I saw them together . . . there was a strange sort of tension there. Kit told me that he was going to the club so much because of the girl. But I wasn't so sure."

"Mary Childs."

"Yes."

"She broke that off about a month ago," I said.

Mackey handed me back the photograph. "What am I missing here?"

"I spoke with someone last night who worked at the club," I said.

"Shrimp had arranged for Kit to throw the first game of each of the championship series that the Blues were in. He didn't come through on that very first game, and we think Shrimp was feeling the heat. I think that what happened was that when the word came in that there was going to be a verdict in the Kelly Bishop murder, Shrimp was wired. His whole scheme with Grady was wrapped up in his holding the murder over Grady's head. I'm guessing that when that reporter showed up, Shrimp just snapped. He lost control. Later that week, Arthur left the club and came back with a bag full of money. We'll have to ask Grady to be sure, but Arthur must have met with him. Shrimp was in deep trouble at that point with Grady's having bungled his agreement about the play-off game. Shrimp and Arthur must've hit him up for another payout right after the verdict came in."

"But . . . Shrimp and his stepbrother."

"You mean their murders. I don't know for sure. Something went wrong. Obviously. Maybe Grady simply changed his mind. My guess is that he tried to strike some new deal with Shrimp . . . maybe something to get this damn picture back once and for all. He must've tried first with Arthur, and when it didn't work, he killed Arthur and then went gunning for Shrimp. Boy's got a temper. We know that. Let's figure that Shrimp knew Arthur had been murdered. Shrimp stashes the photo at the bottom of the bag of money and hands it over to Solomon Biggs for safekeeping. Even if Shrimp is killed, which he was, at least he knows that the evidence against Grady is still out there. Revenge from the grave, as it were."

Mary was coming down the corridor with a pair of coffees. She slowed when she saw me standing with Mackey. His back was to her. She was mouthing something at me, but I couldn't catch it. Mackey turned and saw her.

"What's she doing here?"

Mary stepped over to us. "Hello, Mr. Mackey. I'm sorry about Kit." She handed me my coffee. She held the other one out to Mackey. "Do you want this? I don't really need it."

"Thanks. No." He turned to me. "Do you think they'll let me in to see Kit?"

"I don't know. I haven't tried. He's over there in that room on the left. Right across from that watercooler."

"I—I've got to go see him."

Mackey headed down the corridor. I peeled back the plastic lid on my coffee and took a sip of the liquid cardboard. Mackey reached the door and paused. He dragged his hat off his head. Good manners. I realized that I'd never seen the guy without his ugly hat on before. He entered the room. I turned to Mary.

"I don't want to get you in trouble about the money," I said. "Breaking and entering. Assault. Robbery. I'm not a trained professional, but you've got to figure those charges at the very least."

"I guess I can't expect you to turn the other way."

"The thing is, it's the photograph," I said. "That photo of Grady and the girl. That has to be explained. It can't just drift in from nowhere."

"Then turn me in," Mary said. "Or I guess I'll do it."

My gaze had gone back down to the doorway where Hank Mackey had just disappeared. I was seeing the phantom image, the man pulling off his hat and entering the room. Something about it was feeling peculiar to me.

"Actually, you know what? Maybe this photo *can* just drift in from nowhere," I said. "Look. We'll put the picture in an envelope. 'Detective John Kruk' on the front. I'll go down to the police station and pay some kid to run it inside. Kruk won't need to know how the photo got to him. It's the evidence he needs to nail Grady, that'll make him happy enough. Pete and I were already planning to tell him what Edgar told us last night about the game fixing and all the rest. It's his dots to connect now, not mine."

Mary Childs went through a perfect pantomime of Mary Childs's Greatest Body Language Hits. She took a step back from me, crossed her arms, tilted her head, put on a crooked scowl. I glanced again down the hallway, then back at Mary. "It would be easier for you to turn me in. You're breaking the law if you don't," she said.

I shrugged. "I guess I'm not a Boy Scout after all."

"You're going to hold this over me, aren't you?"

"What do you mean?"

"The fact that you're letting me off free. You're going to have this on me." Her face suddenly opened up as another thought occurred to her. "Well, you're a good old-fashioned regular son of a bitch, aren't you? You're a smooth one."

"Am I?"

"The money," she said. "You want the money."

"It's not your money," I reminded her.

"It's not yours either."

"I never said it was."

"I don't care about the money," she said defiantly. We were standing looking at each other. I went ahead and mimicked Mary, crossing my arms, cocking an eyebrow. Her eyes narrowed with suspicion. And with a touch of mirth.

"I don't think I like you," she said.

"I think you do."

"You're pretty sure of yourself."

"I guess I have my days."

Munger was coming down the corridor toward us. He passed right by the room where Grady and Mackey were. I realized that something was still bugging me, something about Hank Mackey and Grady and . . . I couldn't place it. Munger came up to us, a little out of breath.

I asked, "Did you find Jerry?"

"I did."

"Where is he?"

Pete hesitated. "I just dropped him off with the admitting nurse."

"Oh?"

"Yeah. He wasn't looking too good."

"Oh?" I said again.

"I gave him the choice of apologizing to you, Hitch. Seemed only fair. He didn't take it."

"And that was a bad choice?"

Pete nodded. "I've just been in a real crappy mood lately. Maybe you've noticed."

I started to fill Pete in on what was what. I showed him the photograph of Grady and Kelly Bishop. He nodded sagely. "Well. One down, two to go."

"What do you mean?"

"One murder solved, two to go."

"Pete. You're missing it. Shrimp was blackmailing Grady with this picture. He had him throwing games, he had him handing over loot. Grady must have had enough of it and snapped."

Pete looked perplexed. "Hitch, hold on. Kit Grady didn't kill Martin."

"Yes he did."

"Explain. Give me a scenario."

I shrugged. "Come on, Pete. Somehow he must have heard that Shrimp was at Union Memorial after Lucy shot him. He went over to the hospital and somehow managed to slip into Shrimp's room and stab him."

"A guy who is six-six and has had his face plastered all over national magazines is going to 'slip' into a hospital unnoticed?"

"Well . . . I . . . I mean—"

Pete went on. "Not to mention that a television audience of, oh, several hundred thousand at least were watching him put a whopping to the Knicks at the exact moment that Martin was killed?"

"How do you know that?"

"I'm one of them. I was watching the game that night. Grady was phenomenal."

"But—"

"It wasn't Grady, Hitch."

"No, Pete. It had to be."

"I just told you. Grady was dropping buckets on national television. In New York, Hitch. The guy wasn't anywhere near Baltimore."

"But then . . ."

I stared down the hallway again at the door to Grady's room. It was closed. Again I saw the phantom image of Hank Mackey shuffling down the hallway, looking defeated, dragging his ugly hat off his head. His hair was heavily salted. Cut short, military style. Bristly. Close to the scalp.

Flattop.

"Come on!"

I took off down the hallway. Pete was right behind me. We burst into the room directly across from the watercooler.

Hank Mackey was standing on the far side of the gurney that was holding Kit Grady. Grady's right arm was suspended in the air, held there by a shiny pulley-rig. Equally shiny was the knife glinting in Hank Mackey's hand.

"Drop it."

A pistol was floating just next to my face. It was Pete's. It was aimed at Hank Mackey. Pete repeated, in an eerily calm voice, "Drop it."

Grady was conscious. Groggy, but seemingly aware of what was going on around him. He murmured something at his old coach, but it was too faint for me to make it out. Mackey heard it. He placed his free hand on Grady's shoulder. "It's all right," Mackey whispered. "It's okay, Kit."

Suddenly a scream rang out at the door. Mary Childs. I whipped around for just a fraction of a second. So did Pete. Mary screamed again.

"Kit!"

I turned back in time to see the knife sinking into the chest and to hear the groan. Mary's screams had brought several nurses and doctors running into the room. Someone cried out "There's a gun!" and a craze of cries kicked up. Pete snapped, "Doctor! *Now!*" I wheeled on Munger.

"Put the gun away!"

A doctor pushed past us just as a large guy in surgeon scrubs lunged at Pete, trying to wrestle the gun from him. Grady was trying to sit up on the gurney, but he couldn't manage. Hank Mackey was sinking to the floor, one arm draped across Grady's chest. The doctor lunged across the gurney but failed to catch Mackey before he slid out of sight. Grady's arm shook loose from the pulley and came down across the back of the doctor's neck. The wail of pain that came from the basketball player as his arm flopped onto the gurney was, in a word, horrific. More people rushed into the room. I leapt deftly to the side—out of their way—then crouched down to my hands and knees and peered beneath the gurney.

Hank Mackey lay on the floor on the far side of the bed, on his side. His shirt was a deepening red. He was looking directly at me, in obvious pain, in obvious shock. His lips were moving, but I don't believe he was saying anything. A hand landed on his shoulder and began to turn him onto his back. As he settled onto the floor, Mackey grabbed out with his right hand and took hold of his snot-green hat, which had fallen to the floor. The knuckles of his other hand, still clutched around his penknife, were white.

He didn't begin to convulse until the knife was slid out of his chest.

CHAPTER 24

Kelly Bishop had been an A-student, Honor Roll. In addition to her position as head cheerleader for the Westlake Wildcats, Kelly had also been in the school's photography club and was a member of the school chorus. She was an avid tennis player and Rollerblader and by the end of her senior year, by all reports, was damn near addicted to line dancing at the local popular dance club. Kelly's younger brother suffered from lupus, and Kelly had tirelessly aided in organizing fund-raisers to support research into the disease. She helped organize several walkathons during her high school years, as well as an old-fashioned danceathon, and in her senior year convinced her school to cosponsor an amateur tennis tournament to help raise money for the cause. Kelly enjoyed outdoor activities. On the mantelpiece in her parents' home is a twin picture frame. One of the photographs is of Kelly on the south rim of the Grand Canyon, a bandanna in her hair, a pack on her back and an insanely bright smile on her face. The other photo shows Kelly in a raft on a white-water rapids on the Colorado River. Kelly is at the front of the raft, wearing a life preserver, both hands planted on the front rubber as the craft has just reached an apex of lifting off the water. Kelly's blond hair is flying, and she looks like nothing less than a freshly scrubbed masthead, her neck taut, her chin jutting forward toward the water. Friends say that Kelly could not talk enough about her trip to the

Grand Canyon and her ride down the river. She tried to put her feelings into poetry, though it was pretty pedestrian and a bit overwrought.

> Rocks of ages, older than the sky
> The secrets of canyons carried on whispering winds.
> Vast and ancient, and I am so small and brief.
> On the wild river, do I even make a splash?

Pretty lame, you have to admit. But then Kelly Bishop wasn't pretending to be the next Emily Dickinson. Her plan had been to go away to college in the East, study political science and journalism, minor in languages. Kelly had wanted to get married someday and to raise a family. She loved the camaraderie of the high school sports teams and enjoyed her role as head cheerleader, especially as it allowed her to devise all sorts of fun and wacky cheers and routines for the squad. Her friends knew that Kelly never took the cheerleading terribly seriously. She was certainly not fanatic about it in the least. But she was a girl with a lot of energy and enthusiasm. She liked playing sports and she enjoyed watching them. In spring, she was on the field hockey team. But in fall and winter, it was all basketball, and in Kelly's school, boys-only basketball. Kelly had considered not keeping up with the cheerleading in her senior year. A lot was happening in her life at that point, and she had to admit, she was beginning to feel a little silly jumping around in the skimpy yellow skirt. She told some of her friends that she was "being retro" in continuing with it. Kelly was keenly aware that the onset of college would forever close the door on this time of her life, and so ultimately it didn't really bother her to play it all out one more time. Besides, the Wildcats were kicking ass in the Midwest Conference. Kelly was having a blast. The stands were always filled to the rafters; the noise and the energy coming out of the crowd were phenomenal. It was just plain fun. The Wildcats were awesome. Especially the junior, Kit Grady, who was clearly a rising star. The guy was a joy to behold on the court. Grady was a farm kid from Ohio, tall and lanky and handsome in a quiet, Gary Cooper kind of way. Kelly thought he was kind of sexy. A lot of the girls thought so. He seemed a little moody sometimes, a little too focused on the game, the game, nothing but the game. But still, Kelly Bishop had managed one Friday during an away game in Toledo to pull Grady's focus away from the court a little bit, and over to the sidelines. She wasn't even sure why she was doing it, but she had flirted with the team's center outrageously all through the second half and on a pure impulsive whim had offered Grady a ride home after the bus had returned to the school. She was right there when Grady got off the bus. Grady accepted. But Kelly hadn't driven him home. Instead she drove to the far side of the thicket of trees behind the IGA's rear parking lot, turned off the car's engine and turned on her own. Things were a little rougher than she had anticipated, but not so rough that she hadn't enjoyed the romp. But it was strictly a romp. Grady had approached her several times subsequent, and Kelly made it clear to him that she was not going to be getting any further involved. She was graduating in the coming spring and heading off to Johns Hopkins in Baltimore. It had been a onetime thing, something crazy that had come over her. A trophy moment. Star player and head cheerleader. Kelly made a joke to Grady that scrambling together in the backseat of her car was, in its way, destiny. Almost an obligation. One of those retro things. No harm done.

Except that it got her killed.

Kit Grady had indeed sought out Kelly Bishop this past fall in Baltimore. Soon after leaving North Carolina and signing on with the Blues, Grady had remembered that Kelly was attending Hopkins. He recalled how even after their one time together in the back of Kelly's car, the senior hadn't made a big deal of having slept with Kit Grady. In fact, she had kept him at arm's length after that. Kelly Bishop had been a popular girl in high school. All that work she did for that disease that her brother had, all the cheerleading and the dancing she enjoyed doing. Kit was pretty sure she had said that she was going to be a journalist after she got out of college. A real job. Something of substance, something that could maybe make a difference.

Kit sought her out. He met up with her at Hopkins. She had cut her hair. Put on a little bit of weight. She was still very attractive. But she was certainly no longer a peppy high school cheerleader. She was much more serious than he had remembered. She talked politics a lot. No, she said, she really didn't follow sports much; she was way too busy. She knew about Kit and his move to the Blues, of course. She congratulated him, but she didn't do any back flips. She didn't leap into the air and do a split. She didn't grab a handy set of pom-poms and spell out K-I-T with her arms and body.

And she declined his suggestion that they go out on a date. She really was, she said, just way too busy.

Kit told the police that it really wasn't Kelly's rejection of him that got under his skin. In fact, just the opposite. He respected her for not fawning all over him. He respected her for not going all gooey and stupid over him like so many other people were now doing. He said that it was incredibly refreshing. Also, she knew him. Not terribly deeply, it's true, but still, she was a friend from back home. A friend of sorts, anyway. She knew him not only as a millionaire basketball star but simply as a guy you pass in the hallway. A guy hanging out with other classmates after school. Pressed by the police, Kit also admitted that, well, yes, the sex on that one occasion had been outrageous. Kit had been a junior, this incredibly pretty girl was a popular senior. The backseat tumble had been one for the record books, as far as Kit had been concerned. God damn it, why wasn't she willing to see him again? Just now and then. Like a regular person. Take some of the pressure off his celebrity. What the hell was so wrong with that? Just what the hell was her deal, anyway?

Is it stalking if you just do it once? I'm not sure. Whatever you want to call it, Kit did it. Just once. Just that one night. He parked outside Kelly's dorm at Hopkins and sucked on a bottle of Jack Daniel's. He followed her over to an apartment building on St. Paul Street, where she parked and got into a car with a man, somewhat older. Decent-looking guy. Mustache. Kit followed them downtown, to the Canton area. He parked off Boston Street, where he had a clear view of the nightclub that Kelly and her date had gone into. He worked on the bottle of Jack. And he fed a fire of rage. Grady had no other way that he could describe it to the police. By the time Kelly and the man emerged from the club, it was all Kit could do to keep from starting up his car and running them both down right there in the parking lot. He didn't, of course. He managed to not crash his car as he tailed after them back to the man's apartment. Again Kit held vigil. About a half hour later, Kelly emerged from the apartment. Kit was ready. He pulled the car up to her and pushed open the passenger door. Kelly recognized him, of course. He asked if she would talk to him for a minute. He said that something terrible had happened and that he really needed someone to talk with. She got into the car. Grady told the police that he never said a single word to her. He said that he looked over at her. And that the next thing he knew, his fingers were on her throat and he was squeezing as hard as he could. He doesn't even recall a struggle, though there must have been one. He had practically blacked out. One moment Kelly Bishop was getting into his car to talk . . . and then she was limp. Dead.

Grady drove back to the club. He parked again off Boston Street. He waited until the club was closed and the parking lot had emptied out. He pulled into the parking lot, drove around to the back. He was halfway between the car and the Dumpster when he heard a noise, looked up and was blinded by a flash. Arthur Wisner. Dutifully staying late, cleaning up. His ever-present camera near at hand. The rear door of the club has a porthole window. Kit figures that Arthur must have seen Kit Grady getting out of his car, recognized him and run to fetch his camera. By the time he got back and pushed open the back door, Kit was dragging Kelly Bishop's body from the car. Arthur snapped the photograph, then dove back in the back door and threw the lock.

Kit took off. He dropped Kelly right on the spot and he leaped into his car and he flew. He drove, without thinking, out of the city. It was an hour or so after driving off from the club that Kit determined he had better figure out a way to get rid of his car. He knew well enough that modern forensics would be able to reconstruct with stunning accuracy the events that had gone on in the front seat of the car. If the authorities had any reason whatsoever to suspect Kit in the murder of Kelly Bishop, his car would tell the story. Kit saw a railroad crossing. He saw lights flashing. Without thinking any further, he drove onto the tracks and put the car in neutral. He pulled on the final two inches of the bottle of Jack Daniel's, finishing it off, as he sat watching the train lumber around a bend some fifty feet away. He felt no fear. In fact, Grady told the police that he felt no desire to get out of the car. This had been his plan, but suddenly it occurred to him that the best way to handle the entire situation was to simply stay put. Take his medicine.

But he jumped. He cleared the car in plenty of time. The train was braking and had slowed somewhat, but it was still going fatally fast when it plowed into the car and dragged it a good two hundred feet, before the car finally squibbed away and landed on its roof . . . what roof even remained. Kit was sitting on the side of the road when the police arrived. He was arrested. His misadventure was never for one instant linked with the misadventure of the Hopkins coed who had been discovered behind a nightclub back there in South Baltimore. Kit's car was junked. Mission accomplished. The Blues took a publicity hit . . . but they had already grown accustomed to that.

Mackey survived his self-inflicted stab wound. He might have been accurate in landing the blade in the hearts of both Arthur Wisner and Shrimp Martin, but when it came to taking aim at his own ticker he had hit left of center. Still, had Mackey not stabbed himself in a hospital, he might not have survived his wound. As it happened, he had been dragged off the floor and rushed off to the emergency room, gotten the best treatment insurance will buy, then given a private room and his very own police guard. Not outside the room, but in. Suicide watch. The police had a few questions they wanted to put to Mr. Henry Mackey.

Munger brought the story to me several days after the arrest of Kit Grady and Hank Mackey.

"Kit was screwed from the get-go," Pete said to me. "Arthur took that picture to his stepbrother, and Martin immediately knew what he wanted to do with it. Kincaid had already been pulled in for the Bishop murder. Grady says that Martin told him from the start, if Kincaid is convicted, the photo is going to have to surface. Martin seemed to have no real problem with Kincaid's life being destroyed, but he wouldn't stand by and see him wrongfully convicted."

"Big-hearted guy, our Shrimp," I said.

"Oh yes. A real sweetheart."

And so Shrimp stuck it to Grady. At first, it was cash. Grady handed over three hundred thousand dollars, and then a few weeks later, another hundred thousand. Then, as I had surmised, Martin decided to diversify. He demanded of Kit that he come to the club on a regular basis and that he bring along his cronies from the Blues as well. I can only imagine the bile that must have risen up in the young ballplayer's throat as he posed time and again for Arthur Wisner's camera. If anyone needs proof of the existence of the Supreme Ironical Being, it's right there.

Pete and I were sitting in his backyard going over the gory details. Susan was inside. Pete told me that the two were working out the terms of a truce. Pete had confronted his wife about her sleeping with Roger the asshole. She told him that it was already over, and he believed her. This had taken place the morning after the basketball game, around about the time, I figure, that I was dangling my legs off the end of the pier and entertaining my silly musings about leaning forward and dropping in. Pete told me that it was still going to be very touch and go between them. He didn't think she listened very well to him. She accused him of not communicating. "I don't know what we do with that," Pete said to me. I couldn't tell him. Out of the corner of my eye I kept seeing Susan Munger passing back and forth behind the sliding glass door leading out onto the backyard.

"Why doesn't she just come out and join us?" I asked Pete. "What's she doing? Spying on us?"

"I don't ask, Hitch."

After leaving the hospital, Pete had gone over to Roger's office and confronted Roger about sleeping with Susan. Roger had made the mistake of denying it, and Pete had gotten some of his aggression out. He grinned at me when he told me.

"It's good to express your anger, Hitch. All of my books tell me that."

"Do your books say to clobber people in the face?" I was thinking not only of Roger but of Jerry as well. Same day.

Pete raised his palms to the sky. "Every situation is unique. If you listen, it will tell you how it should be handled."

"Oh, you're deep, Pete. You're very very deep."

Shrimp arranged with Grady for him to throw the first game of the play-offs against the Knicks. Shrimp had pulled in a lot of wagers—Grady really didn't know how much—and was then left with egg on his face and a lot of angry people when Grady suddenly came to life in the second half and powered his team on to victory over the Knicks.

"Not a smart move," Pete said.

One of the angry people was Barry Fisher, who had trusted his business partner's claims to having Kit Grady in his pocket. Fisher had dropped a hundred grand on the game (a 50-50 split, it would turn out, with the fellow at the pension fund with whom Fisher arranged all of his loans). Another very angry person was our very own Toaster Hands. Jerry

Mulvane; I finally had a last name. Mulvane made it quite clear to Shrimp, come up with the money or get ready to rumble.

"This was that Monday," Pete said to me. "Word was out that the verdict on Kincaid was due the next day. Martin must have been shitting major bricks. I think you're right, Hitch. I think he just snapped when that guy came out to his club to do the report. So Grady says that Martin hit him up for two hundred grand. And he also told him that the deal was still on for throwing the first game against the Pacers. And this time, Grady had better not pull anything fancy. Arthur was the bag man. He picked up the money from Grady that Thursday night. Grady says that he pleaded with Arthur to destroy the photograph and just end this thing now. Robert Kincaid had now been cleared of the murder. Martin had seen close to half a million dollars in blackmail already, and Grady was going to cooperate with throwing the games. He asked Arthur what more his stepbrother wanted, for Christ's sake."

The sliding glass door opened just then and Susan Munger came out into the backyard. She was carrying a tray with iced tea and some tuna sandwiches.

"Do you like tuna?" she asked me.

"Sure do. Thanks."

"No problem."

"Thank you, Susan," Munger said. Susan Munger set the tray down and looked up at her husband. It looked to me as if she rejected whatever her first response was going to be.

"You're welcome," she said, then went back into the house and slid the door closed.

"That was civil," I said, picking up a sandwich.

Pete picked up a sandwich as well. "Civil. After twenty-six years of marriage, we're civil?" He took a bite of the sandwich.

"It's a start," I said.

Pete was chewing slowly. His head shook slightly. "You've got a funny way of thinking."

Kit Grady did not know precisely what had taken place after his last meeting with Arthur Wisner. He had handed Arthur the Hecht's shopping bag filled with two hundred thousand dollars, made his pitch for the end of the blackmail, then boarded the Amtrak for New York City. He didn't hear about Shrimp Martin's murder until he returned to Baltimore on Sunday. Grady had his suspicions, but he kept them to himself.

As his old high school coach had done some six months before.

Hank Mackey was kept at the Greater Baltimore Medical Center for three days, until his doctors assessed that his injury no longer required hospitalization. He was then taken off to jail. The story came out in dribs and drabs. The bottom line was Mackey knew that Kit had been the one who murdered Kelly Bishop. As Mackey himself had told me, he was summoned to Baltimore after Kit's drunken run-in with the train in hopes of helping to settle down the Blues' prize catch. Of course Mackey had seen the other big story that was in the papers at the time, the murder of the local girl, popular cheerleader and all the rest of it . . . and he knew. He remembered Kelly Bishop. Hell, he had seen her jumping up and down and shaking her pompoms for nearly four years, of course he remembered her. What told Mackey immediately that Kit was involved in her murder was the simple fact that Grady had never brought the subject up with him. Mackey knew full well that Grady was aware of the murder—all of Baltimore was being reminded of it relentlessly for that first week after it happened—but Grady never once mentioned to his old high school coach anything about "you remember that cheerleader? Kelly whatshername?" Nothing. Mackey watched his brooding young protégé's mute silence on the subject. And he knew.

And he kept quiet about it.

After Mackey was moved from hospital to prison, he confessed to the murders of Shrimp Martin and Arthur Wisner. Mackey told the police that he had been keeping a special eye on Kit during the Robert Kincaid trial. Most people around Grady simply assumed that his darkening moods had to do with the play-offs and the special pressure that was on the young ballplayer to carry the team along to victory. But Mackey knew better. And on the evening that Kit met with Arthur Wisner and handed over the two hundred grand, Hank Mackey was nearby. He had trailed Kit and he saw the whole thing. He confronted Grady later that evening, and the boy confessed. Grady's stoic façade finally broke, and he collapsed into tears, telling Mackey what had happened with Kelly Bishop, and about the photograph that Arthur Wisner had taken and that Shrimp Martin was dangling over his head. The official account—the public account—never said as much, but Pete and I deduced that Hank Mackey had then made a desperate play not only to extract his young friend from the trouble he was in but also to prove to Grady his undying loyalty. Mackey knew that he was being marginalized by Grady. Kit resented that his old coach had been brought in to hold his hand. His attitude toward Mackey had been growing more and more distant from the day that Mackey arrived. Loyalty might sound like an awfully twisted motive for murder, but if someone can tell me when the motivations for murder aren't twisted, I'm all ears.

Mackey met with Arthur Wisner the night after Grady had delivered the cash. Friday night. Mackey had simply phoned Arthur and told him that he had to meet with him right away, life or death. He told him to bring his camera and to bring the photograph of Kit and Kelly. Arthur showed, but without the photograph. Less than an hour later, Mackey was snapping Arthur's picture as the boy lay dead on the ground in the woods near Loch Raven reservoir. Munger had been right in his guess. Mackey had the photograph delivered to Shrimp that same night, along with a note that said simply, "This is over now. Tomorrow, please. The photo. No more deals." The next day—Saturday—Hank Mackey reached Shrimp's apartment just as Shrimp was being loaded into the ambulance. He asked after which hospital the ambulance was going to, and then after the EMS crowd took off, went into Shrimp's apartment and located the photograph of Arthur. It had been right there on an end table, facedown. He looked for the photograph that incriminated Grady, but by then it was already safely stashed away at the bottom of a shopping bag, stowed away in Solly Biggs's hiding place. Mackey made his way to Union Memorial, discreetly determined where Shrimp Martin was being kept and found a time to slip in and out of the room, leaving a fatal stab wound behind. The closest he came to being discovered was when he saw Mary Childs sitting in the waiting area. However, she never saw him. She had been engrossed in a magazine article—"100 Ways to Spice Up Your Marriage."

Without Kit Grady, the Blues failed to win any more games after their home opener. Chad Singleton did himself proud, but in the end, the team needed its million-dollar hotshot and his hot shots. The Pacers took the title. At last.

Grady had no compunction about identifying Jerry Mulvane as Shrimp Martin's prime gaming partner. Nor did he have a problem ratting on Barry Fisher, who had called on Grady the evening of Shrimp's wake and instructed him that the game-throwing deal was still on. Kit could either cooperate or answer to Jerry Mulvane's toaster-sized hands. Kit got himself tossed out of the first game of the series against Detroit. But his broken finger ruse during the home opener against the Pacers backfired when Chad Singleton came on so strong and more than filled the star center's shoes. And so Jerry Mulvane had been dispatched to send the message to Grady that his failure to deliver was not going to be tolerated. And Mulvane delivered the message emphatically. Kit Grady's knee was mangled. The doctors were talking knee-replacement. For a basketball player, that's an acronym for *retirement*.

Lucy was free. All charges were immediately dropped. Her lawyer made a lot of blustery noises about lawsuits . . . but what kind of a lawyer would he be if he didn't make such noise? Lucy was not interested, and her lawyer dropped it. She peppered me with kisses and tears during an Alls-Well party at the Oyster. Munger was supposed to show, but he stood us up. I hadn't seen him since that day in his backyard. I had spoken to him on the phone the next day. He told me that he had been avoiding going to see Eleanor Martin but that it was something he was ready to get out of the way. Pete and I had never discussed what Mrs. Martin had told me, about Pete's anguish over what had happened to Dan Wisner all those years ago. Somehow, though, Pete seemed aware that I knew the story. "Finding out who killed her boy," he said to me over the phone. "It doesn't make it any better." I told him that he was too hard on himself. "You let me know when I have a choice," he had said, and then he hung up.

Solly dropped by the Oyster. He even drew a wonderful little sketch of Lucy on a napkin. Julia congratulated him.

"So you do know your stuff. I really wasn't sure."

Solly puffed up, went red, coughed and laughed. "Took a correspondence course in prison," he said. "Marvelous. You start with a circle then you just build from there."

Solly drank too much until Sally threatened to hustle him out her illegal back door that leads directly into the harbor. "Too much drink and you're in the drink." That's one of Sally's several mottos. She came around from behind the bar at one point and joined us in a round. She sang one of her dirty songs and Julia wrapped her lovely arms around the fat gal and nearly broke her face smiling. Frank remained behind the bar, doing his best cigar-store Indian imitation. Father Ted even stopped in. He spent a few minutes telling us what exactly was wrong with the world today, then he spotted us all a round as well. Solly challenged him to an arm wrestling match and Father Ted accepted. Father Ted spit his cigar onto the floor, took hold of Solly's hand and flattened it against the bar as if it were a leaf. "Praise be!" Solly cried out. "Praise be!" Father Ted told him to can it, slapped some money on the bar and took off.

Later in the evening, Lucy was by herself at a table near the back, crying softly. I pulled up a chair next to her and she fell in on my shoulder. Billie had made a rare appearance at the bar some ten minutes earlier, and I sat watching her talking with Sally. Billie was perched on a barstool, looking like a beautifully aged Mary Poppins. She and Sally were tickling each other's funny bone about God knows what. They've known each other for ages, these two. Since well before I moved in with Billie and ugly Uncle Stu. I watched the old friends laughing and teasing each other, and it was a good ten minutes or more before I realized that the wetness on my cheeks wasn't all from Lucy. I must've been more tired than I realized.

Lee Cromwell was knocking the absolute piss out of George Gershwin. You think you've pretty much heard the various versions of how those old standards can be done . . . but the Edgar Jonz Experience had found a way into brand-new territory. Lee ran a string of the tunes back to back to back. "Summertime." "Someone to Watch Over Me." "Nice Work If You Can Get It." And speaking of back, Lee was showing hers off in a black velvet number that looked like it had been poured over her body from an oil tank. She was even wearing elbow-length white gloves, along with high heels, dangly earrings and fire-engine red lipstick. Lee was ignoring the club's No Smoking policy, and kept a cigarette going in an ashtray on the floor. The things that happened when she twisted and bent down to pick up the cigarette were damn close to illegal.

After the Gershwin combo, Lee and Edgar shared a duet of sorts on "The Way You Look Tonight." These two were like a pair of trained snakes, circling and entwining, Lee's voice, Edgar's trumpet . . . just perfect. Halfway through the tune, I was joined at my table by none other than Pete Munger. He dropped into the chair opposite me, grunted his greeting and kept his eyes riveted on the small stage. I grunted back, but he paid me no attention. He was wearing a sports coat I hadn't seen before—rumple-free—and an open-collar shirt. Lee and Edgar were sharing a single spotlight at this point, the spot getting smaller and smaller throughout the number, closing in so that by the end of the tune, only their faces remained. On the very last note of the song, the light went out. Cute.

"How did you know I was coming here?" I asked Pete as the two of us joined in the applause. The stage lights came back up. Edgar and Lee took their bows. Edgar announced that the band was taking its break. "We're going to take a pair of fives, boys and girls." Lee had stepped over to the steps leading down from the stage. She took hold of her dress and lifted it slightly, stepping with care in her high heels down onto the main floor. Munger was standing up as he answered my question.

"Who the hell knew you were going to be here?"

Big smile as Lee stepped forward. Her gloved hand was floating up toward Munger. "Peter. I'm so glad."